I0585379

SOUL OF LIGHT

BOOK FOUR OF THE HIDDEN WIZARD

VAUGHAN W. SMITH

FAIR FOLIO

ISBN: 978-0-6481931-3-5

Copyright © 2018 by Vaughan W. Smith

All rights reserved.

No part of this book may be reproduced in any form or by any electronic or mechanical means, including information storage and retrieval systems, without written permission from the author, except for the use of brief quotations in a book review.

For Hugo

PROLOGUE

Alyx was lost in a haze of grey and black mist. Her diminishing eyesight had gone to an extreme she never thought possible. She felt her body moving and doing things, but she had no idea how it was happening.

There were flashes of images. She saw the missing Tracker. Alive then dead. She felt somehow involved in that, but it was such a strange and distant memory. Like it was in a previous life. Or something not yet done.

What's happening to me? she thought. The more she tried to wrestle some control back, the more pain she felt and the more she drifted away. Something terrible had happened, but she wasn't sure what it was.

Suddenly, she felt drawn to something. The landscape started to clear, and she recognised the terrain. She had somehow travelled a long way from the scene of the battle. The last thing she remembered properly.

There was a figure standing before her. She had trouble making out any features. But she could tell from the silhouette that he was armed. A sword and shield, and possibly armour as well.

"Well, well, well. What have we here?" the figure said. It sounded like a man. But it was not a normal voice. There was something wrong with it. Alyx tried to speak, but nothing happened. Just silence.

"Perhaps that was cruel of me, pausing. I know you can't respond. In fact, the only reason you can even hear my words is that I am allowing it. So, I guess that does make me cruel. Not that it would be a surprise to anyone." The man paused again. Alyx wanted to scream something, but she couldn't move or do anything else. She was just aware of him and his voice.

"You're not who I came for. It was that meddlesome wizard. He had outlived his usefulness, but I'm not one to let that stop me. I would have enjoyed turning him to some lesser purpose. But you, you're a better prize." The man walked closer and reached out. Alyx had to assume he was touching her head, but she felt nothing.

"We have never met, so I should introduce myself. My name is Darvin. I go by other names, but that will do for now. I've been so preoccupied that I never thought to look for you. And had you not been infected, I probably wouldn't have found you. But that fool Wraith did one good thing for me in the end. Yes, this is too perfect." The man stepped back and looked her over.

"When you killed my brother, it was a dagger through my heart. That's how I felt it. The sharp, sudden loss. The unexpected nature of it is what hurt me so badly. I thought he was invincible, undefeatable. But he made a crucial error. He underestimated you. I won't make that same mistake."

Alyx, even in her haze, had started to piece things together. No doubt her mental faculties were available to her on his whim, which made it worse. But she knew who he was now. And it scared her.

"I felt that. The tremor of fear. Good, you know me. You should be afraid." Darvin started pacing around.

"I've had this feeling within me for some time now, and I didn't know what it was. It was a burning desire for revenge, to hurt you for what you did to us. But I hadn't identified it and acknowledged it. But now it's all rushing out. And I have the answer. I know what will fill the void I've been feeling." Darvin stopped right in front of her. She had trouble making out his features. But she couldn't miss the wicked smile.

"You are a Shade now, which is nice, but not enough. I won't underestimate you. You have a strong will, and maybe you would find a way out. No, I've got something special in store for you. I can bring you into the fold. I can transform you into one of us, and you can sit at our table." Darvin paused, watching her. Alyx had no idea what he was getting at, but it sounded bad.

"If only you could respond. Oh well, in time. But I won't keep you in suspense any longer. To right the wrongs that you did to us, you can serve us. You can fill the gaping hole in our number. You will become the Skull Queen and serve in place of the one you so cruelly stole from us." Darvin clapped his hands, the excitement so obvious.

Alyx understood the words and felt complete and utter horror.

"Noooooo!" she screamed. Some part of it must have gotten through because Darvin took a step back.

"Interesting. I didn't expect that. Never mind, come with me. We have a lot of preparations to make." Darvin turned and left, and Alyx felt herself moving with him.

I can't let this happen, she thought, steeling her resolve. But the fog was coming back, and she was soon lost within it.

1

THE POWER OF SOUL

A lrion sat back, and let the ideas collect and form together.
"I know we've only read a little, but it's been enough for me to puzzle something out," he said. Vincent and Marla looked at him with interest.

"Are you going to keep us in suspense?" Vincent said after a while.

"I've figured out how my grandfather cured Avaria." Alrion looked around, and both his father and Marla looked shocked. He enjoyed that for a moment.

"Go on then," Vincent said.

"He needed two things: access to the Blight and access to Soul Power. Neither of which he had."

"I understand the need for the Soul Power. Why did he need access to the Blight? You were cured yourself when you cured Wraith," Vincent said.

"Yes, but I found a way to insert the Soul Power into Wraith's body. He was right in front of me. I didn't need any special connection to target him."

"I see. But my father managed to create a net so large it covered the entire country of Avaria." Vincent nodded along.

"Therefore, he needed those two things. How did a wizard do that, when he had access to neither?" Marla said.

"Because he mastered the skill of transferring them into vessels. One for Soul Power, one for Blight. The crystal I wear has both. It's proof that he could do it."

"That's good. But how does that help you?" Vincent looked sceptical.

"There's no way I can source and store enough Soul Power to cure everyone of the Blight. It won't help me there. I'm mostly just glad that I've puzzled out how he did it. Considering his limitations, he did such incredible things."

"He really did." Vincent let out a deep sigh. Alrion could sense the regret in his father. He decided to quickly move on.

"Anyway, I'm starting to think of other applications."

"Such as?" Marla said.

"If I can put Soul Power into a vessel. And if the right amount of Soul Power inserted into a body can drive out the Blight. Then what's stopping me from creating something that someone else can use to cure the Blight?" Alrion looked over at his father and Marla. They had confused looks. But he saw them thinking it over, and the realisation showing.

"You're absolutely right. Why did my father never try that?" Vincent said.

"He would have had a finite amount of Soul Power. He never returned here to get more, so he must have been using it sparingly, knowing that he needed it," Marla said. Vincent nodded with understanding.

"It's all theoretical right now. But I know I can get this to work. Those generals of the Blight won't see any of this coming. It's time for the tide to change. We're going on the offensive now." Alrion saw doubt in their faces.

But he believed it, and soon they would too. In the back of his mind, there was the nagging doubt about how he would end this war and cure the Blight. But he silenced it. There was time to figure that out. For now, he had to trust in himself and those who were on the journey with him. They had defied the odds repeatedly. What was one more impossible task?

If this works, I don't need to be there to cure Alyx.

Lara crested the snowy hill and paused to catch her breath. She looked over at Celes and saw the older woman breathing heavily.

No need to put on appearances then, Lara thought. She let down her guard and showed how exhausted she was. They had spent enough time together that she no longer felt like she had to prove herself. Celes caught her breath enough to laugh.

"Good to see that you tire as well. I thought it was only me."

"I'm not really the hiking type. I think I've done a lifetime these last few weeks." Lara surveyed the landscape. There was enough greenery poking out from the layers of snow that it felt alive, and not completely whitewashed. The sweeping hills and rocky mountains in the distance were awe inspiring.

I should try to appreciate this while we're still here. I wish I could get Alrion out to see it.

"Ready to push on?" Celes looked like she needed another minute.

"I need another two minutes." Lara watched Celes's reaction and saw the woman's face relax noticeably.

No need to be rude.

"Do you think this mysterious trader will turn up today?" Lara looked at Celes, curious.

"I hope so, we've got no other leads. We have so completely canvassed this whole area." Celes sighed. "We need to be moving, not making camp."

"If we bring him something, he'll move. But not before. He's obsessed with this project of his."

"The Soul Orbs?" Celes brushed the snow off a nearby rock and sat. She cleared a spot next to her. Lara sat next to her, trying to ignore the cold. A chill ran down her spine.

"Yes. He won't talk about anything else. Well, except news of Alyx of course."

"He's always been stubborn, even as a child. Once he gets his mind set on something, he won't budge. But I don't see why he's so fixated on this. If he wants to save her, shouldn't we be out doing more than just looking?" Celes stared out into the distance, deep in thought.

"I've been thinking about that too. I think I know the answer." Lara noticed that she suddenly had Celes's full attention.

"And?"

"He doesn't want to be in that situation again. Where he has to choose."

"Choose?"

"He chose to cure Branthor, and he could do nothing for Alyx in the moment." Lara could see the scene playing out again in front of her. The desperation on Alrion's face. The defeat in the face of his amazing victory. She pushed the images away.

"And if he develops this Soul Orb, he can cure someone while still retaining his Soul Power?" Celes clarified.

"If it works, then yes. I think that's what this is about."

"You're right. He's grown so much, but he hasn't changed. Not one bit."

"Isn't that great though?"

"Oh, it is. Despite all this, he's still my boy. I still see him that way. It's not really fair to anyone, but that's how it is. I have to keep reminding myself that he's saving the world." Celes rose awkwardly.

"I'm not made for this intense cold. Let's keep moving."

"The sooner we get to this outpost the better." Lara blew warm air into her hands and took off after Celes.

The hike didn't take that much longer. Soon, they saw the top of a wooden shack rising out of the snow. It was nestled amongst tall fir trees and looked like the landscape had grown around it. A small plume of smoke wafted out of a small chimney.

"That's our place." Lara pointed to the shack.

"Good. I hope this trader is legitimate. How do you want to do the interrogation?"

"Interrogation?" Lara stopped suddenly.

"Perhaps that was too strong a word. But we need to figure out what he knows, and I don't have the patience for some ego-driven idiot."

"I'm curious what you would consider normal?" Lara felt a sudden pang of fear. Maybe she didn't know Celes at all.

"Oh, don't give me that look, I'm not like that. I meant more along the lines of 'the cudgel and the honey'."

"Oh, I see. In that case, why don't you choose? I'll follow your lead."

"I'll be honey, you be the cudgel."

"Sounds like fun." Lara winked and Celes returned it. Lara upped the pace and took the lead before heading into the shack.

A wave of warmth rippled out as soon as she pushed open the heavy wooden door.

Finally! Lara lingered for a moment in the doorway, then remembered Celes. She quickly shuffled inside, held the door and closed it quickly. There was a raging fire which explained the warmth. Otherwise, the shack was very simply furnished. There were a few chairs and couches, and one writing desk in the corner. Two men occupied the room. One silver-haired gentleman in adventurer's gear sat at the desk, and another man lounged in front of the fire. He was younger and dressed like a well-to-do merchant. He was reclining in the chair and playing with a silver ring.

He's not dressed for the elements at all. I don't trust him already.

The man at the desk nodded towards the hearth, and Celes approached first. She took a seat directly opposite the merchant. Lara pulled up a chair next to her. The merchant paid them no attention.

"Excuse me, I was led to believe that you have some information of the recent Blight attacks." Celes's voice sounded sweeter than usual. Lara almost laughed. The merchant looked up.

"Oh yes, good of you to finally join me. I was promised coins." He held his hand out.

"Certainly." Celes handed over a small bulging sack. "My name is Celes. And you are?"

"Gunthram." He pocketed the coins without delay and started to resume his previous position.

"And the information?" Celes maintained her polite voice. Gunthram looked annoyed.

"Yes, yes I can confirm the attacks. I was there at one. Ghastly business." He turned his attention to the hearth.

"We're quite interested in hearing more. What was unusual about these attacks?" Celes tried again.

"I'd rather not say." Gunthram started spinning his ring idly. Celes nodded at Lara. The young thief stood quickly and snatched the ring from Gunthram.

"Well, I never!" He started to rise. Lara shoved him back down, making a show of inspecting his ring.

"Nice ring, if a little plain. Does this have some special significance?" She looked him directly in the eyes. Gunthram gulped but did a good job at hiding it.

"No, not really. Just a trinket I picked up."

"You won't mind if I keep it then." Lara pocketed the ring. Gunthram's face grew red. Celes reached out and held his hand tenderly. She looked back at Lara.

"No need to be rude, Gunthram has been through a lot. Clearly, the attack was quite traumatic."

Gunthram seemed to relax and nodded. But he kept his eyes on Lara.

"Why don't you share some more details, I apologise for my associate. She's really quite hasty. I tell her every day, but she just doesn't listen!" Celes was almost using a motherly tone. Lara had to stifle a laugh.

"Very well. I, well I'm. It's just... it wasn't normal." Gunthram seemed quite preoccupied. He started fidgeting. Celes nudged Lara and she returned the ring. He took it without looking and resumed twirling it around.

"The truth is, I can't believe what I saw. There was a creature unlike any I've seen before. She was jet black, dressed in a simple black uniform adorned with silver. But she wielded a giant great sword and her face." Gunthram stopped speaking. He grew pale, and a haunted look came over his face.

"Go on. Please." Celes encouraged him.

"It was like you could see her skull. It was horrific. The few that stood up to her, she was like a whirlwind of death. There seemed to be another standing back and laughing. I ran." Gunthram sank into the chair. He closed his eyes.

"That's quite a story. We're so appreciative of the information. I know that must have been hard for you."

"I see that face in my dreams. I try to pretend it never happened."

"Why did you come here? Why admit you saw it?" Lara softened her voice slightly but still challenged him. Gunthram looked up, fear in his eyes.

"I lost everything. I bragged about my survival in taverns to get the odd drink, and conversation. I felt that I was somehow moving past the whole thing. Then I was offered the odd coin for more details on the story from concerned travellers hoping to avoid trouble. I thought I could keep going and get enough money to travel back to Avaria, without truly reliving it. But no. As many times as I kept it back, it wouldn't stay back." Gunthram slumped into the chair. He focused on the hearth, the flame dancing around and chewing on another log. Celes pulled out another sack of coins and pressed it into his hands.

"What did they call it?" she said softly. Gunthram's lips quivered.

"The Skull Queen." Lara stifled a gasp and looked over at Celes. She nodded, and they turned to leave.

"What are you going to do?" Gunthram said, apprehension in his voice.

"We're going to cure her of the Blight." Lara shoved the door open and rushed out into the freezing cold.

2

DIFFERENT PATHS

A lrion held the crystal delicately and examined it from all angles. From normal inspection, it looked quite average. You could not discern anything special about it. But by accessing his Soul Power, he could see the surging of Soul within the crystal. Not a lot, but definitely there. A knock on the door interrupted him, and he placed the crystal down on the table next to him.

Vincent walked in, nodding to Alrion. He eased himself down in the chair next to Alrion.

"How's it going with this?" Vincent pointed to the crystal.

"See for yourself." Alrion handed it over and watched his father's reaction. Vincent turned the crystal over and seemed to see something. He handed it back.

"It looks successful. What does this mean for your plan?"

"It's a major win. I just need to settle on the right vessel and the right amount of Soul Power." Alrion turned the crystal over once more, before setting it down.

"Provided that it works as intended?"

"Yes, I will need to test it on a Blighter initially. But the applications are vast once I get going."

"Is that your plan? To become a craftsman creating tools to fight the Blight?" Alrion was caught off guard by his father's question.

"What are you talking about?"

"You've been holed up here for weeks, tinkering away while the world moves on." Vincent looked Alrion directly in the eyes. The challenge was obvious.

"It was a good use of my time, while the search for Alyx continued."

"We both know this is not critical to saving her, or your quest. You're just buying time. You're stalling." Vincent paused, watching.

"It's, not like that." Alrion almost stammered the words out.

It's true, isn't it? You're hiding here.

"I'm doing the best I can. It's been relentless getting here." As he spoke the words, Alrion realised how bad an excuse it sounded.

"I know that, nobody's judging you. You've overcome incredible hurdles to get this far, moved mountains. But this is not the kind of situation where you can just put things on pause." Alrion picked up on the sense of urgency from his father.

What's driving this? Maybe it's time to find out.

"I never properly explained to you my last dream." Alrion watched his father's reaction. His face changed quickly, to one of curiosity. The hard edge fell away.

"Go on."

"I saw a vision of the source of the Blight. And my grandfather." A look of recognition passed over Vincent's face in an instant, but Alrion was watching. He noticed.

"Really?" Vincent spoke evenly, keeping his composure.

He's feigning ignorance. But he knows.

"But you already know what I'm about to say. Because you've always known." Alrion's voice raised slightly in volume.

"I'm not quite sure what you are referring to, son. Just tell me."

"He touched the source of the Blight, and it changed. He caused the problems that we now face. That's why he was so hell-bent on solving the problem of the Blight. It was guilt. And you knew about it. All this time. There's no way you didn't." Alrion was on a roll now.

The emotions of the past few weeks, the discovery that he had kept to himself, all combined into a single moment.

"That had to be why the two of you were so estranged. He wanted you to take on his legacy, but you couldn't. And you ran away. Now that I'm here, and I'm doing it, you're here to push me forward again. To make sure your father's unfinished business is done." Alrion was shouting now.

Where did that come from?

He saw his father shrink back. Vincent lost that sense of assurance and confidence. He looked pained.

"Alrion, I." Vincent paused. "I understand how you feel. You're right. I did know about my father's part in this. It was what drove us apart. I am sorry that I kept it from you."

"Why didn't you tell me? Even now?"

"I didn't want to put that burden on you. It's a heavy toll, and you had enough to contend with." Vincent reached out, but Alrion shrank away.

"When were you going to tell me?"

"At the end, once we were done. It would have been a nice close to this whole chapter. We could both put it behind us."

Alrion didn't know what to say. He could hear the sincerity in his father's words.

But another lie?

"I... there's no words right now. Don't worry, I'm not abandoning my quest. I'm just trying to prepare something to be one step ahead. I'm sick of having to make bad choices."

"Which one are you hoping to avoid?"

"Having to choose who to cure." Alrion's voice was soft and trailed away. Vincent stepped forward and enveloped his son in a tight hug. Alrion didn't return it initially but then gave in.

"This does not make things right. You better not be hiding anything else from me?"

"That's it. How many more skeletons can I have in the closet?" Vincent laughed. Alrion was about to respond when he noticed the door opening. Lara and Celes entered the room.

"Oh good, you're both here. There's something we need to tell you," Lara said. Alrion could see from the look on her face that it was bad news.

Something about Alyx. Oh no.

"Do we need to get Marla?" Vincent said.

"No, not yet. We found word of Alyx, and we're pretty sure it's a real lead." Lara looked over at Celes, who nodded.

"And?" Alrion said.

"And it's worse than we expected. She's become something else."

"Something else?" Alrion saw Lara look down briefly before meeting his gaze.

"She's become the Skull Queen."

"What?" Alrion looked from Lara to his mother. Both wore serious and apologetic looks. Even his father looked shocked and saddened.

"I don't understand. She was turning into a Shade. What's this?"

"The enemy must have found a way to transform her further. It's quite cruel really, considering her past." Vincent shook his head.

"She killed the Skull King. I can't believe this. I knew I should have been out looking. Instead, I've been wasting time with these toys." Alrion threw the crystal to the floor. It clattered with a loud noise but didn't break. Lara stepped over and picked up the crystal, examining it.

"Does this work?" She handed it to Celes.

"It should do. But I need to test it. I don't know how much is needed and if the effect will be the same." Alrion started pacing.

"Alright, we need to get moving. No more waiting around. Where were the sightings?"

"Some smaller towns at the foot of the mountains. They must be moving towards bigger settlements."

"Do we have maps? Let's figure out where we need to get to. Maybe we can predict their destination and cut them off."

"I know where some are, give me a minute." Lara left immediately.

"Alrion, I'm not sure we should be pursuing this right now,"

Vincent spoke gently.

"Did you just say that? After we just had that conversation?"

"It's your quest, and you've worked on your tools, your extra options. You can continue to refine those on the road ahead. But you need to learn the spell you need and the place to cast it."

"Listen to your father, Alrion. We are here to support you, but you need to keep moving forward. On the task at hand. You can't save everyone?" Celes reached out and held Alrion's hand. After a moment, he pulled away.

"Alyx is not just anyone. She sacrificed so much, and now the worst has happened to her. It was bad enough her running around as a Shade. But now she's been transformed into her worst nightmare. That should make it more important to save her, not less."

"You can save her by saving everyone. I know how important she is, and what she did. But isn't saving the world more important?"

"You don't understand. I can't save the world if I can't save her first." Alrion slumped down into a chair.

How could I let this happen?

Vincent put a hand on Alrion's shoulder. Alrion felt the warmth and reassurance. He looked up and saw his father smiling.

"You need to do the right thing for yourself, this is your quest. I only want to provide you with some perspective. I've been around a while, I have learnt a thing or two." Vincent winked.

"So you think," Celes said, laughing. Vincent feigned injury and turned back to Alrion.

"All jokes aside, I've just had a realisation. We are your support team, I shouldn't forget that. And I understand that keeping things from you has made it difficult. So, here's my suggestion." Vincent paused and drew in a deep breath.

"Your mother and I will go hunt down clues for the location of the source of the Blight. You can pursue and save Alyx. We can meet up later and go together to end this quest." Alrion nodded, taking the words in. It wasn't the first time they had split up to achieve different things. He looked over at his mother. Celes nodded her approval. But he still noticed her giving his father a questioning look.

So, it wasn't planned. I'm sure he'll get in trouble for that, splitting us up again.

"It's a good plan. If you perfect your Soul Orb, then either one of us could cure Alyx. And once we have her back, we will be much stronger." Lara spoke slowly but seemed to be gathering in enthusiasm with each word.

"But how can we even coordinate ourselves? Where will your search take you?" Alrion said to Vincent. The blacksmith rubbed his chin in thought.

"I was just thinking, that while we don't know where the source of the Blight is, we do know where it is near." Vincent paused.

"Where?" Alrion said.

Don't tell me you've been hiding more!

"Remember the story of the four generals of the Blight?"

"Yes, of course."

"Where did those generals come from?"

"Valrytir." Lara gasped after speaking. Alrion looked over at her, shocked.

"It makes sense, doesn't it?" Vincent raised the question. Alrion didn't know what to think.

"Are you sure?"

"Well, it doesn't really matter if I'm right. They successfully reached the source of the Blight from there, so it's as good a place as any to stage our final approach. They are well-versed in fighting the Blight and have the world's largest and most sophisticated armed force."

"He's right, if you're looking for raw firepower, that's the place to go," Lara said.

"You've been there before, haven't you?" Celes said to Vincent. He nodded.

"Many years ago, before we met. I'm not in a rush to return, but I think it's the right place for us to go."

"This is all very sudden." Alrion sighed. But he thought about what his father had said.

I do need to move forward, I can't delay it any longer.

"I guess this is it. We shall investigate appearances of the Skull Queen. Then we will look for a lead concerning the source of the Blight. If we don't find one, we can meet at Valrytir. Does that sound right?"

"Exactly. Your mother is quite skilled at information gathering. I'm sure she will have this solved within the week." Vincent winked at Celes.

"Right, don't set any reasonable expectations." Celes laughed.

"I think it's the best path, considering the circumstances." Lara's voice was quiet. Alrion could sense some hesitation in her, despite her agreeing to the plan.

"Is everything alright, Lara? Is there something about the plan?" Alrion thought a moment, it was more than that. "About Valrytir?"

"I was born there, but I've not been back in a long time. It will be... strange."

Don't pry, there's some sort of history there.

"That's fine, I'll do whatever I can to make it easier. But first, we need to save Alyx." Alrion looked around the room. Everyone acknowledged him. His father with a tight nod, his mother with a warm smile. Lara gave him an apprehensive smile.

"We will make preparations and leave." Vincent guided Celes towards the door. She stopped and stepped back to Alrion.

"Take care, son. We shall see you soon. Don't forget, that we're so proud of you." Celes pulled his head over and lightly kissed the top of it. Alrion fought down embarrassment.

"Send my regards to Alyx." Vincent opened the door and, after Celes left, followed her.

"I guess it's just us again," Lara said.

"So it is. Just like old times."

"Maybe we can skip the whole 'take on a field of Blighters and almost die in the process' though this time?"

"I'll consider it." Alrion gave her a grin, then his mind started working through the consequences of his decision. But he was still firm.

Alyx, we're coming.

3

AN IMPOSSIBLE CHOICE

Alrion hugged Marla and stepped back.

"Are you sure you have everything you need?" Marla gestured to the storeroom again. Alrion let his eyes wander over the shelves and mentally catalogued everything.

"Yes, any more would weigh us down. And the crystals you gave me to experiment with the Soul Orbs are reusable. We are ready."

"Thank you for your help. Do we know when we will return?" Lara said, looking at Alrion. He shrugged.

"I don't expect to return until it's over. But I will come back and see you. I'm not going to follow in my father's footsteps." Alrion sighed, but Marla laughed.

"Good, we look forward to seeing you back here. You are a part of us, so you belong here. But I understand if you decide to spend your life somewhere a little warmer."

"You do have a tendency to get snowed in." Lara gave an exaggerated shiver.

"Well, thank you again. I will try and send word if possible." Alrion paused, thinking it over.

"Yes, if you leave word with any Mystics you come across, we will get the message. Good luck and look after each other." Marla waved, and Alrion pushed the door open, waiting for Lara to exit.

A blustery wind assaulted them immediately.

"Not looking forward to the initial hike one bit." Lara kicked at some snow and pushed forward. Alrion noticed small clusters of Mystics out and about. They all seemed to slow and stop, watching them leave.

"Do you think they're glad to be rid of us?" Alrion said.

"In a way, yes. We brought so much death and destruction with us. Even if it wasn't our fault."

"True. That's why I'll set things right. This won't happen again. I'll make sure of it."

"And I'll watch your back while you do it." Lara pivoted around and walked behind Alrion, fending off phantom adversaries.

"Maybe save that for later?" Alrion laughed. But he appreciated Lara trying to lighten the mood. The news of the Skull Queen had sent him reeling. He thought that he was prepared to help Alyx, but now he was not so sure. There was a niggling doubt that maybe he would be unable to help her.

First things first—I need to find her.

The path outside the Mystic's home was foreign. Alrion hadn't paid much attention on the way, he had been preoccupied. While staying with the Mystics, he hadn't strayed beyond his accommodation at all, leaving the job of combing the countryside to his mother and Lara.

"You must be an expert in this area now," Alrion said.

"By necessity. We spent more than enough time traipsing around, looking for hidden paths and alternate tracks. It will come in handy now."

"I hope so."

"I can take us the most direct path out of here. But where are we heading to?"

"Do you know where that lead came from? Where the Skull Queen was last sighted?"

"A small town really. Called Londarth."

"Londarth it is. I'm not naive enough to believe that she will still be there, but we can find a trail."

"There's always a trail."

"There wasn't one here. How did we lose her?" Alrion practically mumbled the words. Lara stopped and grabbed him by the arm.

"You have to stop beating yourself up. Sometimes you can't do it all. We'll make it right." Lara looked directly into his eyes. Alrion could see the same pain that he felt. It was reassuring.

"Good." Alrion strode forward, "let's get a move on."

"Try and keep up." Lara darted forward, picking an odd path between the large stones littered along the path. Alrion almost lost sight of her.

Here we go. He started to really move, and the exercise awakened him in a way that was surprising. It was invigorating.

I've been too static. This is good. It was time to just lose himself in the journey for a little while.

～

Hours passed, and Lara finally slowed.

"You really do know these lands now. I didn't think it was possible to cut a path through here that wouldn't require us to take a break." Alrion heaved in a deep breath. He could augment his physical endurance somewhat with the Soul Power, but it had nothing on actual training. The more he learned, the more he realised that it wasn't a shortcut. It was more of an augmentation. He couldn't create fitness. But he could create speed and strength in short bursts.

"Trust me, it became pretty boring heading out time and time again. We needed to find ways to make it more interesting. And cut the duration. There's a limit to how much you can explore in a day." Lara drew in measured breaths. It seemed like she had used this as a rest place before.

"I need to figure out a way to travel faster with magic."

"And take away another thing I can still beat you at?" Lara grinned. Alrion was thinking of a witty retort when he noticed something suddenly hurtling towards them. He reached out by instinct, sending a wave of force. The object stopped immediately and hovered in the air. Alrion stepped over to investigate. It was a jet-black arrow.

"Good reaction." Lara had a dagger in hand and was staring into the distance.

Alrion activated his Soul Power and examined the arrow. He could see the taint of the Blight on it. He could even see traces in the air, where the arrow had displaced it.

This is interesting. He followed the signs, tracking the arrow's point of origin. A flat rock in the distance. There was a man standing on it, but at this distance was only a silhouette.

"There. Let's go ask him a few questions." Alrion grabbed the arrow out of the air. He could feel the Blight within it. A familiar and unsettling feeling.

Don't worry you are past that.

Alrion approached carefully, Lara by his side. She stalked along, sweeping left and right looking for threats. Alrion maintained his focus on the figure ahead of them. The man remained still, looking in their direction.

Details began to emerge. Alrion could see the bow and quiver clearly now, as dark as the arrow. The man was wearing a black hood over his face, with a black leather jerkin. His legs though, they were something else. They were black and wiry, and the stone beneath him seemed to ooze blackness. Alrion conjured a fireball and held it in front of him as he moved closer.

"Ahoy there. Don't shoot the messenger!" The man's voice was almost normal, but there was a strange accent to it that sounded off. He quickly raised his hands and backed away a little.

"Don't trust him, keep alert." Lara started to circle around to approach the man from behind.

"You shot first," Alrion said.

"Just to get your attention. I didn't want to make the wrong impression."

"Too late," Lara said. She was almost within striking distance. However, the man seemed unfazed by her.

"Trust me, it would have been a lot worse had I done this." The man seemed to become a blur and ran rings around them before settling down in the same spot. It was almost too fast for Alrion to react. But rather than loose the fireball, he had held on to avoid friendly fire.

"See? I'm rather fast."

"And you leave a trail." Lara pointed to the ground. A black tar coated the ground in a circle around them, showing his path. It quickly dried up and started to flake away.

"What are you?" Alrion said. He had encountered nothing like this at all. Not even the Trackers were like this.

"I prefer who. Fermur, pleased to meet your acquaintance. You may have heard of me?"

"You're one of the generals of the Blight."

"Alrion, wasn't it?"

"How did you find me? Why are you here?" Alrion created a second fireball. Fermur backed away more, but then noticed how close Lara was.

"Easy now, as I said, don't shoot the messenger. That's all I am. I have a message for you." Fermur seemed a little apprehensive.

He's probably heard of what I can do. Alrion let both fireballs dissipate into nothing. They were a distraction and were probably too slow to deal with this thing anyway.

"Pass on your message then."

"With great delight. I have a message for you from our fearless leader, Darvin. He sends his regards." Fermur paused, watching Alrion.

"And?"

"And he would like to inform you of two events. First, his new comrade the Skull Queen will be leading an assault on a town nearby called Carth."

Alyx. We've found you.

"Why should we trust anything you say?" Lara inched closer, with her dagger still poised to strike.

"I am honour bound to relay only truth. I am a messenger after all. Never liked fighting, not really. It was a benefit of my transformation then, that I could have a legitimate reason to avoid it. Do you want to hear the second part of the message?" Fermur looked at Alrion. He nodded. Fermur beamed a smile.

"Excellent! Now, the second event of note is that Darvin himself will be leading a separate assault on the city of Hurdenor. He provides you an opportunity to confront him as the hero you are." Fermur stopped again and assumed a waiting pose.

"That's it?" Alrion said. *What are they playing at?*

"Yes, that is all. Were you expecting something else?" Fermur grinned like he was expecting the reaction. Alrion looked to Lara. She shrugged her shoulders lightly and kept her focus on Fermur.

"What do you think he's trying to tell us?" Alrion said. The grin faded from Fermur, and he took on a confused look. He leaned back and pulled out an arrow. But rather than preparing it to fire, he rubbed it between his fingers, deep in thought.

"You know, nobody ever asked my opinion. They either tried to kill me or chase me away."

"You seem quite intelligent to me. I would like to hear what you think." Alrion could see Fermur coming around. The general put the arrow back in his quiver.

"Very well, that's not against the rules. I think that he is taunting you. He wants you to choose between going after your friend and saving a city."

"Why?"

"You are his adversary. He wants to know how you think, also, I believe, to cause you pain. That is his way. But as I said..."

"Yes, you're just a messenger. We get it." Lara didn't hide the frustration in her voice.

"You do listen. Fantastic. I must be away then, message delivered after all." Fermur started to whir and move away. But Alrion was ready.

You're not leaving. Alrion sent out a wave of force and wound it around Fermur. It prevented him from moving from the spot.

"Curious." Fermur looked around his feet while straining to run.

I have to try. Alrion started releasing his Soul Power, using his magic as a conduit. He activated his enhanced vision, watching the Soul Power travelling along hidden waves. It started to wrap around and permeate Fermur.

"Oh no, that's cheating." Fermur quickly drew and fired multiple arrows at Lara. She dived down and Alrion quickly refocused his wave of force. Two arrows hit the ground and two others were diverted away by Alrion's spell. In that instant, Fermur was gone, the only sign the trail of black ooze. It seemed to be drying up and flaking away faster than before.

"I'm fine." Lara stood and Alrion ran over. He helped her up.

"No, really I'm fine." Lara turned and looked over the slowly disappearing trail behind Fermur.

"Do we want to follow him? It might be possible."

"No, he's probably going to return to Darvin. Our focus needs to be Alyx." Alrion noticed surprise in Lara's face.

"You've already decided?"

"I can't move on otherwise, no matter the cost. If we don't act now, we will lose her again." Alrion saw doubt in Lara's face before she looked away.

"You don't agree, do you?"

"I thought you were about saving everyone. Maybe there's a way we can?"

"Not this time. Please, support me on this." Alrion looked into her eyes. She held his gaze.

"Always. Let's go save our friend." Lara gave him a hug. The warmth was reassuring. But it was like he could feel it weighing on her.

I won't do this again. I promise.

4

INVESTIGATION DIVERTED

Vincent paused and looked around. The sweeping hills and clear sky were breathtaking. The contrast of the bright green leaves with the remnants of the snow made the surroundings much more colourful than he had expected.

"Beautiful country around here." Vincent brushed some snow off a knee-height rock and eased himself down.

"You really should have tried visiting sometime." Celes gave him a wry smile.

"I know, I know."

"What do you think we will find out here? Lara and I found so little." Celes leaned against a tree and brushed some snow off her shoulder.

"As thorough as you were, your search was constrained by how far you could go and easily return to the Mystics. There's a lot more going on around here, the news about Alyx is just one thing." Vincent sighed. Alrion had taken the news harder than expected.

He's so blind to anything else right now.

"He's been tasked with the impossible. And you haven't made it easy for him."

Here it is. I've been waiting for this conversation.

"Our family history? I was protecting him!"

"You may have started by protecting him, but you ended up protecting yourself." Celes pointed at his chest with a finger and he felt real pain. She was right.

"I know. I hope he understands. The weight of something like that, it's crushing. I didn't want to put it on him, nor did I want to have to deal with the fact that I had kept it silent." Vincent paused and shook his head, "that's always the way, isn't it?"

"What is?"

"Secrets come out at the worst times."

"Always. I think it's a golden rule. Makes life interesting though." Celes chuckled, and Vincent showed a tiny smile.

"So, was there a plan here? Or did you just want to run away from our son?"

She's on fire today.

"Definitely a real plan. I wanted to get you to a bigger city, so you could get to the bottom of what's happening around here. I think any major Blight activity will turn into a lead towards the Source. It's inevitable."

"And I suppose that it's a complete coincidence that the big city around here will be the only place with decent blacksmiths?"

"Of course. If we need to do some investigation at the smithy's, then, of course, I will reluctantly accept the responsibility." Vincent grinned at Celes.

"You are having way too much fun." He pointed at her in a mock accusatory way.

"I know. But I feel like we're finally free again after twenty years of just living a different life. Not a bad one, but different. And it's the last one."

"The last one?"

"This quest, journey, adventure—whatever we are calling it. It's the last one, I can feel it. So, I'm enjoying it for what it is when I can."

"I can't argue with that." Vincent rose and shook off the weariness. He needed to be active and strong.

"Let's push on and find civilisation."

Vincent put down the mug of ale and settled into the warmth. The little tavern was packed full of people, which was a nice change from the lonely wilderness. He gave Celes's hand an affectionate squeeze.

"Feeling more comfortable now?" She smiled.

"I hadn't realised how remote that area is. This feels better. We're still on the fringe, but there are people and activity."

"Shhh." Celes nudged her head towards a nearby conversation. Vincent nodded and tried to pick out the voices.

"I'm telling you, I saw them. Headed towards Hurdenor. A whole horde of Blighters. But they're using the forests to hide their movement," an old man said. He was nursing an ale and, as he spoke, flecks of spit flew across the table. His friends laughed him off.

"Gurt, you old dog. You've been on the piss again. You wouldn't spot a horde of Blighters if they were in here with us!"

"I swear, I hadn't even been drinking. But now, now I need to forget all about it." Gurt downed the rest of his drink and wiped his mouth. One of the men at the table jumped up to return to the bar.

"Good man, Frand. You know I'm telling the truth." Frand turned back.

"Not really, I just want to hear what kind of ridiculous story you'll be telling us next!" The rest of the table burst into laughter and Gurt grumbled with annoyance. Vincent leaned over.

"Sorry, friend, I couldn't help but overhear. Which forest was it?"

"Finally, someone with some sense! It's just over to the east. Easy to avoid, it's not the way you'd normally travel. Although I'd avoid Hurdenor just in case. They couldn't have been heading anywhere else."

"I wouldn't want to risk that, not after hearing your story." Vincent fished out a coin and flicked it onto the table in front of Gurt, "for your trouble." Gurt quickly pocketed the coin.

"Thanks." He looked about to say something else, but Frand returned with his drink. Vincent looked over at Celes.

"I know that look."

"Good, we can skip the conversation where I convince you to follow me into the woods." Vincent finished off his ale and slammed the mug down.

"You know, you're lucky that I love you." Celes rose carefully and threaded her way between the bodies and tables and found the door. Vincent followed close and paused before he left, relishing the heat.

The cold chill was worse than he expected. Night had fallen, and a stiff breeze brought the temperature down even more. Vincent nodded towards the edge of town, and Celes followed close.

"Do you really believe there's an attack brewing?"

"I believe enough to go tramp through the cold and drag you with me."

"Good. This is one of those situations where I would rather you were wrong and had dragged me out here for no reason."

"Likewise. I can't explain it, but it just feels like something is brewing. I can't ignore this." Vincent found a path between two houses, that headed into the trees. He noticed a lantern by the side of the path and bent down to pick it up.

"Looks like we're not the first to venture down here. Can you light it?" Vincent handed it to his wife. Celes retrieved something from her cloak and knelt on the ground. Within moments, she had a flame going and handed the lantern back to Vincent.

"After you." Vincent accepted the light and walked ahead. He noticed Celes walking closely behind him on the narrow path.

"Do you think we are being followed?" Vincent didn't stop to wait for a response and kept walking. The path was easy enough to follow but didn't seem to be much in use.

"No, all clear."

"That's a relief. I'm so hasty sometimes, this whole thing could have been a setup."

"That's why I'm here, to keep you out of trouble. Speaking of which, what have you been up to these last weeks?"

"What do you mean?"

"While I've been out in the countryside, you never ventured out. What have you been up to?"

"Keeping an eye on Alrion mostly and making sure he had what he needed. At other times, practising with the Soul Power."

"You just couldn't help yourself, could you?" Celes laughed.

"What do you mean?"

"First chance to do something that I think of as magic, you're all over it!"

"Hardly. I did it to be responsible and not shirk away from my duty. It should be helpful in our quest." Vincent expected a quip back, but there was silence. He continued to forge through the forest, pausing occasionally to look for signs of activity. There were none.

"What can you do? With the Soul Power?"

"I'm still figuring that out. But I seem able to heal myself and enhance my body. Gain extra speed or strength, push it beyond its normal limits."

"That sounds useful. I assume there's some sort of limits to how much you can use it?"

"Of course, once it runs out, I need time to recover. Stop a moment." Vincent thought he could hear something. He handed the lantern to Celes and motioned for her to stay put. She nodded. Vincent enhanced his vision and was able to see in the dark. He crept forward, straining his ears for confirmation of what he had heard. Nothing yet. Then, a quiet rustling.

Vincent stalked forward, using care to glide through the forest. Stealth wasn't his strength, but he knew enough to avoid twigs on the ground and errant branches. The rustling became louder, spurring him on. He reached a tree and clambered in, bracing himself on the lowest branches. Vincent stifled a gasp.

Before him marched an army of Blighters. With care and minimal noise, they were slowly advancing through the forest. Each one looked intensely focused and in control.

What is this? The tip was good, he needed to warn Celes. Vincent spun quickly and almost lost his grip. He paused, feeling his heart pounding. After a few deep breaths, he lowered himself down and ran back as quietly as he could.

"What's wrong?" Celes hissed as he approached. Vincent slowed.

"Blighters. A whole army."

"What?" Celes's voice was raised, and she quickly covered her mouth.

"I've never seen anything like it. They're marching slowly and quietly, like well-trained soldiers. This is not good."

"This is terrible. You were right to investigate this." Celes looked out into the darkness and shook her head.

"I'd rather be wrong."

"How far ahead did you think this through? Are we going there now?"

"Yes, we must. I wish I could warn them…"

"But they'll never believe you, even if you could get there in time," Celes said, finishing the thought.

"Let's get a horse and try and get ahead of this. We can figure out a plan on the way."

Not long after, Vincent stepped back out of the inn, following an old and bemused farmer holding a lantern out in front of him.

"You young'uns and your urgent tasks. I was once like that. A long time ago. Always rushing around."

I'm not a young'un!

Vincent was about to object but Celes put her hand on his arm. He grumbled to himself and swallowed the retort.

"We appreciate you helping us out on such short notice," Celes said.

"Oh, don't you worry, I'm being amply compensated." The farmer chuckled and started whistling. It only took a few minutes to reach the stables. The farmer used his lantern to light another just inside the entrance.

"Now, I know you're in a big rush, but I can't spare my best stallion. You can take Brenda over there." The farmer pointed to a medium-sized mare, staring out at them with a vacant expression.

Vincent handed over a small sack of gold. The farmer weighed it up, peeked inside, then pocketed the sack.

"I trust you can sort the rest out. Good night, and good luck." The farmer waved and left the stables.

Vincent had the horse out and saddled within minutes. Despite first impressions, Brenda seemed responsive and energetic. He helped Celes jump onto the back.

"Now the fun begins." Vincent guided the horse out onto the main path and gently nudged her into a canter.

"We are on the way to warn a city that won't believe us about a horde of Blighters that are going to attack. But look at you, you're still having fun." Celes grabbed him and held on tight.

"I did say this was the last journey. But we're not at the end yet."

I hope Alrion finds a way here too. These people are going to need all the help they can get.

5

TRACKING THE QUEEN

L ara ambled up the hill, keeping slightly ahead of Alrion. She paused to take in the view. A cluster of houses nestled together amongst the woods. Snow was lighter here, and the trees more densely packed together. She watched Alrion make the last few steps. There was a heaviness to him.

His decision is weighing on him. It was the opposite to what he had done before. When the stakes were high, he used his power to cure Wraith and restore Branthor. It was the greater of the possibilities. But doing so had lost them Alyx. Now he was ignoring an opportunity to confront the leader of the Blight and potentially save a city in the process.

Is it guilt that he let her go before?

"You look deep in thought," Alrion said with what looked like a forced smile.

"As do you."

"There's much to think about." Lara watched his expression darken, but he hid it quickly.

The weight of the world on his shoulders.

"Let's go find the inn down there, I'm sure they have something approximating one, and warm up. Then I have an experiment I want you to help me with." Lara watched Alrion's face. It lit up with genuine excitement and interest. Her heart jumped a little, she loved that about him. His eager curiosity and how genuine he was.

"I'm intrigued."

"Good, hold that feeling." Lara crested the hill and headed down to the buildings below.

The town, if you could call it that, was named Plort. Lara didn't even bother asking about the origins of the name. But she did confirm their bearings and destination. She found Alrion tucking into some spiced chicken and potato. The warmth and the food were returning some of his usual behaviour.

"Where's my food?"

"Coming, I ordered you something special." Alrion winked.

I don't even care what he ordered, it's worth that spark in him.

"You'll be pleased to hear we are just a day's hike from Carth. We can rest here tonight, hike all day tomorrow, and we will arrive late in the day. Then we can see what's happening there."

"Shouldn't we go tonight?" Alrion had a questioning look.

"No. We won't hike all day on no sleep when we think we're going into a battle."

"But maybe we'll be too late?"

"It doesn't matter if we get there before or after the battle, it just matters that she's there. You've made that quite clear." Lara let her frustration out a bit.

"It does matter, we shouldn't put lives at risk unnecessarily."

"We've already done that by coming here instead of confronting Darvin." Lara took a deep breath. "Look, you've made that choice already. Now we need to make sure that you achieve the objective. There's no point to this if you can't save Alyx." Lara watched his face, wondering if she had been too direct. He looked pained.

"You're right. Whatever we need to do to ensure we get the job done." Alrion returned to his food, reluctantly picking at it. Lara's food arrived. It was a plate of steamed vegetables.

"Looking after my weight, are you?" Lara gave him an angry look, and Alrion looked shocked. He almost spat his food out.

"No, no. Not at all. I was just getting you something healthy. You were complaining about too much meat." He suddenly stopped. "Hang on, you're smiling now."

"Got you."

"That wasn't fair."

"You becoming despondent wasn't fair. I think sometimes you need to remind yourself of what you are."

"And that is?" Alrion looked her in the eye. Lara leaned close and whispered.

"The greatest wizard of our time, wielding the power to cleanse the Blight. Also, you have the attention of the most beautiful and graceful thief of all time." Lara leaned back, satisfied. Alrion had a grin on his face.

"I thought you weren't a thief? More of a collector of things?"

"That's not as catchy."

"You're right again." Alrion sighed.

"Right again?"

"About me. I'm sorry, I do lose sight of things sometimes. I thought that when I was..." Alrion looked around at the crowd, "cured, everything would be fine and easy. But it's not. Because now I need to find a way to do something my grandfather couldn't."

"And you will." Lara forced some steamed broccoli into her mouth and kept smiling.

"See! I knew you'd enjoy the vegetables." Lara couldn't tell if he was being serious or not.

Later that evening, they settled into the guest room. Two low beds, and nothing else. But Lara was satisfied, it was somewhere to rest before the long hike ahead of them.

"You mentioned an experiment?" Alrion said. He looked at Lara with curious eyes.

"Yes, I've been thinking about your Soul Power. What did you say it could do again? Other than of course drive out the Blight."

"It seems to amplify your body. Healing, improving performance. Somehow the Mystics can use it to help heal others too, but I'm still not completely sure about that." Alrion looked confused by the question.

He's really so focused in one direction.

"And you managed to cure Wraith of the Blight by using your magic as a way to infuse him with Soul Power?"

"Essentially, yes."

"And finally, you are developing a way of containing Soul Power within a vessel for the purpose of making someone else capable of using Soul Power?"

"Yes, exactly that." Alrion's face turned into a frown. "I don't see where this is going?"

"Oh, Alrion. You are so single-minded. All about the Blight." Lara crossed the room until she was right in front of him. She was practically breathing on his face.

"Ever thought that I could use that Soul Power?" Alrion's reaction was priceless. He gaped at her like a fish out of water.

"How?"

"If you could inject a Shade with your Soul Power, then why not another person?" Lara watched Alrion's reaction. He withdrew from her, sitting down on the bed behind him. He was staring into space, concentrating.

"Why did I never think of that?" Alrion looked up at her.

"That's why you have me, for doing the thinking that you'll never get around to." She cracked a smile and he returned an even bigger one.

"Try it now. Without that orb, just give me your Soul Power."

"I'm not sure."

"How did you do it to Wraith? Or even Fermur? You were doing something to him, right?"

"Well, I touched him with my magic, which was like a conduit to apply Soul Power."

"Then do the same to me." Lara put her arms out like she was welcoming him into a hug.

"Alright. Sure." Alrion concentrated, and Lara slowly rose above the floor, floating in the air.

"This is quite interesting." Lara tried walking, but it didn't work.

"You want to move? Let's figure that out later. For now, I think I have a way to transfer to you." Alrion scrunched his face up in concentration. Then his eyes flashed and seemed to reflect the light differently.

Lara was about to ask him how he was going when she felt it. A strange warmth creeping up her body. It started in her feet and kept on rising.

"I think it's working."

"You can feel that? I'm not sure how much to do."

"Keep going." Lara concentrated on the sensation. It was quite strange, but somehow comforting. Her hand tingled, as the Soul Power passed through it.

Time for a test.

Lara drew her dagger and quickly cut her palm. She pushed away the initial pain and clenched her fist.

"What are you doing?" Alrion cried with surprise.

"A test. See what this Soul Power can do." Lara saw him nod absently, then continue to focus on what he was doing. She didn't feel any different. She tried focusing on her hand, urging the warmth to go there and fix it. Nothing seemed to happen. She tried again and again, labouring the point. Finally, she gave up and opened her hand. The cut was healed.

"It worked!" Lara stared at her palm amazed. Alrion strode over and examined it.

"Hmm, good. Let me borrow that." He took the dagger from her hand and sliced his own hand the same way.

"Huh?"

"Comparing," Alrion grunted. He was concentrating.

"What are you thinking?"

"I think the Soul Power is less efficient in your body. It looked like you consumed a great deal to heal that wound." Alrion looked back at Lara, examining her. She felt a little uncomfortable.

"What are you seeing?"

"I can see the Soul Power within you. There's still some left. It seems to be staying around."

"That's good, right?" She could still feel the warmth when she concentrated, but it was less enveloping, less intense.

"If it can persist a long time, that could be very useful." Alrion looked lost in thought.

"Well, well, well. Guess I was right, wasn't I?" Lara laughed.

"You really were. This is a whole new way of thinking that I never explored."

"It wasn't in that big book you were reading?"

"Not much. The Mystics were quite concerned with keeping their practices secret and to themselves. With good reason. But either they didn't document much of this, or never experimented much." Alrion looked Lara in the eyes, "thank you for suggesting this. We need to really see how far we can take it."

"I agree, but tomorrow on the journey over. The first experiment can see if the Soul Power is still present in the morning."

"Agreed." Alrion started preparing to turn in.

I can't believe that worked. It's like everything just changed dramatically.

Alrion awoke first. Within moments, he remembered their experiment from the night before and enhanced his vision. He couldn't see the Soul Power clearly.

"Lara."

"What?" She sat up immediately, looking around.

"It's daylight. And I need to check your Soul Power. Can you stand?"

"Good morning to you too," Lara muttered. She stood and let the blanket fall away. Alrion could see remnants of Soul Power within her, but not as much as the night before.

"The good news is that there seems to be some left over. But it has diminished."

"Why do you think that is?"

"Do you feel any different?" Alrion couldn't see anything different about her. Lara looked down and went through a quick routine working her individual muscles.

"Everything seems normal, I had a good night's sleep?"

"I can only guess the Soul Power found an outlet within you, but it doesn't seem to have done much."

"That's fine, how much did you use last night?"

"I think around half? I wasn't really paying attention. It could be less, I don't have a full gauge of my strength yet. I was also supplementing it while at the Mystics."

"We can figure that out as we go. And since we have a long hike ahead of us, best we get prepared."

"Absolutely." Alrion started packing his things. The discovery about Soul Power was exciting, and a good distraction. But his mind had quickly turned back to thinking of Alyx. Within the day they would find her. And he would have to face her. Face what she had become. All because of him.

You had no choice, you needed to stop Wraith. The words made logical sense, but it still gnawed at him. He still didn't feel confident that he was even doing the right thing now, targeting Alyx above all else. But at least he knew that a part of him would finally rest. A burden would be lifted, and he could focus more on his quest.

It's almost done. I just need to be strong enough to save her.

6

LOOMING BATTLE

The city walls of Hurdenor loomed above them in the early sunlight. The city was just waking, preparing for a new day. *They have no idea what's coming.*

"I think we're here in time, no signs of panic or a battle yet."

"They can't be far away. What do we do?" Celes said.

"We can't say anything to the gate guards, they'll turn us away. Call us crazy and troublemakers."

"How can they mount a defence without the guards at the ready?"

"They can't. We need to find someone with authority who might listen."

Easier said than done.

Vincent eased his horse down to a light trot. As he approached the guards, one let out a loud yawn without even bothering to cover it.

"You lot are up early. State your business."

"I'm a blacksmith looking for work. Do you know where I can find the smithies in town?"

"I'm not your tour guide. The market district is well signposted." The guard waved them through, his companion now yawning as well.

"That bodes well," Celes said.

"Indeed. Let's go take a look at the smithies and see what we can find."

"I hope you have a plan." Celes sounded doubtful, and she poked him in the back.

"A glimmer of one. We need to start with what we know." Vincent spotted a tattered sign pointing to the Market District and guided the horse to the right. There weren't many people out and about. Vincent pressed on, trying to make good time without going into a full-on gallop. There was no need to raise alarm, just yet.

Here we go. As he suspected, the smithies were all up and working. Vincent could feel the heat from the forges. He slowed and glanced at the different establishments.

"What are you looking for?"

"High-end armour or weapons. The kind favoured by the captain of the guard."

"Oh, I see where you're going with this." He thought he could hear some surprise and admiration in her voice.

"It's a long shot, but worth a try." Vincent brought the horse to a stop. They were outside a shop called *The Haughty Helm.* Vincent jumped down and helped his wife dismount more gracefully. After tying up the horse, he opened the heavy door and ushered her inside.

The shop was richly furnished, and a wide array of armaments hung on the walls. Some smaller items were arrayed on tables, mostly knives, daggers, and small armour pieces. Vincent spotted a bored man sitting up the back. He awoke with surprise, almost falling off his chair.

"Never had a customer this early. Old Henry always insists I man the shop at first light, but usually, I'm catching a few extra winks of sleep. Oh, how we will enjoy this!" the man said. He seemed genuinely intrigued.

"I certainly hope so. Could we talk to him? I'm a blacksmith myself and have something of importance to discuss."

"He didn't mention he was expecting anyone, but why not. Come through here." The man lifted a panel in the bench and gestured towards a door set in the back of the shop. Vincent and Celes entered and followed closely behind him.

Vincent drew in a breath as they entered the workshop. It was much bigger than he expected. The only person present was an older man with wiry hair and a short, slim frame which made his arms look enormous. He was sitting on a stool staring at a sheet of paper.

"Henry, I've got some guests for you." Henry looked up, assessing them both.

"Very well, get back to the shop, Jones." Henry watched Jones head off then looked back at Vincent and Celes.

"I don't recognise you. Travellers?"

"Yes, my name is Vincent, and this is my wife Celes."

"Henry, as you may have gathered." Henry stopped abruptly and just waited.

"You must be wondering why we have dropped in on you so early and unannounced," Vincent said.

"Still wondering."

"Of course, sorry. It's just that we need help and I thought that a fellow blacksmith could be of service."

"Again, I'm still wondering."

"There's an army of Blighters headed towards the city," Celes blurted out. Vincent looked at her, shocked.

"Well, when were you going to get to the point?"

"I like her." Henry grinned, "if what you are saying is true, why come to me? Why not go to the guard?"

"There's no time, they will be here within hours."

"And we think the guard will send us away and think we're crazy," Celes said.

"What proof do you have?"

"None other than my statement. The truth will be quite obvious when they attack." Vincent hoped that he was swaying Henry. But the old blacksmith didn't seem too keen on helping.

"You're completely mad. But what if you're right?" Henry muttered. He started pacing around the room.

"I can't vouch for you, I'm sorry. Even if they believe me, it's too late to do anything. And if you're wrong, I have nothing to fall back on. You've literally walked in here off the street." Henry looked at Vincent like he was challenging Vincent to dispute his words.

"You're absolutely correct."

"But we have to do something. If you're not helping us, we'll find someone else." Celes started to walk off.

"I didn't say I wouldn't help." Henry looked thoughtful. "You're a real blacksmith, right?"

"Yes. Do you need me to prove it?"

"No, we're out of time. I'll supply your materials and you can fortify the entrance to the market district. If you're a maniac, all I lose is some materials which can be reclaimed if need be. But if you're right, then I was prudent to take measures. How does that sound?"

"Done, we'll take it!" Celes spun around and ran up to Henry, grabbing his hand and shaking it. Henry looked at her with surprise.

"She's always full of surprises." Vincent shrugged at Henry.

"You can use anything from that corner." Henry pointed to a far part of the workshop with stacks of lumber and different types and sizes of metal. "I'll open up the side door, so you can get out without using the shop." Henry stalked off.

"Let's get to work." Celes started off towards the materials.

"What's gotten in to you?" Vincent said as he trailed after her.

"You blacksmiths are stuck at slow speed. We need to get something happening before this city is slaughtered."

"I can't argue with that." Vincent picked up the pace and rushed ahead of his wife.

Vincent paused and brushed the sweat away from his face. He ignored the curious looks of passers-by, often stopping to watch him work. Celes handed him another sheet of steel and he lay it across the stakes he had dug into the ground.

"We're running out of time, you can rest later." Celes slapped him on the back.

"Any sign of Alrion?" Vincent said in between hammer swings.

"Nothing. I'll go have another look." Celes took off and Vincent paused again to draw in his breath.

I hope this is not for nothing.

With a final swing, he stepped back to survey his work. A rough fence had been constructed, leaving only a small gap for traffic to pass through. A guard strolled up.

"You, there. Who authorised this work?"

"Old Henry. There's been word of an incoming attack, and he thought it prudent to shore up defences. Here I am, creating a way of funnelling enemies into a smaller space."

"This is not going to work. Why now?" The guard muttered something and slapped the steel sheet in annoyance.

"Don't ask me, I'm just the help. I was instructed to get something up for now, then we can look at how to integrate it better for continued use."

"This is ridiculous. I'm going to have words." The guard strode off, heading towards the smithies. Vincent watched him go.

Sorry, Henry, I needed to buy some time.

Vincent noticed Celes run back through the makeshift doorway.

"Prepare yourself, it's time."

I know that look. This is no game.

Vincent put down his hammer and retrieved his sword. His muscles ached, but there was nothing else he could do. He calmed himself and searched inside for his Soul Power. He directed some to the muscles that ached the most. A wave of calm swept over him, and the complaining was dulled.

That will do. I should save something for the battle ahead.

"Is there somewhere else we can fight?" he said.

"There are some good places just past the main gate. We should ideally start there and fall back here."

"So be it." Vincent drew his sword and led the way. Celes followed close behind.

Alrion, where are you?

~

Vincent heard them first. The snarls and cries, the sounds of metal on metal, metal on flesh. Guards poured into the gates, reinforcing the fallen. But there was no end to the Blighters. Each time one fell another eagerly stepped in. The guards were holding well but tiring. Vincent looked around and spotted a guard with a red sash over his shoulder.

Captain.

"Wait here a moment." Vincent gestured to Celes and she nodded. He then jogged forward to talk to the captain.

"Excuse me, Captain."

"Fall back, use the shelters." The captain didn't even turn to look.

"We have reinforced the entrance to the Trade District. There're some walls in place to stem the tide of Blighters. They won't last forever, but they should make a difference." Vincent waited for a response, but the captain was silent.

"Judging the fight, you will have to retreat within minutes. This is an opportunity to regroup and buy some time."

"Buy time for what?" The captain turned, and his expression was grim.

"A miracle."

"Start praying." The captain turned back to the fight and walked towards the active fighting. Vincent retreated, finding Celes.

"What did he say?"

"Start praying. I think he heard me though and will fall back to the Trade District."

"We can't win this, can we?" Celes whispered.

"You're right as usual. Maybe you can find us a way out?"

"You're dreaming. Find a way out of this city we've never seen that is being assaulted by a horde of Blighters?"

"Yes." Vincent gave his wife a smile.

"Sometimes I wonder how you ever survived without me." Celes shook her head, but Vincent noticed a small smile. But it was quickly gone, replaced with a worried look.

She's right to worry. This city is doomed.

Vincent gestured to a few guards lingering on the fringes. They gave him confused looks and turned back to watching the battle.

"OVER HERE. NOW!" Vincent shouted in his best commanding voice. The confused guards almost jumped and cautiously approached.

"There's no place for watchers here, we need every man. Come with me and fortify this choke point." Vincent didn't wait for acknowledgement, he just stalked off towards the makeshift walls he had constructed. As he walked, he listened out and heard the crunch of footsteps behind him.

Good, something has survived from their training. He showed them where to stand, putting the two nervous ones behind the wall.

"You two are to clean up any that get through. Understand?" The two guards nodded. One nervously adjusted his gauntlet. Their armour was mostly chain, with a few plates on the arms and legs. It looked like it had never seen real battle.

Either they're new, or there's not really a Blight presence here normally. Either way, they're not equipped for this.

Vincent heard shouts and turned quickly to observe. The guards were breaking rank. The captain shouted furiously at them, whipping some back into a formation. But the gates were lost. Vincent saw the captain leading the retreat, drawing the enemy towards the Trade District.

Here's where it gets interesting. If you're going to show up, boy, now's the time. But Vincent had the distinct feeling that they were alone in this fight.

7

FIGHT FOR A FRIEND

The Town of Carth lay before them, nestled amongst some rolling hills. Alrion looked for signs of distress but couldn't see any.

"Did we make it in time?" Alrion looked to Lara. She had a good instinct for these things.

"Maybe." Lara wrinkled her nose.

There's something she's not telling me.

"We better get in there then, maybe we can get the advantage." Alrion started to walk off but noticed Lara was standing still.

"What's wrong?"

"We don't know what we are walking into. How are you feeling? We have just hiked for most of the day."

Tired.

"Pretty refreshed, all things considered."

"Have you been using Soul Power to maintain your strength?" Lara pointed at him with an accusatory finger.

"Some."

"See, you need to be aware of that. She's not going to play fair."

"I know. Because she's probably not really there."

"Good. Remember that. Because when you see her..."

"It's going to be difficult." Alrion sighed and tried to steel himself. *You must save her, no matter what.*

"Do you have any of those Soul Orbs?"

"I have one that's filled. Why?"

"Give it to me." Lara held out her hand.

"But, it's untested."

"Doesn't matter. Hopefully, we don't need it. But if it works, it works." Lara beckoned again for him to hand her the Orb. Alrion reached inside his robe and removed it. He activated his enhanced vision again for a moment to verify its contents.

"Still there." Alrion started to hand it over and stopped. "Just be careful with this." He handed it over and Lara deftly hid it away.

"After you." She pointed at the road ahead. Alrion nodded and started walking.

This is really happening. Time to set things right.

Carth wasn't particularly big. In many ways, it reminded him of home. A few trades, a few homes. But the streets were empty.

"It's too quiet. Could you tell from back there?"

"I had an inkling. But we don't know what it means."

"True." Alrion kept walking. He peered around houses as he went but didn't see any people. Or signs of fighting. He stopped suddenly. In the middle of the road was a deep hole and displaced earth all around.

"What happened here?" Alrion knelt to inspect the ground. There were traces of a black sludge. He looked them over with enhanced vision.

"Traces of Blight." Alrion stood and looked at Lara. Her eyes were on the distance.

"Must be something up ahead. There have been no other signs of a struggle. Keep your guard up."

"Don't worry about that." The truth was, Alrion couldn't be more on edge. He continued, looking more closely for any signs of what might have happened. But the town seemed quiet and undamaged.

Left just as it should have been. The road curved around behind the town.

"Whatever it is, it'll be back there." Lara pointed to where the road went out of sight.

"I hope we're not too late." Alrion's pulse quickened, his heart pumping faster and faster.

You can do this. This will save your friend. Just get the job done.

Alrion walked faster. He needed this to be over already. Lara kept pace, her dagger out. The sounds of their footsteps crunching louder than expected, the still air seemingly amplifying any sound.

"Well, there's the townsfolk." Lara pointed. Alrion could see them all. There was a clearing behind the town, and all the people were bunched together. They murmured softly but were otherwise quiet and still. Alrion could see the reason why. Before them stood a creature, one that inspired terror. His first instinct was to look away, but he forced himself to face it.

The creature had Alyx's frame, although its skin was black and seemed more muscular. It wore a modified black tunic, with light armour on the arms and legs. But its face was unadorned. It was black except for the exposed bones of the skull. And the piercing white eyes. He understood finally.

"The Skull Queen," Alrion whispered.

"I can't believe what they have done," Lara said softly. The Skull Queen reached behind and retrieved a massive black great sword. It was jet black and the edge seemed to ooze with something.

"That's no ordinary blade. It seems to be somehow infused with the Blight."

"This is not good. This is not good." Lara shifted her stance. She seemed to be weighing up her options.

"We just need to engage and get it done. I doubt she's as fast as Fermur, we should end this quickly." Alrion took a deep breath and prepared.

It's time at last. Don't hesitate. Go.

Alrion drew up his Spark, preparing a spell. The Skull Queen instantly turned and hefted the giant sword. She started to swing towards the mass of people.

"No!" Alrion screamed. He threw out a wave of force to try to knock the Skull Queen aside. But the strike was unusually quick. Instead of carving through the people, a trail of black collected into a cloud and sunk down over them.

"What was that?" Lara said. Her mouth hung open. The Skull Queen stepped aside to show her handiwork. The gathered people started to cough and choke as the black substance infused them.

"This could get really ugly." Lara fidgeted, spinning her dagger. She looked between the Skull Queen and the transforming people.

"No. No. No." Alrion muttered. "Not again." Something was building within him. Frustration. Fury. Pain.

"Don't forget that Alyx is in there somewhere." Lara put a hand on Alrion's shoulder, but he shrugged her off.

"Don't involve them in this!" Alrion shouted. He gathered everything he had. Spark and Soul Power. And he ran straight at the Skull Queen. He saw a wicked smile form on her face, and she held up the great sword in a ready position.

"Here we go," Lara said quietly and ran alongside him. She threw out some daggers aimed at the Skull Queen's head. The creature didn't move, and they bounced harmlessly off.

Alrion's focus grew smaller and smaller. He was only barely aware of Lara's attack. Something was happening, and he wasn't getting in the way. He was acting on instinct. A part of him thought that maybe he was losing himself, that he should regain control. But he didn't want to. He had to let this happen.

Alrion continued, travelling faster and faster. Only he didn't stop and confront the Skull Queen. He headed straight for the middle of the townsfolk. He was amongst the writhing and screaming as they were forcefully transformed into something else. Alrion stopped quite suddenly. And he gave in to the feeling, he let go of the force that had been building up.

It was like an explosion of force and Soul Power. It felt like the time he had attacked Ashra in desperation, but instead of the deadly white-hot power that removed everything from existence, it was like the Soul Power was used as the medium. He lost all sense of time, surrounded by a haze of white gold.

Slowly, his vision returned and he surveyed the scene. All the townsfolk were knocked down and looked unconscious. The ground was clear of dust, and the strange black cloud had been dispelled. Realising his own lack of awareness, he quickly turned to look at the Skull Queen. She was crouched down, glaring at him. Something appeared different.

"The sword. The black edge is gone." Lara crouched down next to Alrion.

"Good."

"Are you alright? What was that?" Lara looked worried. But he couldn't find the words to explain.

"I can't say, it was something else. I think it worked."

"It must have." Lara rose and focused on the Skull Queen.

"She looks relatively unharmed. Do you have any Soul Power left?"

"Not really." He felt a pang of despair. He had squandered his best chance at restoring Alyx. Even though he had done the right thing.

It's like I can't save her. Why?

"Don't worry, that's why I'm here." Lara was turning the Soul Orb over in her hands.

"It might not have enough power."

"We'll have to take that chance. But we only get one shot." Lara's gaze focused even more. She was planning something.

"I'll follow your lead." Alrion stood and dusted himself off. His Spark was still available, and his Soul Power would recover in time. At least the townspeople were out of the picture. It was just them.

The Skull Queen swung her sword and readied herself. She looked from Alrion to Lara. Waiting.

I need to be careful. I need to restrain her, but not kill her. Then we can try the cure.

"Let's try and shut down her mobility," Lara said.

"Sure. You distract, and I'll try and lock her down." Alrion watched Lara run off and he approached with caution.

How much of you is in there?

Lara ran straight at the Skull Queen, and the creature prepared to engage. At the last minute Lara changed direction, trying to flank. The Skull Queen turned also, doing a short swipe to keep Lara away. Alrion seized the opportunity, manipulating the earth to swallow up and encase the Skull Queen's feet. She didn't react initially, just looked down after it was done.

"I hope it holds." Lara stayed out of range of the giant sword. After a few moments, the Skull Queen casually moved her legs and the ground broke away. Like she was dusting off sand.

"Try again." Lara darted off, trying to circle around the Skull Queen. She ducked in quickly and tried a slash with her dagger. It glanced off a piece of armour, but Lara managed to retreat safely.

"She's quite fast, but still needs time to manoeuvre the giant blade. I have some options."

"Hopefully, you won't need them." Alrion started to prepare another spell. He sent a wave of force at the Skull Queen, trying to wrap her up completely. She swung her great sword, the movement seemingly cutting through the waves of force and rendering them useless.

What? That's not possible.

Taking advantage of their surprise, the Skull Queen launched a sweeping attack at Lara. The young thief only narrowly dodged away and quickly retreated.

"Too close. Your spell failed?" Lara said in between breaths.

"She somehow cut it down. I need to keep trying." Alrion went back to basics. He launched a small fireball, aiming for the Skull Queen's head. This time she batted it away like it was nothing. Lara had to dodge the fireball, and it exploded into the ground nearby.

"Her sword, it's magical somehow."

"I can see that," Alrion muttered. He tried again. Drawing upon even more Spark, he raised a cage of fire around the Skull Queen, ensuring the flames rose to twice her height. She used her sword like a giant fan, blowing away a section of the flames and stepping through unharmed.

Is she grinning? This is so frustrating.

He needed something else. Ranged attacks were not working. But he had to conserve what little Soul Power he had. It took a long time to regenerate.

Desperate times. Alrion drew his sword. The diamond on the pommel shone brightly in response to the Skull Queen.

"Alrion, no. That's too dangerous. She's an elite fighter." Lara started to retreat further, approaching him.

"There's no other way. I can protect myself." Alrion gripped the sword tightly, then remembered Alyx's training. He forced himself to relax, although it didn't quite hold. But at least he had the right idea.

"It's me you want!" Alrion yelled. He strode forward in a defensive stance, closing the gap. He stared her in the eyes. Those pure white eyes on a ghastly face. He tried to picture Alyx within.

There's no way a bit of Soul Power can fix this.

The Skull Queen closed in. Alrion stepped forward, launching into the most common sword routine they had practised.

Remember. Remember, Alyx.

The Skull Queen parried easily, anticipating each strike. Alrion kept pushing, going faster and faster. A strange unearthly laugh came from her. Despite his upping the intensity, she wasn't even slightly challenged. As he prepared the final strike he stopped suddenly and dropped his sword. The Skull Queen had already begun to swing to counter him. However, the strike extended further out putting her slightly off-balance but sending the great sword hurtling at Alrion's chest.

"No!" Lara screamed. Alrion could sense her running in. Two knives bounced harmlessly off the Skull Queen. As the blade came in, Alrion used the remaining Soul Power he had to infuse into his hands. He caught the blade with his hands and threw it towards the ground.

The swing in momentum threw the Skull Queen off balance, and the sword clattered away as she lurched forward. Alrion threw himself forward, tackling her, and they both fell to the ground. He found himself on top of her, staring into her ghastly face. Lara joined them immediately, helping to pin the Skull Queen to the ground.

"You're crazy," Lara whispered.

"Yes." Alrion could say nothing else. He just stared into the eyes of his friend.

8

THE FALL OF HURDENOR

The initial rally was heartening. The captain and the remaining guards defended the makeshift gate that Vincent had constructed. And initially, it worked. But Vincent could see a looming problem.

Now that they're in the gates, they can reinforce much faster and swarm us. Where's the relief?

Vincent sliced through a Blighter's arm and kicked it to the ground. He turned quickly to look for his wife.

No sign yet. Hopefully, she's found something.

Vincent returned to the fight. He was slowly draining his Soul Power, trying to keep his body from tiring too quickly. It was unfortunate that he had exerted himself so much in the frantic rush to build some fortifications. And they were paying dividends. But he was tiring way too quickly.

How are we going to win this? Where's Alrion?

The battle raged on. Vincent pushed forward to the front line. His Runesteel was working wonders, quickly and efficiently slicing through Blighters. But he was just one man, and he was not a young man. Despite his level of activity and proficiency, the blade could have done more in the hands of an elite fighter. Vincent was not that man, although he accounted well for himself.

The assault slowed, and the Blighters started to hold back.

"Hold!' the captain shouted. Vincent nodded at him. The man knew when to keep the men in line. The guards waited, a strange silence falling over them. The Blighters parted, and a man walked out. He was dressed in black armour, with white trim along most of the edges. He had a sword and shield strapped to his back.

"I wondered who I would find here. I so wanted to meet Alrion, but I knew that the bait was just too tempting." The man spoke loudly, to no one in particular. The guards murmured amongst themselves.

"Blacksmith, show yourself. I would speak with you." The guards looked amongst each other, then noticed Vincent. Vincent checked again for Celes, but there was no sign.

Play along for now.

Vincent sheathed his sword and slowly picked his way through the defenders until he was alone in front of the Blight horde. The man regarded him.

"I don't believe we have formally met. I'm Darvin. I..."

"I know what you are." Vincent interrupted him.

"Good, that makes things easier. Your name is... Vincent?"

"Yes."

"Well, not your true name. But, you see, I can play along with everyone."

"I appreciate that."

What is he playing at?

"You are probably wondering where your son is. He's with the Skull Queen right now. I gave him a choice, you see. Come here and save a city or go there and save one person."

"I see."

"Not very good at arithmetic, is he?" Darvin laughed.

"There are different ways to save people."

"How interesting. I'm so glad that you came, this was going to be quite a bore otherwise." Darvin started pacing around. Vincent watched him with caution, hand on his sword hilt.

"That's a nice blade you have there. But it's not enough." Darvin paused his pacing and regarded Vincent. A cruel smile came across his face.

"Ah, I have it. I am going to give you a choice as well." Darvin chuckled. Vincent tightened his grip on the sword.

Where is Celes?

"Everyone, pay attention. If this man here accepts a one-on-one fight with me and wins, I will spare this city. If he runs away, or if he loses, then you all die." Darvin watched the crowd. Murmurs ran through the guards. The captain walked over to Vincent.

"Are you going to accept?"

"Likely. Although I have no chance."

"We have no chance of winning this battle. Any chance is better than that." Vincent nodded.

"I am sorry this falls to you, although you seem to have some connection to this. Perhaps you can perform a miracle this day." The captain clapped Vincent on the shoulder and started to walk away.

"The name's Douglas by the way. We should call you Vincent?"

"Yes."

"Good luck, Vincent."

"Thanks." Vincent looked again for a sign of his wife but found nothing.

I'll try and drag this out as long as possible.

"I accept your challenge. What are the terms?"

"We duel, and the loser loses."

"To the death?"

"I'll see how I feel about that." Darvin laughed and started to arm himself.

I need to be careful, he could do anything. I don't even know what his real strength is.

Vincent unsheathed his sword and took a ready stance. He felt within himself for his Soul Power. There was very little remaining.

I need to save it. Use it for an advantage.

Darvin was ready, his shield strapped to one arm and his sword in the other. He banged the shield with the sword, and the dread shield reverberated through the space.

"Let's see what you can bring." Darvin started advancing. Vincent took a deep breath.

Here we go.

Vincent struck first, stepping into a sequence of blows, alternating low and high. Darvin led with his shield, blocking the strikes easily. The Runesteel bounced harmlessly off. Darvin then parried the final attack and lashed out with his shield. Vincent noticed just in time, tumbling to the side and quickly scrambling back onto his feet.

"You are resourceful. But as you can see, your weapon does nothing. I can withstand your blows all day." Darvin advanced again, looming in front of Vincent. The general was of average height, but he had a huge presence.

Just focus on the basics.

Vincent stepped back and waited. Darvin became inpatient and launched into an attack of his own. He led with his sword, opening with a criss-cross pattern of slashes that forced Vincent to parry, dodge, and retreat. Darvin grew bolder, launching another series that interspersed his shield seemingly at random. The clangs of sword on sword, sword on shield rang out through the space. Vincent was holding his own but couldn't press Darvin. The general's defences seemed impenetrable.

I need to create an opening. But even if I do, how would it work?

Vincent felt within for his Soul Power. It sat there, waiting. He could try to use it for a burst of speed or strength. But neither seemed like enough. There had to be more he could do.

Purely by instinct, Vincent started channelling the Soul Power into his hand. But then further. He tried to force it into his sword. He could sense the resistance. Then it started to give way.

It's working.

It was a slow progress, but it seemed to be holding. Darvin hadn't seemed to notice, and as the blows continued Vincent didn't notice any difference in the clashes between blade and shield.

It's almost like I need to have more, or I need to activate it.

Vincent dashed back and found more space. He continued the slow infusing of the weapon.

"I'm getting bored, Vincent. You started with a bit of fire, but now you're just playing for time. I won't put up with that. Let's get this really going." Darvin charged forward.

I need to be ready.

Vincent waited cautiously, gauging the right time. With every shield block, he did his best to notice the way the shield had been constructed. Gradually, he built up a mental map of the shield's formation and potential weak spots.

It's clearly special, but it was still built. I can do some good here.

Vincent let the last of the Soul Power go. He was ready. Launching a flurry of blows, he took Darvin by surprise. Again, and again Vincent moved forward, seeking the advantage. At the end of each strike, he pivoted and found another angle. Vincent could sense the frustration in his opponent and built on it. More and more he pushed. Finally, the blacksmith had a good opening.

This is my only chance.

Vincent wound up a powerful strike. Darvin shifted back and held up his shield to absorb the blow. Vincent adjusted his arm slightly, aiming for a spot where he thought the shield was weakest. At the same time, he unleashed whatever Soul Power he had been saving. The blade glowed white hot, the light and heat streaking off in a fiery blaze. Vincent heard gasps from the crowd as the blade fell, biting into the shield.

Darvin stumbled back, swearing. Vincent stumbled, having put everything into that blow. He looked up to see his handiwork. There was a great big crack through the dark shield. It wasn't broken, but it was weakened.

I've laid the foundation. That's all I can do.

A cheer rose up from the guards. But they didn't realise, not yet, that this wasn't the start of a comeback. That was Vincent's best and only shot.

"Nice trick, blacksmith. But the shield still held." Darvin practically snarled the words. His eyes were alight with a fiery anger that wasn't present before.

Should I feel proud or distinctly afraid now?

"You may feel like you've won, but all you've done is annoy me. The real fight starts now." Darvin rushed forward with incredible speed. Vincent watched the sword closely, teasing out the real strike amongst all the movements.

There! He picked it up and went to parry. Even with perfect timing and execution, he was knocked back by the pure force and intensity of the strike. The noise from the onlookers suddenly dropped. It was clear how the rest of the fight was going to go.

I can't fall here. There's too much at stake.

Vincent rose from a crouch. He felt weaker, his strength was fading.

Not now. Not now. With weariness, he forced himself into a ready stance.

"We both know you're done for. Now you've shown them all the true power of the Blight. I wonder how I'll finish you off?" Darvin gave Vincent an evil grin.

"You're wrong. I broke your unbreakable shield. I am not the one to take you down, but I've shown it's possible. Word will spread, don't you worry."

"Fear will spread when they hear of what I've done to you!" With each word, Darvin's voice escalated until he was shouting.

"Not on my watch, creature!" Celes shouted, drawing his attention. He didn't spot the thing she had hurled until the last second. The vial shattered at Darvin's feet, a mini explosion staggering him and the ensuing smoke screening the battlefield.

"Now!" Celes shouted. Vincent turned and ran. There was no honour in dying here, as much as it pained him to leave these people.

"I don't like this," he said.

"Be thankful that you're alive to not like it." Celes led him back through the makeshift fortifications, deeper into the Trade District.

"But what of them?"

"They've already started evacuating, you bought them some time. Now it's time for you to leave." Celes tightened her grip on his hand.

"I'm not arguing." Vincent tried to shake his hand free, but Celes just tightened her grip.

"And I'm not letting go. There's a tunnel we can use to escape the city." Celes dragged him into a shop and rushed towards the back. There was a rug pushed to the side, and a square trap down in the floor.

"Open her up." Celes pointed. Vincent dropped down and heaved the trapdoor up. He could see a set of stairs descending into darkness. Some rather bad smells wafted up as well.

"Quick. Go." Celes almost shoved him into the hatch. Vincent started climbing down, then stopped.

"Hey, what about you? Don't worry about hiding this."

"I've got a guy lined up for that. Just keep going so I can join you."

Vincent continued climbing and noted with relief that his wife was joining him. As they reached the bottom, there was enough light to see their surroundings. It was an old and disused tunnel. Murky and wet.

"Grab that torch and let's get moving. You really riled that monster up."

"He asked for it. Do you think he'll follow us down here?" Vincent said as he retrieved the torch. He started walking quickly down the tunnel.

"Absolutely. He wants to make an example of you, that much is clear."

"Hasn't he already done that?" Vincent picked up the pace.

"No, you have a way with people. And monsters." Celes let out a small chuckle.

"I really wish that wasn't the case." Vincent felt conflicted running from the fight. But he knew he couldn't win. And it was reassuring that Celes had helped the townsfolk evacuate.

Alrion, I hope you're safe. What are you doing?

9

FALL OF THE SKULL QUEEN

The Skull Queen hissed at him and struggled to throw him off. But Alrion held on, and Lara's weight helped pin her down.

"This is not going to last long."

"I know. We have to try." Lara grunted and shifted her weight again.

"Hand me the Soul Orb." Alrion held out his hand. Lara fished it out and handed it over. The Skull Queen shifted suddenly, knocking the orb to the ground. It clattered away out of reach.

"I'll get it." Lara scrambled off to retrieve the orb. The Skull Queen capitalised, shaking Alrion off. He quickly rose, keeping close. The Skull Queen looked cautiously between the two, eyeing off her blade. She needed to go through Lara to get there.

"There's no time. I'll make a distraction, you try to finish it." Alrion started advancing at the Skull Queen.

Without her sword, my Spark is more useful.

Alrion decided to be cautious. He threw a wave of force at one leg, trying to upset her balance. The Skull Queen noticed the magic but mostly shrugged it off.

Let's try some fire.

Alrion let loose a series of small fireballs, aimed at her chest. The creature let some impact, the flames licking at her armour and burning out. She swatted two away.

Keep your eyes on me.

Alrion tried something else. He needed something with more power, that wasn't so easily dealt with. He combined wind and fire, and something else. The combination was instinctive, drawing from his desire for a new form. Lightning arced from his hand, surprising the Skull Queen. She roared in pain, and crouched down, trying to shield herself. But there was nothing to be done.

"This won't last long," Alrion shouted. He could see her testing her strength, fighting against the lightning. He saw Lara sneaking up behind the Skull Queen, the Soul Orb in her hands.

"You need to find a way to insert it. On my mark." Alrion didn't know how the lightning would affect Lara. He waited until she was in position. The Skull Queen was writhing around more, looking like she could break free. Alrion increased the intensity briefly, then let go.

"Now!" he shouted. Lara dashed in, leading with her dagger. She made a small slit in the Skull Queen's back and rammed the Soul Orb in. The Skull Queen's back seemed to start to repair the wound and integrated the Soul Orb. She stopped thrashing and, for a moment, everything was still.

Is it working?

The Skull Queen started to shudder and glow. She screamed out in pain. Light flared within her, pulsing from location to location. Lara ran over to Alrion's side.

"Something's happening."

"I hope it's enough." Alrion checked within and found that he only had the slightest amount of Soul Power.

Please work.

The Skull Queen seemed to be changing, but the process was slowing down.

"It's not complete." Alrion started to quickly think what else he could do.

"What will happen?" Lara looked anxiously from the Skull Queen to Alrion. The wizard closed his eyes and reached out. He embraced the Skull Queen and she grew calm. He withdrew and placed a hand on her chest.

"This is the last." Alrion transferred the last of his Soul Power. He suddenly felt weak and dropped to his knees.

"Alrion!" Lara rushed over and helped him up.

"It's not good to fully deplete it, but I'm fine. Look to her." Alrion pointed. The Skull Queen was lying down now and seemed to be restful. Suddenly, a flare of light exploded out and black particles started to float away like a mist. Once it cleared, Alyx lay on the ground.

"It worked!" Lara stepped over to check Alyx. "She's breathing."

"Good." Alrion slumped back and allowed himself a moment to rest. The townsfolk were stirring too. One by one they woke and looked around in confusion.

"I'll stay with her; can you go help them?" Alrion gestured to the crowd of people. Lara nodded and took off.

"Everything is fine now, the Skull Queen has been defeated," Lara shouted. A few weak cheers rose from the crowd.

"Return to your homes and rest," Lara continued. After a short pause, the first people started leaving.

"Lara!" Alrion said. He had noticed Alyx moving. The weapon master opened her eyes, then squinted immediately.

"So bright." She looked at Alrion and Lara.

"You saved me. I... I can't explain the nature of it. I can't thank you enough."

"I got you into this, so I can't explain how relieved I am that you're back." Alrion looked over at Lara, and she was smiling too. Alyx sat up with a little help.

"I hate this armour, but it's better than nothing. I can't remember so many things, it's like a fog." Alyx stared out into the distance.

"That's fine, information is the last thing I'm worried about."

"Wait," Alyx said, an urgency to her tone. "There's something else." Lara looked at Alrion and he shrugged.

"There's a strike force coming. To mop up regardless of the result of our encounter. We have to get away." Alyx tried to get up, and Alrion assisted her. He then transferred her to Lara.

"Get Alyx somewhere safe and prepare to travel. I'll deal with the strike force."

"But you're exhausted!" Lara gave him a sceptical look.

"That's fine, I have plenty of Spark left. I didn't save Alyx and the townsfolk to just let the Blight come back and reclaim them." Alrion watched Alyx to see her reaction. She gave a weak nod.

"Use the pass behind the town, they'll come that way." Alyx indicated the direction with a slight head movement. Alrion gazed over, recognising the path.

"Thanks. I'll take care of this, you take care of our exit." Alrion lingered a moment, then strode forward. He wanted to appear more confident than he was.

Theoretically, I'm fine, I just need to push through.

Despite trying otherwise, he had saved the people again. And almost lost the chance of saving Alyx. But he had succeeded, if barely. He tried not to think about the city that he had abandoned.

I need to be realistic. I couldn't focus myself knowing that Alyx was out there.

Now he needed to protect what he had achieved. He had sacrificed to save both Alyx and the townsfolk. But Darvin wouldn't let that stand. Of course, he had sent more forces.

You're a wizard, and you've learned a lot. Show them.

Alrion stopped and surveyed the scene. He could see the Blighters coming down through the pass. The relatively narrow path hid their numbers, but they stretched so far that Alrion knew the force was big.

What can I do from here?

He considered creating a landslide but dismissed the idea. He couldn't control it enough, and there could be real danger for the town. But he did have another thing to try. Alrion gathered his Spark and created an intensive wave of fire. He sent it down the path, using waves of force to hem the fire in and keep it on the path.

It's working!

Now that it was on its way, he worked on increasing the speed. There was no point if the Blighters had too much opportunity to avoid it. The fire sped along, following the track of the path. Alrion found that with minimal effort he could keep steering it. But soon enough, he would not be able to see where to direct it.

The Blighters were caught off guard. Those at the front turned to run or jump off the path. However, the bulk that Alrion could see were in a narrow section between rocks and had nowhere to go. The fire slammed through them, charring and incinerating as it went.

I need more.

Alrion gathered more Spark and tried working it as he did before. He imagined a dark cloud forming above the track, then sent down bolt after bolt of lightning. Chunks of earth and Blighters exploded from the ground as each bolt struck, wreaking havoc on the Blighters. Since most of them were trapped by the surroundings or other Blighters, they had nowhere to go.

One last try.

Alrion gathered the rest of his Spark and altered the landscape. A large section of the path opened, dropping the Blighters within. By guessing the nearby landscape, he sculpted the path such that it became a steep incline leading into the newly created pit. He could barely see but did notice Blighters falling in. After a few moments, he closed the ground up, burying all the Blighters in the area, alive or dead. There was suddenly silence and no movement.

Alrion collapsed down onto his knees. He drew in some deep breaths.

You pushed too far again.

He forced himself to look up. If there was another wave of Blighters, he would be in trouble. But there were no signs of any other Blighters.

I got them all, or the rest left.

Unsatisfied, he stood. The act did not leave him feeling as he expected. He expected to be triumphant, turning away a host of

Blighters. But he just felt sick. So much death on his hands, even if it was justified. He turned and stumbled away, one step at a time.

That's why I'm doing this quest. The needless death and destruction can stop.

He pushed forward, looking for Lara and Alyx.

Lara saw Alrion approaching and her heart leapt.

He's fine.

He did look exhausted and stumbled. But he was there, and alive, and there was no horde of Blighters to be seen. She looked over at Alyx and noticed the same relieved expression. Not much time had passed, but they had managed to secure horses. The townsfolk had been bewildered, but thankful.

"It's done," Alrion said with weariness. His shoulders seemed to slump even more.

"You did great." Lara ran forward and gave him a hug. He almost fell into her. "The townsfolk offer their heartful thanks. We have horses and directions to somewhere to rest." Alrion looked over at the horses.

"Only two?"

"We didn't want you being too comfortable. Besides, don't you remember our approach to the Mystics?" Alyx forced a laugh and drew a small smile from Alrion.

"Very well. Who am I riding with?"

"Me. You're in poor shape, and Alyx isn't great either."

"But I'm well enough to keep myself on a horse."

"No complaints here."

"I suggest we leave then." Lara ensured that their bags were secured to the horse and helped Alrion up. She joined him and took the reins, in minutes, they were on their way.

Lara looked around and saw the faces of people staring from their windows.

"They're terrified of us," Alrion said.

"They just don't understand."

"They are right to be, Lara. I destroyed that Blighter force from afar. It wasn't pretty, but it was effective. And horrible."

"It had to be done. I'm sorry you had to do that." Lara reached back and found his hand, giving it a quick squeeze.

"I know. But it shouldn't be like this. I thought being a wizard would be about helping people."

"It is."

"There's too much destruction. I don't want that to be my journey."

"This is good."

"What do you mean?"

"Remember when we arrived at Brangtur?"

"I do. I was a little reckless," Alrion said quietly. Lara imagined a sheepish expression on his face.

"You were downright deranged. And almost pushed too far."

"I wasn't in a good place."

"I know, which is why I'm saying this is good. You're maturing."

"As long as I don't mature so much that I can't get the job done." Alrion went quiet, and Lara didn't know what to say back. She sought out Alyx, and the weapon master caught her gaze and nodded slightly.

Alyx will know what to say.

Lara focused on the path. It was mostly dirt, with the occasional signpost to show another path. It looked like once upon a time there had been small stones littering the path, but they were all displaced now. Finally, she started to see their destination.

A tiny cottage appeared out of the surroundings. It had a large porch and some grass around it. But otherwise, it was just plonked in the middle of nowhere, surrounded by trees and shrubs.

"What's this place?" Alrion said.

"A retreat. They don't use it often and said we could rest here before moving on."

"That's nice of them," Alrion said. But his tone meant something else.

"Yes, it was nice of them. Don't judge them too harshly."

"I know, I know." Alrion sighed and leaned against her. It felt good to have him close again.

I can't carry that burden that you do, but I can help. You just need to let me.

10

BACKTRACKING

V incent observed the town before him. The cluster of houses huddled together seemed tiny and the main street looked too quiet. Not at all like he remembered.

"You were right, there is a town here." Celes couldn't hide the surprise from her voice.

"Well, it's been a while, so I wasn't completely confident. Things do change. But something is off down there." Vincent grabbed the pommel of his sword. As soon as he noticed, he forced himself to let it go.

"I feel it too. Let's go investigate." Celes led the way, tramping ahead.

I'd rather not uncover another disaster.

The main street was deserted. Vincent saw people occasionally peering at them through a window, but otherwise, the townsfolk stayed out of sight.

"I wonder what happened here?" Celes whispered. Vincent wondered too. And he understood why she had whispered. It felt like they were disturbing something, encroaching on the townsfolk.

"That looks like an inn, surely they will talk to us." Celes pointed and charged off. Vincent quickened his pace and followed close behind. The inn was titled Ample Ale and looked incredibly small.

Just a watering hole, no need for accommodation in a town like this.

Celes pushed open the door and Vincent held the door, looking inside. The inn was almost empty, with a bored portly bartender leaning back against a cabinet at one end of the bar. Vincent stepped inside and let the door close behind him. The bartender looked up and seemed to debate moving. He did finally haul himself up and leaned over the bar instead, one hand resting on his head amongst his thick curly black hair.

"Visitors? What brings you here?"

"We're just passing through. What happened here?" Celes said. The bartender paused, searching for words.

"A bad thing. Folks don't really understand it." The bartender looked from Celes to Vincent.

We need to gain his trust.

"We know all about that. We just fled Hurdenor. The city fell to the Blight." Vincent opted to speak simply and see how the bartender reacted. The man spat on the floor and cursed.

"We fared better." The bartender shook his head. "Those animals!"

"They really are. I'm Celes and this is Vincent. And you are?"

"Bruce. Sorry, you've come at a bad time. We had an attack here too. But no one can really understand it."

"Seeing as where we just came from, maybe we can make some sense of it?" Celes gave Bruce a reassuring smile. He perked up a little.

"Perhaps. At least you won't think me crazy."

"Not at all. We've seen some crazy things lately, there's no judgement here." Celes looked to Vincent and he nodded.

"It was the strangest thing. This evil creature turned up brandishing a giant sword. I think it was a woman, originally. All dressed in black and its face. Oh my god, its face." The bartender poured himself a brandy and threw it down in one go, wiping his mouth and shivering.

"What about its face?" Celes said.

"You could see its skull, it was unholy, let me tell you. They spoke of it as the Skull Queen."

Alrion.

"They? Who are you referring to?" Celes said. She closed the gap between her and Bruce and peered into his eyes.

"Uh, you know. The travellers. A man and a woman." Bruce looked away and licked his lips.

"Was the man by any chance a wizard?" Vincent kept his voice calm and friendly. Bruce seemed to flinch at the word wizard, but then seemed to calm down.

"Aye, that's a good way of putting it. The two of them freed us from some sort of spell that the creature cast over us. It was like some strange black fog." Bruce looked like he was going to keep talking but suddenly stopped.

"Please relax. We believe you. We think we know the two people you mentioned. We were travelling together until recently." Celes placed her hand on the bartender's arm. His breathing slowed, and he seemed less anxious.

"Terrible business. We're just waiting around to see what else happens." Celes drew a gold coin and pressed it into his hand. Bruce adeptly whisked the coin away and began to speak again. This time he seemed a little bolder.

"This, you won't believe. The woman returned to the town with another woman. And the man joined them later. People were whispering that the other woman used to be that creature, but I don't believe it."

"I do. Go on, please." Celes flashed Bruce a warm smile.

"We told them of a house they could stay in, away from town. That seemed to satisfy them, and they left immediately."

"On foot?" Vincent said.

"Oh no, they bought horses." Bruce looked from Vincent to Celes, and back again.

He's waiting for something.

"There's something else, isn't there?" Celes said. Bruce stared into the distance for a time, before refocusing on them.

"Just more stories. Some folk said they saw some strange lights coming from the track out back. But everybody's too scared to go investigate."

"That's a completely normal reaction. Why don't we go take a look?" Celes said to Vincent.

"We should. We'll return shortly." Vincent turned to leave, but the bartender grabbed his arm.

"You have to tell us it's safe again. Not for me, you know. For the others." The look in his eye betrayed his true emotions.

"It's safe again. If there's anything to concern you, I'll deal with it." Vincent looked Bruce in the eyes and he nodded. He visibly relaxed and settled back against the bar.

"Happy travels." Bruce waved. Celes smiled and waved but Vincent turned and started walking.

"He was helpful," Celes said.

"To a degree." Vincent opened the door and held it open for his wife. She brushed his shoulder gently and left the inn. More eyes followed them as they walked through the town.

"The people are petrified."

"I can understand why. It sounded horrific. The Skull Queen?" Celes shivered.

"Now I know why Alrion didn't come to our aid. He had to be here."

"Do you think he even knew about the other attack?" Celes said. Vincent stopped walking and thought about it.

"He might have. Darvin was being quite strange. I wouldn't put it past him doing something like that." Vincent resumed his walking, faster now. It had been a long time since his last visit, but the town itself hadn't really changed. Just his perception of it. The path behind Carth was much as he remembered it. But as they progressed, he began to see evidence of a battle.

"Something's not right with the path. Look ahead." Vincent pointed into the distance.

"You're right, the path looks disturbed. And not in a normal way for the passage of time." Celes went forward. Vincent let her run ahead, curious about what she would discover.

"It doesn't make sense. We need to go a bit further and see for sure." Celes didn't even wait for Vincent, she just took off again and disappeared around a corner. Vincent took his time approaching. He had an idea of what had happened.

Alrion, what did you do here?

Vincent found his wife standing at the end of the path. It looked like it should have continued but the ground was completely different. The earth had been broken or disturbed and there was only the occasional sign of there ever being a path. The ground wasn't flat anymore, it was uneven and had frequent marks or holes.

"If you look up there it looks like there are some remains. Likely Blighters." Celes took off again and Vincent followed closely behind.

I don't like the look of this.

Celes was standing over a black leg sticking out of the ground.

"This Blighter looks like it has been buried."

"Not by hand." Vincent looked over the scene. Magic was definitely at play here.

"You think?"

"Alrion. This is his handiwork. I wonder how many he dealt with." Vincent could see scorch marks on the nearby hills and the aftermath of explosions on the ground.

'This is huge. It was probably a whole force of Blighters. Our son did this?" Celes whispered.

"He did. And he saved Alyx. He's growing beyond our influence now." Vincent turned and started to walk back.

"What do we do now? Should we go after him?" Celes ran ahead and stopped in front of Vincent, blocking his path.

"No. We need to let him go."

"And what? Continue this search for the source of the Blight?

Based solely on a vague lead? There are real people dying around us."

"No, I've been thinking about that. The aggressive nature of our enemy changes things. Alrion doesn't have as long as he thinks." Vincent sighed. He stepped past his wife and kept walking.

"Where are you going? He needs us more than ever. Whatever he did here, it's not good. He must be hurting. And finally getting his friend back? That's huge!" Celes kept getting louder until she was almost shouting. She grabbed Vincent's arm and stopped him.

"He needs to walk this path alone. The best thing we can do is find the information he needs."

"And take him the information?" Celes's voice was quieter.

"Yes. We should give him the space he needs but come in with the location of the Blight in case he does not discover it himself."

"And what if he does? We'll be left behind." Celes crossed her arms in front of her.

"It's a risk. But it's reduced if we go to a place guaranteed to have the answer."

"Guaranteed?" Celes gave him a sceptical look.

"Guaranteed. We need to go back to go forwards."

"That doesn't sound quick to me."

"Trust me, once Alrion gets his head straight he will come to the same conclusion. Only we'll get there first." Vincent showed a tiny smile.

Yes, this will work. We can be one step ahead of him.

"You seem quite pleased with yourself."

"I think we can pull this off. And I'm also looking forward to your reaction."

"My reaction to where you want to take us?"

"Yes. You ready?" Vincent saw Celes narrow her eyes and stare at him.

"Just get it over with."

"Paperton." Vincent said the word quickly and waited for a response. Celes started to speak, then stopped.

"I see you're speechless."

"That's a long way."

"We can pass through Brangtur. Take care of some unfinished business."

"Oh, you're good." Celes paused, thinking. "I wouldn't mind settling the score with that rat Wilhelm. The fun opportunity aside, what happens when we get ourselves to Paperton. Are you suggesting we drink from the Pool of Knowledge?"

"Possibly. Or we work with someone there who already has. Either way, we get the information. It's the only place that we know for sure has it."

"It seems like a reasonable plan. I have to admit, I found the idea of Paperton and the Pool of Knowledge fascinating when Alrion told me about it."

"No guarantee they will let us see it. They're probably a little jumpy since the last incident there."

"I'll take my chances. If you think this is the best way I can help my son, then I'm in."

"This way then." Vincent pointed to a trail and they started hiking.

I hope I'm doing the right thing.

11

A CURIOUS PROPOSAL

Alrion handed Alyx a cup of water and she accepted it graciously. After a long drink, she set it down with care and cleared her throat.

"Better?" Lara said.

"Yes. I'm starting to feel more human." Alyx visibly shivered.

"We're just glad to have you back." Alrion gave her a reassuring smile.

"I am glad to be back, I thought I was lost forever. In a way I already was. My consciousness and awareness shifted back and forth. I was a passenger more than anything." Alyx stopped talking and looked uncomfortable.

"I can't possibly understand how that felt, but I understand what the Blight can do. And feeling like you're losing yourself. I won't let it happen again."

"We won't," Lara added. Alyx pondered for a moment before replying.

"As painful as that was, you should let it happen if it needs to. The quest is more important than any of us."

"Don't worry, I won't allow that situation to happen again." Alrion was firmer in his voice, and that seemed to stop the line of conversation. A stillness sat over the group.

"So where to next?" Lara said. Alrion sighed and leaned back in his chair.

"Now that we've saved Alyx, we need to find the source of the Blight and I need to finalise the spell required. I can finally stop all this." Alrion started to speak again but quickly stopped. He jumped up from the chair and ran outside. Lara and Alyx scrambled to follow.

Alrion saw the flames leaping through the air. He immediately swept them away with a wave of force then looked beyond, seeing the wizard. Without waiting, he sent more waves of force at the wizard, hoping to destabilise him without causing damage.

The hooded wizard just made a minor gesture with his arm and the waves of force fell away. He approached slowly, and the flames in the air winked out.

"Just announcing myself. I come in peace." The wizard pushed back his hood.

"Branthor!"

"That's my name. Well, now that I'm back to myself. I see you fixed your friend too." Branthor gestured at Alyx and smiled.

"What are you doing here? How did you find me?"

"Wizards have ways, as you know. First, I had to escape the immediate danger and I did. Lucky for me, Darvin went after your friend there and had his fun with her. But now that I'm recovered, it's time for a little payback. And you came to mind."

"I saved you. I stopped the Blight from corrupting you further." Alrion raised his voice, showing his frustration.

"I know, which is why you're the perfect partner to assist with my revenge. I'm after Rindale."

"Rindale? The other general?" Alrion looked at Alyx.

"I don't remember seeing him."

"He was behind your transformation." Branthor pointed at Alyx. "And mine. He's the architect behind all the developments of the Blight."

"What do you mean exactly?"

"He's the one behind the evolution of the Blight. The new variants coming out. Destroy him, and you cut off the Blight's advantage." Branthor spat on the ground.

"I can see why it benefits us. But why you?" Lara said.

"He was instrumental in using the Blight to control me. But more than that." Branthor trailed off. A brief look of pain flashed across his face as he remembered something.

"Rindale was the one that captured your father and was the reason my wife was infected. He needs to be stopped for good." Branthor clenched his fist, and his posture straightened. He looked ready to fight.

"That's all great, but why should we trust you? You've been working against us every step of the way." Lara looked to Alrion and he nodded.

"Have I really? Yes, I wanted to stop you and control you. But I stayed my hand. Even in my grotesque form, I still fought you fairly and gave you a chance. I tried to recruit you rather than kill you. And you freed me from their influence."

"If you're so powerful, why not just do this yourself."

"I can't risk failure. And I want this over quickly. The Blight are drawn to you, I will find them faster this way. They can't escape us working together."

"What do we get out of this?"

"Other than ridding the world of that monster Rindale? You need a sweetener?" Branthor paused and gave thought. He snapped his fingers. "Tell you what, I will offer something else to show how serious I am. I'll reveal the location of the source of the Blight. That's something you want, right?" Branthor grinned. Alrion started to talk and stopped. He composed himself and tried again.

"Possibly. But how can I trust that you actually know that?"

"Oh, Alrion, please give me some credit. I'm a master wizard after all. I've drunk from the Pool of Knowledge and divined many of its secrets. Particularly those concerning that quest you are on." Branthor watched Alrion's reaction and laughed. Alrion looked torn and turned to see Alyx and Lara. They both shrugged.

"If you don't completely trust him, that's fine. I'll be watching your back, and his every move." Lara removed her dagger and twirled it with menace.

"You know what they say about your enemy's enemy," Alyx said. She continued before Alrion could respond, "revenge is a powerful emotion. He is unlikely to turn on us while our goals are aligned. Just be careful he doesn't pull you down with him." Branthor looked at them both, then turned his gaze back to Alrion.

"See? It's worth a try. Isn't the reward worth the risk?"

"What information do you have. About Rindale." Alrion turned and looked towards the nearest mountains. He stared out, waiting for Branthor's answer.

"I've been tracking the Shade Wizards. I think I know where they're coming from. That must be Rindale's base of operations. That's all I'm willing to share, for now."

"I see." Alrion sighed and tried to think through his options.

Why must I continue to be assaulted by these situations. Having to work with that traitor who killed Falric, I'm not sure if I can do it.

"I'll do it on one condition. You surrender yourself to the Wizard Academy after your revenge. You took the life of our leader, and you must pay the price. Perhaps you can serve as an example." Alrion turned and stared at Branthor, daring him to reject the offer. Branthor scratched at his newly grown beard.

"You drive a hard bargain. But once this is done, I don't care what happens to me. I accept."

"Wait here, we have preparations to make." Alrion strode inside and was closely followed by Lara and Alyx.

"That was unexpected," Lara said. Alrion nodded and looked to Alyx.

"You haven't had long to recover. Can you travel?"

"I've been worse, we should take advantage of this opportunity."

"Thank you." Alrion started rounding up his possessions. He had a blank expression on his face.

"Are you going to be fine working with him? Considering what he has done? Nobody would blame you for hating him." Lara put a hand on Alrion's shoulder and pulled him close. He turned and looked into her eyes.

"After what I have gone through, I understand him better. But, more than that, I cannot handle the depths that hate would take me into. The thought of it is exhausting, and painful even. He is not a good person and has made mistakes. What he is doing now is a mistake too. But he is set on this path, and maybe we can help him and help ourselves at the same time."

"You think of helping him at a time like this?"

"He has suffered more than any of us. Think about it." Alrion gently stepped back and continued packing. He walked around the room, picking up anything that resembled a container and stuffed them into his satchel.

"If you say so. I still don't trust him." Lara sighed.

"I think Alrion is not saying that we trust him, but trust that he wants his revenge on Rindale." Alyx leaned against the wall, waiting for them to finish. Lara grabbed a few things and stood next to Alyx. Alrion saw them ready and strode outside.

Branthor was stroking the mane of one of the horses.

"I take it you have no mount?" Alrion said.

"No. I have no problem walking, but it may slow us down."

"You can ride with me." Alyx walked up and slowly started untying one of the horses.

"Thanks. You know, I can help you. I understand the process you have been through." Branthor stepped closer and put a hand on Alyx's arm. Alyx remained still and calm.

"What are you doing?" Alrion said, advancing on Branthor.

"What you did is quite brilliant, Alrion. Amazing even. But I have to say, it was like curing someone with a hammer. It was quite destabilising. Take it from someone who just experienced your assistance." Branthor chuckled. He then concentrated on Alyx. Alrion could feel Branthor manipulating his Spark. Alyx closed her eyes and shivered.

"Every place the Blight had its tendrils, is a place of damage. Once you understand the signs, you can fix them. As a wizard, I could not reliably fix myself. That took time. But I understood the damage quite well." Alrion concentrated more, trying to see what Branthor was doing. He activated his Soul Vision and he could see the strands of Spark going from Branthor into Alyx. By peering closer, Alrion could see the areas Branthor was talking about. They were right there, clear as anything. Subtle, but obvious signs of damage.

"If you're going to do something like this to the entire world, you may want to refine your technique a little." Branthor chuckled again and stepped back. Alyx opened her eyes and flexed her arms. She took a few steps.

"I feel a lot better." Alyx put a hand on her chest and breathed deeply.

"You're welcome." Branthor turned to Alrion. "No offence, but you have a lot to learn still."

"No offence taken." Alrion bristled at Branthor's manner, but he couldn't fault what the wizard had said. He did need to do better, and he had lots to learn.

"Ride with me," Lara said. She climbed onto one of the horses and leaned forward, making room for Alrion. He joined her and looked over at Alyx. She seemed comfortable with Branthor riding behind.

"It's not that far, don't worry. We can resolve this awkward travel arrangement shortly." Branthor made himself comfortable and closed his eyes.

He's just infuriating, the way he behaves. Strides in here like he knows better than everyone. But I need him, at least for now. I need to learn what I can. There's wisdom in there, despite his flaws and his corruption.

"Take this trail," Branthor said, pointing. Alyx took the lead, and Lara and Alrion fell in close behind. Alrion closed his eyes and thought about what he needed to do. He could at least try to use the travel time for something useful.

He carefully leaned over and rifled through the saddle bag, retrieving a glass flask with a cork stopper.

"What are you doing back there?"

"I'm doing an experiment."

"For what? You're not going to explode us, are you?" Lara laughed. Alrion could tell it was a bit forced, but he appreciated the effort. These were strange times, and a little laughter couldn't hurt.

"No promises. I'm going to see if I can store my Soul Power in an ordinary flask."

"Really? So, I can drink it?"

"That's the plan." Alrion smiled. Lara let out a genuine laugh that went right through him, warming his soul.

I'm on the right path now. It's not what I expected, but it's the way forward.

12

UNCERTAIN STEPS

Lara slowed the horse, signalling the rest to be quiet. She heard sounds ahead. Alyx drew close and leaned in.

"I heard something ahead," Lara whispered.

"Do you want to investigate?" Alyx said. Lara nodded and carefully dismounted. She turned to look at Alrion and he gave her a slight nod too. Lara glanced at Branthor out of the corner of her eyes, but he seemed to be still and disinterested.

I don't know what to make of him.

Lara crept forward, veering off the path and finding a way through the shrubs and trees that lined the road. She hoped that it was nothing, but her intuition was eerily accurate. As she progressed, sounds wafted over. Definitely conversation.

Lara realised that she was quite close but couldn't see without revealing herself. Her view of the path was blocked by a dense collection of shrubs and leafy plants. She glanced at the surroundings and saw a promising tree. The lower branches were accessible and sturdy.

Here goes.

Lara clambered up, almost slipping as she reached for the first branch. She grabbed it securely, bracing herself as her feet looked for somewhere to rest. She found small knobs on the trunk that would suffice and rested for a moment. Next, she hauled herself up and perched in the crook between the branch and the tree trunk. She could see more now, but it was just vague shapes. The view was obscured by the leaves of the tree.

Probably for the best.

Lara found another branch to try to ease along, trying not to make any sudden movements. Any suspicious movement from the tree would draw attention, and she didn't know what was before her.

I bet it's the Blight. With my luck, probably a Shade or worse.

Lara gingerly shimmied along the branch until she had a better view. Leaning the right way, she could just peer through the foliage and see what was below her. Finally settled, she allowed herself to concentrate on the dialogue.

"This is definitely the right town," a male voice said. There was a strange rasp to it that grated and made Lara's skin crawl.

"You don't seem sure," another voice replied. It was deeper but had the same rasping quality. Lara couldn't decide which voice was worse.

"I don't see you confirming anything, you should know as well as me."

"We could ask?"

"And look foolish? Never. I don't want to be an example like Wraith."

Something about them seemed familiar, although she could barely see with the fading light. A flame burst into being, flickering next to one of the men. In the light, she could see more details.

A Shade Wizard! Now it all makes sense.

Lara carefully retreated, being extra careful to not make any noise. One twig snapping could out her completely. She was not equipped to really deal with a Shade Wizard, let alone two.

We need to agree on a plan. At least I'll go report this.

Lara reached the trunk and skirted down a little faster than she had hoped. Her feet scraped against the tree and there was a loud crunch as she reached the ground. She heard movement nearby and cries of surprise.

No time now. Move!

Lara kept quiet, but sped through the brush, weaving between trees. She could sense fires being lit behind her but dared not look back.

Push on, let them be distracted looking for you.

As Lara put distance between them, she allowed herself to be a little noisier and increased her speed. It was paramount to alert everyone. She arrived suddenly and quickly stopped, allowing a moment to catch her breath. It seemed as though everyone was already alert.

"We sensed trouble. Wizards or worse?" Alrion said.

"Two Shade Wizards. I didn't notice anyone else."

"See? I told you."

"Nothing is confirmed yet, but it's a good lead. What do we want to do?" Alrion looked around at the group.

"I say kill them, they're an abomination and could get very dangerous. The less the better."

"I could cure one at least," Alrion offered.

"We could see that one for information too," Lara added. Alrion looked to Alyx for an opinion.

"Either way we need to kill one or both. I have no particular preference."

"Let's advance then and try to separate them. That way we have a chance at capturing one."

"You're the boss," Branthor said with sarcasm. He hurried away without waiting for anyone else.

"Lead the way," Alrion muttered under his breath. He took off at a fast pace, Lara and Alyx by his side.

"They were on the path but noticed me leaving and started torching the nearby area."

"That's fine, it will make them easier to find."

"Not in that smoke," Alyx said. With the sun setting, there was much less light. And the smoke from the ongoing fires was hanging over the whole area. It looked like the Shade Wizards had let the fires continue burning.

"What are they doing?" Alrion said. He shook his head.

"Smoking me out?" Lara shrugged. She remembered Branthor and looked ahead. "The wizard is gone."

"What's he going to do?" Alrion sighed. He suddenly perked up and changed direction.

"This way." Alrion pointed and drew his sword.

Why is he doing that? He's more powerful than the sword. Lara noticed that the diamond was glowing blue, as expected.

Lara kept pace with Alrion and saw a white-hot glow explode from the distance. She increased her speed, sprinting as fast as possible. After a brief delay, Alrion caught up to her.

He must be using his Soul Power. The smoke was beginning to disperse, and Lara observed what looked like a wizard. She slowed and approached carefully, Alrion taking the lead.

"It's just me," Branthor shouted. The smoke quickly disappeared, and the scene became clear. Before Branthor was a small crater.

"What did you do?" Alrion shouted. He roughly shoved his sword back into its scabbard.

"They were too dangerous, I had to react." Branthor shrugged. Lara saw a mischievous smile cross his face.

"That's a forbidden spell." Alrion was outraged.

"For good reason. But it suited my purposes here. They have ceased to exist, and there are no remains either. It covers our tracks."

"Won't it be obvious when they've completely vanished that a wizard was behind it?" Alrion paced over and knelt, looking at the crater. He dug fingers through the dirt.

"At worst, they will expect me. This is not how you fight them, so they'll be off guard."

"Seems like an extreme response." Lara didn't like how carelessly Branthor had employed such a spell. She still remembered vividly when Alrion had used it back in the desert. He had come so close to destroying them all.

"I have a little more control than this one." Branthor chuckled. "Magical control, I should say."

"What do you believe in now?" Alrion said.

"Revenge. Didn't I say that?" Branthor's voice was hard and he turned from them to view the road.

"Charming." Lara noticed movement and turned to look. Alyx emerged from the brush on the opposite side of the path.

"No other enemies in the area."

"Thanks for looking out for us," Alrion said. He looked a bit embarrassed.

"I have no weapon, it was the best use of my skills."

She still looks dangerous.

Alrion started to fumble with his clothes and removed his sword belt.

"Take this." He offered the sword to Alyx. She stepped back and put her hands up.

"No, that is your blade. You need it."

"It's holding me back. You can borrow it for a while." Alrion threw the sword onto the ground. Alyx glanced at him, then turned her gaze onto Lara. She nodded and smiled, trying to encourage the weapon master. Alyx gave a short bow and retrieved the sword. She strapped it around her waist then drew the blade. After a quick circular motion, she expertly sheathed it.

"As you wish." She turned to observe the path ahead.

Alrion strode over to Branthor and roughly pulled him around so that the wizard was facing him.

"If we're going to work together, I can't have you going off on your own." Alrion glared at Branthor, and the master wizard's eyes glinted with delight.

"Oh, how interesting. And what then am I supposed to do?"

"Agree a plan and stick to it. Clearly, we've encountered worse than two Shade Wizards and survived. We do this my way, or we don't do it at all."

"Oh, is that a threat?" Branthor arched an eyebrow and observed Alrion. "Are you really that willing to let my information go?"

"I can find a way without you, if need be. But I can't continue if I can't trust you to behave in a way that's acceptable to me." Alrion stood taller and stared intently into Branthor's eyes.

"Fine, you can dictate terms. I will, however, offer my expert opinion on whatever plans you come up with." Branthor stuck out his hand. Alrion grabbed it and shook firmly. After a brief pause, he turned and addressed the group.

"Well, that's done. We have at least some confirmation of Branthor's information. Let's go investigate the town." Alyx kept staring out into the distance but nodded. Lara stepped closer to Alrion and leaned in.

"Well done. I'm proud of you, standing up to him." Alrion blushed but quickly hid it. He turned to face Branthor.

"Do you have anything to add?" Alrion started walking and didn't wait to hear the answer. Branthor paused then followed. He still retained an amused look on his face.

I still don't understand him. Maybe he's just broken now?

They walked in silence, observing the town as it rose before them. A nearby path converged with theirs, and a constant but slow stream of people filtered along, heading for the town gates. Puffs of smoke rose up giving an idea of the size, and Lara could already see quite a few tiled roofs and a few bigger structures stretching taller than the rest. Branthor finally spoke.

"While I suspect Rindale is based here, I don't think it's his home. I believe he has some lab somewhere else, where he conducts his... work." Branthor spat audibly onto the path. The gesture drew the horrified looks of a few travellers.

"This is where you think the Shade Wizards come from?" Alrion said.

"I think they are perhaps trained here, but they are not made here. I haven't quite figured out the connection. But there's always a presence."

"We will have to be careful. Perhaps they can detect us as well as we can detect them?"

"I doubt that. As you are aware, the Blight connection adds an element of noise. That would be quite distracting. I think we have an edge there. Well, I do. I suspect you haven't quite honed that skill yet."

Branthor looked at Alrion, clearly to gauge his reaction. Alrion looked a little annoyed, but he quickly hid it.

"I've not yet seen the need, but it's something I can work on. How do you suggest I do that?" Alrion spoke slowly and purposefully.

He's really maturing. He's not as defensive now.

Branthor seemed surprised at the response. He didn't reply immediately.

"We can look at that later, it's not critical to discuss right now. Obviously, I have agreed to defer to your judgement, but I suggest we focus on locating the base of operations for the Shade Wizards and see if we can track them to Rindale." Alrion looked to Lara.

"What do you think?"

"Well," Lara said before pausing. She thought carefully about her response. "Given the information we currently have, I think that's the most prudent course. If Branthor can pinpoint a location, I can infiltrate and follow them."

"I can live with that. Just don't get spotted next time," Branthor said. "We can't have them turn you into a monster too. We've all had a turn." Branthor laughed and pointed at Alyx, Alrion, and himself.

I couldn't think of anything worse. Lara shivered and pressed forward.

13

BRANGTUR REVISITED

Vincent pulled his horse up short and took in the sight. Brangtur was not nearly as impressive when viewed from the minor service entrance, but his mind filled in the blanks.

"This is where it all started." Celes slowed her horse and brought it alongside her husband's. Vincent gazed at his wife and recognised the nostalgic look on her face.

"Our great adventure together. We have Wilhelm to thank, after all." Vincent chuckled and Celes broke into a delighted laugh.

"We'll have to give him an appropriate thank you present." Celes winked.

"What did you have in mind?"

"I'm thinking it through. Let me work out some of the knots then I'll talk you through it."

"As you wish." Vincent nudged his horse forward, knowing that his wife wouldn't share any details until she was ready. But he could already guess at a few options. Celes wouldn't settle for anything less than would pull the rug out from under Wilhelm. He was far too comfortable in his position and enjoyed lording it over everyone.

"Is there anything you need to do here?" Celes said. Vincent took in a deep breath and looked around.

"Nothing I can think of." Workers bustled around in the early morning, none of them paying any attention to travellers entering via the service entrance. They knew better than to ask questions. Anyone coming in and avoiding the main entry had good reason and usually the authorisation to do so. Something Vincent himself had learned many years ago.

They rode in silence. Vincent kept an eye on any approaching guards, but none seemed interested in him or his wife. Celes seemed to be in her own world, and Vincent had to frequently remind her to make space between townsfolk that she didn't seem to notice. Yet somehow, she seemed to be pressing ahead with purpose, as they were clearly heading towards the entertainment district. Celes suddenly stopped and looked up.

"Good, I'm ready. Let's get a meal and I can fill you in."

"Sure. Anywhere in particular?"

"Hmm." Celes stared into the distance, concentrating on something else.

"The Lucky Lance."

"That old place?"

"It's a classic. Don't you remember the significance?" Celes's eyes flashed with humour but also something dangerous.

"Ah yes, I could never forget that. It's where you plied me with drink to agree to help you with your fool's errand." Vincent grinned.

"Exactly. It worked last time, it'll work again." Celes winked and led the way. Vincent sighed and followed close behind. Within a matter of minutes, the Lucky Lance was before them. It seemed to be the busiest inn around, and the clamour of drinks and music seemed to be cheerier and more genuine than the others.

The energy in the room was almost overpowering as Vincent pushed the doors open. Two musicians were frantically playing, one on a stringed instrument and the other on a giant flute. The patrons were loving it, some clinking their tankards together, others dancing on the tables.

"Business is booming." Celes tapped Vincent on the shoulder and pointed to a table.

"Your usual?" Vincent said. Celes didn't even respond, just waved him on. Vincent chuckled and wove his way through the crowd. He couldn't remember the place being so busy.

"What can I get ya?" the bartender said, leaning close to try to hear Vincent over the noise.

"Two chicken plates and two ales." The bartender started to walk away, but Vincent reached out and grabbed the man's arm.

"Sorry, but what's going on here? I don't remember this place being so busy."

"I've no idea, but it has to be related to that vagrant we had here. Business really picked up after that."

"Vagrant?"

"Yes, he was an odd fellow and did the rounds begging for drinks. One person tried to run him out, but it ended rather poorly, so we all suffered the rag-riddled man. But one day, a young couple came in and drank the vagrant under the table. He left with them and never returned. The story spread, and I guess the rest is history."

"What a remarkable story." Vincent handed the bartender the coins and struggled back through the crowd.

"That took a while." Celes was still observing the room and didn't look at Vincent.

"It's incredibly busy. Bartender said that things took off after a young couple drank a vagrant under the table and convinced him to leave with them."

"Of all the places for them to find Certan. I suppose it is the Lucky Lance after all. We'll have to tell them about how famous they became."

"I hope it doesn't encourage him to drink more." Vincent laughed.

"Have you met that girl before? I'd wager she helped him more than you'd expect." Celes relaxed into the chair finally.

"You've settled on a plan then?"

"Yes. It's really quite brilliant." Celes paused, looking over Vincent's shoulder.

"And now we can discuss it." Celes accepted an ale and held it up waiting for Vincent. They clinked glasses, and each took a deep drink.

"Hopefully this time you won't need as much encouragement."

"Really? I'd hoped to top Alrion's record." Vincent smiled and Celes shook her head.

"It is so nostalgic here. Ah. Well, onto the plan. Do you remember the Silver Sceptre?"

"From Valrytir? The one owned by the Regent General?"

"Yes. The very same one that I swapped out and smuggled all the way here."

"Where is it now?"

"It's in Wilhem's collection. I was double-crossed by a supposed friend who was paid off by Wilhelm."

"You want to steal it back?"

"Even better. I want to get caught stealing it."

"Again? Are we that old now that we can't do things properly?" Vincent burst into laughter. Celes retained her smile and waited for him to finish.

"Not only is there a bounty on that Sceptre, but the Regent General has an outstanding extradition order on whoever stole it."

"If you can convince them he stole it and has been hoarding it all this time..."

"Then the guards have no choice but to ship him out to Valrytir, away from all his precious goods. Many of which will be under suspicion." Celes had a wicked grin on her face and took a sip of her ale.

"That works for me. But won't you still be arrested for thieving? He can still out you as the Shadow Fox."

"That's my problem, don't you worry about it." Celes flashed a smile, but it didn't help. Vincent was still worried. He grunted and shook his head.

"Relax. Drink your ale." Vincent took another deep drink. He suddenly felt suspicious.

"You haven't mentioned me. What part do I need to play?"

"Oh, yours is so easy. Just visit some of your old blacksmith friends so they know you're back in town."

"Word will spread, you know. Is that what you want? Wilhelm has spies everywhere, and now he knows what to look for."

"It's no fun if he doesn't know it's coming. He will be up all night wondering what I'm going to take next. Oh, this is good, you can't imagine how much I've missed it." Celes was practically glowing.

"I'm glad to be of assistance." Vincent finished his ale quickly.

"I best make some appearances then?"

"Please. I'd prefer we strike tonight, and I want Wilhelm to have time to prep the guards."

"As you wish." Vincent leaned in and gave Celes a quick kiss before heading back into the crowd. He gently forced his way through until he was outside.

The shadows were growing longer, signalling the end of the day. They had decided to leave the horses at the inn for the time being. Vincent needed to move with real pace to the Blacksmith district if he was going to plant some information in time. As he strode, Vincent thought about his old contacts, some of which he had seen on his most recent visit. One, in particular, sprung to mind. Vincent chuckled to himself.

I bet that old codger will run straight to Wilhelm himself!

Vincent picked up the pace so that he could arrive in time.

The Blacksmith district was still full of life. Many craftsmen were still working away, some had pre-emptively lit lanterns to ensure consistent light over the transition to night. Vincent almost stopped a dozen times to observe what was being crafted, but each time dragged himself away.

You have a job to do. Your former life is on hold.

He gave wide berth to a few of his favourite places, knowing that the smiths there were loyal and friendly. He needed the opposite.

There we go.

Vincent stepped inside *The Jewelled Marvel*. The owner, and skilled goldsmith and silversmith, Benton, was still inside. He was tall and thin and wore his work apron, with small glasses hanging off the top. Rather than working on anything new though, he was swanning through the shopfront observing customers and offering advice. Although he unashamedly was scrutinising all his wares to make sure nobody was thinking of stealing. His eyes widened when he saw Vincent and he hurried over.

"Vincent! Why it's been a while. And you left under such strained circumstances."

"Benton! Great to see you. Yes, being chased out of the city by the guard is thankfully a rare occurrence. I see business is good."

"Always, I work hard to keep this running. What brings you back here?" Benton ran a hand through his curly, greying hair and quickly ran his eyes over the customers and his goods.

"Just passing through, don't have time to sort out that whole misunderstanding with the guard. My wife has some unfinished business, so I thought I would attend to my own business." Benton quickly turned back and gave Vincent his full attention.

"Which is?"

"Well, I wanted to get her something as a memento. Since we probably won't be back for a while. Women love jewellery, and I know we've had our disagreements, but you're the best. I can't argue with that." Vincent gave a forced smile and Benton broke out with a wide grin.

"My friend, you are right there. You have come to the right place. What did you need? I have rings, amulets, bracelets, pendants, you name it. All at a special price for you." Benton started off, beckoning for Vincent to follow. The goldsmith pointed out different pieces, clearly highlighting the expensive ones.

He wants to make a lot of money off me today. I better oblige him.

"I want something that she can wear on her neck," Vincent said. Benton paused and scratched his forehead.

"Yes, I have the perfect thing." He performed yet another look around the cramped room and didn't seem satisfied. Ducking behind a door he yelled something and a timid apprentice in an apron shuffled out into the store.

"Go on, make yourself useful." Benton gave the apprentice a light shove and the apprentice started walking the aisles.

"So hard to get good help. Ah, here we are." Benton held up a thin gold necklace with a stunning stone set in the bottom. It was pure white with veins of blue throughout.

"A beautiful and rare piece, and a perfect companion to the Pure Diamond, don't you think?" Benton gave Vincent a knowing look. Vincent laughed and winked at Benton.

"I don't know what you're talking about. But I do like the look of it." Vincent retrieved a pouch of gold coins and opened it to look inside.

"How much am I in for?" Benton snatched the pouch and looked inside. He then closed the pouch and tucked it into his clothes behind the apron.

"The whole lot, and that's a discount. I expect you'll want a pouch for this?"

"Please." Benton huffed about and found a purple velvet pouch, carefully dropping the pendant inside.

"Give my regards to your wife. Will I have the pleasure of seeing her wear the piece?"

"I doubt it, I think we will need to leave shortly. But I promise I'll come visit next time we are here."

"I look forward to it. Have a pleasant evening." Benton didn't even wait for a reply and strode off to talk to a customer. He waved the apprentice away, who seemed all too glad to be escaping to the back of the store.

I could see his mind ticking over. I'm sure he thinks that he can get paid tipping off Wilhelm, and maybe even recover what he just sold me. What a piece of work. At least, though, I've set things in motion. Now to find Celes and make sure she's ready for this. It's not going to be easy.

Vincent rushed out of the store and walked with purpose.

14

THE MESSENGER

Alyx kept her hand on the sword hilt as they entered the town.

"Welcome to Twingley," Branthor said with a grandiose gesture. The town was relatively busy but quite small. It was over-shadowed by a large structure behind.

"Looks like a fortress back there," Alyx said.

"That seems to be where the Shade Wizards are too. Not surprising when you think about it. There's nowhere to hide in this town otherwise." Branthor sighed and curled his lip in disgust. He kicked at some small rocks on the dusty path.

"Let's enquire at the local inn." Lara pointed out the largest building in their vicinity and took the lead. Alrion nodded and followed along. Alyx waited for them all and surveyed the area before bringing up the rear.

I'm not sure who to trust.

"The Sprained Spear," Lara announced. She shared a laugh with Alrion, but Branthor wasn't paying attention.

"You two sit and be quiet, I'll go ask for information. Care to join me, Alyx?"

"Sure." Alyx looked over the room and joined Lara. There didn't seem to be anyone dangerous, so it seemed fine to leave Alrion alone. Lara didn't need as much protection, she had good instincts.

"I'm not sure you need my help," Alyx said as they approached the bar.

"Probably not but having a sword around sure does keep people polite." Lara glanced back at Alrion. Alyx followed her gaze and saw the two wizards sitting as far from each other as possible and facing different directions.

"I also want them to get used to each other. For now, at least." Lara turned back to the bar.

"I would not be so understanding. But perhaps my way was not the best."

"It must be quite a burden, holding onto that feeling of revenge for so long."

"After a while, it becomes part of you." Alyx shuddered. She inadvertently started to remember her time as the Skull Queen. It seemed that any such feeling easily brought on that experience. She needed to be careful. As crazy as it sounded, it felt like she could be drawn back at any time.

"Four ales, and a moment of your time," Lara said to the innkeeper. This time it was a middle-aged woman with curly black hair. She had it tied back with a scarf and was in constant motion. She nodded and poured the ales expertly, bringing them over immediately.

"I'm not the chit-chat type." The innkeeper held out her hand. Lara dropped in five coins.

"Then I won't keep you. I just want to know what the deal is with that giant fort back there." Lara looked over the innkeeper's shoulder. The woman pocketed all the coins.

"Not much to say really. Back in the day, this town was a staging area for the Valrytir army. They used to camp out in that fort and do manoeuvres. Run small campaigns. Said this was a strategic location due to its proximity to certain routes. I was quite young at the time, so I don't know the whole history." The innkeeper walked away a few paces and started cleaning some glasses.

"What about now? Doesn't look deserted."

"Some rich recluse moved in. Has a lot of visitors but there doesn't seem to be a large staff there. We get more customers here, more traffic through the town." The innkeeper hesitated but stopped talking and returned to her work.

"Sounds like there's more to the story." Lara tossed over another coin. The innkeeper pocketed it without any acknowledgement and kept working.

"Just rumours. Some say they're practising dark magic up there. There's often strange lights and sounds. There are folk that stop by here that don't seem right. They don't talk, just keep their faces covered and pay well. So, we don't ask questions." The innkeeper strode away to the far end of the bar and busied herself with something else.

"That's about it. Help me back." Lara picked up two mugs and Alyx grabbed the others. They returned to the table, and it was still quiet.

"I thought you hated this stuff," Alrion said.

"It was easier to buy more. We learned a bit about that fortress."

"The information checks out. As soon as she started talking, I remembered there being something out here. But I never came here myself." Alyx took a sip of the ale.

"Good to know. Essentially, it used to be a Valrytir outpost but now there's an eccentric recluse living there and rumours of dark magic." Lara looked over at Branthor.

"Yes, well we already knew that. You could have asked about access routes." Branthor sighed.

"And take the fun out of it? Alyx and I can scout. In fact, why don't we do it now. You two wizards can sit here and talk wizardly stuff." Alyx gulped down half her ale and stood quickly.

"But don't you need help?" Alrion said. He looked quite uncomfortable. Branthor leaned back and started drinking his ale.

"Do you think there's anything Alyx and I can't handle out in the open?" Lara gave Alrion a pointed look and Alyx started to draw the Runesteel sword.

"Let them go, rest and recover while you have the time," Branthor said. Alrion nodded and leaned back.

"Have fun, let me know what you find."

"Of course. Don't go anywhere," Lara teased. She took the lead and Alyx followed her out.

"More bonding time?" Alyx said.

"Doesn't hurt. Also, I trust them to watch each other. I'd rather we determine what options there are, without having to worry about either of them jumping in head first."

"I agree with that." Alyx liked Lara's caution. It was something she had lived by for so long. Even with her considerable abilities, she had also acted alone. You needed to maximise your chances and tip the scales in your favour. Otherwise, you were dead. Or worse. Alyx shuddered again.

The one time you let loose and gave in, you were infected. You can't do that again.

"Not the talkative type, are you?"

"I have a lot on my mind."

"Since we're alone, maybe you can talk freely. One comment of yours has been bugging me for a while." Lara stopped walking and looked straight at Alyx.

"Yes?"

"You said I looked familiar, but you would discuss it with me later."

"Yes, of course. I recognise you, and I know your father. Alrion doesn't know, does he?"

"No, I haven't said anything. It's not relevant anyway." Lara turned away.

"I'm no expert in these matters, but surely he needs to know if you two are to continue to be together."

"In time."

"I think it is inevitable that the truth will come out on this journey, sooner or later."

Lara turned back and faced Alyx. "I know." Lara bit her lip. "It's fine, I'll deal with that later. Please don't say anything."

"As you wish." Alyx pointed to the road ahead and Lara started walking once more.

There was only one path out of the town that headed towards the fortress, and they followed it without discussion. Alyx let Lara lead, interested to see the thief's approach. There wasn't much to look at on the path, only the odd tree and plant. Mostly it was just slightly yellowing grass. Halfway to the fortress Lara suddenly stopped.

"Look over here." She paced towards something on the edge of the path and Alyx hurried over. There was some sort of black residue on the ground, flaking away. Something about it seemed familiar to Alyx, but the more she grasped at it, the more it escaped her.

"Looks important. Do you know what it is?" Alyx said.

"Yes, I've seen this before. Recently. It's a trail that's left by Fermur, the Messenger."

"Oh. That explains why it looks familiar. I must have interacted with him... before."

"You must have. We met him recently." Lara saw Alyx's expression. "Wait, we don't necessarily need to kill him. He was interesting and seemed more neutral than you would expect. Like he's forced to do their bidding."

"Isn't that just something he's put on to confuse you? They don't exactly play fair."

"I'm just saying to not be too hasty about how we deal with him. But we must hurry, this trail won't remain for long. He must be close by." Lara pointed to the area she had first flagged, and the black flakes were almost gone.

I could get my revenge right now. Darvin was so angered by the loss of the Skull King, I could make him hurt by destroying his messenger.

"I'll do my best, let's follow the trail." Alyx started to jog and matched Lara's pace. The trail was getting more defined the more they followed it.

"We must be getting a lot closer. He's super-fast if he wants to be, I suspect he's leading us somewhere intentionally." Lara didn't slow, however.

"Do you think it's a trap?"

"Possibly. Just be prepared." Lara removed a dagger from her jacket and maintained her pace. Alyx let her hand hover above the sword pommel.

Surely Runesteel can end these things.

She caught Lara glancing at her, but Alyx didn't try to hide her emotion.

She should know what I am capable of.

The trail veered off the path, taking them away from the fortress. They pushed through bushes, crossed rocks, and ended up amongst a dense copse of trees flanked by rock and hill.

"There's no escape here," Alyx said.

"For him too? Let's slow down." Lara dropped down to a walking pace and Alyx did the same. They emerged into a clearing, and Fermur was sitting on a giant rock, waiting. Alyx was instantly repulsed and drew her sword. She felt Lara's hand on her arm and allowed herself to be temporarily restrained.

"You took your time. I had to write you an entire invitation and drop breadcrumbs. I felt like I was in a fairy tale." Fermur laughed and grinned at them both.

"Why are you here? Why bring us here?"

"Why, I have news, of course. Updates. So nice to see you again, Skull Queen. Although something dreadful seems to have happened. You look mighty pale. And what's with all that colour in your face?" Fermur laughed even harder, and almost toppled backwards.

"Monster, just tell us what you want and be gone before I permanently house this sword within your chest," Alyx growled. The fact that he was so fast was probably the only reason she had remained still. If she made a move he would be gone, and their chance would be lost.

"Oh, I'd love to converse with you two, it'd be quite enlightening. But, sadly, I invited your friends to join us and I really can't disappoint them."

"Alrion and Branthor are on their way here?" Lara said.

"Of course, it would be very rude otherwise. Oh, and here they are." Fermur pointed behind them. Alyx turned and saw Alrion and Branthor rush into the clearing.

"There it is. Oh, and Lara and Alyx too," Alrion said. Branthor looked ready to start fighting.

"Good, good, you're all here and now I can deliver my message."

"Just die," Branthor said. He made a move but Alrion stepped in front and the two glared at each other.

"Eventually, of course. But if I did so before telling you of the secret entrance to Rindale's fortress wouldn't that be a terrible waste?" Fermur batted his eyelashes, or at least what seemed to approximate them. Branthor appeared to stand down, and Alrion relaxed a little.

"Why? Are you betraying your own?"

"Hardly, I do as I am told. But I am here to tell you there are two ways into that fortress. And Rindale is within."

"Go on." Branthor gestured for Fermur to get on with it.

"As always, I am here to give you choices. Do you charge in through the front door, appeal to Rindale's ego and topple him when he thinks he has the upper hand? Or do you take the secret passage behind me, and appear when he least expects it?"

"That sounds obvious," Lara said.

"Oh, you think so? You must be smarter than me. So glad that you're so confident."

"Why are you like this? Like a person?" Alyx said. She didn't bother to hide the distaste from her tone.

"Oh, that's so nice of you. Darvin fought for us, to keep our personalities. Of course, a lot changed. But we evolved, rather than become something else. It keeps things interesting, doesn't it?"

"Why is your master giving us this information? We'll just make good use of it and continue to defeat him and his supporters. It doesn't make any sense." Alrion stepped in front of the rest, addressing Fermur directly. He didn't seem to be that wary of the strange creature. Alyx stepped forward to within reach of Alrion.

"Now, I can hardly speak for my master, but perhaps I'll offer some words of wisdom to one who speaks so plainly. Do you think that your Soul, the special power within you, is omnipotent and infallible?" Fermur peered into Alrion as if appraising it himself. Alrion thought for a few moments before replying.

"No, it's just a tool."

"So is the Blight. Now, considering that you can use your tool to overwhelm and remove the Blight, don't you think that the opposite is also possible?"

"Perhaps."

"Don't you think it interesting that we've never really tried to kill you outright, instead we," Fermur looked at Branthor," and our agents have been trying to bring you to our side?"

"That's because I was vulnerable before."

"True, true. But do you think you won't be vulnerable when you arrive at the source of the Blight, where its true power is gathered all in one place?" Fermur cocked his head and looked at Alrion. The wizard gasped and stepped back.

"You don't think we know what you are up to? Grow up, young wizard."

"You can't scare me away," Alrion said, regaining his composure.

"Not trying to, not my job. Alas, it seems I have said too much. I do take this messenger thing far too seriously. Or maybe not seriously enough, since I invariably say more than the message. Well, for now, one more thing." Fermur paused as if to speak, and suddenly he became a black blur and disappeared into the large hill behind.

"Impossible creature," Alyx cursed and sheathed her sword. Branthor put his hand on Alrion's shoulder.

"I hope you know what you're doing, kid." Alrion shrugged it off and stared into the space where Fermur had disappeared.

Next time he won't get away.

15

JUSTICE OF THIEVES

C eles stood before the tiny door, almost imperceptible in the twilight. It looked rarely used, which suited her just fine. She fished a dull key out of her pocket and turned it over in her hands.

Will it still work?

This was her ace in the hole, one of the things that she had convinced Vincent to make for her all those years ago. But she had never used it. Not on the ill-fated Pure Diamond heist, nor the more recent and ultimately successful attempt. She had been saving it for this moment. Because once Wilhelm knew she had this sort of access, she would never get another shot.

Darkness had not yet set in but would soon. She was sure Vincent had succeeded. He knew the right people to talk to, and just being seen might have been enough. With any luck, she could make the right moves before Wilhelm had a chance to prepare.

When has luck been on your side? Really?

It did seem like she had more than her fair share of terrible luck. But she still had her freedom, and that was something. One more heist would be fine. Then she would retire for good.

Celes carefully inserted the key and turned it slowly. At first, there was no movement. Gradually she increased the force until the lock roughly clicked and the door jumped open slightly. Peering around she could see nobody looking and slipped inside.

The room was completely dark and silent. Celes let her eyes adjust and took it in.

Yes, just as expected.

It was a dusty and rarely used storage room. By itself, completely boring and unworthy of attention. But it was right next to another room of considerable interest. Celes padded through the room, taking care not to disturb anything. She expected this area of the mansion to be quieter but still didn't want to take any unnecessary risks. With each step, she moved further in, and her heart started to thump faster and faster. There was no denying it. She had dreamed of this opportunity for years.

At the far end of the room was a long corridor. Celes crept up to the edge and peeked out. There was nobody around. The room directly opposite called to her, and the door was left ajar.

Shouldn't it be locked?

After another glance, Celes stalked across and pressed up against the door. She quietened her breathing and strained to hear a noise. Nothing. She slowly pushed the door open, hearing a jarring squeak from the hinges. Wincing, she kept going, trying to keep the noise to a minimum. In a few moments, it was over, and she was inside.

Finally, after all these years.

The room was packed full of wooden crates, each stuffed with paper. Way too much paper. Impossible to look at with the available light. Celes took in the rest of the room, focusing on the walls. She noticed a few lanterns and moved closer to one to investigate. It was an oil lantern, and with a few adjustments, it was lit.

Oh, it would be a joy to accidentally knock over this lantern. But then I'd waste this opportunity. Ah well.

Celes sighed and refocused on her task. She picked up the nearest box and started rifling through.

Not even close, although they do seem to be of similar age. Keep looking.

She systematically worked her way around the room, increasing her speed as she went. Her plan only worked if she found what she needed. Suddenly she paused, feeling unsafe. She listened carefully and heard footsteps. Scrambling as quietly as possible, she doused the lantern and hid behind the door. The footsteps kept approaching at a steady pace. They stopped right at the doorway.

Celes held her breath, running different options through her head, should she be discovered. The presence lingered, waiting.

"Must be my imagination. He never uses this room anymore anyway. We should just torch it and be done with it," a male voice muttered. The footsteps continued once again. Celes kept listening until she couldn't hear them anymore.

The guard wants to torch this place? Lucky I'm not doing their job for them.

Celes waited as long as she could tolerate, then relit the lamp. Time was running out. If she didn't appear in the expected place, they would start to suspect something else was up. And she couldn't afford for that to happen.

Finally, she was done. Celes looked up and swore under her breath. She had searched the entire room and come up empty.

What's Plan B?

Celes stared at the door she had entered through and was considering what to do next when something caught her eye. A rough box, smaller than the rest. It was shoved up against the door and she hadn't noticed it when entering.

No way.

Celes ran over and rifled through the box. One of the papers stood out and she snatched it from the box and looked over it carefully.

Yes! I have it!

She folded the note and pocketed it, heading over to the lantern to extinguish it once again.

Why couldn't that have been the first box I opened? Oh right, because that would be too easy!

Celes shook her head then stopped in her tracks. She needed to get back into the right frame of mind, else she'd make a mistake.

Just hold it together a little longer.

She eased herself into the corridor and headed deeper into the mansion. After a few turns, she found herself in familiar spaces. None of which held any guards.

I suppose that's to be expected if they want to catch me red-handed.

Going by that logic, she needed to just head directly for her prize and the way would be clear. But it was too risky, and she needed to play the part even if they were making it easier. She took a circuitous route, checking for guards and thankfully noticing a few. Even if they were in odd places.

At least the place isn't completely deserted.

Celes slowly descended until she reached the lower level housing the secret vault.

Maybe not so secret now.

There were two guards posted outside, but the vault was open.

Maybe Wilhelm himself is inside?

Either way, she needed a way in, without causing too much of a fuss. It was time for something tried and tested. Celes removed a tiny smooth stone from her boot and tossed it across the room. It skidded and rattled, drawing the attention of the two guards.

"Movement over there, go check it out." One of the guards rolled his eyes and stomped off to investigate the noise. The other watched him go with a grin. Celes crept up behind him and grabbed the guard in a hold. The guard tried to call out, but the thief was too precise and too fast. She smothered any noise from his throat and soon he was collapsing to the floor. She dragged him into the shadows nearby and darted into the vault before the other guard noticed her.

The vault was much larger than she expected. Lanterns were lit along the walls, showing the array of riches. Celes almost gasped as she recognised the many artefacts.

"I thought I was a big-shot, but compared to this I was just dabbling," she whispered. Celes pushed the line of thought away and focused back on the task. The sound of the vault door slamming shut made her jump, and she looked around to see if she had been spotted.

"Come forth, Shadow Fox, I know you're hiding there," Wilhelm said. Celes composed herself and strode forward with feigned confidence. Something about the situation didn't feel right. Wilhelm stood at the end of the vault, holding the Silver Sceptre. To his right was another man that Celes didn't recognise.

"Ah, there you are. Right on cue. I'd like to introduce you to a good friend of mine, Magistrate Ronder." The magistrate nodded.

"Is he here to arrest you finally?"

"Quite the opposite. When Wilhelm told me he could give me the Shadow Fox, why I was willing to do quite a deal." Ronder chuckled and started advancing.

"You don't remember me, do you? I wasn't always a Magistrate. I used to work in the town guard. I was assigned to every single crime you committed. I failed in my duty, and today I can finally make things right."

"But Wilhelm is a bigger crook than I ever was! Look at this place!" Celes gestured at the many riches lining the walls.

"What can I say? Except that I caught the Shadow Fox red-handed, trying to steal from a local icon. That's all that needs to be said. Everything else here is irrelevant."

"But that Silver Sceptre, that's a matter of national security. Valrytir could start a war over that thing if they find out you have it!"

"Oh, they don't care anymore. It's been over twenty years! And they won't find out anyway." Ronder wore a wide grin and Wilhelm burst into laughter.

"I won't let you get away with this."

"I already have." Ronder joined Wilhelm in his laughter.

This is bad, they've caught me in the trap intended for them. Vincent better have remembered the original plan.

"Well, laugh it up. While you still can. Because my coming here was the easy option for you. And now we're going to invoke something a lot more painful."

"We? And how do you suppose you do that while you're in my custody?" Ronder sprayed spittle as he talked and ended it with a little laugh. He was quite pleased with himself. His face, however, suddenly changed when a large crash sounded at the entrance of the vault. A large section of the vault door fell in and Vincent stood before it, his Runesteel sword gleaming in the lantern light.

"We, as in me and the guy with the Runesteel sword. That's my cue." Celes turned and ran, after taking a moment to remember the looks on Wilhelm's and Ronder's faces.

"Impeccable timing," Celes said as she neared Vincent.

"Of course. Things not go to plan?"

"I'll explain later. My optimism got the better of me." Celes turned to the bewildered men and shouted, "when your world comes crashing down, just remember the Shadow Fox made it so!" Vincent stepped back and ushered Celes out. She ran through the vault entrance and Vincent sheathed his sword. The two of them quickly ascended the nearby stairs.

"I assume there's some sort of backup plan?"

"Of course. I assume you're still chummy with Mason?"

"Sure. If by chummy you mean I've not seen him in twenty years, severely disappointed him when I abandoned Valrytir and actively avoided him in Brangtur. Then yes, extremely so."

"Good, since we'll be dropping in tonight." Celes grinned and Vincent groaned. They faced no opposition leaving the mansion, the few guards that spotted them weren't sure how to react and did nothing.

Within minutes they had arrived at a large stately house. A single guard was posted outside the large gate.

"No visitors. Make an appointment in the morning." The guard yawned and waved them away. Vincent drew his sword. The guard stiffened and put his hand on his sword.

"Show him this. He will ask to see us immediately." Vincent handed the guard the sword. He looked it up and down, sceptical. But he eventually nodded, unlocked the gate and disappeared inside.

"I had a thing too," Celes said.

"This requires less explanation. You can talk to yours once we're inside."

"Such a show-off." Celes smirked at Vincent. He gave her a wry smile. True to form, the guard returned within a few minutes and wordlessly waved them in.

The house was beautifully but starkly furnished. The few pieces inside were a dark wood, immaculately finished but simple in design. A white-haired mountain of a man stood behind the dining table, examining Vincent's Runesteel sword.

"I'd recognise this work anywhere. Quite a surprise, considering how we parted ways. You said you'd never make another weapon. What are you playing at, Vincent?" Mason spoke without looking up, his deep voice echoing around the large room.

"My wife has some business with you, I only enabled the conversation," Mason grunted and looked at Celes.

"Out with it then. Vincent has already wasted enough of my time."

"I sincerely doubt that." Celes removed a piece of paper from her pocket and offered it to Mason.

"What's this? An inventory receipt?"

"Yes, for the Silver Sceptre. Note the date. Wouldn't you like to recover that?" Celes watched Mason's reaction. He looked up sharply.

"I can't ignore such an opportunity. Who has this?"

"Wilhelm. You're familiar with him, I suspect?"

"Of course. And you've seen the item?"

"Tonight, in fact. I had hoped to steal it back as a sign of good faith. But it seems the local magistrate Ronder is also in on this." Celes watched Mason's face harden.

"Valrytir will not stand for such treatment. We are supposed to be allies and friends."

"Then I suggest you move at once. They might get spooked and start moving things out. You may even find more national treasures, he's been collecting for a while." Celes watched with delight as Mason started pacing the room. He stopped suddenly and addressed them both.

"Thank you for this information. This should be enough to get me back home. I've done my best to... enjoy this posting, but I grow weary of it. If this plays out, you've redeemed yourself, Vincent."

Mason held out the Runesteel sword and Vincent accepted the blade, sheathing it.

"But you shouldn't tease me with such weapons. That is a cruelty." Mason shook his head.

"My apologies, but time was against us and I needed your attention. As you see, this is not a matter that can wait."

"Indeed. Off with you, I have work to do."

"Thank you, and good night." Celes and Vincent turned to leave. Before they could walk out, Mason called out.

"Send my regards to the Shadow Fox."

16

OUTMANOEUVRED

A lrion walked over and sat down on the rock Fermur had been on. He carefully avoided the black residue and stared at the wall where Fermur had disappeared.

"From this close, you can see the entrance. That's quite clever." Alrion reached out and his hand touched no resistance.

"Well, the secret tunnel entrance checks out, if we believe that it goes into the fortress," Lara said.

"His information was good last time, it led us to Alyx. For whatever reason, he's been telling the truth."

What Fermur said is concerning. Are they just leading me on because they think I'll convert to their side?

"What did he say last time?" Branthor walked forward and glanced at Alrion then Lara.

"He told us about two options. One was the location of Alyx, another was a town that would be attacked," Alrion began.

"And both options were real. We chose to save Alyx."

"I see. Well, I'm not one to discount a chance to catch Rindale. There's four of us here, why not split up? We can follow both approaches." Branthor pointed to the group and let the question hang.

"That's not a bad idea. We meet where Rindale is, and there will be no escape." Lara looked thoughtful.

"It does reduce the risk of selecting the wrong option. If we set the groups accordingly it should be relatively safe." Alyx nodded along as she spoke.

"Time is crucial; therefore, I won't belabour the discussion. One wizard with each group then? Who should I take?" Alrion looked to Lara.

"Take Alyx. I'll go with Branthor."

"Are all fine with that?" Alrion gave each person a chance to respond, but Alyx and Branthor just nodded.

"I'll go up the guts. I'll draw their attention and Lara can sneak in behind me and avoid detection. It will put Rindale at ease, in a manner of speaking. He will feel like he knows my approach and skills," Branthor said.

"I actually think that could work," Lara said.

"Fine, we will explore the tunnel and find a way to meet you. Just remember, if you get there first, we need Rindale alive. He's too valuable to just slaughter." Alrion glared at Branthor. "No excuses, you can restrain yourself."

"That's fine, once he's secured, I have no qualms holding back. Just as long as you hold up your end of the bargain and deliver him to me."

"Fine." Alrion stood up off the rock and stepped towards the secret entrance. He could feel a cool breeze tickling his skin.

I still don't feel like I can trust Branthor. Hopefully, Lara can keep him in check.

Alrion felt a touch on his shoulder

"Take care and take your time. There might be traps." Lara leaned in and gave him a quick hug.

"Thanks, you too. Don't let him riot too much."

"Of course. I have a few tricks if I need them." Lara gave him a wicked smile.

"See you on the other side." Branthor started walking off and Lara rushed off to join him.

"Let's go investigate this tunnel." Alrion started to move but felt Alyx holding him back.

"Me first. You can provide light." Alyx stepped inside and Alrion shrugged and joined her. He created a ball of light and hung it above them. He adjusted the size and glow to illuminate them and a short distance ahead.

"Let me know if you need more, but I assumed we didn't want to create too much of a beacon."

"This is fine." Alyx walked on. Alrion looked around at the tunnel. It seemed to be a natural formation. At least originally. The ground was well worn from footsteps.

"What a strange tunnel, it doesn't look man-made," Alrion said.

"Perhaps the fortress was built in that location for this reason. It had a dedicated exit."

"Perhaps." Alrion walked a bit further but felt something strange from Alyx. It had been bugging him the whole time.

"Alyx, how much do you remember of your time with them?"

"Very little. I was like a passenger encased in fog. Occasionally I could grasp glimpses of what was happening."

"But you remember Fermur?"

"Not clearly. But he is familiar? Does that make sense?" Alyx walked faster and Alrion almost stumbled on an errant rock trying to keep up.

"Then why does he make you so angry? We could all see it." Alrion paid more attention to the path as he waited for a response. There was silence for a long time.

"It's not so much that creature, although he is repulsive. It is what he means. And he is one of their leaders, even if he's used for errands."

"Shouldn't you pity him then? Knowing what it's like to be used?"

"I should but I cannot. I'm sorry, that's all I have to say." Alyx went quiet and Alrion decided not to pursue it.

I'm not sure what to make of them. What if that had happened to me? How would I want to be treated?

The cavern began to change and have more human elements.

Wooden planks to smooth out certain sections of the ground where there were dips or holes. A few handrails here and there. Soon enough, there were supporting structures and frames to no doubt maintain the stability of the tunnel.

"This isn't just a secret passage. This looks well-trafficked," Alrion said.

"I agree. It just depends on how frequently it is used, and by whom. If we're lucky, Rindale has not told many about it."

"True." Alrion decided not to talk too much, in case they drew attention. After a few more turns they encountered a large wooden door with metal handles.

"This must be where it connects to the fortress." Alrion reached out, but Alyx pushed his hand away.

"Wait. Let me." Alyx gently touched the door, feeling it all over. She suddenly opened a tiny panel and Alrion heard a metallic click.

"It should be open now." Alyx gently pulled the door and it opened with a creak. There were torches lit inside, showing a stone hallway and steps leading up.

"Here we are. Did you know about that?" Alrion said.

"No, I just had a feeling." Alyx entered the fortress, holding the door for Alrion. He let it close gently behind him.

"And here we go." Alrion followed Alyx's lead as they crept through the bowels of the fortress. It was cold and felt damp.

"I doubt it's as easy to drop in on Rindale as Fermur said," Alrion muttered.

"Of course not. But as Lara pointed out, the information is good. Let's just hope we can capitalise on it." Alyx drew the Runesteel blade and stalked forward. They continued along a corridor, Alrion noting nothing of interest along the walls. Finally, they came to an intersection with two options: left or right.

"We have a fifty-fifty chance of picking the right option," Alyx said.

"Wait a moment. Let me think." Alrion remembered what Branthor had said about sending wizards. There was a chance that he could do it as well. Surely the presence of any wizards would be a sign of Rindale's location.

Alrion closed his eyes and imagined his Spark. He held onto the feeling then went searching for something like it. He sensed something out there but couldn't quite figure it out.

"I'm at a loss. Any ideas?" Before Alyx could speak, a large boom sounded in the distance and seemed to send shockwaves through the fortress. The ceiling rattled, and flakes of stone fell from the ceiling.

"That definitely came from that direction." Alyx pointed to the left tunnel.

"Agreed. I hope that's not Branthor."

"I admit I don't know the man that well, but he doesn't seem known for his tact."

"No, and he seems to be worse after being cured." Alrion shook his head slowly and followed Alyx. The tunnel they had selected was the same as the main corridor. All built in stone and with regular torches, but nothing else of interest. They continued at the same pace, looking for signs of life or the enemy. Finally, they came to another intersection.

"Do you want to wait for more signals?" Alyx said.

"No, we need to press on. I'm feeling quite nervous about this." Alrion looked left, then right. Nothing was visibly different.

"Let's go right." Alrion pointed and Alyx started off. She didn't even question his direction.

I hope I picked right. I don't even know what I based that on.

Sounds started to echo through to them. Voices, banging, and other general commotion. Each time a new sound came through they paused, but there was no immediate danger and no way to tell where exactly the sound had come from.

"I suspect we should just press on."

"Agreed. Let's see where this takes us." Alrion continued, the slow progress was agonising. He kept imagining what Branthor was doing, and none of it was good.

Please be safe, Lara.

"Here's something." Alyx stopped and let Alrion take it in. Ahead was a large metal door. It looked incredibly strong and thick. Before it, on each side of the corridor, looked like smaller doors leading to rooms.

"Good. Let's explore the smaller rooms then investigate the big door. Maybe it'll lead to Rindale?"

"Not with our luck, but I won't discount it." Alyx took off with a bit more speed and Alrion stayed close behind. Once they reached the rooms, Alrion waited behind and Alyx crept into each one, checking for enemies.

"Nothing but boring supplies. Maybe these tunnels are for deliveries after all?"

"Perhaps. But that door is something." Alrion walked up and examined it at close range. There was a keyhole in the middle, but otherwise, it was quite solid. It seemed even sturdier than he imagined.

"We need a way inside."

"True. But first, we need a way to see what's on the other side," Alyx said.

"I'll see what I can do." Alrion leaned close to the keyhole and had a look inside. It was pitch-black and there seemed to be something restricting the light from the other side. But if he concentrated, he thought he could hear something.

Think. You've amplified your voice before, maybe you can do something here.

Alrion gathered his Spark and imagined creating a wedge of force that he could stuff into the keyhole that would amplify the sounds coming through. He finished the visualisation and finalised the spell. At first, nothing, then a few whispers.

"Did you do something?" Alyx said.

"I think so, but it needs more work." Alrion tried increasing the volume of the spell. Nothing happened. He injected more and more Spark into it. Words started to come through.

"It's up to you, Branthor, what will you do?" a male voice said.

"Recognise that?" Alrion said.

"Not sure, maybe?"

"I won't let you get away," Branthor said. The anger in his voice was obvious.

"We need to get in there before he does something rash." Alrion stepped back and looked at the door.

Are there any weak points?

"I doubt we can get through this with any subtlety unless you can lockpick?" Alyx paced around the door, examining it.

"I could maybe destroy the surrounds or cut a hole in the door. Hmm."

"You can't escape me!" Branthor shouted.

"Time's running out." Alyx stood back and braced herself.

No choice now, we need to get in there.

Alrion built up his Spark and created a fire spell. He shot rays of extreme heat around the edges of the door, burning right through. He outlined the shape of the door and, once he had finished, the weight of the door, now free from the hinges and stonework, fell in with a crash. Smoke and rubble went everywhere. As soon as it was possible Alyx darted in and Alrion followed. They clambered over the remains of the door into the massive room beyond.

There seemed to be a lot more rubble than expected. Looking around the room, Alrion saw Branthor and Lara emerge unscathed.

"There you are," Lara said. She had a strange expression that Alrion couldn't quite pick.

"You imbecile, you ruined everything," Branthor roared.

"Where is he?"

"Who knows? He escaped through a Wizard Gate and you DESTROYED IT!" Branthor waved his arms in frustration and stormed off.

"A Wizard Gate? We heard they were getting away, so I had to act. Branthor sounded like he was going to kill the lot of them!"

"He was actually playing along. He wanted them to escape so we could follow them to their real base," Lara said quietly. Alrion looked from her to Branthor.

Oh no. I have ruined things. Rindale escaped because of me.

"I'm sorry, I had no idea."

"Amateur! I followed your rules, I could have wiped him out."

"How was I supposed to know that a Wizard Gate was here, let alone what one is!"

"If you had paid attention, you would have felt it. You sensed enough to find your way." Branthor threw his hands up in despair and a nearby fallen chunk of stone disintegrated.

"So, we got good information. But it was incomplete. Dangerously so," Alrion said. He tried to make out what from the rubble was this supposed Wizard Gate.

"What else should we expect?" Lara said. Alrion looked to Alyx. She had sheathed her sword but was looking at Branthor warily.

"You acted on instinct, which is usually better than not acting. Tough luck on this one. There's a lesson to be had."

Alrion knew she was right. But in the moment, he couldn't think of it that way. Branthor's insults were hurting too much. Mostly because they had a lot of truth in them.

17

A FAMILIAR FACE

C eles pulled the horse up, surveying the land before her. Beyond the rolling hills, she saw the spires of an odd little city.

"Is that Paperton down there?"

"The very same. We're not far now, although we should take our time on the descent."

"When were you here last?"

"A long time ago. I had to skip it when Alrion journeyed there. Had I known the dangers he would face, I would have chosen differently." Vincent looked dismayed as he recalled. He was acting a lot more thoughtful lately and reflecting a lot. Even at times being nostalgic.

"You know, I've been thinking. We didn't need to pass through Brangtur. In fact, given our recent history, it was actually a risk to do so."

"We've got a pretty good record of not being detained there. Low risk, don't you think?" Vincent gave her a quick grin.

"But not without risk. You did that purposefully. Why?'

"An incentive to make this long journey worthwhile, remember?"

"No, that's not it. I'll get the answer, you may as well just tell me."

Celes gave Vincent her best direct glare. He actually laughed but quickly recovered.

"I wanted to tie up some loose ends and have a little adventure with you. Everything has been about Alrion and his quest, I thought it would be nice to do something for us on the way." Vincent stared out towards Paperton.

He does look very thoughtful. What's going on?

"But why now?" Vincent started to speak but paused. He began after a little while.

"We don't know how this quest will end. We've all been in incredible danger at one time or another. Things are not going to get easier. We lost Falric on the path to Paperton. There's a chance that we're not all going to journey home at the end."

"That's rather defeatist of you, isn't it? We always scrape through!" Celes was alarmed by the tone.

He's always optimistic and supportive. There's definitely something going on. And he's all reflective too and tying up loose ends.

"What aren't you telling me? Is there more to this that you aren't saying?" Celes crossed her arms and challenged him. Vincent sighed.

"It's just a feeling. Hopefully, I'm wrong, but what we did back there was completely right and completely necessary."

"That's at least something I can agree with. Let's just hurry up, I can get the truth out of you later." Celes spurred her horse on and took the lead. Vincent quickly caught up and matched her speed.

Just a feeling? We'll see about that.

The ride to Paperton was swift and easy. The paths were well-maintained, and even the route down to the town was enjoyable, even if they did need to occasionally pull the horses up to be safe. Celes's first impression of the town was that it looked like a mess of papers with ants crawling all over.

"Such a literal name," she muttered.

"It's perfect, isn't it? Hasn't changed at all." Vincent was smiling.

"I didn't take you for a scholar."

"Oh, I'm not, but they do have a wealth of knowledge here on blacksmithing. It's amazing."

"Of course they do." Celes laughed at her husband and he shrugged. As they reached the town, they saw quite a few people out and about. But none really paid them any attention.

"I expected scholars to be more sedate. And inquisitive." Celes looked at the people with wonder.

"They're all incredibly busy. Or busy looking like they are busy. They don't need to know about us yet."

"Very different. Do you know how to get to the Pool of Knowledge?"

"Alrion explained how he accessed it, but we won't fare well just trying to sneak in. We better announce ourselves and follow the proper channels. I think there's an administrative office around here somewhere." Vincent took the lead and Celes was happy to let him navigate through the completely haphazard assortment of buildings.

"Let's try in here." Vincent held the door open and Celes stepped inside. It was a relatively small building with a large desk in the entry and an old couple sat behind the desk. Both wore thick glasses and were inspecting stacks of paper.

"Excuse me," Vincent said. There was no response. He repeated himself, "Excuse me."

"We need to visit your Pool of Knowledge," Celes said. The old woman looked up and adjusted her glasses. She stared at Celes for a full two seconds before bursting into laughter.

"Oh, that's a good one. Did you hear that, Earl?"

"Hear what, Mona?"

"These people want to visit the Pool of Knowledge!"

"Ha! Fairy tales!" Earl didn't even look up but did bury himself deeper in the paperwork.

"I'm happy to fill out the required paperwork. But I don't really have time for games, my son is a wizard and was here recently and drank from the Pool. He needs help accessing critical information." Vincent waited after he spoke. Celes watched the older couple carefully and noticed them discreetly pass a look between them.

"Earl, do you have someone who can set these people straight?" Mona said. Earl sighed.

"Fine, I'll interrupt my work again." Earl rose slowly, stepped around the desk carefully and marched out of the building.

"We really don't want to cause any trouble, but we're here on quite an urgent need."

"Sure, sure. Just wait on those chairs." Mona pointed to two wooden chairs, well-worn without any cushions. Vincent and Celes sat down and waited.

A while later Earl returned, with a much younger man. He was short in stature and quiet and looked at Vincent and Celes thoughtfully.

Now, he looks like a scholar.

"Nice to meet you. My name is Caleb and I'm here to assist with your enquiry."

"Hi, Caleb. I am here on behalf of my son Alrion. He's a wizard who visited you recently," Vincent said.

"Is that so?"

"Yes. He spoke highly of the citizens of Paperton and their sacred duty of protecting the Pool of Knowledge. However, we need your help. Perhaps you can direct us to someone who can confirm the information I have just provided."

"Is there anything more you can say, to assist?"

"Well, Alrion was sent here by his mentor, Falric, a master wizard. Unfortunately, Falric passed away. But Alrion used Falric's spellbook as proof of his claims."

"Do you also have the spellbook with you?"

"No. I do not."

"Were you also acquainted with this wizard, Falric?"

"Yes, we travelled together but were separated before Alrion arrived at Paperton." Vincent waited for another question, but there was nothing. Caleb closed his eyes and appeared to be thinking.

"When can we talk to someone who can help us?" Celes said, exasperated.

"I apologise, but I must fulfil my duty and ask the appropriate questions. This process assists us both. Without it, I cannot verify your story and introduce you to the right person to further your query."

"Very well," Celes grumbled.

"However, I have heard enough to continue your application. Please follow me." Caleb gestured to the door and immediately left. Celes looked at her husband, who just shrugged, and held open the door for her. Caleb was waiting for them outside. He began walking at once.

"It won't take long, please keep up." Caleb walked at a brisk pace, weaving through the wandering scholars on the streets. They seemed to be heading to a rather large building at one end of the town.

"I think that's the main hall," Vincent said.

"Makes sense. Does that sound like the right place to be going?"

"Definitely." Vincent looked optimistic so Celes decided to keep her hopes up.

Maybe this next person can help us break through all the bureaucracy.

"This is the main hall. Visitors are not normally allowed within, but you seem quite sure of your story." Caleb pushed open the giant doors and kept walking, not waiting for them. Vincent and Celes rushed through and kept pace with the shorter scholar.

"Quite a grand hall." Celes looked up at the ceiling and took in the immense size. They were heading towards a large stage at the back. However, rather than step up to the stage, they turned and entered an old wooden door to the side.

"Please step inside." Caleb waited next to the door but did not enter. Vincent entered first, then Celes. Inside was a small chamber with a scholar in robes behind a desk. He looked up at them.

"Who brought you?" he said.

"Caleb," Vincent replied. The scholar nodded.

"Go on through." He waved them over to a passage in the back of the room. Vincent went first and Celes whispered her thanks as they passed by the scholar. After a short walk, they entered a much larger room. Bookcases lined the shelves, each one stuffed with books in every possible orientation. A ladder was propped up against one bookshelf. In the centre of the room, an old man with a brown robe sat writing. The hood was up, obscuring his face. He kept writing, not acknowledging their presence. After they stood for a few moments, the man put his quill down and looked up.

"Not going to say hello?" he said. Celes gasped and ran up.

"Falric? You're alive!"

Falric gave her a wry smile. He looked over at Vincent.

"Good to see you both. Welcome to Paperton."

"It's good to see you too. A lovely surprise. But you better start explaining what you are doing here." Vincent didn't look impressed after the initial shock.

18

CHANGE IN APPROACH

Alrion looked around the room, his mind reeling with what had just happened. He tried to think of what to do next, and his mind was blank. Lara gave him a reassuring smile, but he knew that it was just for support. She knew that he had blown it too. Branthor finished his rant and wandered back. He had a strange grin on his face.

"Alrion, Alrion, Alrion. What are we going to do now?"

"I don't know. That's what you expected, right?"

"Of course, we just lost our lead. But it was the one they gave us. Always trouble that. I think something else is required." Branthor eyed off Lara and Alyx.

"You two can search this fortress for any clues. I doubt Rindale left anything, he's a careful operator. But we need to know. Alrion and I need to do some creative planning. What do you say?" Branthor waited for a response.

That's not a bad idea. Maybe I should listen to what he has to say. We can't keep ignoring each other and trying to work separately.

"Sure, let's try that. Please meet us back at the inn with your findings."

"We'll leave no stone unturned." Lara led Alyx to the opposite end of the room.

"Shall we take the secret tunnel? I'd love to see it."

"If you must." Alrion started picking his way over the rubble and they started down the tunnel to return to town.

"Nice work with the door, by the way, that was very clean." Branthor noted the cuts in the stonework as they entered the tunnel.

"You didn't seem so impressed a few minutes ago."

"I was caught up in the moment. I expected more awareness, but your precision was good. Credit where credit is due."

"Sure. Thanks." Alrion continued walking, after giving Branthor an odd look.

I can't figure this guy out. He's all over the place.

"Not much to this tunnel, is there?" Branthor said as they progressed.

"No, the only thing to note is over there." Alrion pointed to the storage rooms and Branthor quickly checked them out.

"Ah, secret supply tunnel. Nice one. Nothing more needs to be said."

"Fair enough. I'm amazed it didn't collapse while I was in it."

"And why would that be?"

"Whatever you did rocked the entire place. Stone was falling from the ceiling." Alrion looked at Branthor and the wizard was grinning.

"Pretty amazing, yes? And note the tunnel did not collapse. I didn't even disrupt the Wizard Gate."

"Are they quite sensitive?"

"Not really, but I wasn't sure exactly where it was." Alrion stopped walking.

"You didn't know where it was, but you berated me for not knowing about it?"

"Precisely. You didn't detect it, you were practically on top of it. There's quite a difference." Branthor resumed walking and Alrion sighed.

"You have much to learn." Alrion shook his head and kept walking.

The trip back to town was uneventful, but Alrion was curious where Branthor was heading. It wasn't too surprising when they ended up back at the inn.

"We've done this, haven't we?" Alrion said.

"No, that was the prelude. The warmup. This is the main event. Take a seat." Branthor didn't specify where, he just sped over to the innkeeper. Alrion picked a table in the corner. The plump seat was damaged and sagging, but the location was good. It provided a wide view of the rest of the inn. He saw Branthor negotiating with the innkeeper. Whatever it was about, the innkeeper seemed quite dissatisfied. Finally, Branthor produced a rather hefty sack of coins and the innkeeper relented. Branthor ran back with excitement, brandishing a nondescript brown bottle.

"Ah, we are in luck. Managed to score the innkeeper's special reserve. This stuff will put hair on your chest, and other places I imagine."

"I sincerely doubt that."

"I can put a spell on the bottle?" Branthor winked.

"Just open it." Branthor stood and fetched a few glasses from the bar and returned, pouring two thumb-widths in both glasses.

"First glass, down the hatch. We can sip the rest."

"This is going to help us. Two wizards getting drunk?"

"You'll thank me later." Branthor lifted his glass and waited for Alrion. The young wizard raised his, they clinked glasses and quickly downed the contents. Alrion's throat burned away into nothing, leaving him wondering if he'd even manage to swallow anything ever again. The pain eventually subsided, leaving a warm glow.

"That was ridiculous!" Alrion barely squeezed the words out, his voice hoarse and a coughing fit followed soon after. Branthor laughed and slapped Alrion on the back.

"Good on you for not lessening the impact."

"I'm not going to give you the satisfaction of commenting on that."

"Very well." Branthor chuckled, and Alrion could tell that the wizard had probably done something to reduce the effect of the alcohol.

"Why don't you start with your ideas," Alrion said carefully, trying to avoid another coughing fit. Branthor refilled both glasses to the same point. He pointed to the glasses and they both had a sip. It still burned terribly, but not as bad.

"We'll get to that. But first, I think we need to understand each other a bit more. That will improve our cooperation."

"Yeah, you can explain how you did all that evil stuff and can look at yourself in the mirror."

"I see the special reserve is already working. Happy to discuss my own shortcomings, but right after you answer this: why do you need information from me on the location of the source of the Blight?" Branthor had an intensely serious look on his face which surprised Alrion.

"Why? Because that's where I need to go. You know that."

"Ah-hah, yes now we're getting to it. Yes, I know the location. I know the purpose, the general workings of the spell too. Because I drank from the Pool of Knowledge. As did you. Why don't you know?" Branthor kept his gaze fixated on Alrion. The younger wizard looked away and took another sip of the drink.

"That detail has not been revealed to me yet."

"Obviously. I learned a bit about how the Pool works, from those guardians. Mostly they threw it in my face as reasons why I would fail, but it was useful all the same. The short explanation is that your mind brings out the information when you need it."

"Are you saying I don't need it?"

"Well, you reached the Pool. You completed that Vault of Silence trial and pulled a big ol' trick afterwards. And you cured me. That sounds like you should be ready. Why aren't you?" Branthor downed the rest of his drink and poured another. Alrion was floored.

What is he getting at? Does he know why?

"I don't know why. You tell me."

"Oh, I think you do. I can only guess. Why can't you complete your quest? Why, Alrion?"

"I don't know why. Lucky you can tell me what I need to know."

"No, not this time. We have a deal, so I will eventually. But you don't need me. Why? Why? Why? Why can't you see it!"

"Because I'm not good enough. I'm not ready," Alrion blurted out, louder than he expected. He looked around the room sheepishly. Nobody seemed to notice.

"And why is that? You managed to beat me without any real training. You have all that knowledge in your head. Why not?" Branthor kept pushing. Alrion was tired and frustrated.

"Because I keep failing people. Falric was killed, by you no less. Alyx was infected then turned. And transformed into the Skull Queen. My grandmother sacrificed herself to save me. I sacrificed a whole town to save Alyx. The list goes on." Alrion slumped down in the chair and sipped the drink again. It was empty and Branthor refilled it. He leaned back finally, looking satisfied.

"You're taking it all too personally." Branthor took a deep swig of his drink. "And don't get hung up on Falric. That old paper-pusher went down far too easily. I wasn't even trying!"

"That's not helping."

"Listen, kid. I'm not your mentor, not cut out for it. At least Falric seemed to be good at that. But it doesn't take a genius to see what's going on here. You need to sort this out, or you'll fail. Because I can tell you the location, but if you don't correct this..."

"Then I'll never figure out the rest of the spell?"

"Precisely. And take it from me, you're going to want to know the full details before you step in there." Branthor leaned back and closed his eyes, deep in thought.

"That's all you're going to say?"

"Yes. Perhaps we should move on to discussing our plans for Rindale?"

"What about you, though? Why are you the way you are? You don't get to change topic so easily."

"What's there to say? Sometimes people get broken one too many times. Now I just want to get my revenge on those who have wronged me."

"Rindale?"

"Yes, he's my main target. There were others responsible, but of lesser importance." Branthor finished his drink once again and refilled it.

"Like who?"

"Your family."

"My family?" Alrion drained his glass and Branthor quickly added more from the bottle.

"Your grandfather, your father to a lesser extent. More recently you've been a thorn in my side. Your mother, well she seems alright actually." Branthor laughed.

"You're twisted."

"I told you, didn't I?" Branthor sighed. "Today is not a day for my darkness." Branthor slammed down the drink in his glass and lounged back, his eyes closed.

"The plans then. We need another way to track down Rindale, one that we trust."

"I doubt we can track the Shade Wizards again," Branthor added.

"Maybe not, I'm not sure if they caught on to that as an approach. But if they were training them here, we may have less luck." Alrion took a sip of his drink.

"Do we know anybody that can get to Rindale." Branthor kept his eyes closed.

"Not really. We know Fermur, but he's not quite in the trustworthy camp." Branthor sat up and opened his eyes.

"Yes, but he could be persuaded to speak something that we can trust in a relative sense, yes?"

"If we had no other options."

"Do we have other options?" Branthor stared at Alrion.

"None come to mind."

"Then we should see what your companions think." Branthor made himself comfortable, leaning back in the seat and assuming a sleeping position.

"You're going to nap?"

"Why not? You can keep drinking if you want." Branthor pushed the bottle closer to Alrion and closed his eyes. Within moments, Alrion could hear him snoring.

"I'll never understand him," Alrion muttered under his breath. He tried to think of alternative options while waiting for his friends.

Hours later, Alyx and Lara stumbled into the inn, weary. They sat down roughly next to the wizards.

"Any luck?" Alrion said.

"No. We combed that place, and it was picked clean. I think Rindale was ready and waiting." Lara looked to Alyx who shook her head.

"I agree. It was a fool's errand. But we eliminated the possibility."

"Alrion had a bright idea," Branthor added. He didn't change position, but he did open his eyes.

"Which is?" Lara said, prompting Alrion to speak. But Branthor jumped in.

"Fermur. He's the only one that seems to know of Rindale's movements. We just need to figure out a way to get information from him that is complete and trustworthy."

"No easy task," Lara said.

"And we need to figure out where he is. I'm not sure stumbling around until we find the trail he left for us is the most prudent option." Alyx was looking over at the bar as she spoke.

"Hold that thought." Branthor jumped out of his chair and rushed over to the bar. He returned swiftly with two new glasses. Placing them before Lara and Alyx he filled them to the same level he had been doing previously. Lara smelled the liquid.

"You've been drinking this? How bad is it?"

"I thought I would lose my ability to speak," Alrion said. Lara laughed.

"You better not drink it, he promoted it as putting hair on your chest." Alrion laughed and Lara smirked, taking a swig. She made a pained face and Alrion could watch her forcing it down. Alyx threw it down like water and looked bored.

"Great, great! Good teamwork, all," Branthor said. "In the interests of teamwork, I thought it helpful to mention that I can track Fermur's location." Alrion stared at Branthor.

"How?"

"When we met earlier, I imbued a speck of dust with a unique signature from my Spark and attached it to his leg in a way that will not come off." Branthor poured himself another glass and took a sip.

"You started tracking Fermur but didn't think it worth mentioning until now?" Alrion said, anger building in his voice.

"It's not as simple as that, and I didn't want to jump to conclusions. Besides, we just did some valuable bonding."

"You're impossible!"

"Truly. But, as I said, I am a master wizard who has visited the Pool of Knowledge." Branthor shrugged.

"All that aside, it means we have a lead on Rindale and a way to find him. We just need to figure out how to get what we need from Fermur," Lara said. Alyx grunted, and Alrion didn't like the expression on her face.

This could get ugly.

19

CAPTURING THE WIND

Alrion waited for silence before speaking.

"I think the most important question, to begin with, is: where is Fermur now?"

"That will take some pinpointing," Branthor said. Alrion kept his gaze on the older wizard.

"You'll need to give us something to both back up your claim and begin our planning," Lara said.

"Very well." Branthor closed his eyes. His breathing slowed, and he looked deep in concentration. After a few minutes, his eyes snapped open.

"There's another town not too far away. He seems to be circling it but not staying put. My guess is that he's waiting for something and is staying out of sight." Branthor gave Lara a smirk.

"Town have a name?" Alrion said.

"Not sure, but I can see how to get there."

"Good enough to start with. We need a way to deal with his speed once we get there." Lara started drumming her fingers on the table.

"Alyx, I remember you being good with a whip. Does that extend to ropes and other similar items?" Branthor asked.

"Yes, of course."

"That's our best bet of restraining him. I don't believe he's that strong, if we can get enough steel chain around him, he won't get away."

"I can handle that, provided he is stationary or moving at a walking pace," Alyx said.

"Maybe we can just ask him nicely?" Lara chuckled.

"I might be able to catch him with a force spell," Alrion mused.

"That's too obvious, but a good idea." Branthor poured himself another drink and slowly drained it.

"You know, I wonder if you can pull a similar trick like you did back at the desert temple. You trapped me quite handily."

"Yes, you never saw that coming. I'm not sure though."

"Why not?"

"At the time I had just cleared the trial, and I think the location of the temple somehow amplified the effects."

"We don't need something of the same magnitude. Just enough to disrupt that speedster." Branthor looked to Alyx and Lara for support.

"If you can do something on a smaller scale, that will help."

"Maybe focus more on slowing him down rather than trapping him?" Alyx added.

"Happy to try, but we need a proper test. We can't waste the next opportunity." Alrion finished his drink and blocked Branthor from adding more.

"A test!" Branthor stood immediately, his chair falling behind him. He scooped up the bottle of alcohol and tucked it into his robe.

"No time like right now," Alrion muttered. He stood a little shakily and eagerly accepted a steady hand from Alyx.

"You have a sobering up spell?" Lara said to Branthor.

"No, that would ruin my fun. Follow me." Branthor left the inn and strode away with confidence. The light was fading but he didn't seem bothered. They walked down the path a little until Branthor led them into a clearing.

"This will do." With a wave of his arm, four big balls of light appeared and ascended into the corners of the clearing, bathing the area in bright light.

"How is this supposed to work?" Alrion said.

"I'll create a projectile of the appropriate speed. Alyx here will…" Branthor stopped suddenly. "Alyx will go back to town and find a suitable steel chain then return." Alyx sighed and left.

"You will practise slowing down the projectile. Once that is working, Alyx will practise catching it with the steel chain."

"How should I slow it down then?"

"Use your Will or whatever you call it. I'll leave the mechanics up to you."

"And what about me?" Lara said.

"You can tell us what we're doing wrong."

"Happy to." Lara winked at Alrion. He nodded and thought about the test.

I need to alter reality so that the projectile moves slower. But it will be quite hard to focus on it. Maybe I can alter the properties of the area it is going to move through, and that might work better.

"I have an idea of how this will work, but let's start with something small." Alrion looked around for a small stone. Branthor clicked his fingers and a stone floated in front of Alrion.

"Was that absolutely necessary?"

"Yes. Now tell me where to send it." Alrion walked into the middle of the clearing. He picked up a stick and drew a large circle in the dirt. He stepped over beside the circle.

"Send it through here. You may want to catch it on the other side, regardless of what I manage to do to it."

"Sure. Let me know when you are ready."

"Wait. Before you do it, show me how fast you think it should be," Lara said to Branthor. He sent the rock flying across the space and it stopped just past the circle Alrion had drawn.

"It's not fast enough. Try again." Lara pointed back to the starting position. Branthor sent the stone flying again, so fast it was barely visible.

"Too fast, slow it down a bit." The stone floated back to the start position and flew again. Slower, but still barely perceptible.

"That's it. Alrion, do you agree?"

"Looks about right to me." Alrion wondered how he was going to slow it down so much. But then he remembered it was just a small stone. He started to prepare his mind. He created the visualisation, that the space within the circle was different. The air was thicker and slowed everything down.

"Go now." The stone flashed by as before.

"Nothing happened," Lara said. Alrion nodded. He needed to focus more.

Remember, you aren't thinking about it, you're adjusting reality. Remaking it as you need.

"Again." The stone flew but something happened. It seemed to alter its trajectory slightly and slow down. But it was still incredibly fast.

"Something happened there. What were you doing?" Lara said.

"I made the air thicker and slower."

"I don't think you should mess with the air. What if we're breathing it?"

"Good advice there," Branthor added. Alrion pondered that.

"You're right. I don't think I need that detail anyway. Let's try again." Alrion held his hand up to make them wait. He concentrated on changing the reality within the circle, so that everything moved slower. Much much slower. Then he clicked his fingers and knew that it was so. He let his hand down and nodded to Branthor. The projectile flew with incredible speed and, amazingly, once it passed into the circle it moved in slow motion. As soon as it exited the circle it sped up quickly until Branthor stopped it.

"Now that, that can work." Branthor sounded impressed and a little surprised. Lara beamed up a smile.

"That's incredible."

"I have surprised myself a little, to be honest." Alrion wiped away a bead of sweat on his brow. Even though he wasn't expending as much direct concentration, the effort was taking its toll.

"This will be tricky to maintain for long."

"Luckily I'm back with the steel chain." Alyx had the chain coiled around one arm, with a length trailing down and almost touching the ground. She expertly flicked the chain around, doing circles and other movements so fast that the chain was a blur.

"Try it in the circle." Lara pointed. Alyx walked over without pausing her display of skill. She flicked the chain across the circle boundary and part of the chain moved very fast, whilst the other part moved very slow.

"This is hard to judge." Alyx moved within the circle. As soon as she did, she also moved in slow motion. She immediately left the circle. Alrion dropped to his knees and was short of breath.

"That was quite an experience. What you did is great, but we can't be within that space."

"Agreed." Alrion paused and tried to catch his breath. "Influencing you was a huge burden. We need to be smart about this. I'll struggle with Fermur, for sure."

"Don't worry we can trial it more tonight."

"And I can start using human-sized rocks." Branthor actually sounded excited.

One thing's for sure, I'm going to sleep well after this.

Alrion awoke with a terrible headache. Cradling his head, he looked around the room and barely recognised it. Lara was leaning against the wall next to the doorway and turned to look at him.

"You're up. How are you feeling?"

"Terrible." Alrion remained seated, he didn't trust himself just yet.

"Branthor expected this. Said you've probably never worked that hard in your life."

"He would say that." Alrion forced himself up and he was steadier than expected. He tried focusing some Soul Power and directing it into his head. Maybe that would help.

"Grab some bread on the way and join us outside. We need to head out immediately." Lara darted out of the room and Alrion started moving too. Each step felt like his head was pounding with the same rhythm, but he kept his momentum. Slowly but surely, he did feel better, and once he emerged downstairs into the inn, he felt relatively normal. Grabbing a bread with seeds on top that looked like there was cheese inside, he moved swiftly through the empty room and emerged into the sunlight.

"Good morning. Just." Branthor acknowledged Alrion with a slight nod and mounted his horse. Lara and Alyx were already mounted. Alrion saw what was to be his horse, and took his time getting on. Luckily, his body seemed fine and he eased into the saddle. Retrieving the bread he had selected, he took a big bite.

Wow, I'm really hungry.

"We need to get a move on, our quarry hasn't moved but he's fast and may take flight at any time." Branthor spurred his horse on and took off.

"I see you've been busy," Alrion said to Lara.

"Your recovery was critical for the success of the plan, so we did what we could to expedite things once you were ready. Approved?"

"Yes, this is quite delicious." Alrion quickly polished off the rest of the bread.

"Did you even chew that?"

"Probably. Do you think this will work?" Alrion gave Lara a long glance.

"Probably. Now let's keep moving, we can discuss tactics when we're closer."

"No problem." Alrion focused on the ride and let his thoughts wander. But he didn't let them dwell on the encounter ahead.

Within a few hours, they could see the town.

"There she is, the quaint little town of Quagmire." Branthor showed off the town with a flourish of his hands.

"Sounds delightful," Lara said.

"It's quite apt, isn't it? The name?" Branthor responded with a chuckle.

"Let's hope so," Alyx grunted.

"Where's Fermur?" Alrion went straight to the point.

"Hold on." Branthor closed his eyes again. Alrion thought about probing Branthor on the spell some more but opted to do it at another time. Within moments, the master wizard snapped his eyes open.

"There's a field at the edge of the town. Fermur is sitting in the middle."

"Doesn't like surprises, does he?" Lara said.

"No, I suppose he likes to use his speed. If anyone approaches, he's got ample time to flee, often before they've even spotted him." Branthor stroked his chin.

"We have to bank on the fact that he wants to talk to us and feels safe. I can't be effective at long distance," Alrion said.

"Then let's make ourselves known. If we don't hide our approach he may feel more in control." Alyx drew her sword and started moving forward. The rest followed. They skirted the edge of the town, battling through shrubs and plants until they found a serviceable path. They continued in silence.

Alrion ran through the plan over and over in his mind. It was a good plan, and they had practised it well. But he still wasn't sure if he could pull it off.

Don't overthink it. Just stick to the plan.

Soon enough Alyx emerged into a clearing. The grass was low like it had been recently cut. In the middle of the clearing stood Fermur, arms crossed. He was motionless and stared at them.

"So far so good," Lara said.

"Just keep going." Alrion moved just behind Alyx and matched her pace. He wanted to be as close as possible. Closer and closer they went, and Fermur was still motionless. Finally, he unfolded his arms and spoke.

"I see you've tracked me down. I hear things didn't go quite to plan."

"You gave us bad information," Alrion said. He continued to

advance. They weren't far now from the range he had been practising.

"It wasn't good or bad, it was just information. As I was instructed. You made the most of it, approaching on two fronts. A shame then that you missed your opportunity."

"Maybe you can give us another." Alrion kept approaching, passing Alyx. Fermur started to back away. As soon as Alrion stopped, so did Fermur.

"We can speak from here if it makes you more comfortable." Alrion sized up the distance. It was further than he liked. Not terrible, but not guaranteed. Alyx sheathed her sword and put her hands behind her back. Fermur relaxed a little. Alrion watched Alyx prepare her hands, ready to pull out the steel chain when required. Lara and Branthor fanned out, not going any closer but forming a wider line.

"It does. After your last disaster, I don't feel entirely safe."

"Yet you let us approach," Alrion said.

"So that we may talk further. I suppose you want more information? A precise location for Rindale?" Fermur laughed.

"Yes. Very much so." Alrion started preparing his visualisation. He kept his eyes open, which seemed harder. But he didn't want to tip off Fermur. Lara glanced at him and Fermur twitched. He seemed ready to flee at the slightest hint of danger.

"Would you kindly tell us what we need to know?" Alrion said. Fermur smirked and prepared a response. Alrion closed his eyes and finished his visualisation. He started to apply the speed adjustment with his Will. Without a circle, and at a further distance, it was more difficult to get the right area and the right power. So, he threw everything into it.

Fermur must have felt something was off because he started to run. He looked startled as he ran slowly but sped up faster and faster. Alrion felt a strong resistance blocking him. He took in a deep breath and disregarded it. There was no opposition to his Will. Even so, he felt tiny cracks forming in the strength of his resolve.

Alyx was running in but she was too far away. She wasn't going to make it in time. Rocky formations grew out of the ground and started to wrap themselves around Fermur. He knocked them away forcefully, but they did manage to delay him. Alyx was there and hurled out the steel chain. Fermur slowly turned to see what it was and missed another piece of stone that had risen and blocked his path. He stopped momentarily, and the steel chain connected, wrapping itself around the general. The stone formations disintegrated into dust and slowly fell to the ground. But they obscured the whole scene.

With a gasp, Alrion let go of his modification and turned on his Soul vision. He could see Fermur still there.

"Go confirm," Alrion rasped and fell to the ground, drawing in more and more rapid breaths. He could see his team rushing over to the scene.

20

A WIZARD'S TALE

F alric motioned for Caleb to fetch chairs and leaned back in his chair.

"You have every right to say that. I will tell you my story." Falric paused and waited. Caleb fetched two chairs from an adjoining room and presented them to Vincent and Celes.

"And you?" Vincent said.

"No need. Please make yourselves comfortable." Caleb stepped to the side of the room and stood near the door. Vincent waited for Celes to sit then he joined her. Falric looked at Celes, then Vincent.

"I imagine much has happened. But first I will tell you a story." Falric drew in a deep breath, sighed and began.

"I awoke suddenly on that morning, sensing something was wrong. I was able to detect a wizard nearby, which was quite alarming. For two reasons. The first is that the wizard had never announced himself before. The second is that there seemed something familiar." Falric coughed and looked around at the table. Caleb disappeared and returned quickly with a glass of water. Falric gulped it down and seemed more content.

"Right, yes so I detected this other wizard and resolved to confront him immediately. We were so near our goal I couldn't risk anything else happening. It didn't take long for me to find him, he was waiting patiently. He laughed and challenged me for facing him alone, and it was then I realised what was so familiar. It was Branthor." Falric looked up at their reactions and seeing none kept talking.

"I was completely shocked, and I couldn't understand what had gone wrong. Branthor was not forthcoming either. He just began a battle. He seemed to be toying with me, holding back. He was always better at battling, and he knew it too. I played his game, matching his attacks and thinking of a way out." Falric reached for the glass and took a small sip.

"It was around this point that I noticed young Alrion. He had found us, and I worried terribly about his safety. I made a split-second decision right there, to try to protect him from Branthor. I waved him away and let Branthor's next spell take me down. Luckily, it was big enough to do the job admirably. I did help it along though."

"What do you mean?" Celes said.

"I have a few tricks of my own. I used a tiny spell of equal parts Will and Spark to burrow myself further down than should have occurred naturally. By controlling my own burial, so to speak, I was also able to provide myself a way to breathe. Small pockets of air, connecting to the surface. The spell was small enough that Branthor didn't notice. He did hang around I believe to check if I would emerge, but he finally left."

"And then?"

"Of course, I waited for some time. I felt a presence and noticed magic above my position. I initially panicked and thought that Branthor was back, rooting around for me. I dug myself deeper still and waited patiently. However, I believe it was actually Alrion looking for me."

"Why didn't you reveal yourself then?" Vincent said, not hiding his anger.

"I was weakened and had dug myself a lot further down than expected. I did not have enough power to spring myself quickly and safely, nor to communicate. I had to slowly and carefully extract myself. The whole effort took days, I barely survived."

"Alrion was gravely injured in his encounter with Branthor. Surely you could have still made it to see him?" Vincent said.

"Yes, I could have. I approached Paperton with caution, unsure of what I would find. My enquiries led to the discovery that Alrion had survived in his quest and that the enemy wizard was nowhere to be found. I resolved then to let Alrion continue, knowing that he would meet you in Brangtur. I decided to wait for him to leave, then begin my stay in Paperton." Falric stopped talking and waited for a response.

"Why did you not attempt to join him? I know nothing of wizard training, but Alrion's had barely begun." Celes sounded annoyed too. Vincent sat back and let Falric answer.

"He had accessed the Pool of Knowledge. He had proved himself and he had a way to further his training. I thought that it would be best to let Alrion continue his growth and his journey, and I could learn the secrets of the Pool of Knowledge."

"You left him alone, so you could do more research?" Vincent's voice grew in volume with every word.

"Branthor bested me too easily. I am well-travelled, but the knowledge is old and out of date. Alrion had found a new companion and had you to join him. It was a risk worth taking." Falric paused but started again. "And I knew that if he had a roadblock in his journey he would return. And I would be ready to help him in whatever he needed. Imagine my surprise to see you both here instead."

"I expected more from you. I didn't expect you to abandon him when things became difficult," Celes said.

"And what of the Wizard Academy? Surely you're needed there?" Vincent said.

"There are protocols that I have already established. Things will go on as they should. I spent my life building up the Academy. You can fault me on many things, but not that."

"I'm still not happy with this. I went along with everything, I supported your approach the whole way. Surely you could have guided him from the shadows, supported him in other ways?" Vincent studied Falric's reaction. The wizard did look a little guilty, embarrassed. He turned away before returning his gaze.

"I took the easy option and justified it to myself. Luckily for me, it worked out. I would have to live with it if something happened. But I believe all is well?"

"He's alive, and he's accomplished quite a lot. He can cure the Blight now." Vincent felt annoyed by the pride and joy in Falric's features.

He started this, but I feel like he betrayed us.

"Then he's so close. What is his goal now?" Falric said.

"He needs to determine the source of the Blight to complete the final spell I believe," Vincent said.

"Which is why we are here," Celes added. Falric looked confused.

"If he's come as far as you say, he should have the information already. It's a crucial part of the spell. And if he needs it, why is he not here with you?"

"I suspected he would be here or would be soon. He had other matters to attend to."

"I see." Falric rubbed his chin. "Something has gone wrong. The mechanics of the Pool of Knowledge are infinitely complex, but the concepts are simple and reliable. What he needs should have been revealed to him already."

"Then your training has been incomplete," Vincent said. Falric nodded.

"Perhaps. Well, I must say I doubt that he will find what he needs without coming here, based on what you have said. I am glad that we will be reunited."

"We could take the information to him?" Celes said. Falric shook his head.

"Telling him details is not the answer. He needs to understand it all, together."

"Then come with us. You can help him," Vincent said.

"No, this is not a matter we can just wave away. Alrion needs to continue the journey to learn the answers he seeks. There are no shortcuts. That's a primary rule." Falric closed his eyes and looked deep in thought.

"Take me to the Pool then. I'll learn what needs to be done and assist." Vincent stood and stared at Falric defiantly. Falric cowered back quickly but regained his composure.

"I'm afraid that won't be possible. Caleb?"

"Yes, as Falric said. The Pool has been closed off and no further access is allowed."

"Surely we can discuss…"

"And only a wizard can properly incorporate and use the information that Alrion seeks," Falric said. Celes placed her hand on Vincent's and he sat back down.

"We just want to help our son. Surely we can do something?" Celes said.

"You can start by telling me everything that has happened. I may have some ideas on how to help Alrion once I know the full details."

"You should find yourself a chair," Vincent said to Caleb.

Vincent sighed and looked over at Celes.

"That's it all, isn't it?"

"Yes, now you know everything, Falric." Celes picked at a leftover scrap of bread. Caleb had disappeared and brought food on two different occasions while they spoke.

"There's one thing I can't figure out. This wizard who has been helping Alrion. It doesn't make sense," Falric said.

"What doesn't make sense?" Celes said.

"You need to come into contact with that magical notebook to send messages. It should be obvious, then, who you have come into contact with." Falric paused, deep in thought.

"Those messages started after the Pool of Knowledge, correct?"

"To the best of my knowledge. We haven't really spoken at length about it," Vincent said.

"There's a Wizard Store near here. Because of its location, it has some additional security. All wizards who visit must provide a name which is recorded in a book. We may find some clues there." Falric eased himself out of the chair and straightened out.

"Right, let's go then." Falric started walking off.

"Is this really the most important thing we could be doing?" Vincent jumped out of his chair and almost knocked it over.

"Yes, this is at the heart of it all. Caleb, you can join us."

"It would be an honour." Caleb gave a short bow. Vincent pulled him aside.

"Look, even if I can't get access you need to explain more about the Pool, so I can help my son."

"Of course. That is within my power and I will happily so do."

"Good. Thanks." Vincent rushed to catch up with Falric and Celes.

They emerged into the night air, the slight chill surprising Vincent. Falric walked with an almost fevered pace. He led them through buildings until they came to a run-down shed.

"This is it?" Celes said.

"Of course. Hiding in plain sight." Falric walked up to the door and knocked three times. After a bell sounded, he said, "Falric." After a few moments, the door unlocked and Falric opened it.

"Let's go." Falric ushered them in and close the door. The Wizard Store was quite small. There was a corner with clothing and travelling supplies. But the rest was filled with books.

"Seems fitting," Vincent said.

"What's that?" Falric asked.

"The store here in the scholar's town is full of books."

"These are the recordings of those who have studied or experienced the Pool of Knowledge."

"Good to know." Vincent started browsing the shelves. Falric walked to a bench set in to one of the walls and unlocked something underneath. He pulled out a dusty book.

"Come over and look at this." Vincent closed the book he had opened and walked over. Celes was already there hovering over Falric's shoulder.

"Now, see here is the entry that we just created." Falric pointed to a space in the book. The word 'Falric' was written in script with the date.

"That's quite impressive!" Celes slapped Falric lightly on the back.

"I'm afraid this was Granthion's doing. I know enough to maintain it, but the exact way it was created escapes me. I suppose with sufficient study I could recreate it, but never felt the need." Falric started paging through the book.

"Obviously, all the recent entries are me. Here, it should be around this time." Falric ran his fingers over the page.

"This one is me. And above it are..."

"Branthor. And Aydan?" Celes said with surprise.

"Branthor didn't even try to hide his identity. Not that it would be easy, and I suppose he had already dealt with me."

"And the other name? Is it familiar?" Vincent said.

"It's an odd one. It's in the old language. Nobody uses it now, except scholars. Or wizards."

"What's it mean?" Celes asked.

"Lost One," Caleb said. Celes spun quickly to face the scholar.

"I learned the language as part of my training. I'm no wizard, Falric can attest to that." Caleb held his hands up and chuckled.

"This may just be the clue we need," Falric pondered.

"Do you believe it's a real name?" Vincent said.

"It needs to be. Well, actually not explicitly." Falric paused and gathered his thoughts. "It needs to be a name that the person believes is true. I suppose an alias could fit if it was used for a long time."

"And it has to be a wizard?" Celes asked.

"Yes, absolutely. No way around that. Aydan it is then. Now we need to find the man behind the name." Falric walked away from the book. Vincent leaned over and observed the script himself, then he closed the book.

"Any other mysteries in here we should be aware of?" he said. Falric didn't hear, he was already poring through another book.

"Maybe we can find something here ourselves," Celes whispered in Vincent's ear. He nodded and strode over to select another book.

21

THE RIGHT WAY

Branthor closed the door, the creaking sound annoying him. He surveyed the room and gave a satisfied nod.

This will do. The kid actually pulled it off.

Fermur was seated on a wooden chair in the middle of the room. He was chained up and immobile and quiet.

"Are you sure I can't fully encase him in stone? We only need his head," Branthor said. Alrion glared at him.

"This is sufficient. He knows that he's in our custody." Alrion made eye contact with Fermur and the general nodded weakly. Lara hovered nearby, checking the strength of the restraints.

"Fine, fine. Now, I got us this opportunity. What are we doing with it?" Branthor started pacing the room.

"We achieved this, and we're going to ask Fermur some questions." Alrion dragged over another wooden chair and sat in front of Fermur.

"We're not monsters," Alrion glanced over at Branthor, "well, most of us aren't. Please cooperate and tell us what we need to know. Where is Rindale?"

"I can't tell you," Fermur almost whispered. His voice had lost its confidence and strength.

"Can't or won't?" Branthor added.

"I cannot betray them. It is impossible."

"Would you? If it were possible?" Alrion leaned in.

"I'm not sure. It's not the answer you want, but it's the truth." Fermur shuffled against the chains, clearly uncomfortable.

"He's too conditioned. We can't trust what he says." Branthor grew irritated and sent a pile of dust flying under the door.

"We have to try. What was the point of capturing him anyway?" Lara walked up to Branthor.

"There was always a chance he would talk. But if not, he's leverage. They will want him back. Or we could just remove him now, save everyone the trouble." Branthor grinned. He knew it wouldn't win them over, but he enjoyed their annoyance and disgust too much. Although, he did notice a serious look from the weapons master.

She's on my side. She's experienced it as I have. There can be no middle ground, no quarter. Since she understands, this may go well.

"Absolutely not. We need to figure out a way to get the information safely. I'm not like them, or you." Alrion pointed a finger at Branthor.

"As you wish. I'm just pointing out the inevitable conclusion to this affair." Branthor walked back and leaned against the wall.

Time will bring them around. They won't get anything from that creature.

"We need to think about how to release him from whatever restriction is holding his tongue." Alrion stood quickly and moved the chair away.

"You could cure him, wouldn't that do it?" Lara said.

"Possibly. Alyx, do you remember much of what you experienced before you were cured?"

"Not much. What little I do remember, I think was because they allowed me more consciousness."

"True." Alrion turned to Fermur. "Didn't you say that when you were transformed you were allowed to keep your personality?"

"Yes."

"That would suggest that he's conscious of his thoughts and

actions and would more likely retain them. Don't you remember everything?" Alrion turned to Branthor.

"Don't compare me to that!" Branthor dismissed Fermur with a hand gesture.

"Alyx?"

"I can't offer anything concrete supporting this course of action. It may work, it may not." Alyx spoke with no emotion, her voice flat.

"You would treat this monster with humanity? He's no longer human." Branthor spat on the ground. Fermur remained still, his head bowed. Alrion walked up to Branthor and looked him in the eye.

Kid's got some steel in him. Good.

"I don't think there's anything you can say that can sway me from this. He will be removed as a tool of the Blight, and he may offer the information we need. But he is not a tool to be used. That makes us the same as them." Alrion kept a steady gaze on Branthor.

"It's your show." Branthor backed away a little. "I'm just offering the voice of reason. Just because you return him from being a monster, doesn't mean it's permanent. There's every chance he will get recaptured and reconverted."

"A risk worth taking. It's the right thing, and soon enough everyone will be cured." Alrion glared at Branthor. The older wizard chuckled.

"Be my guest." Branthor gave them space and observed. Alrion walked up to Fermur slowly.

"Is there anything I should know before we try this?"

"Does it really work?"

"Ask them. They're living proof." Alrion pointed to Alyx and Branthor.

"That one's still quite mad, I think you made a mistake." Fermur pointed to Branthor and Alrion laughed. Fermur had managed a wry grin.

"No, I think unfortunately that's just how he is."

"You're welcome!" Branthor shouted out. He hung back and let the young wizard work.

It will be interesting to observe this process.

Alrion closed his eyes and went still. Branthor monitored the wizard, watching and waiting. He noticed Alrion gathering his Spark. He was forming it into some sort of spell. But it was a nothing spell, not special in any way.

Maybe you do need those Mystics to make it work.

Fermur went rigid suddenly. He strained against the chains. Branthor readied a spell, just in case he needed to subdue the general. A warm light began to envelop Fermur, and soon he was obscured by it completely. Branthor heard the chains drop to the ground. He readied himself. Alrion dropped to his knees, panting. Lara rushed to his aid and Alyx went over to investigate what had happened.

Fermur lay on the ground, motionless. Black flakes drifted off him and dissolved in the air. There was more colour to his face, and he seemed more human.

Branthor felt a cold shiver run through him. Knowing it was possible, having it happen to him was one thing. Seeing it happen was another.

Maybe he can do this? No, saving one at a time is manageable. What he must accomplish is impossible. Don't get fooled.

Branthor wandered over, clapping.

"Good show! I'm no expert, but I think it worked."

"He appears to be breathing normally. The Blight markings are gone." Alyx examined Fermur.

"He needs to rest then?" Branthor said.

"Yes, Alyx needed time. Maybe he needs more." Alrion looked around the shed. Branthor saw what the wizard needed.

"There's enough here to work with." Branthor created the visualisation in his head, then summoned his Spark to complete the spell. An earthen bed sprung up through the wooden floor. With another quick spell, some rough cloth and straw flew over to the bed, acting as a makeshift blanket.

Alrion picked up Fermur under the arms, Lara helping him with the feet.

"I could have done that. So could you, much easier," Branthor commented.

"Didn't feel right." Alrion lowered Fermur down. "I need to rest now. Try to keep him alive if you don't mind."

"Sure, boss." Branthor chuckled. "I'm going to go for a walk, that way I won't accidentally do anything." Branthor channelled some Spark to fling the door open and sauntered out.

Once outside Branthor continued walking. He didn't aim for anywhere in particular. He found himself standing beneath a tree. He formed himself a stone chair and sat down.

What is this feeling?

He scoured his body for any signs of the Blight, but there were none. The boy's cure had worked, even though he kept doubting it. He let himself enter a meditative state and floated for a while, his mind not latching onto anything in particular. Suddenly he sat up.

There. There it is.

It was like a wound festering within him. His pain. His desire for vengeance. Even the thought of Rindale's name brought up waves of anger and anguish.

I can't be normal again, can I?

He couldn't continue the journey with Alrion. He was torn between wanting to be there, and not wanting to. He believed that there was a chance, however slim, that Alrion would succeed. But there were consequences for that too. Better not to be there. One way or another it would end with Rindale.

Branthor detected movement back at the shed and rose slowly. He let the chair collapse back into dirt and dust. With purposeful strides, he made his way back to meet them.

Your journey will end soon. His will go on.

The thought was oddly comforting. Branthor even smiled when he opened the door.

Inside, he saw Fermur sitting up and sipping some water. His eyes darted around the room feverishly. He looked like a spooked animal ready to bolt.

"He's awake. Does he understand you?" Branthor said. Fermur almost jumped at the sound of Branthor's voice.

"I think so. He seems better by the minute, although he's quite nervous as you probably noticed." Alrion remained crouched near Fermur, and Lara was feeding him the cup of water. Alyx hung back, but she had a hand on her sword. Branthor strode forward, pushing Alrion aside. He hauled Fermur to his feet and held the man's head in both his hands.

"Where's Rindale? Do you know where he is?" Branthor was loud and forceful. Fermur looked terrified, staring directly at the older wizard. Fermur managed a tiny nod.

"Is that a yes? Where is he?" Branthor continued, although he noticed Alrion had risen and was looming nearby. "I'm not hurting him, he needs to be focused."

"Rindale," Fermur said quietly. He nodded again.

"Can you tell us where to find him?" Branthor spoke a little softer but retained his tight grip. Fermur started to speak but stopped. He looked distraught. He started waving his hands.

"He's trying to tell you something," Lara said.

"I think he wants to show you," Alyx added. Branthor removed his hands and stepped back.

"Will you show me the way to Rindale?" he said. Fermur nodded feverishly. Branthor nodded and turned away, looking to the door.

"Good. I will destroy him and prevent him from doing any more experiments. I'll save the world, in my own way. No more vile creatures will haunt us." Branthor clenched his fist. He knew all too well that he was part of that category. But his words were still true.

"There's no guarantee that there isn't more like him. Or that they won't convert him again. Isn't that what you said?" Alrion remarked. Branthor wheeled around to face Alrion, not bothering to hide his anger.

"When I'm done with him, there will be nothing anyone can do to bring him back or use him further. It ends with him." Branthor stormed outside before his rage completely unleashed itself.

22

THE SCHOLAR'S PATH

Vincent closed the book and stood. He stretched, relieving the stiffness from sitting for such a long time. Celes and Falric seemed quite content and comfortable, glued to their books.

"Is this really productive?" he said.

"The pursuit of knowledge is always productive." Falric closed his book and turned to Vincent. "Just, sometimes you don't need that knowledge right away."

"I need to keep moving. Do we have somewhere you can point us to?"

"Like the source of the Blight?" Falric said.

"Sure, that'll do." Vincent headed towards the day as if he were leaving immediately.

"No point being there without Alrion. You also can't ignore Aydan, that other wizard. Whatever his game is, he's interfering. I fear that if we don't do something, he may cause problems at the end."

"You think he's waiting for Alrion to do the spell?"

"Why else would a wizard help, hover, yet refuse to make himself known? He has an agenda and until we know what it is, it is a huge risk to allow Alrion to complete his quest." Falric looked quite concerned.

"Sounds like a bit of a wild goose chase to me. If this wizard is really up to something, then we just need to prepare and head him off when he arrives. What do you think?" Vincent looked to his wife.

"I'm more inclined to find and confront this wizard sooner rather than later. Then we can focus on ensuring Alrion has what he needs."

"Your wife is quite wise." Falric smiled and Celes batted her eyelashes at Vincent.

"I see that I'm outnumbered. Where do we go from here then?" Vincent sighed.

"You'll need help to continue following the trail." Falric rose and started pacing around the room.

"Trail?" Celes said.

"Well, you'd want to investigate other Wizard Stores. They will paint a picture of his movements, and you may find other clues."

"The trail might not lead anywhere. What if he only visited this one?" Celes said.

"If this wizard is interested in Alrion's quest, then he would definitely have visited the Wizard Store at Valrytir." Falric stopped pacing.

"Why is that?"

"It's at the heart of this. And near Alrion's destination."

"Ah-hah!" Vincent pointed at Falric. "That's what I needed to know."

"Oh, but it's not the final destination. And I haven't told you where the Wizard Store is."

"You're going to guide us then? That's a good plan." Celes looked like she was working through some ideas.

"No, I cannot. I must wait here for Alrion. Plus, I can further my knowledge at the same time."

"Can't Caleb do that? Help Alrion retrieve the knowledge he needs?" Vincent looked over at the scholar.

"It is true that I may be able to help Alrion," Caleb began to explain.

"But as he's not a wizard he can't learn all the details that Alrion needs. He will likely want another wizard to talk it through," Falric said.

"If you're staying here, how do we visit Wizard Stores?" Celes said.

"Excellent question. For that, we will need to return to my quarters." Falric paused for a moment then strode off to the door. Vincent gave Celes a questioning look and she shrugged.

"Let's see what he has," she said softly. Vincent nodded, and they followed Falric out of the room.

Falric led them back to Paperton, and they retraced their steps to the room where they had found him. He asked them to wait a moment and started looking through a dusty wooden chest.

"Ah-hah!" Falric dusted something off with his robe then presented it to Celes.

"What's this?" Celes turned the object around in her hands. It was a metallic disc with some inscriptions on it.

"It's a Wizard's Marker. One that I made. It's infused with my Spark and can be used to open Wizard Stores."

"How do we use it?" Vincent said.

"Instead of knocking with your hand, use that. If the door doesn't open, then state your name. The door will do the rest." Falric grinned, looking quite pleased with himself.

"This solves our problem then." Celes looked to Vincent.

"True, we just need to know the location of the Wizard Store we are supposed to visit."

"Yes, yes. I should write that down for you." Falric sat down at his desk, pulling out a sheet of parchment and a pen. He wrote copious notes and even scrawled a small drawing.

"This will make sense once you reach Valrytir." Falric handed the paper to Celes who studied it.

"Are you sure about that?" Celes handed it to Vincent.

"Trust me, you'll find what you need. I can't explain it better without making it usable by anyone. It's imperative that we keep this location secret." Falric gave Celes a serious look. Vincent handed her back the page.

"I think we can work with this. We need to trust Falric."

"You want to trust him now? You didn't seem too happy with his behaviour earlier?" Celes gave Vincent a pointed look. The blacksmith raised his hands in a surrender gesture.

"We're at his mercy on this. As much as I don't agree with some of his decisions, his knowledge about Wizards and related matters can't be argued with. If we're on this path, then we can trust his information." Falric gave them a satisfied smile.

"I suppose you're right on that. This better work." Celes shook the medallion at Falric.

"Go try it now, I'll wait here." Falric pulled out a book and started reading it immediately.

"After you." Vincent gestured to the door. Celes sighed and started walking. They kept a quick pace through the town.

"I just feel like we're missing something. I can't explain it," Celes said.

"I know what you mean. I think Falric knows something but he's not telling us. He wants us to discover it ourselves." Celes stopped abruptly.

"You're right. That's it. It makes sense now." Celes shook her head. "Now I know what you mean about wizards. You just feel like they're manipulating you."

"For your own good, they'll say." Vincent chuckled.

"Maybe so. But I have to agree with it. We need to deal with this wizard that is shadowing Alrion. It'll be catastrophic if we don't. I'm not going to interfere with his quest, but I am going to make sure nobody else can."

"That I can agree with. Let's test out this trinket." Vincent started walking and Celes rushed ahead.

They arrived at the dusty shed quickly. Celes retrieved the medallion from her jacket and knocked it on the door three times. Nothing happened. Vincent nudged her and pointed to her mouth.

"Celes," she said. The door opened a crack, and Celes smiled at Vincent. She pushed the door open and entered the room.

"Let's check out the ledger," Vincent said. Celes headed straight for it and flipped it open. It didn't take long to find the right page.

"Here it is." Celes pointed to the newly added entry.

"There's your name. Oh, and it says, 'on behalf of Falric'. Very clever." Vincent chuckled.

"Yes, I can see why Falric was so pleased with this. I'm glad it works." Celes looked around, "do you think we can find something of use in here before we go?"

"Perhaps. You start looking around, I have a hunch I'd like to investigate." Vincent returned to the book and flipped through the pages. He was looking at all the entries. Apart from the recent activity, there was very little. Soon it became years between entries. Finally, he stopped flipping pages and tapped on the page with his index finger.

"Celes, come look at this." Vincent waited for her to join him and stepped back.

"Aydan. He's been here before? When?"

"It looks like it's almost twenty years. A long time."

"How interesting. So, that would suggest that he is older."

"Indeed. That helps narrow it down, doesn't it?" Vincent looked at Celes and she smiled.

"Fine, yes you're not too bad an investigator yourself. That was a very helpful discovery." Celes looked back to the room. "What else could we find here?"

"I'm not sure, but let's see what kind of information is here. We might find something to help Alrion." Vincent started on the nearest bookshelf, his wife started at the opposite corner of the room.

Vincent noticed that the tomes seemed to be organised by wizard. The volumes corresponding to the same author were all clustered together. Many didn't involve dates, but with a bit of reading between the lines, you could spot something which aged the information. By sampling from different books, he started to notice a trend.

"They're grouped by author, but also chronologically." Vincent stepped back and mentally traced the timeline through the shelves.

"What are you looking for?"

"Books by my father."

"I see. Where do you think they will be?"

"That corner most likely." Vincent pointed then joined Celes. They looked through the books, carefully looking for information about the authors and the contents.

"So much of this is unreadable," Celes sighed.

"Yes, it must be about spells. But surely there is other information too." Vincent pulled out a book and recognised the handwriting. He excitedly turned through the pages.

"Look at this." Vincent offered the book to his wife. Celes took the book and examined it.

"I can read this. Who wrote this? I don't see any signatures."

"My father, I recognise the handwriting."

"Wow, this is quite a find. Maybe we will learn something from this. Do you think we can take it with us? It looks quite dense." Celes flipped through the book and sampled different pages.

"Why don't you try, you have the medallion."

"Good idea." Celes closed the book and strode over to the door. She opened the door, paused then walked outside. Vincent rushed over to the ledger and flipped to the most recent page.

A treatise on the Pool of Knowledge and information transfer, by Granthion. Borrowed by Celes on behalf of Falric.

"So far so good." Vincent closed the book and left the room, joining his wife.

"Looks like it worked?" she said as he approached.

"Yes, I even saw a line in the ledger. Falric will know that we have taken it."

"Fine by me."

"Likewise. Why don't we call it a day then? We have a long journey ahead of us." Vincent started off towards Falric's lodgings and Celes kept pace.

"I'm excited. It feels like we have something we can help with." Celes was positively beaming.

"Me too. It's a good feeling." Vincent put his arm around his wife and they kept walking.

23

THE ANCIENT TRIAL

Certan struck out his palm, feeling the force of the strike then holding his position. After a few moments, he relaxed and bowed. The monk opposite him bowed too and quickly retreated.

"They'll trust you more if you actually hit them," Graem said.

"It's a matter of respect. I am restraining myself."

"It looks like disrespect, you assume that they can't take a hit." Graem shook his head and started leaving the room. The rest had already left, and the giant stone room seemed unnaturally still. Certan rushed off to catch up with his fellow monk.

"I feel like I brought destruction here," Certan said.

"That creature? It would find its way here eventually anyway. You brought the wizard, that was helpful. And he did marvellously. Helped me out too."

"You as well?"

"Yes, he cleared out some Blighters trying to scale the walls. In return, I led him down to the Vault of Silence."

"Have you done the trial?" Upon Certan's words, Graem stopped dead still and turned around.

"That's not something you can ask a fellow monk. It's not respectful."

"It's a simple question."

"No, not really. Perhaps I have not reached that level of seniority, and as I am your senior that questions my ability. Perhaps I tried and failed and carry that wound with me. Or perhaps I have succeeded, yet you haven't recognised my mastery despite my success. Which of those options seems respectful to you?" Graem gave Certan a stern look.

"I'm sorry, I hadn't thought it through like that. Perhaps I've been away too long."

"No, you're just clutching at anything because you have no purpose." Graem started walking. "Although, now I bet you're wondering whether I've actually done the trial in the Vault of Silence."

"I think I've worked it out."

"And your answer?"

"Will not be revealed." Certan grinned and Graem laughed out loud.

"Now you're thinking like a monk. There's hope for you yet." Graem stopped suddenly. He looked back at Certan with curiosity. Certan joined Graem, wondering what had given the monk pause.

An elder monk stood before them. They almost never left the Vault of Silence, even now that the extensive repair work on the temple had turned everyone's routines upside down.

"Certan, you have not accepted our summons," the elder monk said in a low monotonous voice.

"Summons? There's been no summons."

"Directly? No, we don't work like that. But you have been shown the signs, you've had the Trial mentioned to you. Even by this one." The elder pointed to Graem.

"Perhaps you're right."

"Perhaps?"

"Yes, you're right."

"Why have you ignored us?"

"I don't know." Certan looked at Graem, the monk was staring at Certan with no emotion.

"Don't look at him for help, tell us the truth." The elder's voice had a tinge of annoyance in it.

"I don't deserve to take the Trial. I failed the order once and acted poorly. Even by attempting to redeem myself I brought ruin and death to this sacred place. It is enough that you suffer my presence so that I might earn my place among you." Certan bowed deep. The elder stood perfectly still, not reacting. After a long pause, he spoke.

"Are you done?"

"Speaking?

"Yes."

"I am done."

"Good. Follow me now." The elder dismissed Graem with a gesture and turned the corner. Certan followed closely behind.

What's going on? Is he taking me to the trial? I'm not prepared. This is not the right time.

Certan recognised the route they were taking. All the monks knew the way, even though many would never be asked to join the elders in that place. With each step, he felt a pit in his stomach. Fighting evil, dying if need be, did not concern him. He had already thrown his life away when he turned to drinking. But this, this was terrifying. His life would be examined by the monks, and if he was to do the trial, then that would be something else.

Every whispered tale of horror concerning the trial flooded back to Certan's memory. He was more anxious by the moment, the intense shame of his behaviour when he had been banished came back even stronger.

"Enter." The elder stood by the door and ushered Certan in. He entered the room and saw the three other elders all sitting. The last elder took his place with them.

"Why do you approach us, Certan," one elder said.

"Because you summoned me."

"Why did we summon you?"

"To do the trial and enter the Vault of Silence."

"You are not ready," another elder said. Certan was taken aback by the comment. He thought about it for a moment.

"You're right, I should come back another time."

"Refusal of the trial is the same as failure. Only, with failure, you are sometimes given another chance."

"Why summon me if I'm not ready and I cannot refuse without forfeiting my chance forever?"

"You should be asking yourself that. Why have you forced us to act this way?" Certan felt like he had been given a gut punch. He felt faint.

I'm set up to fail. They're punishing me for what I've done.

"The Vault of Silence is the catalyst that removes doubt. You will move forward, stronger, or you will be broken. It is the next step that you must take."

"Why? I've done everything I can to keep my place here. Can I stay if I pass the trial?"

"No," another elder shouted, his voice ringing through the space.

"I don't understand."

"Your place is not here. Your place is with him."

Alrion.

"The wizard?"

"You should never have left his side. He has suffered much but continues to gain in strength. Yet, he cannot succeed alone."

"There are others to support him. Let me prove myself here first."

"Pass the trial. Go aid your friend. Only then will you be worthy of a place here."

"There is always a choice. But if you wish to remain a monk, then you must accept our price," another elder said. In unison, they bowed their heads.

Maybe I made a mistake, and Alrion is in more trouble. I thought I could fix my situation. This feels so rushed, but perhaps it's as it should be.

"Very well. I accept your terms." Certan stood forward with confidence. There was nothing to lose. If he refused, everything was lost anyway. He had gone down that road, and it had ruined him. It was time to stand up, whatever the cost. Certan saw a doorway opening in the distance, white and shimmering. He walked towards it, slowly but carefully. He tried as much as he could to peer in, but he couldn't see anything.

Here goes.

Certan stepped into the light and in a flash, he was somewhere else. It looked like a bar. Wooden floors with a thick wooden bar, with only one table and chair. The walls were lined with shelves, and each shelf was crammed full of alcohol.

No, no, no.

Certan spun around, taking the room in. He could smell it, the intoxicating mix of vapours that hung in the air. He thought he might get drunk from the smell itself.

This is just a test. I can do this.

Certan strode over to the nearest shelf and grabbed a bottle. He opened it, looking inside. Certan dropped the bottle in shock and it smashed soundlessly on the floor, the contents oozing out. The smell was stronger now.

They're not empty or fake. It feels real.

Certan realised something was wrong though. He kicked the biggest piece of the bottle to the corner. The bottle spun and ricocheted off the table legs on its way over. All without making a sound.

The Vault of Silence? It's not all for dramatic effect.

There was definitely no exit, just bottles upon bottles of different drinks. Spirits, wines, ale, it was all there.

I will clear these from the way.

Certan started at one part of the room and methodically broke every shelf and bottle as he worked around the perimeter.

The exit will be hidden here somewhere. I need to withstand the lure and pain of the alcohol to get out.

Certan kept himself focused on the task, not letting himself notice the alcohol being scattered everywhere. After a time though, he started to tire.

Why am I tired so fast?

The monk stopped and stepped back to observe the room. The

shelf before him was reforming before his eyes. He looked back, and every shelf had completely restored itself.

How many times have I already cleared these same bottles?

An answer lay on the ground. The bottles were slowly disappearing, but the alcohol was not. The more he broke bottles, the more the floor was soaked through with alcohol. Much of it was pooling as well.

I'll eventually drown myself.

Certan laughed. He had never imagined drowning himself this way.

I can't destroy the alcohol, and I can't drink it. How do I get out?

Noticing his elevated heart rate and breathing, he walked to the nearby chair and sat. He calmed himself and closed his eyes. Once he felt composed, he opened his eyes and saw an open bottle and a chunky glass full of a brown liquid. He resisted the urge to swat it away, and carefully carried the drink to the bar and set it down. After returning to the table, Certan sat down on the table instead, cross-legged.

No more creation of alcohol here now that I'm covering the space.

He closed his eyes and kept his mind clear, as much as possible until sleep came.

Certan opened his eyes, for a moment forgetting where he was. But the vast amounts of alcohol quickly reminded him. He felt incredibly thirsty and started to reach for a bottle instinctively.

Is the room smaller than before?

Certan noticed several bottles of what had to be flammable liquids floating in front of him. He knocked them away, the bottles crashing and contributing to a pool of liquid. Something looked strange about it. Certan quickly rose and climbed off the table, walking over to inspect the puddle.

It looks quite deep, surprisingly so. He plunged a hand in and couldn't feel the floor. Leaning in further and further, he finally reached something. But he wasn't sure what it was.

I could dive in.

He instantly rejected the idea. But then, he couldn't shake it.

This is a trial of Will. Perhaps I need to immerse myself in that which I cannot control.

Certan took a deep breath. This test was never meant to be easy. He released the breath and drew in one even bigger. Then he dove headfirst into the strange puddle. After the initial shock, it felt like swimming. It only took a few strong strokes to get down to where the strange surface was. He couldn't see properly but did manage to feel around. It was definitely some sort of doorway. He searched frantically for some sort of handle or latch. But there was nothing. Certan clawed at the door, looking for a way to open it. But it didn't budge. His breath was running out, so he turned and leapt back out of the puddle.

He stood on the edge, drawing in deep breaths and ignoring the potent alcohol running down his face and clothes. He absolutely stank of alcohol.

This isn't working. I immersed myself and it wasn't enough.

Certan looked around the room. He was missing something. He sank down and closed his eyes, meditating once more. The answer would come to him in time, he was sure of that.

Certan awoke quickly, feeling disoriented. He had fallen asleep without realising. The room was exactly as he remembered it. Only there was a wood chip floating slowly over the strange puddle of alcohol. It triggered a memory.

I demonstrated Will to Alrion and Lara this way. The fundamentals of Will.

Certan remembered the lesson. How Lara had been so good at effortlessly hovering the chip of wood. Certan did the same here, this time making the wood float a long way above the puddle.

I've been foolish. I have not seen what was right in front of me.

Certan stood and looked around once more. He picked a section of wall and reimagined the room with the door in that location. But not just imagined, he remade it the way he wished. Certan closed his eyes and opened them again. The door had moved. But it still had no way of opening. He walked forward with confidence and placed his hand on the door. It opened inwards, bathing him in a white light. With a smile, Certan stepped through the door.

He found himself back in the same chamber. The elders looked at him and nodded.

"You have passed the trial. You have proven yourself as a master of Will."

"Thank you for the opportunity."

"Do you know what you must do?"

"I do." Certan gave them all a deep bow.

"Do you know where to go?"

"No, but I can find out."

"No need. Head to Valrytir." The elder gave Certan a wry smile.

"I will. When we meet next, the world will be free from the Blight."

"Good, that is the right time for you to return." The elder closed his eyes and Certan knew he was dismissed. He turned and left.

Thank you again. Your faith in me has been unwavering, and I will not let you down. Alrion, I am coming. We will finish the journey we started.

24

PLANNING THE ASSAULT

Alrion looked at the landscape before him. The ground slowly descended into a deep valley. The grass thinning and becoming dirt. And within looked like a rounded stone fortress. Unlike anything he had ever seen.

"You're sure this is the place?" Alrion said. Fermur nodded.

"It makes sense. This will be Rindale's tomb." Branthor clenched his right fist.

"It looks really old. I don't think he built this, it would have been here before," Lara said.

"Agreed. This will be a very difficult place to attack. It will be heavily fortified." Alyx folded her arms and shook her head while she took it in.

"Sentries will spot us coming from a mile away. Have you guys got a spell for that?"

"Invisibility I can do. It's hard to maintain for the whole group, however. Much easier to do on myself," Branthor muttered.

"He can scout then if we trust him." Lara looked to Alrion. He shook his head.

"It's not a matter of trust. We all need to be there. Rindale can't get away again." Alrion turned to Fermur. "Is there something you can tell us, to give us an edge?"

"Hmm," Fermur muttered. He still seemed to have trouble speaking.

"We will protect you. Nobody will transform you again."

"There... is a path." Fermur strained, the words sounding quite difficult to utter.

"And that will get us inside?" Lara said.

"Avoid most traps." Fermur looked relieved that the words came out.

"Sounds like a good idea to me. Any objections?" Lara looked around the ground. Nobody said anything.

"Then..." Lara started to say but was cut off by Branthor.

"Are you completely stupid? He did this to us last time. That didn't end well, did it?"

"It's different. He's cured now, and Rindale isn't expecting us," Alrion said.

"Not expecting us? Are you that naive? Fermur hasn't checked in and actually isn't infected anymore. Isn't it obvious where we will be going next?" Branthor looked quite agitated.

"We're not going to let him get away again." Alrion turned to Fermur. "Can you draw us a map of some kind?"

"Yes." Fermur nodded as well. Lara searched through her jacket for some paper. Branthor formed a table and chairs out of the ground. Tufts of grass littered the table top.

"Be my guest." Branthor pulled up a chair for Fermur. The reformed man looked at Branthor warily but did sit down. Lara handed him a sheet of paper and a rough pencil. Fermur started sketching.

"This is a much better idea. We can plan how we attack the fortress." Alyx was looking over Fermur's shoulder.

"Fine. But you need to let me verify some of the details. I don't want to blindly trust what he says." Branthor glared at Alrion.

"That's prudent. And you have the invisibility spell too. But you must promise that you won't enter the fortress without us there."

"You trust my word?"

"You can swear an oath."

"On what?"

"Rindale's life." Branthor burst out laughing.

"You better not let me down."

"He has nowhere else to retreat to. It ends here." Alrion looked at the group and they all nodded.

"I think he's almost finished," Alyx said. Moments later, Fermur leaned back and pushed the paper across the table. Alrion picked it up and Lara looked over his shoulder.

"The scale looks consistent. This must be the path he was referring to." Lara pointed to a winding path that joined about halfway through the building.

"What are these crosses?" Alrion asked.

"Traps," Fermur said.

"Oh, I see. Yes, the path does seem to enter the building past the main traps. Is this meant to be Rindale's chamber?" Lara pointed out a spot on the map. Fermur nodded.

"His chamber is in the middle of all the traps."

"Can you enter through the front?" Alrion said. Fermur nodded again.

"Sounds to me like we should just take the most efficient entrance if we have to encounter traps anyway," Branthor said. Alrion wasn't sure. There had to be some reason that Fermur mentioned the other path.

"How did you visit Rindale if he was surrounded by traps?" Alrion said. Fermur scrunched up his face a little as he thought.

"Disable. Some."

"There! See, if we go this way, we might be able to disable enough traps to get through safely." Alrion glanced at Branthor.

"Fine. I'll go and investigate. If Fermur's access point and information checks out, we can move forward with that plan." Branthor closed his eyes and concentrated for a few moments. Alrion studied him intently, wondering what he was doing. He noticed the surge of

Spark, but it didn't feel like a huge amount. Suddenly, Branthor was gone.

"That's how a real wizard operates," Branthor said. He was still invisible.

"Very impressive, see you soon," Alrion said. He heard Branthor's feet crunching on the ground as he walked away.

"We can hear you!" Lara shouted after him. But she looked shaken. Alrion drew in close.

"Are you alright?" Lara turned quickly and smiled at him.

"Yes, I just found that invisibility a bit shocking is all. Would be quite useful in my line of work, provided you don't tramp around like a bear."

"I can imagine so. I'll figure out a way to make you invisible if you'd like?"

"As long as you can turn me back." Lara winked.

"Maybe I should practice on something else first." Alrion chuckled and received another smile from Lara. Alyx was just staring off into the distance.

"Are you concerned about him?" Alrion said.

"He is like me, only worse. His rage is so barely contained, something will give way soon."

"How did you contain it?" Lara said.

"I channelled my anger into my training, my deadliness. All in preparation for my revenge. Lucky for me, I was occupied enough by my growth and development. And the fighting was a good outlet."

"But for him it's different?" Alrion said.

"Yes, he's already a master wizard. Has been for a while. And the Blight... it changes you. Amplifies the worst. You would understand." Alyx glanced at Alrion and he gave her a slight nod.

"One way or another, his rage will consume him. Hopefully, we meet Rindale before that happens."

"Or else?" Lara whispered.

"He'll destroy himself and everything else. Him first." Alyx pointed to Fermur. The man gulped and cowered.

"It won't get to that. We'll deal with this now. Then everyone can move on."

"You can't save everyone." Alyx shook her head and looked out in the distance once more. Alrion let the conversation die. Lara pulled him aside.

"You do realise that Branthor will eliminate Rindale. By the most destructive means necessary."

"I do."

"Are you fine with that?"

"No. I'll try to get a better outcome."

"If Rindale doesn't perish, Branthor will go crazy. You even made a deal with him."

"I know, let's just see how things go." Alrion's voice faltered slightly. Lara gave him a disapproving look.

"Sometimes you need to make the hard choice. Rindale has already had his chance. Your grandfather cured him, remember?"

"So we think. Look, I know I should be harder about this. But I know what it's like to have this transformation. I've seen what it does to people, what it did to Branthor. Rindale is a real person, just like us. Look at Fermur, he's a broken shell. That's what we need to protect, that's the reason I'm doing this." Alrion sighed.

"I don't disagree, but I'm warning you. This is going to get ugly."

"It always was. Branthor is too far gone. We just need to do our best with the situation we have before us."

"Of course. As always, I've got your back." Lara smiled and winked, then her face changed completely. A serious look came over her.

"Hey, there's something I need to mention. I've been thinking about it for a while."

"Oh alright. What is it?" Alrion didn't have a good feeling. To see Lara's face change so suddenly, it couldn't be good.

"Don't leave me out," Branthor said. Alrion spun and he couldn't see the wizard.

"Oh, you're back. How long have you been here?" he said.

"Not long. Just enough to hear mention of how crazy I am." Branthor didn't sound annoyed. He appeared suddenly right next to them.

"Good, then we're all going into this with open eyes. What did you learn?"

"The information checks out. The path is as described and allows easy access into the compound. I didn't venture further because I didn't want to set off any traps." Branthor sounded annoyed at that.

"Thank you for following the plan. Do you spot many guards?" Lara said.

"None. It was suspiciously quiet."

"He's inviting us in, you think?" Alrion commented.

"He must be. We should be prepared for anything."

"We are. Alyx, come closer so we can discuss the finer details." Lara waved Alyx over. She strode over and left Fermur sitting against a nearby tree.

～

Hours passed, and twilight was falling. The plan had been discussed and agreed, and Alrion was itching to go.

"Now is the time." Lara started to walk down the path and the rest followed. Alyx escorted Fermur, and Branthor and Alrion stayed close to Lara. As expected, they found no sentries or guards on their descent. The fortress itself was eerily quiet, and dark. Alrion distributed tiny lights for each person to see better as darkness fell. They walked in silence, their boots crunching along the dusty and sometimes stone littered path. Frequent stops were required to ensure Fermur was well, he seemed to have minimal energy and had barely eaten or drunk anything since he was cured.

The fortress loomed above them. As they approached, it looked like it had been carved out of a mountain. Years and painstaking labour would have been used to sculpt it to its present shape, and the enduring years smoothing it out even more.

They took a fork in the path, and they wound through the territory and around the edge of the fortress. Alrion spotted their destination, a side gate. It was an obvious fixture in an otherwise bland and featureless wall.

"Something is not right with that," Alrion said. He couldn't quite make out all the details, but he could tell.

"It's open! That's the problem." Lara stopped and turned to Branthor. "Did you leave it open?"

"I'm crazy, not dumb. I closed it properly and quietly," Branthor replied.

"Then either someone is really careless, or it's an even more obvious invitation." Lara looked annoyed. Alyx stood still, her arms folded. Lara turned to Fermur.

"Is this normal? Is this gate normally locked?"

"Always."

"Great. Just great." Lara stared at the gate again.

"Should we just proceed? If they're expecting us, it's better to convince them we are still coming. Rindale may flee again if he gets nervous." Alrion didn't like the idea of walking into a trap, but he liked the idea of Rindale getting away again even less.

"It's quite foolish, playing to Rindale's tune. He has everything stacked in his favour." Branthor was looking elsewhere on the fortress, no doubt assessing another way in.

"That's ideal. He will get complacent and make a mistake. We can capitalise on that." Alrion took a step forward. Lara grabbed his arm.

"Are you sure about this?" She looked nervously over at Branthor.

"Let's spring the traps. Branthor, you're about to have some fun." Alrion looked at the master wizard. He laughed and rubbed his hands.

"Good, I was beginning to think we were going to talk all day."

I just hope I can keep everyone safe. Ugly doesn't even begin to cover this.

25

SPLIT FOCUS

F alric regarded Celes warmly.

"You two take care, and good luck on your search."

"You take care as well. You sure you won't miss this book?" Celes felt the outline of the book through her bag.

"No, not at all. I think I've practically memorised it. Besides, I'm sure Vincent will appreciate having something from his father."

"I will."

"There, see. Glad you found it." Falric looked away, his mind preoccupied with something.

"I just had a thought. I know you are in a rush and all to get to the location of the Wizard Store near Valrytir. But I thought there was something else worth mentioning."

"What is it?" Vincent had a cautious and almost annoyed tone to his voice. Celes almost laughed.

He's so suspicious of Falric, it's adorable.

"There are some ruins near here. An outpost that used to be a staging area for wizards. Granthion established it, but it's been abandoned for a while. It's not from here, and since you're on a trail that's quite old, maybe there's something there?"

"It's worth considering." Vincent looked to Celes.

"The place isn't destroyed, right?" Celes asked.

"No, no, no. The Wizard Store is protected. Not sure what's left inside, but it'll be safe to enter. I think there's a Wizard Gate there too as well, but that's of no consequence since you can't use it. And I wouldn't even know where it went." Falric trailed off.

"How do we find this place?" Vincent said.

"When you leave town, follow the path north and look for a dirt track. It will lead you to some old ruins above the town. Good spot, it's a real shame."

"What exactly happened?"

"I think it was Blight attacks. Due to the sensitivity of the location, it was decided to not reinforce too heavily in case the Blight took an interest in it and started to poke around nearby. As far as I can tell that all worked because there's been no activity since."

"Great. Fancy a stroll?" Celes said to Vincent.

"Certainly, I thought you'd never ask."

"Off you go then. I'll tell Alrion hello from you both," Falric said with a chuckle.

"And tell him we will see him soon. When he's ready," Celes added. They finished their goodbyes with Falric and Caleb and left the building.

"I'll miss him," Celes said.

"Miss him? The wizard? He was gone and presumed dead, and now he's back. I don't think it's possible to miss him in these circumstances." Vincent grinned at her.

"True. Very logical." Celes smiled back. They hiked up the path out of town without much chatter. Celes was deep in thought and enjoyed the quiet.

How will we ever find this wizard? The trail is over twenty years old. And until recently nobody even thought to look for him.

Celes sighed deeply and kept walking. Vincent glanced at her but said nothing. Soon they had finished the long winding climb and were on the main path.

"Now the hunt begins. Keep an eye out for this dirt path," Celes said.

"Sure. Maybe I'll spot it first."

"In your dreams." Celes pushed further ahead.

I'm glad he's cracking jokes, like the old days. This whole thing feels so aimless. But I've had slimmer leads than this before, we need to follow it along and see what comes up.

Celes kept looking for the dirt track, conscious of not wanting to miss it. She also wanted to beat her husband and find it first. It was silly and meaningless, but it also focused her. There was value in that. For the most part, the path was lined with dense shrubs. But that's where the danger lay. The path could be overgrown and easily passed over.

Vincent started to slow.

"Shouldn't we be spotting this path soon? I feel like we've already come so far already."

"Probably. I'm worried that the path will be overgrown and hard to spot." Celes focused less on the surroundings, and more on the path itself. All she needed to see was evidence of a dirt track beginning. The rest would come after that. Celes looked past where Vincent was standing and saw something interesting. She jogged over, pushing past her husband. There was definitely something.

"There's potential here." Celes could see that the edge of the path was unusually dirty and dusty. She forced back the bushes and could see something different starting.

"Vincent, over here, help me with this." Vincent walked over and placed a hand on her shoulder.

"Stand back please." Vincent had his scabbard angling forward, ready to remove his sword.

"Certainly." Celes stepped back to give him room. Vincent drew his sword in a smooth motion, slicing through the main bush. He followed it up with three more precise strikes then cleaned his sword on his cloak. He kicked one of the fallen shrubs out of the way and grunted.

"I think you're on to something."

"Not going to clear away your mess?"

"I wouldn't want to detract from your find." Vincent winked at her. Celes groaned.

"Always with an excuse." She rushed over and dug the fallen greenery out of the space. Vincent had hacked away just enough to reveal a dirt track. It looked old, and largely worn away.

"I think that's it. Congratulations!" Vincent bowed.

"You should have known better than to challenge me, I'm the best at finding things."

"Oh I know, I just thought that this would be faster." Vincent grinned at her. Celes smacked him playfully on the shoulder and started striding down the path.

"At least we know it's completely abandoned. This path was well hidden," Vincent said as they walked.

"You were worried about it being inhabited?"

"The Blight are always a concern. You weren't worried?"

"No, I have you to deal with them." Celes changed her tone and talked more seriously. "I really didn't think about it. Am I losing my edge?"

"No, I just think you're more balanced than you were. Logically, there was no reason to worry about this place being infested with the Blight. It's certainly seen better days though." Vincent pointed ahead. Celes followed his gesture and saw the ruins. A tall tower sat at the back, with a few buildings in various states of disrepair littered around the space. A tall stone wall extended around one half of the site and had crumbled away from the other. Only littered stones remained.

"Which building do you think holds the Wizard Store?" Celes said.

"Likely the tower. Wizards love them for some reason."

"Is it because they think they're above everyone else?" Celes quipped.

"Couldn't have said it better myself." Vincent chuckled. "Well, to be fair I don't actually know the reason. Maybe it has something to do with how their powers work. Maybe they need to see their targets."

"Maybe. Let's start with the tower then." Celes started off again,

Vincent keeping pace with her. Nature had started to overgrow a lot of the stonework, giving it an ancient look.

"I think some of this damage was deliberate," Vincent said, pointing to a charred wall.

"By the Wizards or something else?"

"Not sure. I don't know who else can wield fire on this scale." Vincent paused to examine the wall further. Celes pressed on.

"This tower looks in good condition, considering." It seemed to be resistant to the worst of the decay and overgrowth. It almost looked like the tower had taken on the look to blend in.

Don't think such ridiculous things, it's not alive.

Celes stopped in front of the door. It was large and wooden and appeared to be intact.

"Time to give your medallion a spin?" Vincent said.

"Of course." Celes removed the medallion and rapped it on the door two times. Nothing happened. Vincent nudged her with his elbow.

"Celes," she said. There was silence, then suddenly the door creaked open.

"It still works. And it needed my name as well."

"Must be the additional security around here. Maybe there's something of value inside," Vincent said. He pushed the door open and waited for Celes to enter.

The room inside was almost pitch-black. Celes felt around the walls and found a metal bracket with a lantern. With a little effort, they were able to light it. Celes held up the lantern and looked over the room.

It was similar in structure to the last Wizard Store they had visited, but it was in complete disarray. Books were everywhere, shelves knocked over, and there were some broken chairs and other furniture.

"This place looks, I would say ransacked, but the books appear to be here still." Celes stepped around a pile of books and investigated the room.

"Very odd. Let's find the ledger." Vincent navigated around to the bench, looking inside. He retrieved a dusty book and placed it on the counter.

"Let's see who last visited." Vincent opened the book and Celes joined him, looking over his shoulder. She accidentally knocked over a pile of books on her way.

"Don't worry, they've survived worse," Vincent said without looking up. He was carefully flicking through the pages.

"There's us." Celes pointed to an entry.

"Exactly. The previous one is..."

"Branthor." Celes looked at Vincent. Her husband shrugged.

"That's not surprising. Maybe he came here after his transformation began? That might explain the redecorating." Vincent cast his eyes over the room again.

"That seems plausible. Let's see who else visited." Celes pulled the book closer and scanned through the entries herself. There were a few names she didn't recognise, in addition to Falric.

"Nothing noteworthy in recent times. Let's go back and see if our mystery wizard paid this place a visit." Celes flipped through the pages, taking care to review the entries.

"Ah-hah!" Celes pointed to a place in the book.

"You found him?"

"Aydan. Not long after he signed into the last place." Celes looked at Vincent with a triumphant smile.

"Looks like your trail is here. I wonder if there's anything to suggest where he went next." Vincent leaned back slightly and appeared deep in thought.

"Hang on. There's an asterisk next to the entry," Celes said. Vincent looked up sharply.

"Oh, that's different. I wonder what that means?" He refocused on the book. Celes looked at the page, there was nothing else to explain it.

"Why don't you try the beginning of the book, maybe there's a guide or explanation of the notation?" Vincent said.

"Of course!" Celes quickly flipped to the first page and skim read the contents.

"How to read this ledger," she said as she read. She used her finger to trace the words until she found what she wanted.

"To make an entry as having additional commentary, use an asterisk. Add your note in the Observations journal," Celes quoted.

"Falric never mentioned that," Vincent muttered.

"No, he didn't. Maybe he doesn't know?" Celes rifled around through the nooks under the bench and pulled out several books.

"This is it." Celes slammed the book down on the counter, unable to contain her excitement.

"Maybe don't destroy the book in the process," Vincent said. Celes ignored him and opened the book and started reading. There were quite a few comments throughout. Each one had a date and a name associated with it. But no details of the person who recorded the comment.

"It's just a matter of finding the right one," Celes said. Suddenly she found it. Without any delay, she started reading out the entry.

"Suspicious visitor today. I scanned the log to see his reported name and was surprised to notice that it was the old language. Wizards are never given these as a name, which further cemented my suspicions. Gareth thinks I am being overly cautious, but there is something not quite right with this one. He does not come across as having much Spark at all, yet he can read from any tome in our library. When questioned about his purpose, he just deflects any questions and responds with as little as possible." Celes paused and looked up at Vincent.

"This is our wizard. Maybe there's something about where he's going."

"Maybe. Keep reading." Vincent looked as hooked as Celes felt. She didn't think it possible, but her excitement increased even more.

This trail is still here, you just need to know where to look. And we've got it!

"In case he returns he has long dark hair and average build. Green eyes and above average height. Whilst I was unable to ascertain his next destination, I did overhear him muttering something about the desert. I am going to send messages to my colleagues in other Wizard Stores along that route to see if they can learn anything. It may be nothing, but I have a strange feeling and I can't ignore it." Celes stopped reading.

"This sounds right. It would make sense for this wizard to be interested in the desert, and the Vault of Silence. He had no trouble following Alrion's journey. Maybe he already did something like it before?" Celes couldn't quite read Vincent's face. It was a mix of confusion and concern.

"Perhaps. It's a good lead. I doubt we will find much else of value here." Vincent waded into the mess of books, picking through some at random.

"Didn't Falric mention a Wizard Gate here as well? What's that?" Celes said.

"I'm not too familiar. But they're supposed to be a means of travelling around."

"And you didn't think to mention these before?"

"I'm no wizard! I don't know how they work, or if they still work. You should be grilling Falric instead!" Vincent sounded annoyed.

"Oh, that's fair enough. Let's try to find it." Celes looked at Vincent to see what he thought. He frowned.

"I don't quite understand why, since we can't use it."

"But maybe Alrion can?" Celes could see Vincent thinking it over.

"I suppose we can look. I can't find anything else here, and we can at least verify if it's been obviously broken or not."

"Great. Let's go." Celes turned and started towards the door. Vincent sighed and followed closely behind.

They emerged into the ruins, Celes looking around.

"I wonder where that Wizard Gate is? Do you think it's big?"

"I assume so." Vincent looked over the rest of the buildings. "None of these look in as good condition as the tower we just entered. Maybe it's here somewhere?" Celes nodded and started circling the tower. Nothing jumped out at first, but after stopping and staring at the rear she noticed something.

"Look here." Celes stepped forward and touched the surface. There was a very faint outline of a door etched into the stonework.

The charring of the stone and other dirt and debris made it almost invisible.

"If that's a door, try your medallion again." Vincent walked up until he was shoulder to shoulder with Celes and peered at the prospective door too. Celes retrieved the medallion and rapped it against the door outline. Light started to shine around the outline of the door, and the wall started to rumble and move. The stonework swung inwards, revealing a staircase.

"Onward and upward!" Celes said.

"As you wish." Vincent waited for her to start ascending before he followed. The stairs were incredibly narrow and quite dusty. But all things considered, they were in good condition.

"No lanterns in here," Celes commented.

"I suppose they didn't need them, what with being wizards and all."

"Seems plausible. Doesn't make this climb any easier." Celes pushed on, taking care to ensure each step she found solid ground before continuing. As they progressed the darkness started to lighten slightly. Even though there were no windows.

I wonder what's up here? Maybe it's causing the light?

Celes let her mind search for answers while she continued to climb. Soon the light became more obvious, and she could tell it was a pale blue glow.

"Something glowing up here," she said.

"Good. Let's see what it is." Vincent sounded close behind. Celes rounded another corner and stopped dead. Vincent almost fell into her.

"Look at that." Celes stepped into the room, mesmerised by the sight. A stone archway sat in the middle of the room, blue light illuminating its edges.

"I'd say it's still working." Celes approached slowly, Vincent joining her.

"What can you tell me about them?" she asked.

"Not much. Obviously, it looks like it is active. Maybe even used recently?"

"Where does it go?"

"Your guess is as good as mine. I think they can be single or multiple destination. But I don't think you can just go wherever you want."

"Predefined options then?"

"That's what I'm thinking. My father never used one with me, so I don't have that experience to pass on." Vincent looked deep in thought. Celes walked closer, examining the stone structure.

"It looks like there are two distinct destinations. Don't you think?" She pointed to some markings, one at each end of the arch supports.

"Yes, it looks like there's an East and West option."

"Didn't that note say that Aydan was heading to the desert? That's East."

"Yes, you're right. Do you think he used this?"

"Why wouldn't you? If I was a wizard I certainly wouldn't walk around if I had access to this." Celes leaned forward, staring into the blank space filling the arch. She touched the stonework describing the East option and it suddenly started glowing.

"Look! I've selected a path."

"This is not a good idea. We don't know where it goes, and if it goes into the desert that's a big risk. Valrytir is the opposite direction." Vincent looked concerned. He took a step backwards.

"What if..." Celes whispered. She withdrew the wizard medallion and dangled it in front of the gate.

"What are you doing?" Vincent said.

"I'm seeing what we have to work with." Celes slowly swung the medallion toward the gate.

"You're really sure about this?" Vincent said.

"If it works, we need to do it. This is the only way I can help Alrion right now." Celes stepped closer. She gripped the medallion tightly and thrust it into the gate.

"Why do you think that's going to work?" Vincent said.

"Clearly this thing is already active, it just needs a trigger. If it worked for the regular door, why not this as well?" Celes looked back at Vincent and winked. He sighed.

The Wizard Gate suddenly roared into life. Blistering heat issued out of the gate, and a shimmering image stabilised in front of them. It looked like a desert scene.

"I don't believe it." Celes almost dropped the medallion.

"I'm in shock." Vincent looked back at Celes with a curious expression.

"Maybe I should be a wizard." Celes chuckled. "How long will this stay open?"

"I don't know, not long. If you go through, I can't follow. One of us needs to be at Valrytir when Alrion gets there."

"We can find another one of these surely, don't be silly." Celes held out a hand for her husband.

"I can't. There's too much at stake. Alrion could use this gate to shortcut much closer to Valrytir and we'll miss him entirely."

He's right. What do I do?"

Celes looked from Vincent to the shimmering image. It was a big risk, stepping into the unknown. She wasn't really equipped for a proper desert journey. But this opportunity was too good to pass up. She knew she could solve this puzzle, follow the trail, and find the answer. She would reveal the identity of the mysterious wizard. And find a way to reach Alrion in time.

"I just feel it in my bones, I have to go."

"I know. If anyone can solve this, it's you. I need to be there for Alrion, just in case. And if I get to Valrytir first I'll check out the Wizard Store there."

"But you don't have the medallion!"

"I'm sure I can find a wizard." Vincent walked forward and gave Celes a quick kiss.

"Go, follow the trail. I'll make sure he waits for you at Valrytir."

"You better!" Celes smiled and stepped through the gate, her whole world being enveloped in an intense white heat.

RECKONING

Alrion approached the door with caution. It looked safe, but he didn't trust it.

"Can someone take a peek inside?"

"Done." Branthor disappeared and his footsteps showed him walking away. Within a minute he was visible again before them.

"Nothing to report. We'll need to rely on some inside information." Branthor looked at Fermur and sneered. Fermur bowed his head and looked down.

"Then let's at least enter and assess the situation." Alrion stepped inside and looked around. They found themselves in a large open room, barely furnished. There was only a round table with a few chairs in the corner. The stone floor was otherwise left bare.

"There's only one way through. Fermur, how far until the traps?" Lara said. Fermur held up two fingers.

"Two rooms? Fine, let's visit the next one." Lara went first, and the rest followed. Alrion glanced at Branthor, trying to assess the wizard's temperament. He seemed to be quietly muttering something, but otherwise focused.

Just hold it together.

The next room was much the same, only there was a statue in the middle. It was cast from a smooth black stone and showed a single figure holding a vial in one hand and a dagger in the other.

"That's Rindale," Branthor said, spitting on the ground before the statue.

"How nice," Lara muttered.

"What kind of traps? Can you tell us anything?" Alrion said to Fermur. The man tried to speak but nothing came out. He sighed and looked down.

"Great. Just great." Branthor strode forward and peered through the next doorway.

"Lara and Alyx will assess then we will come up with a strategy," Alrion said. Branthor lingered for a moment more, then stepped aside. Lara and Alyx walked up to the doorway.

"This room is pretty obvious." Lara pointed. Alrion saw a single path heading through the room. On each side was a sizable drop into pitch-black.

"I think the lack of a handrail is hardly a trap," Alrion said.

"Look at the sides of the room." Alyx pointed. Alrion stepped closer and focused. He saw small tube-like devices all around the room, all at the same height.

"What are they?"

"I bet they fire something horrible when you walk on the path." Lara looked to Alyx. She nodded in agreement.

"How did you get through all those times?" Alrion said to Fermur. He shrugged.

"This is not exactly difficult." Branthor strode ahead and raised stone walls either side of the path. He then broke off a pebble and flung it along the ground. The traps triggered, sending wave after wave of arrows from each wall. They bounced harmlessly off the stone walls and fell into the gap.

"See?" Branthor started to walk along the path. It seemed safe. Alrion waved the others along and walked last, looking out. He couldn't see anything else and Lara seemed satisfied, if still quite cautious.

"Now I understand why you want to do it this way. The traps are childlike." Branthor sneered. After his next step, a clicking sound happened, then a deep rumbling.

"What was that?" Lara said. Alyx pointed to the far door.

"Look!" Alyx started running towards it. A strange metallic substance was sliding down and closing the door. Branthor chuckled and threw waves of force at it. Nothing happened. The spells slid right off.

"Now we're in trouble. Run!" Alrion shouted. Branthor stood motionless, trying different spells. Alyx drew her sword and sliced away a big chunk of stone.

"Use this," she shouted to Alrion. He understood immediately, and propelled the stone under the door, slowing the descent of the metal. But the stone began to tremble.

"We're out of time. Get through the door!" Alrion ran forward with Alyx right beside him. Lara had dragged Fermur ahead and pushed him through the gap first.

"Watch him," Alrion said to Lara. She ducked through next.

"You next." Alyx pointed to the gap. Alrion created a wave of force and whisked Alyx through, despite her protests.

"Branthor, there's no time. Come with us." Alrion held out a hand and beckoned for Branthor to join them.

"C'mon, you can just reinforce the stone and come," Alrion shouted. Branthor stood motionless.

"No, I will not crawl through and abide these traps. I will not suffer the indignity and make that creature feel any delight at my expense. No, I will go back and do what I wanted to do the first time. I will destroy his home and him with it." Branthor turned to leave.

"No, don't be foolish. We can do this together!" Alrion shouted.

"Time's up." Alyx dragged him back. Within seconds the stone crumbled, and the door was sealed.

"Well, that was interesting," Lara said.

"Yes, looks like we can't brute force our way through these traps."

"I meant Branthor storming off by himself. So he can destroy the place." Lara did not look impressed.

"If there are traps here using magic-resistant materials, there will be there too. We might beat him there." Alrion stood and took in the next room. There was a small platform just past where they were standing, then the rest of the space was full of water. The door was not visible.

"Oh great, a water feature." Lara sighed.

"I can understand how Fermur could traverse this, I'm just wondering where the door is," Alrion said.

"I'm wondering why Fermur bothered to enter this way. Either he had a key to deactivate them, or the other route is rather inconvenient."

"It would have to be quite inconvenient to be worse than this." Lara shook her head. Alrion chuckled.

"Let's hope so, for Branthor's sake." Alrion walked to the water's edge. "I wonder what I can see." Alrion enabled his enhanced vision and peered into the water. He could make out shapes below the surface, they looked to be metallic and seemed suspicious. He could see the door just below the surface, at the other end of the room.

"The door is where it should be, just low enough to be in the water."

"Do you think we need to drain the water?" Lara said.

"Or do we somehow move the door?" Alyx added.

"I don't know. Have a look, see if there's anything to interact with." Alrion let his eyes wander over the walls, there was no detail whatsoever.

"Have a look up there." Lara pointed to the ceiling. Alrion could see something sticking out of the ceiling. It looked like a hook of some kind.

"Do we have rope? We could perhaps swing across?" Alyx said.

"I have some, but I'm not confident it's long enough. And how would we get it there?"

"I can help with that." Alrion smiled and winked. Lara retrieved the rope and handed it to Alrion.

"Oh yes, this won't be long enough at all."

"Sorry, I wasn't exactly planning for this. I can't carry a whole store with me."

"No, don't worry I'm glad we have something." Alrion felt the rope in his hands. It wasn't too heavy, but it would be problematic if it fell into the water. He prepared a visualisation, that there was a powerful layer of air covering the surface of the water and would stop things from falling in. He channelled some Spark and set the spell.

"Lara, could you please let me know how cold the water is?"

"Sure." Lara bent down and reached for the water with her hand.

"Hang on, something's wrong."

"What is it?" Alrion feigned worry.

"I can't touch the water, something is stopping me." She looked up to Alrion. He started chuckling.

"Good, it's working."

"That was not funny!" Lara shot him a dirty look but Alrion laughed even more.

"Sorry, I just needed someone to test it. And I thought we could use a laugh."

"You thought you could use a laugh, actually."

"I found it amusing." Alyx had a small smile, which quickly disappeared.

"Careful, you'll be a full-blown Branthor if you don't watch yourself!" Lara smirked and laughed at Alrion's reaction. He couldn't stop the look of horror on his face.

"Anyway, let's give this a go." Alrion threw the rope into the air then tried to catch it with waves of force. He didn't quite get it, and the rope wobbled and fell back to the ground. Thankfully, it bounced and rested on the layer of air. Alrion shuddered slightly.

"What's wrong?" Lara said.

"Maintaining the air while there's an object trying to break through is quite taxing. I don't want to overdo that." Alrion took in a deep breath. Then he used a wave of force to encircle and grip the rope, ensuring it couldn't fall through.

"That's better." He slowly raised the rope until it was level with the large hook.

"Now's the tricky bit." Alrion slowly adjusted the rope until it was above the hook. He gently lowered it, until it was hanging evenly over the hook. He released his spell and waited.

The rope kept moving, sliding around the hook. But it settled down and was still.

"Great work!" Lara slapped him on the back.

"Now we can test it. It's not long enough to reach, but can you pull the hook down with the rope?" Alyx said. Alrion nodded and concentrated once more. He used waves of force to grab the ends of the rope and pull it down. The hook started to move with a groan and a rumbling. Alrion started to release the spell.

"Hold it!" Alyx shouted. Alrion scrambled to keep a hold of the spell and maintain the force on the rope. The rumbling continued until the doorway rose above the water.

"Great work. It looks like there's just enough of a platform across there to stand and open the door. We just need to get across." Lara looked up at the hanging rope.

"I don't think we can use that to swing across."

"If Alrion has created a surface above the water, surely we can just walk across?" Alyx looked at Lara, and the two of them looked to Alrion.

"We can try. It will just be difficult." Alrion sat down near the water, cross-legged. He needed to concentrate very carefully.

"Try to put one foot's weight on," he said. Lara walked over and carefully placed a foot down. As she increased her pressure, Alrion felt a pressure building within his head.

"So far so good, try the other foot." Alrion waited, and he could tell immediately when she had started, because he felt the pressure inside building again, even more.

The Spark component of this spell is minimal. I'm doing this the hard way. I need to remember the Vault of Silence.

Alrion tapped into his Soul Power and circulated it around his body. It seemed to calm him, knowing that he had another source of power, while his mind was under intense pressure. Then he focused, remembering the lessons of the past. The way he had escaped the

Vault, and the way that Certan had taught them about the power of Will.

It's just like the trap you set for Fermur. Set a change and make it part of your beliefs.

Alrion adjusted his mindset. It was like trying to make a puzzle piece fit. But when it suddenly did, the pressure in his mind became background noise.

"I'm stable now. Go on. One at a time." Alrion could tell that Lara was walking, but he tried not to focus on it. Instead, he found a piece of the wall that he could examine in detail. In the back of his mind, he was aware of Lara's walking, but he didn't overthink it. Soon, he felt a wave of relief and turned around to look. Lara was standing on the small platform at the other end.

"Go, Fermur." Alrion pointed to Lara. Fermur hesitated, looking over at Lara, and back at Alyx.

"Go on." Alyx nudged him forward and Fermur stepped out carefully. After testing that he seemed supported, he shuffled forward awkwardly. The strange and uneven gait did prove a distraction for Alrion, but he adjusted things so that it was normal. Before long, he was across too. The small platform was quite crowded with the two of them standing on it.

"Feel free to open the door if you need to," Alrion said.

"We'll wait as long as possible," Lara shouted. Alrion nodded and gestured for Alyx to begin walking. She did so carefully and cautiously, her sword drawn the entire time. Alrion felt a little weariness from maintaining his Will but otherwise felt fine.

This is working well. It should be fine to cross myself.

Alyx could barely squeeze onto the platform as well.

"Open the door, it's fine now. Otherwise, I won't have room to cross over." Alrion stood and watched. Lara tried the door, and thankfully it opened inward.

"Looks clear!"

"I'll make a start." Alrion began to walk across when he heard something behind him. A piece of wall was opening, and something was coming out. It was a Shade.

Time to move!

Alrion didn't trust his ability to maintain his Will-created platform and fight at the same time. He rushed across as fast as he could, trying not to think about the fact that it was carrying him. The Shade had realised that it could chase and was hurtling along.

"Quick, get over here." Alyx held out a hand for Alrion. He felt like the Shade was moments away, and his back twitched. He reached out and grabbed Alyx's hand, letting his Will transformation fall away. Before he was whisked into the next room Alrion heard the satisfying sound of a large splash.

27

SUCCESSION

Alrion surveyed the scene before him. His mind struggled to take it all in. The room was largely destroyed, with large stones wedged into all the walls and ceiling. A giant flaming hole showed where Branthor had entered the room. The bodies of Shades littered the ground, some even looking like Shade Wizards. In the centre of the room, Branthor and Rindale stood, arms locked together, stuck in an epic struggle.

"Stay back!" Branthor shouted. Alrion looked to Lara and Alyx. They were just transfixed on the scene before them. Fermur was cowering in the corner. Alrion took one step closer and tried to analyse what was happening.

Rindale had a long dagger with a jet-black blade pressed up against Branthor's throat. Branthor had one hand protecting himself, and another pressed up against Rindale. Rindale was covering that hand. It seemed like a stalemate.

"I can sense the hatred in you, wizard. Why do you detest me so?" Rindale spoke like he was mocking Branthor.

"You took everything from me, you monster!"

"Oh, I really doubt that. All I did was inadvertently infect your beloved. You should be blaming the boy's family for what happened."

"That was incidental, you caused it!" Branthor bellowed.

"Granthion tasked you with following his son. Andar got himself caught and fled at the first opportunity. And Granthion withheld from you his spell to cure the Blight." Rindale gave Branthor a wicked smile. "I'm almost innocent in this. All I did was pursue a man. You just got in the way."

"But it didn't stop there, did it? You had to transform me into an abomination!" Branthor pushed back with intensity and Rindale almost lost his balance. But he regained his cool and his twisted smile returned.

"You called me, what was I to do? You would have died. I gave you power and a way to get your revenge on the boy."

"No, you twisted my mind so that I was working for you."

"It was in both our interests, surely you can forgive that?" Rindale laughed. Alrion started to move forward but Lara held him back.

"Don't step in prematurely. Branthor is on edge, he might kill us all." The horror in Lara's voice convinced Alrion to hold back.

"You should spare a thought for me. I was cured by Granthion's spell and had to rebuild my life. It was a long and difficult road, with many missteps. For years I was considered an invalid."

"I have no sympathy for you, vile thing. You should have taken that opportunity to start afresh."

"Oh, but I tried. I really did. I found respectable work, even though it was below my capacity. I withheld all my darker tendencies. For a time." Rindale focused on Branthor with an intense look and pressed harder.

"And then you decided to just return to evil?"

"No. That was when Darvin found me. There's no escaping, you see. Eventually, we'll find you. Or sometimes you come to us." Rindale turned and winked at Fermur. The broken man sobbed.

"Never again, I won't let you do this. Your work ends now."

"My best work is already complete, you're too late." Rindale laughed. "There's no win here. You can't even get revenge, because I know exactly how your spells work, wizard." Rindale's voice was harsh.

"I'll do what it takes to eliminate you forever," Branthor muttered. He looked feverish.

"You cannot succeed. The instant this blade touches you, you'll be infected once more. A tool of my bidding." Rindale laughed. Branthor looked furious like he was going to explode. Alrion took a step forward. He shook away Lara's hand.

"I can end this. Both of you stand down."

"I caution you against interfering, young one. You'll get your turn eventually." Rindale turned slightly to stare at Alrion, then turned back to Branthor. "I see your father in you, Alrion."

"I don't care. Branthor, prepare yourself. I'm going to restrain Rindale." Alrion took another step forward. Branthor looked livid.

"You. Will. Not. Take. This. From. Me." Branthor struggled, then appeared to just give up. Rindale smiled as the dagger started to move forward. But it diverted from Branthor's neck, plunging into the wizard's chest. As Rindale was celebrating, a bright white light formed on Branthor's fingertips.

"Don't!" Alrion shouted. But it was too late. In seconds the white light became overwhelming and an explosion rocked the room. Alrion threw up a wave of force to act as a shield but was still knocked down. He quickly stood up again, unsteady on his feet. The power of the shockwave was incredible. The whole room looked turned upside down. It was even more broken and dispersed than before.

Alrion checked on Lara, and she was fine. Alyx had shielded her, and Alrion's barrier had done the rest. Fermur was still cowering in the corner and had started whimpering.

They're fine, but where's Rindale?

Alrion activated his enhanced vision and searched the room. He could find no trace of the Blight General. He did locate Branthor, under some rubble in the corner of the room. But he looked in bad shape. And infected too.

Alrion strode over and knocked the rocks away with a force spell.

"Branthor!" Alrion rushed across now that Branthor was visible.

"It's done. Not a trace of that creature exists." Branthor's voice was hoarse and quiet, and he coughed soon after.

"Just stay still, I'll heal you." Alrion started to prepare his Spark. Branthor grabbed his wrist.

"Don't! I'm done. Please, let me go." Branthor looked up at Alrion, pleading.

"You don't need to be." Alrion looked at Branthor, assessing his wounds. "You'll turn into one of them anyway if I leave you."

"No, I'll die first. This is a critical wound." Branthor tapped his chest, then closed his eyes.

"But..."

"If it's about my promise, then I'm sorry I changed my mind." Branthor took a deep ragged breath and continued. "I was going to tell you the location, but I won't now. That would play into their hands."

"But, why?"

"You're not ready. If you were, you'd know. Maybe you're ready now, I can't say for sure. But there's only one place you can find out."

"Where?" Alrion knelt next to Branthor.

"Paperton." Branthor managed a pained laugh.

"What do you mean?"

"There they can assess you, explain how to unlock the information. There's more to know than just the location. You can't undertake the journey without knowing."

"Thank you, Branthor. There's good in you, there's part of you that can be saved. Let me help you!" Branthor shook his head.

"No, you mustn't. This is momentary clarity, now that my revenge is done. The rage, the anger, and the shame. It consumed me. But this is enough. You must let me rest." Branthor closed his eyes. His breathing slowed. He opened his eyes once more.

"Good luck, Alrion. May you overcome your fate." Branthor smiled and closed his eyes. He took one last deep ragged breath and sagged. The life drained from him. Alrion leaned back, feeling the depth of the loss.

I should have saved him. Why? Why did I let him go?

He felt Lara's arm around him, pulling him up. She guided him over to the rest.

"That was meant to be. He did us a great service." Alyx bowed.

"I don't know what to do now. I could have saved him."

"You already did." Lara gave him a hug. Alrion wiped away a tear.

"That could have been any of us."

"It very nearly was. What did he tell you?" Alyx said.

"He refused to reveal the location of the source of the Blight. He said that it was a mistake to tell me, that it would lead to my undoing if I went now."

"Really?" Lara sounded confused.

"Yes. He explained that I should return to Paperton, to the scholars. There will be experts there to guide me through what I need to know, and that I can't complete this journey without the right knowledge."

"He was dangerous and unhinged, but he was a master wizard. It doesn't sound like he withheld the information in spite." Alyx sounded thoughtful. Alrion turned around to look for Fermur. The man was gone.

"Where did he get to?" Alrion sighed.

"Don't worry, we'll look for him," Lara said.

"I don't know what to do now. I'm just exhausted." Alrion let Lara lead him over to a place he could sit. Alrion glanced over at Branthor's body.

"Well, I need to help him before we go anywhere."

"Of course we will. His journey has ended, and he needs a proper farewell." Alyx bowed again in Branthor's direction.

"I didn't like the guy, but he achieved a great thing today. I know it wasn't how you wanted this to end, but this is a great win against the Blight." Lara gave Alrion a slight smile.

"But then why does it feel like this?"

"Because everything comes with a price." Alyx's face was hard, her expression impossible to read. Alrion dragged himself up.

"Let's attend to Branthor before I go collapse somewhere." He started to walk back through the rubble, Alyx and Lara flanking him on both sides.

How many must die before this quest is through?

28

THE HIDDEN GATE

Alyx rushed back into the room. She didn't like being separated from them, even though she had found no other enemies in the fortress. Seeing Alrion and Lara was a relief, and she sheathed her sword and walked slower.

"You're back. Anything to report?" Alrion said. He was standing over Branthor's body. They had cleared the area around where he had fallen.

"There seems to be a lot of equipment around the place, it all seems like it's quite dangerous. I couldn't find anybody at all, let alone Fermur."

"I think we need to be alright with the idea that he's gone. Hopefully, with Rindale eliminated, Fermur will be left alone."

"I hope so." Alrion stood still and bowed his head slightly. Alyx walked over and joined them.

"I've figured out what to do here," Alrion said. He turned and looked at both Lara and Alyx. "I will destroy Branthor's body and destroy this place. It should never be used again, and it will send a signal to Darvin."

"I suppose, especially if there doesn't seem to be anyone left. And that would take care of the equipment that Alyx mentioned." Lara still sounded a bit hesitant though.

"Don't worry, we won't be inside at that point. Have you explored the annex?" Alrion said to Alyx.

"Annex?"

"There's another building connected to this one. I can feel it."

"No, I haven't noticed anything. It might be on the other side of the building?" Alyx looked to Lara who shrugged.

"I certainly didn't notice anything else on this side either."

"There's something else here. I almost missed it, but the more I think about it, the more I'm sure. Maybe it's wizard related, I can't say."

"Well, let's investigate before we go," Alyx said. Alrion nodded and turned again to Branthor. He motioned for Lara and Alyx to come closer.

"Farewell, Branthor. You lived a hard life, tormented by the Blight and the loss of your wife. I forgive you for all that you did and thank you for your advice and help. I hope that you have reached a place of peace." Alrion paused, silent. After a few moments, he spoke again. "I don't know the appropriate way to bury a wizard, but I also know that you won't want your body to be taken by the wrong people. And we don't want this evil dagger to remain. Therefore, I will take steps to protect you in death." Alrion motioned for Lara and Alyx to stand back. He remained exactly in the same spot, however, and raised one hand.

Bright light started to accumulate on Alrion's hand, just like Branthor had done. However, Alyx also noticed a bit of a golden tinge to the light. The brightness was mesmerising, and she kept staring into it. Suddenly she realised what she was doing and came to her senses. She grabbed Lara by the arm and dragged her away. When they reached the other end of the room, white flashed everywhere, temporarily blinding Alyx. Her vision slowly returned, and she saw Alrion was still standing in the same place.

"At least he hasn't blown himself up," Lara muttered. She dusted herself off and started walking. Alyx joined her. As they neared

Alrion they saw a deep chasm in the ground. It was impossibly smooth like it had been carved out of the ground and cleaned.

"Do I even want to know what happened here?"

"I used a modified light bomb. There's no trace of Branthor or that cursed weapon left."

"I see. You're not going to make that a regular thing you do, are you?" The nervousness in Lara's voice was obvious. Alrion turned to look at her and took on a sheepish grin.

"No, I won't put you in danger unnecessarily. I also don't approve of the destructive power. It's too... final. You're bound to destroy too much, and there's no going back."

"Which was the idea. As long as you can control it and use it sparingly, we will be fine." Alyx gave Alrion a respectful nod, which he returned.

"Absolutely." Alrion's face returned to stony sadness. He shook his head and started walking off toward the hole in the wall that Branthor had made.

"Where's this extra building you mentioned?" Lara said.

"We may need to go outside to find it. But keep your eyes open as we walk through. There may be a path from in here." Alrion walked through without comment, but Alyx was stunned by the destruction on display. The room was ripped apart, and scores of Blighters were scattered all over the room.

"No wonder we can't find anything left alive," Lara whispered.

"I'll never fully understand him. For all that he hated us, he never did this," Alrion said.

"There was a part of him that still remembered how to be human. It's just it became quieter and quieter as time went on." Alyx could sympathise. She had been on a similar path to vengeance. It was not as satisfying as it should have been.

Better that he died, he could not handle the life afterwards.

They passed through another room of horrors until they came upon the main gate. It was mangled and bent like it was a child's toy that had been stepped on. Lara let out a small gasp.

"This is what we are capable of, but choose not to do," Alrion said.

"I can see why you don't." Lara rushed forward and didn't look back. Outside the fortress was quiet and peaceful. There were no sounds of wildlife, and there was only grass and a path. Alrion led the way, following the path around the exterior of the fortress. Around halfway down the length of the building, he paused.

"I can feel something. It's in this direction." Alrion turned left and stepped onto the grass. He continued forward like he was following an invisible path.

"I don't see anything." Lara stopped periodically and peered into the distance. Alyx couldn't make out anything. Just flat countryside and grass, with the occasional rock, shrub, or tree.

"Here," Alrion said. He stuck his hand out, reaching for something. Lara bent down and picked up a tiny stone. She hurled it into the distance. It sailed through the air, and suddenly made a 'tink' sound and bounced off something.

"Well, I'll be," Lara said.

"I'm not imagining it," Alrion said.

"I never suggested that." Lara turned and looked at Alyx

"Clearly, there's something there." Alyx moved forward until she was next to Alrion. She reached out with her hand and felt around. There was something cool and smooth there, but invisible. She used her hand to feel around and get an idea of what it was.

"It's made of stones, smooth stones." Alyx pulled her hand back.

"I'm not really familiar with this kind of magic." Alrion placed his hand on the invisible surface and closed his eyes. He looked to be deep in concentration. His breathing slowed, and he seemed almost asleep. Suddenly his eyes shot open, and he pulled his hand back. Where his hand had been, a transformation was taking place. The invisible was becoming visible, like a wave of light was illuminating it all. Within moments, a stone building with a metallic wooden door stood before them.

"Wow," Lara whispered.

"I wonder if Branthor knew about this," Alrion said. He pushed on the door and it opened slowly. Alrion created a ball of light which floated above him, then he entered the building. Lara rushed after him and Alyx turned to look behind. She could spot no enemies.

Hopefully, we didn't trigger any traps or alarms.

Alyx drew her sword and followed them inside. The room was quite bare, with stone on the floor and all the walls. The only item of note was a carpet in the middle of the room. Lara rushed forward and inspected the carpet.

"As expected." She quickly pulled it aside and revealed a trapdoor.

"Good. Let's keep moving." Alrion started forward and helped Lara haul the trapdoor open. There was a ladder inside, and no way to see what else was below.

"I'm going first." Alyx squeezed in between the others, sheathed her sword and started climbing down before they could protest. The ball of light drifted down until it hovered above Alyx's right shoulder.

"Be careful," Alrion said.

"I can handle a ladder," Alyx said drily. Given that the area was so well-hidden, she didn't expect too much else in the way of security. Nothing the wizards had done before to their spaces was dangerous, to her knowledge. Once she reached the bottom, she sensed a source of light. She turned and took a look. It was faint, but there was a blue glow emanating from the distance.

"There's something down here. Safe to proceed." Alyx stepped aside and made room for the others to descend.

Maybe this is one of those Wizard Gates. It must be functioning too. I wonder if Alrion can operate it?

Lara descended first, then Alrion.

"I think that's a Wizard Gate. Let's investigate." Alrion took off at pace, and Alyx rushed ahead of him. There was nothing else in the long room and no other sources of illumination. As they neared the source of the light, Alyx could see the structure properly. It was definitely some sort of gate. Two stone columns with an arch over the top, glowing blue.

"So that's what they look like when they aren't destroyed," Lara said, nudging Alrion. He chuckled.

"Yes, yes I deserved that. This is really interesting though." Alrion stepped forward and studied the gate up close. Alyx joined him, looking at the symbols.

"Maybe you need to press something?" she said. One symbol stood out for her. It looked familiar. She pressed on the stonework and the symbol suddenly glowed. Alyx stepped back quickly, looking for other activity. Nothing else changed.

"I think you did something. But the gate isn't open yet." Alrion peered closer into the space and examined the remaining symbols. Lara circled around and looked at the gate from the back.

"There's nothing back here, I think the gate acts as some sort of special doorway. When it's working."

"That would make sense. I encountered something similar at the Vault of Silence. Different of course, but similar in idea." Alrion walked around the gate, observing it from different angles and finally stopped in front of it once more.

"Hmm, I wonder..." Alrion reached out, his hand glowing. The gate flashed then roared into life. Blue and white light arced around the room, then settled down. The view was obscured, but there was definitely some other location at the other end of the gate.

That's Valrytir!

The scene was blurred but unmistakable if you were familiar with the city. It was a location on the fringes, one she had visited often as part of her training. Alyx shuddered with the realisation. This gate could take them a tremendous distance. She glanced over at Lara who seemed to be having the same realisation. She must have also recognised the location. Alrion, however, was transfixed by the sight.

"Wow, it works. I wonder where it goes?" He looked to Lara, who shrugged.

"It's too hard to tell from this side. It could be quite dangerous," Alyx said.

"Right, we should think carefully about this," Lara said. Alrion turned back to the gate.

"We'll only know by going. Hmm, there's something strange about this." Alrion looked puzzled. Lara and Alyx exchanged glances.

"What do we do?" Lara mouthed to Alyx.

"I'll go," Alyx mouthed back and pointed from herself to the gate. Lara nodded.

"Here's an idea. Why doesn't Alyx step through first. She can assess the other location for safety, then we can follow?" Lara said. Alrion whipped around, looking at her curiously.

"It sounds logical but, if it works, you'd have no way of coming back. Alyx?"

"It's a good plan, and honestly it's the only option if we're intent on trying out this gate. If I'm separated, then I can easily continue ahead on my own and meet up with you later. Lara, of course, could do the same, but you two have shared a lot more of this journey together and should remain so."

"Absolutely, just what I was thinking. Remember, our best lead right now is to return to the Pool of Knowledge. The chances that this gate goes there are practically zero!"

"That's true. Maybe none of us should go through?" Alrion said. Lara shrugged.

"No, I don't agree. We need to assess the viability of these gates. If they work as intended, they will be crucial to enable us to travel longer distances safely." Alyx looked at Alrion, he looked conflicted.

If I can get to Valrytir sooner, I can prepare them for what is coming. It's the best plan. These two don't need me right now.

Alyx had made her decision. She looked at Lara, and the thief gave her a slight nod.

"Don't do anything I wouldn't do," Alyx said. She pushed past Alrion and dove into the gate. As it swallowed her up, she turned just in time to see the look of surprise on Alrion's face.

I hope this works. Oh well, better me than anyone else.

Alyx closed her eyes and let the gate transport her.

29

THE LOGICAL MESSAGE

I n a flash, the gate closed and Alyx was gone. Alrion reached out too slow like he could just pull her back.

"She's gone," Lara said. Alrion ran his hands over the gate. It still glowed blue as it had before, but it seemed dormant.

"I don't get it, I activated it before. What's going on?" Alrion muttered. He located the symbol that Alyx had pressed and tried it again. Nothing happened.

"Maybe it needs time before it can work again?" Lara offered.

"It doesn't seem like that's how it should work." Alrion hit the gate in frustration. It sat still, motionless.

Alyx is gone. How do I get her back?

Alrion let Lara pace around the room, looking for anything that might be useful. He knew there was nothing else, but he wasn't always right. He had been wrong about this. Or had he?

I sensed something was off. Maybe it was rigged for only a single activation?

"Do you know where it went?" Alrion said. Lara hesitated before answering.

"Can't say for sure. It felt like it was a long way away, from what I could gather." Lara disappeared off to keep searching the space.

"It did feel like a different climate. I can't believe it, she's gone, and I have no idea where she is!"

"You know," Lara said, approaching Alrion, "I know it just happened, but let's think logically about it. Is this really the worst thing that could happen? Alyx is most likely alive and well, and she's armed with her deadly survival skills and a sword that can cut through anything." Lara looked directly into Alrion's eyes. "I think she's going to be just fine."

"I know, of course, she is. I just feel responsible for transporting her to the middle of nowhere!"

"It might be a very nice place. And you didn't transport her, she transported herself. You can't take complete responsibility."

"Perhaps." Alrion pondered the thought and kept poking around the gate. He remembered the moment it had activated. The gate had just responded to his Spark, he hadn't really needed to do anything special. That suggested that it would work independently of him having to power it. With that in mind, he activated his enhanced vision and examined the gate. As expected, the gate was infused with Spark.

This should just work. I don't understand what's going on. Maybe it's been altered somehow.

"Any insights?" Lara said.

"No. It should be working. I can only guess that there's some sort of limitation on it."

"What do you want to do?"

"I can't leave Alyx without at least trying everything. Let's make sure there's nothing else we can do here and figure out the next move."

"Sounds good to me. Should we explore the grounds?"

"Yes. Let's go for a walk." Alrion led the way back to the ladder and they climbed up to the entry room. They left the building and Alrion turned back to look.

"It's invisible again."

"Good. We know where it is, and nobody else should notice it." Lara looked out at the fortress and surrounding area.

"I don't see anything obvious, should we just do a lap of the building?"

"Yes. I'm confident there's nothing else in there that we need to be looking at." Alrion started walking and Lara kept pace with him. As they walked, he let his mind wander, considering the Wizard Gate and what had happened. No matter what path he went down, he kept coming back to the fact that it had to have been altered somehow.

Their exploration of the fortress grounds revealed nothing. There was nothing of note in the nearby area, just grass and some basic stone fencing.

"Nothing here." Lara took another look and returned her gaze to Alrion.

"Agreed. Do you want to take another look inside the fortress?"

"No, there's no need. I'm not interested in Rindale's ghastly experiments."

"Good. Then I can make sure they're never repeated." Alrion picked out a spot a bit further away and started walking over. Once he reached the spot, he turned and sat down on the ground. He patted the grass next to him.

"Sit here, please." Alrion waited for Lara to sit and closed his eyes. "I'm going to set things right."

"Sure."

"Please stay here." Alrion focused his attention on the building. He pictured the building in his mind, creating a visualisation. This would need to be a complex combination spell.

First, he prepared the ground. He prepared the fact that the ground would open up, swallowing up the entire fortress. Like when he had entombed Wraith in the desert. But the earth would need a kick. He added some Spark to the mix and let it go. Exactly as pictured the ground opened, inviting the fortress inside. The massive structure dropped suddenly. But Alrion wasn't done yet.

He twisted the centre of gravity around, making the centre of the fortress attract all the area around it. The fortress began to compact itself into a much smaller space, the materials grinding away into dust as they did so. Finally, before that process was completed, he created a giant ball of intense fire and hurled it into the gap, sealing the ground over the top.

"I think that will do it." Alrion relaxed and lay back.

"I think so." Lara lay down next to him. "You don't think you overdid it at all?"

"I didn't want the place to be there anymore, but I didn't want to destroy the whole area."

"I was right. You are delusional. I'm getting flashbacks to when we took on an army of Blighters by ourselves." Lara chuckled.

"Some things never change I guess." Alrion cut the laughter. "You know, I was trying to do something Branthor would approve of."

"You don't owe him anything."

"I know. He did some terrible things, but I understand. It could easily have been me in that situation."

"Oh, that's true. But he still had a choice. Don't forget." Lara jumped up. Alrion hesitated and Lara offered him a hand. He sighed and accepted, letting her pull him up.

"We can't sit around here all day. Are we going to go back to the Pool of Knowledge?"

"I'm not sure. Let's go try the gate one last time."

"Fine by me." Lara led the way back and waited patiently once they reached the spot. Alrion unlocked the building once more, and they slowly descended the ladder and approached the Wizard Gate. It looked exactly the same.

"Time to try your luck." Lara stood aside and waited. Alrion stepped forward and pressed on the symbol that Alyx had used. Nothing happened.

"Still might work." He activated his Spark and reached into the gate. Again nothing.

"Something is not quite right. It won't work until we figure out what's different."

"Then we need some advice." Lara looked thoughtful. "Hang on, we have someone to consult for advice."

"Who?"

"That mysterious notebook you carry around. It hasn't steered you wrong yet."

"The messages haven't exactly been controversial. But yes, I haven't looked in there recently." Alrion retrieved the notebook and flipped through the pages. Everything looked the same, all was familiar. Suddenly he noticed another entry.

You're missing a vital piece of the puzzle. Return to Paperton and fill in the gaps. Then you will understand the true nature of your quest.

"Oh, now that's interesting." Alrion handed the notebook to Lara.

"That's quite clear in intention. Wow, it does sound like we need to go back." Lara started to hand back the notebook but stopped suddenly.

"You don't think Branthor was that wizard? Do you?"

"No, why would you say that?" Alrion took the notebook back and studied the handwriting. It didn't seem familiar. Not that he could recall Branthor's handwriting.

"Didn't Branthor just give you that exact same advice?"

"Yes, but that's not conclusive by itself." Alrion flipped back and looked at the other entries.

"When was the first one? Wasn't it after the Pool of Knowledge?"

"Yes, I'm sure of it."

"That was after your encounter with Branthor. And wasn't he at the Academy when you joined?"

"Yes, he was."

"So, couldn't he have somehow interacted with that notebook before? Maybe that's how he was tracking you!" Lara looked at Alrion with amazement.

"Hang on, don't get carried away." Alrion read the messages again. "It doesn't sound like Branthor. And for most of this, he was Wraith, he wouldn't have been able to write like this. Like a normal wizard." Alrion shook his head. It couldn't be Branthor.

"He would have said something. At least at the end."

"Not necessarily. He admitted that he decided not to tell you the location of the source of the Blight, remember? He might have decided to withhold other information too, in your best interests." Lara looked convinced.

"I'm not so sure. Let's just see what happens. We'll know soon enough at any rate."

"How's that?" Lara said.

"If there's another message, then it's not Branthor."

"Yes, but that doesn't mean it was never him." Lara gave him a challenging look.

"You don't have to win every conversation you know." Alrion chuckled.

"I'm just saying, it's a good theory don't discount it."

"Fine, I won't discount it." Alrion started walking back to the ladder. They ascended to the hidden building then emerged outside. Alrion headed towards the main path. Lara kept pace with him, occasionally looking behind.

"Alyx is not going to appear behind us," Alrion said.

"Not checking for her." Lara looked again. "Something about this place doesn't feel right, even after you removed that fortress."

"It's fine, we'll be gone soon enough." Alrion stumbled but managed to regain his footing.

"Are you alright?" Lara rushed over, ready to help him up.

"Yes, just a bit tired. Perhaps I overdid it a tad."

"Wow, that's unusual. It's never happened before." Lara gave him an unimpressed look. "Go sit against that tree over there." Alrion listened dutifully and rested against the tree. A gentle breeze blew past, making him feel relaxed.

"I don't suppose you know the way back to Paperton?" he said. Lara settled down next to Alrion.

"Not exactly. But I'm pretty confident if we follow this path past the fortress, we'll come to a relatively big town soon enough."

"That suits me. We can resupply and plan our trip back."

"Does it feel strange? Heading back there?"

"A little. It feels like I'm backtracking, almost retreating. But I can't think of it like that. It's important."

"The wizards seem to think so. And Branthor had all that knowledge too. I wonder what he wasn't sharing with you?"

"I wonder that too. He definitely knew a lot more than he was willing to share."

"That other wizard seems to know too. If that last message was anything to go by."

"Yes, you're right. Maybe he's visited the Pool of Knowledge too? Maybe we can find out something when we return."

"I hope so, I love a good mystery." Lara leaned over and rested her head on Alrion's shoulder. It was a good weight to have.

30

ON THE TRAIL

T he intense bright heat of the gate was replaced by the dry oppressive heat of the desert. Celes stepped out of the Wizard Gate and into some barely shaded ruins.

At least it worked. Can I use it to get back?

Celes looked back at the gate and it seemed like the one she had passed through.

Looks promising. Let's see if I can find myself a clue.

Celes wandered around the location. It was reminiscent of an old temple of some kind, constructed from stone. But it was terribly worn down by the elements. She had no idea how the paltry structure shielding the Wizard Gate was still standing.

"Any clues here are long gone. What a bust," Celes whispered. The wind picked up, as if in answer. Celes stepped into the minimal shade and gave herself a moment to think.

The wizard came this way, years ago. What was he looking for in the desert? It can't be whatever was just here because it's already gone. Maybe there's something nearby.

Celes carefully sipped some water and evaluated her situation. She could afford to search the nearby area for anything of value. But she was not equipped for a proper trip across the desert.

That gate better work, that's for sure.

Celes followed what looked like used to be a path. There was nothing immediately outside, or much of anything to look at. Just sand dunes and the remnants of a path. But something didn't seem quite right.

I need to follow this a bit, I feel it in my gut.

She tried not to think about how foolish this was and set off. The walk was easier than she expected, even though the harsh desert wind and extreme heat made it uncomfortable. Somehow, though, her hunch had borne out. She could see what looked like an oasis up ahead.

I could really use a drink, here's hoping I'm not hallucinating.

Celes pressed ahead with as much pace as she could manage. The sun's rays seemed even more intense, and her throat was parched. But she didn't dare drink the last of her water. She just needed to go a bit further and reach the oasis.

And, like that, she was there. It was a small stone-fenced area, with some shade and water in the middle. Even the sight of water made her feel better. She stumbled forward, eager to drink. Just as she was within reach the water disappeared. Instead, there was a dry hole that she tumbled into. As she picked herself up, she saw a dark shape leaning over her then blackness.

Celes awoke in a cooler place, amongst pillows. She darted to her feet and assessed her surroundings. She was in a small dwelling that was sparsely but comfortably furnished. A jug of water was set before her and a glass. She inspected the water and smelled it, checking for any known additives. It seemed clean. She poured a glass and drank it down fast.

"You're a cautious one. Good instincts." A man with a sand-coloured robe approached and sat on a cushion at the far end of the room. Close enough to enable easy conversation, but not too close.

His hair was a mix of grey and black and his green eyes studied her closely.

"I have you to thank for my accommodation?"

"And the mirage. Perhaps the two cancel each other out." The man chuckled, his thick beard drawing her attention. He pushed it down and waited for her response.

"You're a wizard then?"

"Yes. The name's Ashra, although some call me the desert wizard." Ashra stood and bowed with a flourish.

"Celes. You lure a lot of travellers in with that mirage?"

"Not that many. You came from an interesting direction, and you aren't really prepared for a desert journey."

"Yes, it's a bit of a long story. But suffice to say, I'm here and I likely need your assistance. Since you're a wizard and all."

"Intriguing. And what is it you're after in this rather inhospitable place?"

"I'm following a wizard, well his trail. It brought me here. Perhaps you will know what he was after?" Celes studied Ashra's features. He definitely knew something.

"This wizard has a name?"

"Not a real one, just an alias. Aydan."

"I see. And who set you on this path, Celes?"

"A master wizard named Falric." Celes noticed surprise in the man's features.

"I know him, from a long time ago. I'm sorry to say, last I heard…"

"His death was feigned. He's very much alive." Celes tossed the medallion to Ashra and enjoyed the shocked expression on his face.

"He gave you this?" Ashra asked, turning over the medallion. He then handed it back.

"Yes, to get me into Wizard Stores. That's how I've been tracking this wizard, Aydan. Although the trail is old, over twenty years."

"Falric, that old scholar. I didn't know he had it in him, giving us all such a great scare." Ashra paused and pointed at Celes. "There's something familiar about you, what's your connection to Falric?"

"He took my son away to become a wizard." Ashra burst out laughing.

"Now, this is something. Your son is named Alrion, correct?"

"Yes."

"I know him well, we crossed paths when he came through here. His father too. A very difficult time for them. How is Alrion now?"

"Alrion is well, he cured himself of his affliction. Vincent is also well, we were travelling together until recently."

"When you stepped through the Wizard Gate?" Ashra wasn't dancing around the topic any longer, it must have been obvious where Celes had come from. There was no point in denying it.

"Yes. We've had to take different paths for a time. I'm following the trail of Aydan, and Vincent is pressing forward to prepare for Alrion."

"I see. What does your husband think of your hunt for this mysterious wizard?" Ashra gave her a curious look.

"He's supportive. He agrees that it's important to get to the bottom of who is meddling with Alrion's quest before it's too late. And that I'm the one best suited to find him."

"I see. Vincent is quite wise then?" Ashra chuckled.

"Well, he knows when he needs to let me have my way. Besides, I am uniquely qualified to track this wizard down."

"I can see that. How can I be of help?"

"You've already done enough." Celes pointed to the room around her, and the water. "Although, if you can think of a reason why a wizard would travel here twenty years ago, I'm all ears." Celes watched Ashra's face. He nodded and closed his eyes, deep in thought.

"The temple of the monks is quite a trek, I doubt it was that. There is something near here that might be of interest."

"What is it?" Celes leaned forward, desperate to find out.

"Another Wizard Gate. It's special in that it's only one way."

"So, you need to come here to use it?"

"Precisely."

"Where does it go?"

"A small town, rather unremarkable I believe." Ashra had a glint in his eye.

"You're hiding something, aren't you?"

"What? Me?" Ashra laughed. "Honestly, there's no major mystery in that place that I am aware of. But not many know of this gate. It's a good way to travel without drawing attention. Perhaps it was just a step in your mystery wizard's trip." Ashra poured himself a glass of water and drank deeply. Celes let the information brew in her mind.

Is this all there is to it? The wizard came here to throw people off the trail?

"Wouldn't anyone who could take the gate to get here, be aware of the other gate nearby?"

"I can count on one hand the number of people who have come through that gate in the last twenty years." Ashra chuckled.

"Were you here when this wizard passed through?"

"Twenty years ago? It's unlikely. It was around that time that I first came to the desert. I think it's more likely that this wizard passed through before then."

"I see." Celes wanted more to go on, but this was a good option. She wouldn't need to spend much time in the desert, and with any luck, the next trip in the gate would get her closer to Valrytir so she wouldn't be too far behind Vincent.

"And you're sure there's nothing else here for this mysterious wizard?"

"Honestly, no. I think your best option is to follow that gate and see if you can pick up the trail. Where's Vincent heading?"

"He's going to Valrytir. We're going to meet at a Wizard Store near the city. Falric said that it's a key location for the end of Alrion's quest."

"Ah, that's interesting." Ashra closed his eyes, deep in thought. "I believe the source of the Blight is around there somewhere, which makes sense. This next gate will definitely take you closer, or at least negate this rather large detour you've just made." Ashra grinned at her. Celes gave him a quick smile in response. The wizard stood and stretched.

"It's time we got moving. I feel a storm coming in, and you won't want to get stuck in it."

"Sure, I see no reason to hang around. Especially in such an inhospitable place." Celes paused and looked around. "Excluding your home of course." Ashra laughed without restraint.

"You probably think me crazy for coming out here and living in these conditions."

"Not really, I know what people are like." Celes gave him a grin and he returned it with a conspiratorial look.

"Ah, a fellow enlightened one." Ashra walked over to a ladder and directed Celes up. She climbed up and waited for him. Through the sparse windows, she could see the wind beginning to whip up.

"I feel like we may not have as much time as you thought."

"Don't you worry, I'm a wizard, remember? We're good for some things." Ashra strode outside and waited for Celes to join him. The heat and the dryness seemed a little less intense. She didn't notice the wind as much as she expected either. Before she could say something, Ashra spoke.

"You're probably noticing that I'm shielding you from the extremities of the weather."

"I was just about to say something."

"I know. Just remember that I can do more if we need it." Ashra said no more and Celes kept as close as she could. Whatever he was doing, it made the desert much more bearable and she didn't want to miss out.

They walked along a sand dune, following no discernible path. Ashra adjusted their course a few times, and within an hour he stopped abruptly.

"We're here."

"I don't see anything." Celes looked over the whole landscape and could see nothing.

"You just need to know where to look." Ashra brushed away some sand, revealing a metal ring attached to a square.

"Is that a trapdoor?"

"You tell me." Ashra stood back and let Celes inspect it. She yanked the door open and noticed a ladder going down.

"Ladies first." Ashra didn't make eye contact, he seemed preoccupied with something else. Celes clambered onto the ladder and carefully descended. It was almost pitch-black, even after her eyes adjusted to the gloom. Once Ashra climbed in and closed the hatch it became completely dark.

"My apologies, light is on the way." Ten little lights floated down and attached themselves to different parts of the structure. Celes could now see that they were in a tunnel leading to something.

"We've not far to go." Ashra climbed down quickly and joined Celes at the bottom. He started to walk and Celes followed along.

"Do you know why wizards have such bad reputations?" Ashra said.

"Because you meddle?" Celes said, hoping to get a laugh out of him. But Ashra stopped and looked serious.

"Oh, that is just a matter of perspective. But you're close. The reason that people dislike us, is that we tell them what they need to hear, not what they want to hear." Ashra started off again, letting the comment linger.

"What's so bad about that?"

"It's a matter of perspective. Because the wizard may have a different one, he sees what he does as completely reasonable. Even helpful. But the person interacting with the wizard only sees the wizard as being obtuse and unhelpful. And they get frustrated."

"Well, you're all individuals. Why not just change the way you behave?"

"It's funny that. There's a common thread through us, and not even Granthion can lay claim to it. Maybe there's something we gain through our Spark? Regardless, no matter how they are brought up, all wizards gravitate to this same behaviour. To serve the greater good and longer-term benefit." Ashra stopped to inspect something on the wall, it looked like a tiny carving. But Celes couldn't make out anything interesting about it.

"Branthor didn't seem like he was doing that. Was he an exception?"

"Again, it's all a matter of perspective. He believed himself to be serving a greater long-term goal and sacrificing everything else to get there. Quite extreme, but classic wizard behaviour." Ashra turned a corner and stopped completely.

"Ah, here we are. Looks like it still works." Ashra looked at Celes, to see her reaction. The gate was almost identical to the one she had travelled through. She walked closely and examined it. She could feel Ashra's eyes on her, watching her carefully. She shrugged the sensation off and looked at the markings.

"As far as I can tell there's only one destination."

"Very good. Now show me how you activated the last one." Ashra stood back, continuing to study her. Celes almost felt self-conscious. She retrieved the medallion and thrust it into the opening of the gate. Nothing happened. She left her hand there for a few seconds and tried again.

"No such luck?" Ashra said. He gave her the strangest look like he was testing something.

"Hmm, it was delayed but it worked last time." Celes turned and saw Ashra was standing right there. He held out his hand, and she gave him the medallion. He turned it over again and handed it back.

"Very curious. I hadn't expected it to work, and this has proven me right. I think you lucked out at the last gate. That or whatever happened to this medallion was a one-time deal."

"In that case, I feel incredibly lucky to have your assistance." Celes started to imagine what it would have been like to be stuck in the desert. She gulped.

"Not your wisest move, but it paid off." Ashra reached out and the gate activated, the light taking Celes by surprise and temporarily blinding her. The gate shimmered and showed a different scene this time, but it was quite dark and hard to make out.

"This is where we part ways." Ashra held out his hand, and Celes shook it. Ashra held on to her arm.

"Before you go, I feel I must come clean with you. This wizard you are searching for..." Ashra paused, watching her. Celes stared at him, waiting for his next words.

"I've met him. I know who he is." The shock ran through her like a bolt of lightning.

"Tell me!" Celes shouted. Her ferocity surprised them both. Ashra quickly changed his expression into a friendly smile.

"Think on all that I've said so far. I've told you what you need to know, not what you want to know." Ashra's smile had a hint of sadness and he pushed her back, Celes tumbling into the gate before she could respond.

31

THE SCENIC ROUTE

A lrion tossed a saddlebag onto the horse and hiked up himself. He took a moment to steady himself and look for Lara. She was ready to go and nudged her horse forward the second she noticed Alrion was mounted.

"Keen to go?" Alrion said as he caught up.

"Desperate. I just found this whole town to be sucking the life out of me." Lara cracked the reins, speeding up the horse further. Alrion knew what she was talking about.

Everything they had done since arriving at the town had been slow and drawn out. Finding somewhere to stay, finding supplies, finding horses. Each activity had been like pulling teeth. Everyone had been polite, but unhelpful.

"Good riddance, Beetham," Alrion muttered. He matched Lara's pace and soon they had passed through the town surrounds and were onto the main path.

"How long is the ride?" Alrion said.

"A few days I think, it's not too bad. Hard days though."

"Well, we have nothing better to do. I'd rather not draw this out, the sooner we can return the more comfortable I'll feel."

"Because it's holding you back?"

"Yes. Now that the whole situation with Branthor is resolved, and Alyx is cured, there's nothing left on my list. I can't afford any more distractions."

Alyx, now you've gone and disappeared again. At least this time you can protect yourself.

"It does seem like we need to move things forward. Darvin is getting more and more aggressive."

"He's got nobody left now." Lara turned sharply to look at Alrion, and he could see the realisation dawn on her.

"Alyx had already killed the Skull King, and when Darvin turned her you cured her."

"I cured Fermur."

"Rindale was just obliterated by Branthor, who you also cured."

"That doesn't leave anyone else, does it?" Alrion smiled at Lara. She nodded, a satisfied look on her face. The expression changed quickly.

"I'm still concerned by Rindale's last statement. That we were too late to stop his work."

"Well, he may have achieved something, but whatever it was, nobody else can continue the work. I'm happy with that."

"True." Lara slowed down and came to a complete stop.

"What's the problem?" Alrion said.

"There's a fork in the road."

"Don't we just consult the map?" Alrion watched Lara's face. She seemed quite puzzled by something.

"This fork isn't on the map. It's probably nothing, but it does raise doubts."

"But one of the ways is? We can just follow that?"

"Of course, the way I planned is still there." Lara looked down the alternate path. Alrion followed her gaze. He could see why she was confused. This wasn't a rough-and-ready dirt track. It was an established road. It looked like until recently it had been well-maintained. Alrion rode his horse over, to take a closer look.

The road wound into the distance, he couldn't see where it led.

There seemed to be more vegetation, and it appeared to be less wild, and more curated.

"There's something odd about this. I get the feeling that this way was the better-maintained way. The main road is the one that was neglected, at least until recently."

"I had the same feeling, which is why it's so strange. But, maybe it's just a local residence and therefore no map required."

"You're probably right." Alrion stared into the distance. He felt something. It was almost imperceptible. The more he concentrated, the more he felt it. It was like a pull.

"We need to investigate." The words surprised Alrion as much as Lara.

"Why is that? I thought we were in a hurry?"

"We are. But there's something there. We need to check it out. Maybe it's nothing and I apologise for the detour. But, if it's something..."

"I get it. Well, it's your quest. We can take the scenic route on occasion." Lara sighed and started riding. Alrion pushed forward, taking the lead. Lara seemed content to trail behind, periodically looking behind.

The countryside was vibrant with lots of colourful flowers and an exotic mix of different trees and plants. However, Alrion couldn't spot a lot of animal life.

"Looks nice but seems rather quiet." Alrion looked to Lara to see her reaction.

"You're right. I'd expect an environment like this to have a lot more animals or at least evidence of them."

"Maybe there's something here." Alrion smiled and kept riding. As he turned the corner he stopped suddenly. Peeking over the tree line he could see what looked like a castle or manor house.

"Now look at this!" Alrion pointed.

"Luxury home, as expected. This could still be nothing. And it would explain the unmapped road."

"Still doesn't mean that it's nothing." Alrion took off again, curious to see what was there. As he rode, he noticed movement in the tree line in the distance. It was minimal but noticeable.

"Did you see that?" he said.

"I did. There's something there, and it's probably not friendly. Let's hide the horses and approach on foot."

"Agreed." Alrion found a spot just off the path with enough space for the horses. They tied up the horses and approached the path.

"I think we'll need a few things." Alrion tracked back and retrieved his bag from the saddle. Lara did the same.

"You're right, if things don't go well, we won't have an opportunity to come back."

"Let's see what's going on." Alrion started walking off and Lara held his arm.

"Wait, let me go ahead." Lara took the lead, staying near the side of the path and taking cover as she went. After a minute of this careful approach, she remained hidden and waved Alrion over.

"Take a look over there." Lara pointed out a spot between two tree branches. It took Alrion a few moments, but he saw what she had pointed out.

"Blighter."

"Exactly. Likely a lot more where it came from. We haven't been spotted yet, we could just go back the way we came." Lara watched Alrion, gauging his reaction. He could see that she wanted to return and not invite another Blight encounter.

I understand her thinking, but something is not quite right. I need to investigate this properly.

"My gut says we need to properly investigate. At least figure out why they are here, in the middle of nowhere."

"I thought we were back on track, prioritising the quest?"

"We are. These Blighters are here for a reason, and we're going to find out why. I'm sure it's strongly linked to my quest." Alrion grinned and noticed a quick smile from Lara that was gone as soon as he noticed it.

"In that case, let me go ahead. I'll assess how we approach. If you notice a commotion, come in and bring your spells."

"Absolutely." Alrion nodded and watched Lara leave. She kept to the path a little longer, then completely entered the trees. Alrion lost sight of her, and instead focused on the Blighter they had spotted. That would be his sign.

Nothing happened for a while. Alrion kept looking for Lara and saw nothing.

No commotion, but no sign of her either. Do I need to do something? I'm going to investigate, I can't stay here any longer.

Alrion stepped forward and noticed something. He scanned the distance and realised what it was. The Blighter was gone.

She's there. I'll see if I can approach without being seen.

Alrion continued along the path, looking for the way that Lara had entered via the trees. He found a tiny way through the thick trunks and decided to follow it. Now that he was on the way, he had a relatively simple trail to follow. There was only really one path through the trees from the direction that Lara had taken. Soon he spotted a single Blighter corpse.

More than we expected, at least out here. No wonder she took so long. I don't like dealing with Blighters now that I know that they can be saved. But I can't avoid them until I'm ready to do the spell. And I sure can't cure them one at a time.

Alrion steeled his resolve and kept following the trail. He found another road, this one leading off the main one and heading to the main gates. The gates were open.

"Time to go in. I'll find Lara," Alrion whispered. He continued to stalk quietly, not wanting to sound the alarm. There was a good chance that Lara had already taken out any patrols, but he didn't want to take a chance there were more lingering.

As he passed through the gates, Alrion noticed Lara crouching behind a small outpost building. She noticed him and waved him over furiously. Alrion rushed over, not looking behind him.

"Why are you here?" Lara hissed at him.

"You were taking too long. I understand why, now."

"I had it under control." Lara's attention was diverted by a crash.

The main doors of the keep swung open and a Shade strode outside. It was flanked by a host of Blighters.

"Still have it under control?" Alrion said. Lara flashed her Runesteel dagger.

"Absolutely." As Lara looked on, more came through the doors.

"Shade Wizards," Alrion said.

"Only two."

"Still nasty."

"Isn't this where you channel your overpowered ego and take them all out?" Lara smiled at him.

"Ouch, I'd like to think I've grown a little." Alrion acted hurt. "I'll humbly take them all out." He walked out immediately.

"What are you doing?" Lara whispered after him.

"I'm trying something," Alrion replied. Within moments he had their attention.

"Who's in charge here?" Alrion said. He was met with some confused looks. One of the Shade Wizards eventually stepped forward.

"I'm in command, I'm the highest ranked here."

"I'd like to explore this keep. Would you so kindly vacate the premises?" Alrion smiled broadly. The Shade Wizard sneered.

"I've heard of you. Almost one of us, but you were too good for it."

"You should watch your words. Otherwise, I'll cure you."

"Never!" The Shade Wizard started gathering his Spark and hurled a large fireball at Alrion. He held out his hand and the fireball seemed to be drawn into it and fizzle into nothing.

"What?" the Shade Wizard shouted.

"You're going to have to do better than that." Alrion could feel the absorbed heat and Spark in his hand. He was a bit surprised that it worked. It was a mixture of ideas and memories from all the jumble in his brain. He could use his Will to break down the spell into harmless components. Lucky for him, the spell was so familiar that it worked fine. But it only just worked. Not that he had to let them know.

Wanting to keep the advantage, Alrion added to the Spark and fire essence in his hand and compressed it into an ultra-hot spear of fire. He shot it out at the Shade up the front. The shade collapsed to the ground immediately, black dust starting to flake away.

"What did you do?" Lara whispered.

"I burned away its heart. The transformation is reversing now. Unfortunately, the person inside is also gone." Alrion spoke loud enough so the Shade Wizards could hear as well. They looked at each other and nodded, before taking off in opposite directions to attack Alrion.

"Do you mind taking one of them out?" Alrion said.

"It would be my pleasure." Lara remained in the shadows but started to stalk away. Alrion focused his attention on the other one.

They saw how I dealt with a long-range attack, they're likely to come in close. I can take advantage of that.

Alrion approached the Shade Wizard that was closing in. The enemy smiled and, as soon as he was in range, thrust his hands out, a wave of fire spewing forth. He laughed as it happened.

"Seen it before," Alrion said. "And I had no Spark at the time." Alrion threw up a shield of earth and the flames died away harmlessly. He pulled up another piece of earth, toppling the Shade Wizard to the ground. As the wizard rose, Alrion stepped forward and grabbed the Shade Wizard with one hand.

"It's over." Alrion sent a pulse of force through the wizard. He almost channelled his Soul Power into the strike, feeding more and more into the enemy wizard. As it was happening, he remembered what Branthor had said about the cure. There had to be a better way.

Alrion imagined his Soul Power entering the enemy's body, and gently travelling through the body's own pathways. It found every site of Blight infection and gently overcame it, breaking down the Blight and purging it. Once he had finished, he opened his eyes and watched the Shade Wizard collapse to the ground. The sight was enough to distract the other Shade Wizard, long enough for Lara to plunge the Runesteel dagger into its heart.

With all the leaders dispatched, the Blighters broke ranks and fled. Alrion thought about finishing them off but Lara stayed his hand.

"Individually, they aren't a problem for those around here. Maybe they'll keep under the radar long enough for you to cure them."

"Are you sure?"

"In this situation, it just feels unnecessary. Let's get this one inside." Lara gestured to the unconscious man at Alrion's feet. He enveloped the wizard in a mesh of force and gently lifted him off the ground. Next Alrion turned to the body of the dispatched Shade and Shade Wizard and incinerated them. Only dust remained.

"Let's see what all the fuss was about." Alrion started towards the gates and Lara followed, checking to see if there were any more enemies to worry about. Inside, the keep was like a stately home. Lush furnishings and plush carpet with polished wood and lots of fancy rugs. They found a bedroom on the main floor and Alrion placed the wizard on the bed.

"Do you think he'll be normal again?"

"I hope so, otherwise this cure is going to be a bit of a bust when everyone is touched by it."

"Branthor seemed relatively fine."

"He did. With any luck, this one will mostly regain himself." Alrion took one last look at the sleeping wizard and left the room.

"Up or down?" Lara said.

"Down. We seem to have more luck in the dungeons." Lara nodded and headed towards the stairs down. They reached a stone storeroom with a giant lock on the door.

"Perhaps you would like the honours?" Alrion pointed to the lock. Lara sidled over and pulled out some tools, tinkering with the lock for a few moments. It clicked open and she tossed the lock to Alrion.

"Impressive."

"Thanks." Lara winked and pulled the door open. There were a few empty wooden crates and more stairs down.

"This looks promising." Alrion started down and Lara stayed close behind. He found a torch hanging on the wall and kindled his Spark, lighting it with a tiny flame.

"This is more fun," Alrion said, pointing to the flaming torch.

"Absolutely. Not that I don't appreciate your magic lights."

"They're a bit too perfect." Alrion pressed on, waving the torch slowly in front of him to illuminate the passageway. It was plain stonework with no furnishings. Eventually, he noticed another source of light and extinguished the torch. A faint blue glow was visible in the distance.

"If you were a betting woman..." Alrion said.

"Then I'd bet that's another Wizard Gate."

"Let's see if you're right." Alrion upped the pace, his excitement bubbling over.

I knew there was something here. I don't think they were using this either, just guarding it. It must lead somewhere good. I'll definitely go through this one.

As expected, the closer they walked, the more it looked like a Wizard Gate. Until Alrion confirmed it.

"I've another shot it would seem."

"Do I get to go through this one?" Lara laughed.

"Not without me. I'm not splitting my team up on opposite ends of the world." Alrion moved in closer and examined the symbols marked on the gate.

32

UNEXPECTED RETURN

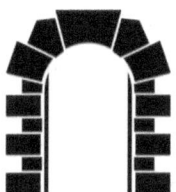

The blazing heat and light subsided and Alyx found herself in a luxurious garden setting. The Wizard Gate was integrated into the stonework and Alyx had never noticed it before. But she knew this garden well. She spent so much time here.

Back in Valrytir. In the Specialist Training camp, no less.

It looked to be early evening and the garden was empty. Not that it ever attracted many people. Few had access, and of those who could come, they weren't the type to appreciate gardens. Initially, Alyx hadn't either. But it was a place she could train without unwanted eyes on her, so the garden had become a regular haunt during her time here.

Alyx didn't dally and started rushing out. She thought about the path she would need to take, and how to best avoid bumping into anyone. That was an awkward conversation she would rather not have.

The layout of the building seemed the same, not that she expected any changes. It hadn't been that long, really. She knew the new recruits would likely be in the mess hall, so she entered the large wooden building near their quarters, hoping the area would be deserted.

The polished floors and trophies along the walls brought back a lot of memories. Mostly good memories. A few painful ones. But she pushed them all aside, this was not a time for reminiscing. Now that she was back, she needed to find a quiet space to plan her time. Alrion would be coming here at some point, and he would need support in the city. Lara's influence would be quite useful, but it wouldn't hurt trying to line up more before they arrived. If she knew one thing about the Blight, it was that nobody took them on single-handedly and got away with it. Although she had almost done it.

At too great a cost. Then I was foolish enough to get infected after the fact.

Alyx made it through the building with speed and exited the giant doors. She was out on the path, heading towards the entry gate when she heard a voice.

"Alyx!" She kept walking, pretending she didn't hear.

Hopefully, she thinks she has the wrong person.

"Alyx, I know it's you!" The voice was accompanied by running footsteps. Alyx sighed and turned around.

"Mary?" The woman had not changed a bit. Still a ridiculous height and long blonde hair. Of course, it was tied up, and her uniform stole away a lot of her femininity.

"I don't believe it. You're here of all places?" Mary looked incredulous.

"I was in town, so wanted to sneak a look. It hasn't changed."

"You were in town? I thought you'd never come back. And stories of your exploits have gone around."

"What exactly?" Alyx asked, nervously.

How much do they know?

"The Skull King? I thought you were just having me on, I didn't realise you were serious. It's unbelievable!"

"I trained my whole life for it." Alyx looked away, trying to find a reason to leave. Mary must have sensed something.

"Look, I don't know why you're back. But come have a drink with me. I can't let you go without hearing your story." Mary's eyes had that look in them. Alyx knew it too well.

"Fine, lead the way. I know I have no choice."

"That's the spirit. And you can tell me where you got that sword too, and what happened to your one."

"This is just on loan." Alyx tapped the hilt with her hand.

"And your old sword?"

"Do you want that drink or not?" Alyx gave her a wry smile and Mary chuckled.

"Can't help myself. Can you blame me? That sword was bigger than you were!"

"I understand completely."

"I just can't believe you're here." Mary led her through the streets to a familiar place, *The Hard Stuff*.

"Did you expect anything else?"

"Not really, I just hadn't thought this far ahead." Alyx followed Mary inside. Mary directed her to a table, and she went up to the bar.

Alyx looked around at the clientele. Luckily, she didn't recognise anyone. But it would happen in due course. This was the preferred bar for all the specialist units. Mary returned with two cups and set them down carefully.

"So, spill. What happened exactly, on the day that you left?"

"We went on a skirmish. Small team. Was supposed to be reconnaissance, but we thought we could take out the scouting party."

"You and who else?"

"Just Adam."

"Oh, I see." Mary grabbed one cup and pushed the other towards Alyx. She drank deeply then set it down.

"It was a trap. The scouts were actually Tainted ones, and they had swarms of Blighters hidden a short distance away. We took two down but were then completely surrounded." Alyx had another drink.

"Did they offer terms?"

"No, they wanted to infect us and hold us until we were almost turning then send us back."

"Urgh. Horrible."

"Exactly. I... I didn't do justice to my name that day."

"What did you do?" Mary leaned forward, concern in her eyes.

"I became enraged, and just started attacking. I dragged Adam along with me. I created enough of an opening for us to make a break for it. But I didn't take it."

"You kept fighting?"

"Yes. I wanted to punish them for trying to trick us. It was a foolish move. Adam chose to stay too, and he got mauled. In the end, I had to do the same thing anyway. I created another opportunity and hauled him out of there. But it was too late."

"The infection had taken hold?"

"Exactly." Alyx drained the rest of her drink. She leaned back and closed her eyes. She could still see his expression. It wasn't anger or hate. That would have been fine. It was sadness at letting her down. That they would be separated. She drove the vision from her mind.

"And the commander went ballistic?"

"You better believe it. Did you know Adam was the general's son?"

"No. Really?"

"Yes. It was done in secret, to ensure he received proper training and didn't get treated differently to the rest. I knew, but most didn't."

"Is that why you left?"

"No. Looking back, I think I just felt like I had failed and couldn't stay any longer. And I don't think it was helping me anymore, I was only staying for his sake at that point."

"I'm so sorry."

"Yeah, well, can't change it now. Just try to make different mistakes." Alyx looked into her empty cup. Mary jumped up and charged over to the bar. She returned soon with two more cups.

"And what of your revenge? The Skull King?" Mary's eyes were alight with curiosity.

"I can't go into the full story. But I'll tell you this much." Alyx paused and took another sip of the new cup.

"I worked my way through his twisted arena bouts. Finally, as the champion, he needed to grant me a boon."

"Did you ask him to stab himself?" Mary laughed.

"That would have been a waste, he'd only regenerate."

"Oh, I see. What a monster."

"Yes, he was a piece of work. I challenged him to a duel to the death. He accepted quickly and laughed."

"And you fought him alone?"

"Alone and in front of a crowd, in the arena. He knew all about my family sword and thought that he had protected himself. But there was a secret he didn't know about."

"Which was?"

"Still a secret." Alyx paused and had another sip of her drink.

"That's no fun."

"I suppose not. At any rate, I won the day. But my sword was destroyed, I left it behind. And fled."

"But you won? Why did you flee?"

"Just because I won, didn't mean I was safe. The shock of what happened gave me an opportunity. But there were plenty of folks who used the Skull King's dominance for their own ends. I had a target on me. The best thing I could do was disappear."

"Wow. Even after all that, you still kept wandering."

"For a time."

"Well, now I have something to share that you won't believe." Mary gave her a secretive smile and slowly sipped on her drink.

"I'm waiting."

"It's about your sword."

"Yes?" Alyx stared at Mary

What is she talking about?

"We retrieved the pieces, they're being held here in Valrytir in an exhibit!"

"What?" Alyx almost shouted. She composed herself. "It doesn't matter, it can't be reforged. The technique required magic and nobody living knows how to do it."

"Not necessarily. But it is true that right now we can do nothing with it. For now, it's just a symbol of your triumph." Mary stared at Alyx. "But now we have you."

"I'm not back for that. I have a new mission." Alyx saw she had Mary's interest.

"Oh, now I have to hear about this."

"I'll need your help." Alyx hadn't thought this through, but it was obvious. Alrion would need military support when he arrived. Mary was the best way to start that conversation.

"You'll need my help?"

"Yes. We're going to need a rather large force."

"To do what?"

"Good question. Crush the Blight? Take down Darvin?" Mary burst into laughter.

"You don't aim small, do you? You don't think we haven't been trying?"

"You haven't had anything worth risking it all for."

"Oh, haven't we? And what have you got that changes everything?" Mary had a strange look on her face. It sounded like she was dismissing Alyx. But her expression, it was different. She was looking for hope. Looking for that spark that they didn't have. And Alyx had it. She had the missing piece.

"I have a wizard that can cure the Blight."

"Nonsense." Mary dismissed her with a hand gesture.

"I've seen it firsthand. He cured himself, and he even cured me." Alyx could see she had Mary's attention.

"I don't believe it."

"He'll be here soon enough, and you'll know then." Alyx leaned back and finished her drink. She had done what she could. Planting the seed would do for now. At least for Mary. She would act differently when Alrion arrived. Then she would claim prior knowledge and pretend like she was pulling everything together. This could still work.

"You think you can just waltz in and drop that information and disappear?" Mary looked annoyed.

"If that's what it takes." Alyx smiled.

"No, it's going to take more than that." Mary finished her drink and stood. She stood over Alyx. "If you want my help, you need to rejoin the unit."

"I have different priorities now."

"You did before as well. I can see your reluctance. It's alright, I'll sweeten the deal. You can duel me for a place in the unit. If you win, I'll take you in and help you build support for your wizard friend. If you lose, you can slink away and return when you're ready to fight."

"Why are you doing this? Helping me is in your interests. The Blight will be done. Ended."

"So, you say. It's not even about that. You abandoned us. You fled and didn't even say goodbye. You need to prove yourself again. If you can't beat me, then you don't want this enough. And that's not going to work for anyone." Mary stormed out of the inn. Alyx chased after her.

"Just like that?"

"Just like that. Follow me back to the training ground, or don't. It's your choice." Mary didn't utter another word.

I didn't realise she was so upset. I thought they understood. But I was wrong. If this is what it takes, so be it. I can beat her. I won't let Alrion down.

Alyx tried to remember how Mary fought, but she couldn't remember anything in particular. They didn't spar much, and Alyx was often on assignment with other squad members. They had mainly bonded because there were precious few women, and it had been because of Mary's insistence. Alyx had been so single-minded, she hadn't really tended to that friendship at all. And this was the price.

As they walked through the main building, people started to notice. Whispers followed them, and people started to trail along as well. Once they reached the training ground, there was quite a following. All wearing the uniform of the elite, the black and brown padded vests with armoured plating on their forearms and legs. Mary walked into the centre of the training ground and waited. The murmurs reduced to nothing. A lone man ran out with a sword, handing it over and rushing back into the crowd. Mary looked up and addressed the crowd.

"We are joined tonight by an old comrade. She was highly respected, a core member of the unit. But she abandoned us in a time of need, to fulfil her own quest. She's returned, not to serve, but to ask for more. For that reason, she needs to prove herself. Right here, right now." Mary clenched her right hand into a fist and whoops sounded all around the training ground.

Looks like I'm quite popular here.

"Alyx here figures herself quite the accomplished warrior, Which is why she has agreed to duel three of us at once." Mary smiled and waved over two other fighters. One was male, and the other was female. They looked like they were twins.

Oh no. Not them.

Alyx recognised them. The terrible twins. An impossible pair, they harried any force with amazing precision, each one instinctively guessing what the other was thinking, leading to manoeuvres that were impossible to see coming. Mary could just sit back and let those two wear her down or create an opening. Then Mary could swoop in and finish it off. It wouldn't even take long. Alyx closed her eyes and focused.

You can do this. You destroyed the Skull King. You survived being infected, you survived being cured. You made it all the way here. Alrion is depending on you. It's time to win them over, it's time to show them why you're the best.

Alyx opened her eyes and drew her sword. A quiet murmur rippled through the crowd as the Runesteel glinted in the light.

"Begin!" Mary pointed with her sword and the twins moved in, their swords whirling in confusing patterns as they approached.

Divide and conquer.

Alyx targeted the male twin, named Shane. She went all-out attack, forcing him into a defensive stance. His sister, Sherry, tried to flank, but Alyx had pressed so hard that Shane was constantly retreating. That gave Alyx a little breathing room. Not for long.

Mary moved in, poking dangerously and interrupting Alyx's assault. This gave both Shane and Sherry ample opportunity to close in. Now it was Alyx retreating, blocking and parrying the multiple sword strikes coming from different directions and heights.

I can't keep this up forever.

Alyx knocked a few attacks back harder than necessary, to force the attackers to pause momentarily. The effort worked and made a strange sound.

What's that about?

Alyx dashed backwards to give herself some space. She was reaching the limit of the training ground. Mary approached from the front with a wicked grin. Shane and Sherry approached from the other sides. As Sherry whirled her sword around Alyx noticed something.

There's a nick on the blade.

Then she remembered. I'm wielding Runesteel. These must be ordinary swords. I can end this fight quickly. Alyx changed her stance, inviting attacks by lowering her guard. She needed to parry quickly and bide her time. But she was running out of space and she was beginning to tire. Fighting three high-intensity sword wielders at once was a huge drain. Suddenly she saw an opening, a slightly sloppy strike from Shane. Rather than parry, Alyx let it slide by and aimed for the sword. She swung with all her might, and the blades connected with a crash. But the Runesteel won out, and after the initial resistance, the other blade snapped apart, the metal dropping to the ground. Shane stepped back, perplexed. There was a murmur of wonder running through the crowd. Alyx took the advantage and turned her focus to Sherry. She hastily parried the strikes, trying to minimise the risk of Alyx also breaking her blade.

Alyx swung high, then kicked a leg out, dropping Sherry to her knees. Alyx quickly recovered and swung her sword down, forcing Sherry to raise hers to defend herself. With the high position and momentum, Alyx sliced through Sherry's blade. She didn't even pause and stepped to the side to continue her movement. She advanced on Mary immediately.

"Nice trick, but it won't work on my blade." Mary laughed. But Alyx could see the frustration behind her eyes.

"Now, we are back to what should have been the contest." Alyx was still tiring, but she felt a wave of renewed energy now that the twins were out of the fight. Thankfully, they accepted their defeat honourably and retreated to the sidelines.

Alyx slowed her attacks and paused. Mary stood at the ready, watching warily.

"It's time to finish this." Alyx steeled herself and prepared to attack. Mary raised her sword, waiting.

Just one opponent and she's human. Should be easy.

Alyx closed her eyes for an instant, drawing upon all her energy and focus. She became one with her weapon and charged it with all her will. She and the weapon were a force of skill and power. Like one they glided forward, nothing was an impediment. Each block, parry, or strike from Mary was just another step towards the next attack. Mary kept up well, but the constant fluidity and single-purpose of Alyx's attack could not be turned back. Bit by bit, Mary retreated, and she started making mistakes. Strikes glanced off her armoured forearms, which caused further mistakes. Finally, Alyx pushed even harder, with a final flurry of attacks. Her final attack was so strong that Mary's weapon was knocked from her hands and she cried out, dropping to her knees.

"Yield." Alyx pointed her weapon at Mary's neck.

"I yield. You won." Alyx sheathed the sword and started walking away.

33

A LIFETIME AGO

A lrion stepped back.

"Looks like this one can do multiple destinations."

"Try it?" Lara said. Alrion pressed one of the symbols. It lit up in a faint blue light and the gate itself roared to life. A flash of light and heat then a shimmering picture hung before them.

"That was easy." Lara stepped forward and stared at it. Alrion held onto her shoulder.

"Don't fall in by mistake."

"Of course not." Lara chuckled and continued inspecting the scene before them.

"It's not clear where this is, looks awfully dark."

"Let's check the other one." Alrion pressed another symbol and there was another flash, the scene changing again. This looked to be somewhere in the mountains.

"There's not really mountains near Paperton are there?"

"I wouldn't say so. We're probably better off with the dark one."

"Provided it isn't a trap."

"I'm sure the two of us are pretty safe. Besides, only wizards can use these."

"Don't forget that we just took two Shade Wizards." Alrion looked at the different symbols. He couldn't read what they were supposed to say. He looked to Lara.

"I'm just saying, we know that one of these is definitely the wrong direction. What harm can it be trying the other?"

"I can't argue with that." Alrion pressed the button and the light flashed again, the scene changing back to the dark one.

"Ready?"

"Absolutely." Alrion stepped forward, bringing Lara with him. He felt an intense light and heat go over him. Suddenly he was somewhere else. It was a dark room, constructed of stone. He created an orb of light and attached it to the roof.

"It's a bit cooler here, definitely not a desert but not mountains either."

"There are no windows in here. Are those stairs over there?" Alrion pointed to the end of the room.

"Yes. Let's investigate." Lara walked ahead and Alrion took his time, trying to work out where they were. But it became clear that they needed more to work with. The stairs were narrow and cramped and were slow to descend. Alrion floated the orb of light ahead of them, illuminating the stairs. Finally, they reached the bottom, and it was a simple entry area with a door.

"It's so enclosed, I have no idea where we are. Did we come down from a height, or did we descend deeper into the ground?" Lara said.

"I have no idea. But it doesn't feel like we are underground." Alrion placed a hand on the door and it activated, opening instantly.

"Curious." Alrion noticed light stream in as the doors opened.

"Good, I wasn't looking forward to being underground again." Lara stepped outside immediately. Alrion followed her and looked around. They were in a small settlement, which looked ravaged by fire and other damage. The building they had been in was a tower, which looked like it had survived better than the rest.

"That must be a wizard tower. Which means there might be other things here of interest." Alrion started walking around the tower, seeing what else was there. He noticed another large door, made of wood, on the opposite end of the tower.

"Let's take a look." Alrion stood before the door and Lara joined him. She tried to open the door, but nothing happened. Alrion placed a hand on the door. He felt something resonate within. But the door didn't open.

"Is it a magical door?" Lara said.

"I believe so. It must be a Wizard Store. In the past, I used a knock to open it. This one seems different."

"Maybe it needs your name?"

"I doubt that." Alrion stared at the door. "Alrion," he said finally. The door unlocked and started to open.

"Maybe I should be a wizard?" Lara said with a laugh.

"I think so, you're more qualified." Alrion stepped inside and took it in. The room was rather dishevelled. He created another few orbs of light and floated them into the space, attaching at different parts of the ceiling.

"Looks kind of trashed." Lara walked inside, stepping around the debris. Alrion picked up a few books and looked at them.

"Nothing interesting here, just general wizard tomes." He kept picking his way through, trying random books.

"This looks like something official." Lara was standing before a desk of some kind, tucked into the corner. Alrion walked over to join her.

"There's some sort of ledger here on the counter." Lara started flipping through.

"What's inside?"

"I think it's the name of visitors." Lara skimmed over the contents, trying to find the last page.

"There's my name!" Lara looked at him with excitement.

"You're right. Hang on, what's this?" Alrion pointed to the next name.

"Celes? Your mother was here?"

"Recently. What's she doing here? In a Wizard Store?" Alrion stepped back. It didn't make sense.

"Didn't your parents say they were going to Paperton to track down information for you? Maybe this is part of their journey."

"Maybe we're closer to Paperton than we realise. Can you open up that map?" Lara retrieved the map from her bag and opened it up.

"I can't tell from here, we don't know what this place is called. And they sure don't have Wizard Stores and Wizard Gates marked on it."

"Maybe something else in here has the name." Alrion looked around the room. He grabbed a book at random and looked in the covers, and the first and last pages.

"Here's something. 'Property of Arnthorn Wizard Store. Please return after you are finished.'"

"Let me check the map, surely that's the name of this area." Lara pored over the map and stuck her finger on a spot.

"This is it. Barely registers, but it's here. You're in luck." Lara looked up and smiled.

"Yes?"

"We're so near Paperton. We could get there by tonight."

"Wow, that's great. Pity we had to leave the horses behind." Alrion sighed.

"I know. I'm starting to think we should just stop getting them. Unless..." Lara trailed off.

"Unless what?"

"Do you think that horses could go through a Wizard Gate?" Alrion laughed.

"I'd like to see you get one up those stairs."

"Don't tempt me." Lara winked and folded the map. She stashed it back into her jacket.

"Let's be off then." Alrion closed the ledger and carefully stepped over to the door. He held it open for Lara and they both left the building.

The rest of the area looked more damaged.

"Something bad happened here, that's for sure."

"At least that tower survived. It really saved us," Lara said.

"I know, I feel like we've traipsed all over the world. It was nice that we found a little shortcut on the way here. Especially when it feels like we are backtracking."

"It's not backtracking, it's returning. You are coming back with more skills, experience, and knowledge." Lara smiled.

"That's a good way of looking at it." Alrion returned the smile and looked past the burnt and ruined buildings. There was a small trail outside and they started to follow it.

"This should link up to a main road, which we can follow all the way to Paperton."

"Excellent." Alrion lost himself in his thoughts and followed along. As Lara predicted they found the main road and kept walking. After a while, Alrion piped up.

"I wonder how Caleb is going?"

"It really hasn't been that long, but it feels like an age has passed. I keep picturing him old and wizened, but I know that's ridiculous."

"I know what you mean. Maybe he will have grown a beard?" Alrion chuckled and Lara joined in.

"He's a good man, hopefully, he can help you."

"I'm sure he can. Both Branthor and the mysterious wizard think so." Alrion sighed.

"One thing at a time. We'll figure out who's behind the scenes. But first, let's act on what we can. You need to learn as much as you can, so you know how to complete the quest. This whole thing won't end until you can perform that spell."

"I know. We've done a lot of good already. But we need to reverse everything. Darvin will keep building otherwise, or someone else will rise up to replace him. The Blight is so resilient."

"It is. But so are we." Lara leaned in and gave him a kiss on the cheek, then sped off. Alrion laughed.

"Where are you going?"

"Just follow me!" Lara kept running, aiming at something in the distance. Suddenly, she stopped. Alrion slowed down and stopped alongside her.

"Now look at that." Lara pointed at the scene beyond. Alrion drew in a breath. They could see all the way into the valley, looking down at Paperton. It was dusk now, and tufts of smoke and a few lights could be seen coming from the odd-shaped buildings.

"There it is, just the same. Do you remember when we first came?" Alrion said.

"Yes. We had a horse then." Lara laughed. "But seriously, it was quite intense. We were racing against time. Falric had just passed. It wasn't a good time."

"It wasn't." Alrion remained quiet for a moment. "But we're in a better place now. Eventually." Lara pulled him close, so their heads were side by side and they could watch Paperton breathe. Alrion felt calm.

"It's time, let's go." They separated and started the descent down into Paperton.

After a long and winding walk, they arrived at the entry to the town. Most of the scholars had taken shelter within their homes and the streets were empty.

"Where do we start?" Lara said.

"Let's try the main hall. It worked last time."

"Sure." Lara started off towards the large building. The lights were on, which was promising. Alrion remembered when he had charged in and disrupted the whole meeting. It was all done on instinct, with a little prompting from Lara. But they had achieved the impossible. They convinced the scholars and he gained access to the Pool. Things should be easier now.

I bet they're not.

Alrion chuckled to himself.

"What's so funny?"

"Oh, nothing. I just thought that even though things should be easier this time, they probably won't be."

"Don't be like that. Think positive. We're going to get the best possible outcome!" Lara poked him in the side with her index finger and smirked at him. It worked, he couldn't possibly carry on that pessimistic line of thinking. Continuing, they soon reached the giant doors of the main hall. Alrion reached out to push open the doors when they started to open of their own accord. A short bald man was leaving at the same time. He stopped, surprised. Then he wore a broad grin.

"Alrion! Lara! Wow, this is a surprise." Caleb looked thrilled.

"Caleb, you haven't changed a bit." Alrion reached out and shook the scholar's hand.

"We thought maybe you would have a beard or something," Lara said. Caleb laughed.

"Not for lack of trying. Come in, come in." Caleb turned around and ushered them into the main building. It was empty, as expected. But Alrion could still remember when it had been full. He chuckled to himself as he remembered his antics on that day.

"Have you spoken to your parents?" Caleb said.

"Not for a while. Are they here?"

"Oh, no. They were here, but they left. They did say you might be coming, but I didn't know whether to expect you or not. I must say, this is a happy reunion!"

"It is. I'm curious, did they leave because they got what they were after?"

"I don't know how to answer that one, but I don't think so. It's something we should discuss further." Caleb led them through the hall and over to a small door at the back.

"How have you been? Studying hard?" Lara asked.

"Oh yes. I have been working closely with my mentor to master my ability to manage the knowledge from the Pool, and coach others in its use. There is a great deal we can share."

"Great, that's why I'm here. When can I start?" Alrion held the door open for Lara and entered last. They were walking down a narrow corridor and ended up at a desk, with a man sitting there.

"More visitors?" he said.

"Yes, they're with me." Caleb turned to Alrion. "We can start as soon as you want, but I need to introduce my mentor to you. We will be working closely together." Caleb beamed another big smile.

Wow, he must really like this mentor. I guess that's good, it may speed things up if he's good at what he does.

"Off you go, you know the drill." The man waved them away, and Caleb led them through another door. A short walk later they found themselves in another chamber. An old man sat at a desk at the rear, wearily turning the pages in a hefty book. As he looked up Alrion stood dead in his tracks.

"No way. You died. I tried to save you."

"I appreciated the effort. But I wasn't going to let myself go that easily." Falric smiled a little sheepishly.

"Falric!" Lara ran over and hugged him.

"Have we met?" Falric said with a laugh. Lara stepped back and looked at him curiously.

"I don't think you ever met me. But I've been with you all for a while."

"Since Carford," Alrion said with a wry grin.

"Yes, Vincent mentioned you. There is a lot we must discuss."

"I agree." Alrion couldn't quite share Lara's enthusiasm at finding Falric. Yes, he felt an overwhelming sense of relief. And happiness that his mentor was alive. But it was also accompanied by a sense of emptiness, of abandonment.

Why did he stay here and say nothing? Or is he that mysterious wizard, trying to help me in other ways?

Alrion walked over to talk to the master wizard at length.

34

DIVING IN

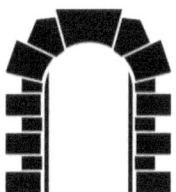

"Come take a seat, so that I might tell you a tale." Falric gestured to the empty seats. Caleb brought them closer to the desk and waited at the edge of the room. Once Alrion and Lara were seated he began again.

"Alrion, your father had almost the same reaction." Falric sighed and shook his head. "I feel like this is just a repeat of that scene."

"What explanation did you tell him?"

"The truth. At heart, I'm a scholar, not a warrior. I made a pretty good administrator as well, and researcher too. This place was my home, so when things played out the way that they did, it made sense for me to stay here."

"What do you mean played out the way they did?"

"I confronted Branthor. Once he was close, I knew it was him, although I didn't understand why. When you saw us, I couldn't risk you being dragged into the conflict. I hoped that by succumbing to him, that he would be satisfied and move on."

"Then why didn't you just rejoin me straight away?"

"I overdid things. My own ruse, whilst protecting me, helped hinder my escape. It was quite an effort to emerge from that rubble. You know better than anyone. I sensed your efforts on the surface."

"I've never felt more powerless. It has followed me ever since." Falric bowed his head when he heard the words.

"I am deeply sorry for that. I never wanted you to feel that. You should never feel responsible for an old wizard like me, I can take care of myself. I'm accountable for my actions and decisions, nobody else is." Falric paused and coughed. "I see now the impact it had on you. More than I foresaw. Which is my oversight."

"I am at least glad you're alive."

"Oh, I know that. I know that. I also expected that you would return, for one reason or another. Because you would need to seek clarification here before moving forward."

"Why would you think that?"

"The Pool works in mysterious ways, but there's a strong theme of protection within it. It hides knowledge from you that you aren't ready to know. It's mostly a practical measure, to protect the mind from being overwhelmed. But the more we study it, we believe it to be more nuanced than that." Falric looked to Caleb. He nodded.

"Especially when it comes to wizards. The knowledge of spells can be catastrophic. There seem to be additional protections in place."

"Such as?" Alrion asked.

"You know how a spellbook will have blank pages until you have the skill and capability to handle the spell?"

"Yes."

"Similar to that. Knowledge pertaining to spells within the Pool will be hidden from you until you are ready to receive it."

"You're talking about the final spell. The one to cure the Blight for good?"

"Yes. I know just about all there is to know about it. But even for me, it didn't all come at once."

"But it's not something you'll tell me, is it?" Alrion looked Falric directly in the eyes. He looked surprised.

"Oh, yes you are quite correct. Why did you say that?"

"Branthor said the same thing to me. That he knew what lay ahead, and he couldn't share it either. That there was something missing if I didn't yet have the knowledge." Falric closed his eyes and looked to be deep in thought.

"You've worked wonders, young man. You didn't just cure Branthor, you saved him. That is the advice I would have expected from him, from the old Branthor." Falric looked like a weight had been lifted from him.

I didn't think about it, but he must have been carrying the weight of Branthor's fate too. Although, he mustn't know how it ended.

"I'm sorry to say that Branthor has passed."

"What? How?" Falric sat upright, keenly attentive.

"He destroyed Rindale but took a fatal blow. I wanted to save him..."

"But he asked you not to?" Falric sighed and closed his eyes again. Alrion saw a single tear escape them.

"He really is at peace then." The master wizard gave them a weak smile, and he looked older than he ever had before. "Thank you for sharing that, and for treating him with such humanity. He walked the wrong path, but it was something easy to do and hard to turn back."

"I know," Alrion said quietly.

"Well, I guess you're keen to get on with things. But before we do, it's appropriate that I briefly mention what your parents are doing."

"Sure."

"We discussed the idea that a wizard has been sending you messages via the notebook you took from the academy."

"Go on." Alrion wondered if Falric was going to be making a revelation.

"It's not me."

"Oh, I thought that it might be since you're alive."

"Although that's a good theory since I'm confident that the wizard must have handled the notebook to be writing in it!"

"Really?" Alrion burst out. That narrowed down the list of people substantially.

"Don't get too carried away," Lara said.

"Why not?"

"Didn't you lose that notebook for a time?" Lara looked at him sceptically.

"Yes, you're right. I recovered it from one of those Trackers. But I was getting messages long before that."

"Let's not get hung up on that detail, for now, there are many ways that a wizard could access your personal belongings, especially if they've been trailing you." Falric gave Alrion and Lara serious looks. He seemed intent on getting back to the topic he had introduced.

"Sure. Please continue."

"I will. We determined that a wizard named Aydan accessed the Wizard Store in Paperton. That is likely an alias, and there's good reason to suspect it is the identity of the wizard that is watching you from afar."

"Aydan. That's his name. Or at least what he calls himself."

"Can't say that I've ever heard of it," Lara said.

"It's in the old language. It means 'Lost One'."

"Interesting. What's this got to do with my parents?"

"We jointly decided that the best way for them to help with your quest was to determine the identity of this individual. So that there were no surprises when you were ready to perform the final spell."

"Is that because you can't tell them things about my quest?"

"Primarily, yes. Although your mother was quite concerned about the risk of this wizard interfering more directly."

"That's why we saw her name in a nearby Wizard Store," Lara said.

"Oh, you found that one?"

"We came in through that Wizard Gate," Alrion said. Falric looked surprised.

"I'm surprised that it's still working. They aren't used much anymore, too prone to failure."

"I've discovered that also." Alrion instantly thought about Alyx, trapped somewhere far away.

"Where are Vincent and Celes off to?" Lara said.

"They're following an old trail. Aydan first passed through here around twenty years ago. They believe that there's more chance of unlocking a clue to his identity in the past."

"That's a good idea. Do you know where they were heading?"

"I know where they will end up." Falric paused for a moment, looking from Alrion to Lara. "They will end up in Valrytir." Lara let out a short gasp but quickly hid it. Alrion still noticed.

"Why Valrytir?" she said.

"The conclusion of Alrion's quest is nearby, and there's also a notable Wizard Store there."

"All roads lead to Valrytir. It all ends there." Alrion's voice was more solemn than he expected. Falric gave him an odd look.

"In a sense, not necessarily a literal one. Right, now that I've brought you up to date, I think we need to address your training. Caleb?" Falric beckoned for the scholar to come over. He strode over immediately.

"Caleb will be your primary instructor in this. I will provide additional instruction and advice from a wizard's perspective."

"How long will this take?"

"As long as it needs. You are the decider of that." Caleb bowed to Alrion.

"You talk like a wizard," Alrion laughed. Falric chuckled too.

"He's right though. A good deal of this is up to you."

"I get it. Can we start?"

"Absolutely. Come with me." Caleb walked back to the doorway and waited for Alrion.

"Here we go. Don't let Falric off too easy on the questions." Alrion winked at Lara and joined Caleb. In moments, they were walking back through the building.

"Are we going back to the Pool?"

"Oh no, there's no need for that. I don't think it's recommended either. What we're going to do is visit the immersion room."

"That sounds interesting." Alrion tried to picture what it looked like but wasn't sure. He kept imagining something like the Vault of Silence but figured it had to be different. Caleb brought them back to the main hall, but he led Alrion to another door, almost hidden around the other side of the stage.

"We're almost at the entrance," Alrion commented.

"Almost, but not quite." Caleb stood before the door and waited. "Please enter." Alrion pushed the door open and walked inside. There was a tiny window in the ceiling letting in the sun's rays, otherwise, the room was quite dim. It looked like a pool in the middle. The walls were all painted white.

"What is this room?"

"This is a tool to help your mind relax and detach from the everyday. You will see a chest over there, that's for your clothes."

"Really?" Alrion looked back at Caleb.

"You would not be comfortable with them weighing you down. We also recommend you scrub yourself down over there." Caleb pointed to a bucket and stool at one end of the room.

"Are you going to stay in here?"

"Oh no, we have thought of that. There is an adjoining room that I can use to talk you through what you need to do. Your privacy will be respected."

"Sure. I guess I better get started."

"Please. I will await your signal." Caleb left the room, closing the door softly behind him. Once the door closed the space seemed extremely quiet.

"It's worth a try," Alrion muttered to himself. He removed all his clothing and dutifully used the bucket and brush to scrub down. He rinsed himself as best as he could and approached the water. It was nicely warmed somehow and felt comfortable. He stepped in and found himself standing at the bottom, the water up to his neck.

"Lay back," a voice said from somewhere else. Alrion looked around and couldn't find the source.

"Lay back, you will float." Alrion realised that it must be Caleb, and he tried leaning back. With careful manoeuvring he was able to lie on his back, floating in the water. He was fully submerged except for his head.

"Good, close your eyes and start to picture the Pool of Knowledge." Alrion closed his eyes and thought back to that day. He had been terribly injured by Branthor and had stumbled over to the Pool. While drinking, he had tumbled into it and blacked out.

I don't think you get more immersed than that.

He kept waiting for Caleb's voice again, but there was nothing. Just quiet. He started to lose track of time, and where he was. His limbs too were almost indistinguishable.

"Imagine that you are diving into the Pool of Knowledge. All that you need is there, right at the bottom. You are diving deeper and deeper." Alrion tried to follow along, and imagine the story that Caleb was speaking.

"What does the Knowledge look like?"

"A chest. But it's locked," Alrion said. He could see the chest now. It was made of wood and reinforced with steel. A large keyhole adorned the front. He knew he couldn't force it open.

"Where's the key?" Caleb's voice said. Alrion searched all around, there was no key. He banged his hand on the chest in frustration. The pain coursed through him, way more intense than expected.

"You must find the key." Alrion held his hands up in annoyance. There seemed to be markings on them. He searched his arms and found more markings.

The key is on me somewhere.

Alrion kept searching, checking his shoulders, legs, and head. Finally, he saw it. The key was emblazoned on his chest. He tried touching it and the heat almost burned him.

Ouch. How do I get it?

He tried again, reaching out. This time he kept his hand on the key, embracing the heat. He let it pass through him. The pain lessened. Dark thoughts started to bombard him. Fear. Doubt. Regret. Anxiety. Rather than resist, he let them pass through as well. He didn't need those, they could go. Suddenly he had the key in his hand. Without any hesitation, he thrust it into the chest and turned sharply.

35

CLOSING IN

C eles stumbled to regain her footing and looked around. She looked like she was in a cellar, with some light leaking in from nearby. The gate itself was almost invisible.

That snake Ashra, he played me. Bloody wizards.

Ashra was right about the gate though, it didn't look like it was working at all. The space felt oppressive, and she didn't want to return to the desert, so she ignored the gate and cautiously walked towards the stairs. They were cut from stone and headed up to somewhere well-lit.

Might as well see where I am.

She took each stair one at a time and listened carefully. It seemed quiet above her, although she did hear the occasional sound of footsteps. As she reached the end of the staircase, she noticed a shadow up ahead.

"Hello?" Celes said.

"Please show yourself," an older male voice said. It sounded strong, but also a bit apprehensive. Celes approached slowly with her hands up, trying to look non-threatening.

"Can I ask who you are?" the man said. He looked like a retired farmer, his grey hair belying his age and his simple work clothes looked faded and worn.

"My name is Celes. It sounds rather incredible, but I just walked through a Wizard Gate."

"Yes, that's the one. Clearly, you're no wizard though." The man eyed her suspiciously.

"No, a wizard activated it for me. I had no idea it opened up in your cellar?" Celes paused, offering the man a chance to introduce himself.

"I'm Lyle, and this is my home. I'm no wizard either." Lyle looked her up and down. "You seem harmless enough, come over and have some tea and you can tell me why you ended up here." Lyle beckoned for her to follow and walked off. Celes cautiously followed, looking around the home. It seemed quite nicely built, but old. It seemed a bit too grand for a farmer's home.

"You're probably wondering why I live here?" Lyle said as he walked into the kitchen. There was a black pot simmering over the stove. Whatever was in there smelled wonderful.

"I was. Not everyone has a Wizard Gate in their basement." Celes smiled and Lyle chuckled.

"No, they do not. Take a seat, please." Lyle sat down at a tiny rectangular table and offered Celes the other chair. They were wooden and old but looked sturdy.

"This place has been in my family for a while. The going story is that a long time ago a wizard lived here. He built this home because he loved the area and constructed that Wizard Gate so that he could return here from his travels."

"I see. Do you have a lot of visitors popping in?"

"No, it's incredibly rare. It's been years since I had anyone. Easy to tell too, that thing goes off like a firecracker. You can't miss it."

"Good to know. So, you can count the number of people you've seen come through here?"

"Absolutely. You're the first that's not a wizard." Lyle gave her a curious look and stood, checking the bubbling pot. He seemed content and pulled out two bowls from a nearby drawer and carefully ladled steaming liquid into both. He gently placed them down on the table and laid down spoons and a rough but clean cloth serviette.

"Now's the part when you tell your story." Lyle carefully spooned some stew into his mouth. Celes looked at hers and decided it was too hot.

"It's a long story, but I suppose I can describe it like this. A strange wizard is following my son around and sending him messages. All we have to go on is a name, so I'm following his trail to try to unearth his identity."

"Oh, now that's interesting." Lyle had another spoon of food. Celes decided to try it. It wasn't as hot as it looked, and the food was delicious. More spices than she expected.

"This is lovely. Quite an unexpected flavour."

"Thank you. It's a local dish, makes use of our produce. The blend of spices is not normally used, so visitors really get a kick out of it." Lyle took another spoon.

"Where is here anyway?"

"Stonebridge. We're in a tiny little town in the hills outside Valrytir."

"Wow, I never heard of this place."

"Not many have. The name comes from the stone bridge connecting this town to Valrytir. Some say it was the only way in back in the day. Who knows?" Lyle shrugged and had some more stew. Celes kept eating and looked down into the bowl. She had almost finished.

"Lyle, I have to thank you for the meal, and the hospitality. I don't want to intrude on you any longer than necessary. But before I go, is there anything you could tell me?"

"About your mystery man?"

"Or the area. Is there anything special here?"

"Other than the gate? I don't think so." Lyle scratched his head and looked thoughtful.

"Now that you mention it, there is something." Lyle leaned forward, a conspiratorial look on his face.

"It would have been around twenty years ago, a man passed

through that gate. I don't remember the name he gave, but it could be the one you are looking for."

"That's great. Can you describe him at all?"

"He was young. Tall with dark hair. Intense looking eyes. Seemed a little bit troubled, you know?"

"Sure. Did he do anything special while he was here?"

"He did ask about the place. Seemed like he knew something. He asked me to take him into the cellar."

"Where the gate is?"

"Yeah, there's a trapdoor there and another room underneath. To be honest, I was surprised that he knew about it." Lyle paused and finished his stew, pushing the bowl away.

"What was down there?"

"Some old trunks, nothing of value that I could see. But then it was the strangest thing."

"What's that?"

"He asked me to hang back, so I retreated back to the room with the gate. I waited and waited. But he just up and vanished. I couldn't see where he went. And he never came back." Lyle sat back in his chair and looked at Celes.

"That's an interesting story." She wondered if this man was trustworthy. On the surface, he looked like he was, but at the same time, the whole story sounded sketchy. And a good way to get a woman trapped in a cellar.

Do I take the bait and investigate, or do I just leave?

Despite asking the question, Celes knew what she would do. It was the same impulse that led her to stepping into that Wizard Gate and landing in the desert. She stood quickly.

"Lyle, if you don't mind, I'd like to see the space that you are talking about."

"Really?" Lyle gave her a confused look. "There's nothing there."

"Something doesn't add up. I know he was a wizard, but my gut is telling me he did something down there. He didn't just vanish."

"Well, if you insist, I can take you there. Certainly gone through myself many a time and found nothing." Lyle stood up and walked around the table, making his way out of the room. Celes was sure he was telling the truth, but she had to investigate. She followed him back to the room with the Wizard Gate. He grabbed a lantern off the wall and ran it back to the kitchen to light it. He returned quickly, lighting the room.

"See over there?" Lyle pointed to the corner of the room. It was barely noticeable, but Celes did see a metal trapdoor.

"That's quite subtle." Celes walked over and investigated. It wasn't locked. As it swung open, she could see a ladder leading down. She couldn't see what was below.

"I'd appreciate it if you..." Celes turned and addressed Lyle but she was cut off. He roughly shoved her, and she stumbled into the hole. She managed to grab one of the ladder rungs with one hand and quickly steadied herself with the other hand. She reached up to climb and saw the trapdoor closing above her. She kept climbing and shoved the trapdoor as hard as she could.

You idiot, how could you let him do that.

Celes banged the trapdoor.

"Don't be foolish, let me out this instant!" Celes kept banging. After a few moments, she paused and listened.

"I'm sorry. I had to promise him."

"Who?"

"He called himself Darvin. Said I had to hold any who came through the gate. It was the only way to save myself."

"He won't know! Just let me out!"

"I'm sorry, I can't take that chance. I really wish it didn't have to be this way." Celes heard something sliding into place. She banged against the trapdoor again and it still wouldn't budge.

I can't believe this just happened. Think, Celes, think.

Celes took a deep breath and climbed down the ladder. It was pitch-black, and she could see nothing.

He hid his intentions well, and I walked right into it. But I know he wasn't lying about this room. I know for sure. Maybe, just maybe, Aydan found a way out of here that Lyle never did.

Celes didn't have a choice. Or anything else to do. So, she stepped onto the ground and felt around for a wall. She found it easily, solid stone. With a little effort, she found she could reach the ceiling as well.

Time to start the search.

Celes felt her way along the wall, taking care to press the entire surface and feel for anything different. So far, nothing. Just more of the same stone. After a while, she kicked something solid and swore. Regaining her composure, she bent down and felt around. The object felt like a chest. It was definitely closed. She found the latch and opened the chest.

Please don't regret this.

She stuck her hand into the chest slowly, feeling around. It seemed empty. She did find what seemed like a scrap of cloth in one corner.

Nothing. Keep going.

Celes stood and navigated her way around the chest, continuing her search. She came across two more chests in the same fashion. And again, after a careful probe each was empty. One had a scrap of paper, but she had no way of looking at it.

So far, you've verified Lyle's story about the contents of this room. Now assuming the wizard could go invisible, he may have just given Lyle the slip. However, he had knowledge of this place. Maybe he knew of something that Lyle didn't. A secret passage created by the original wizard. You have to keep looking.

Celes pressed on, following the rest of the walls. Eventually, she had traversed the whole room and found nothing. She sank down and sighed.

Nothing on the walls. Maybe this is a fool's errand.

Celes suddenly had an idea.

The floor!

She started to crawl along, feeling around with her hands. The stone felt the same as the walls, albeit a bit more worn down. She kept exploring, keeping up the disciplined search. She couldn't afford to miss anything. Systematically she scoured the room, working her way along the floor. Finally, she noticed something. It felt like a depression in the floor. Small and circular. She tried pressing it with her hand, but nothing happened. As much as she felt around it there didn't seem to be any switches or toggles. But it did remind her of something.

The wizard medallion.

It was a long shot, but she had nothing to lose. Celes grabbed the medallion from her clothing and pressed it into the floor. She heard a strange hum and a click, then something moved. Celes scrambled back, trying to see what was happening. A rumbling sound continued, then eased off. Surveying the room, Celes couldn't see anything different. She carefully approached the area and probed with her hands. Something was there. A set of stairs going down. She carefully negotiated her way down backwards, letting her feet find the next step while she clung to the stairs. It was quite a way down. Once she reached the room her feet stepped onto a metal plate of some kind. It made a clunking sound then the stairs started to move. Celes jerked back and found a wall to lean on.

I did it! And now the way is closed. I'm safe, for now. If you can call alone in a pitch-black tunnel safe.

Celes laughed softly and started to make her way.

36

REVELATION

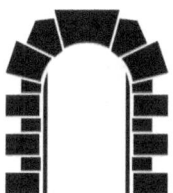

The chest burst open with light, disorientating Alrion. When he regained his senses, he was in a library. Sitting at a desk, scribbling away, was Granthion.

This is just like that dream I had.

Alrion walked up to his grandfather.

"Hello," he said hesitantly. Granthion motioned for Alrion to sit but didn't look over. Alrion pulled up a wooden chair and sat, leaning on the heavy table. After a few moments, Granthion looked up.

"Ah, you're back. Good to see you."

"I suppose I passed that? I'm worthy of the knowledge?"

"I'm not here to judge you." Granthion leaned back and chuckled. "You see I..." he began to speak again but Alrion cut him off.

"Yes, I know. You're a part of my mind, generated as a representation to help personalise this information I have inside me."

"Good, you're a quick study. Well, maybe not quick, more that you seem to retain knowledge well."

"I can see why my father found you difficult."

"Oh yes. He found it testing, and well it wasn't easy for me too. But he'll never truly understand that. Just think..." Granthion trailed off. He seemed to be waiting for a prompt.

"Just think?"

"I was going to say something, but I can't tell you yet. Not my fault." Granthion looked at Alrion disapprovingly. Alrion sighed.

"Of course. Can I at least see the spell now?" Granthion tapped the spellbook and it slid across the table. Alrion stopped it with his hand and started reading.

"Curing the Blight," he read out loud. This time the rest of the text was readable. With his heart pounding, he read on.

That's hardly a revelation. More basic information.

Alrion looked up. Granthion was sitting patiently, waiting.

"This is pretty basic so far. Why was this information held back?"

"I'm not sure. Maybe you weren't ready for even that? Maybe there are subtle hints within the background information that are too crucial to expose?" Granthion shrugged. Alrion turned back to the tome. He kept reading.

Here we go. Some juicy details.

He read about the location. It was described in detail, although he couldn't make sense of the directions. But the directions did start with Valrytir.

"Good, it is near Valrytir." Alrion looked over but Granthion didn't respond in any way. He turned back to reading. There was a section about how the Soul Power needed to flow through to the Source of the Blight. That made sense. More details that weren't particularly exciting. He knew there was something more to this, separate to all these incidental details. Suddenly, he spotted it. Alrion reeled back, almost falling from his chair.

"No. No, this can't be. Why would you do this?" Alrion stood, pointing at Granthion. The wizard looked saddened.

"I'm sorry, I don't make the rules."

"That's not fair. Why should it be like that?"

"There is a balance to all things. Do you believe the power of the Light is all-consuming and all-powerful?"

"Yes."

"It's not. Your will and purpose propel it forward. But it does not make you untouchable."

"I'm not asking to be untouchable."

"It sure sounds like you are. You want to withdraw the power of the Blight from the world, stuff it back where it came from, and suffer no consequences?"

"Yes. Isn't this journey sacrifice enough?"

"No, far from it. The journey you are on is a privilege. The opportunity you have is a privilege. The cost is fair."

"My life? That's not fair. Not after everything." Alrion sunk back down into the chair. Now he understood why he had been kept in the dark. He understood why he had been shown that vision of Granthion touching the wall of darkness. It wasn't about his family history, it was a preview of what Alrion would be dealing with. A sign of the true nature of his quest, and what it would require. Alrion slammed his fist down on the table, the spellbook closing in response.

"That's a normal response, I suppose," Granthion said. He looked sympathetic, but also slightly detached.

"Is this what you were like?"

"I can only assume so since my knowledge and memories have been contributed to the Pool."

"Don't you care?"

"Very much so. In fact, you could say I cared too much. Why else would I sacrifice myself to save my son with an incomplete spell?"

"You knew it would kill you?"

"Of course. Even though it wasn't the proper spell, more a cheat, the principles were the same. The reversal of so much Blight, it has to go somewhere. Better death than the alternative. You've seen it." Granthion gave Alrion a serious look and he felt chills. He remembered the process happening within him, he could vividly recall what it had done to Branthor and Alyx.

"So, I'm to just push forward and give myself up?"

"No, don't give yourself up. Give of yourself. It's a winning trade. One life for thousands. You'll do more good than anyone who ever lived. You'll set things right."

"But I'm so young. Why me?"

"You were looking for a purpose, were you not? Unsatisfied with your life. And here you are, with the most important and fulfilling purpose of us all. Is that not enough?"

"I just need time. And you're far too logical and reasonable. That's not fair either."

"True. But I'm also not real. I'm just an image in your mind, taking the form and manner of a great wizard and drawing upon the knowledge of those smarter and wiser than us all." Granthion grinned and Alrion shook his head. It was too much, and while a small part of him thought it made sense, but he couldn't let himself go.

"I can't deal with this now. I just need to move forward and see what my options are."

"Charging ahead and hoping for a different outcome? That's definitely going to work." Granthion stood and turned, examining the bookshelf that was behind him. Alrion stood and wandered over, curious.

"Is there anything useful over here?"

"Oh no, nothing. I was just waiting around for you to leave."

"Great. You've been a great help." Alrion turned to go, but a hand held him back. Granthion stared into his eyes.

"Don't forget, you're not alone in this." The intensity in Granthion's stare was unnerving and Alrion pulled away. He took a few steps away from the scene before he stumbled into another pool of light.

Alrion opened his eyes, seeing the dark chamber slowly rise around him. He was still floating on the water, but no voices could be heard, just silence. He started to speak, but it felt wrong disturbing the stillness. With some effort, Alrion swam over to the edge and dragged himself out. His limbs felt loose and useless. With great difficulty, he managed to dry off and dress himself. He all but stumbled out of the chamber. Caleb rushed over, concern all over his face.

"You were gone a long time. You should not have risen without help. Your limbs will be sluggish and limp. You could have drowned!"

"Nope, a different fate awaits me." Alrion let the scholar help support him. They walked slowly back, with no further words exchanged, to the room where Falric was working. The master wizard noticed them come in but didn't look up, he kept working. Only once Alrion was seated did Falric address him.

"You look like a man who has seen a ghost."

"I have, in a fashion."

"Did you get the answers you were looking for?"

"Yes, but not what I was looking for," Alrion said bitterly. Lara rushed in.

"What did I miss?"

"I have learned the location of the source of the Blight, and also what must be done."

"That's great. Isn't it?" Lara said, trailing off. She looked between Alrion and Falric.

"There is a price involved. My life." Alrion directed his attention at Lara. She gasped and looked concerned. She pulled over a chair and sat near him.

"Surely that's just one possibility."

"You tell her." Alrion looked to Falric.

"Whilst we shouldn't discount the idea, the facts don't look good." Falric shook his head slowly.

"What do you mean? What are we talking about here?" Lara said with alarm.

"Alrion will interact with the source of the Blight. And in order to strip it from the entire world, he must be the conduit for it. The entire power of the Blight will flow through Alrion back to the source."

"Which will destroy my body, and likely my soul, in the process. Great, huh?"

"We don't know that for sure."

"Look at what happened to my grandfather. If he couldn't avoid it curing a country, how can I avoid it curing the entire world?"

"That's still not a foregone conclusion. You're different from your grandfather!"

"I appreciate your optimism, and I won't discount it." Alrion sighed. "But we need to accept the fact that this quest will likely destroy me if I succeed." Alrion watched Lara's face. She looked from Falric to Caleb, and neither gave her any reassurance.

"There's always a way. No need to be glum about it." Lara beamed a smile around at them all and got none in return.

"Let's focus on what we can do. You said you knew the location of the source of the Blight? Can you describe where it is?"

"Hmm, it was described to me, but I don't know the area well. But I suspect I could point it out on a map. Do you have one?" Alrion said to Caleb.

"Oh no, sorry. Valrytir are very precious about their maps. Detailed maps are kept close to their chest. Perhaps for reasons such as this. At any rate, we only have very high-level charts showing different regions and major routes into the country."

"I have one." Lara rummaged through her jacket and retrieved a neatly folded thick piece of paper. She unfolded it onto the desk in front of them. Caleb walked over and investigated it.

"This is amazing. Where did you get it?"

"I have my sources." Lara winked at Caleb and guided the map closer to Alrion. "Do you think you could point out the location?"

"Let me see." Alrion absorbed the details of the map, looking at the different roads and landmarks. Without realising he started to move his hand to the right spot. He hesitated.

"Is this a bad idea showing everyone?" he said to Falric.

"That's a good question. I believe those in this room can know, but I wouldn't show others. The fewer people who know, the better."

"You already know anyway." Alrion let his hand navigate the map, pointing to a spot. Lara gasped.

"I know where that is. It's not far from the city at all!"

"That's a bit unnerving, but there we go. I think the best course of action is to start our journey."

"How do you intend on getting there?"

"Are you offering your assistance?" Lara said.

"No, no. I've done my share of adventure and performed rather dismally. I was going to suggest the Wizard Gates."

"Go on."

"There's a special gate combination that gets you close to Valrytir. Not many know of it."

"And it's nearby?" Alrion said.

"Yes, it's in a tower not far from here."

"We came back through that one." Lara looked puzzled.

"Indeed, one thing to remember is that Wizard Gates aren't necessarily the same in both directions. Sometimes you cannot travel back to where you came from."

"I see. Is there anything else we should know? There's been one occasion where I was unable to activate the gate again."

"That sounds like a restriction of some kind. Quite rare, but then again, we don't have all the answers. I was going to say that the passage of time is inconsistent within the gate. You will not travel instantaneously."

"What do you mean?" Lara said.

"It will feel like only a few moments between when you stepped into the gate, and when you arrive. But it's longer than that. Each gate is different, and the areas you travel to make a difference. At any rate, I just wanted to alert you."

"It's not the same as actually walking, is it?" Alrion didn't feel like these gates were all that reliable. No wonder he hadn't heard about them prior.

"Oh of course not. But you might lose a day in some cases. Just something to keep in mind."

"Thanks. And that combination you mentioned?"

"Take the desert option." Falric looked at Alrion. "Then you'll need to search out the next gate. Are you confident enough to do that?"

"I have managed before."

"Good, I assumed so because you managed to find and use a gate already." Falric stood and walked over to Alrion. He leaned back against the desk and took Alrion's hands in his own.

"Lad, this is too much for one person to bear. But I cannot help you with this. As far as the spell goes you are on your own. I can't say exactly what will happen, but you need to be prepared for the worst. Otherwise..." Falric looked away.

"Otherwise what?"

"Otherwise the worst will happen. Alrion will fail, and he will be consumed by the Blight. Transformed into something terrible." Falric sighed, and his hands trembled.

"There can be no hesitation. No doubts. Travel now, yes. But don't rush in before you are ready. There's only one chance, and the consequences are dire."

"Great pep talk." Lara shook her head.

"Listen, I know that I've failed you. I haven't been the support you've needed, you've had to go elsewhere. But it's made you stronger, and you have people to watch over you. You can do this, but don't walk in there if you have doubts. It's better not to. We can make do, there are other options." Falric rose and stepped over to join Caleb.

"This is goodbye then," Alrion said, a little more stiffly than he intended. He stood with some effort and ambled over to Falric, hugging the wizard and almost toppling him over. He did the same with Caleb.

"It's been an honour to serve you. We will await your return. I know you'll find a way." Caleb smiled and bowed.

"Well, that's one of us." Alrion turned and left the room, Lara by his side.

37

THE FELLOWSHIP REBUILDS

A lyx adjusted her uniform again.

I can't believe I'm wearing this.

She had avoided it as long as possible, but there were no excuses left. If she wanted to join, she had to look the part. The black and brown did help her blend in, and the padding and design were good for fighting in. The armoured plates were more of a hindrance than anything else, but she could use them as required too. Mary walked into the room, looking Alyx up and down.

"Good, it was about time. I was beginning to think you had forgotten how to get dressed."

"I did." Alyx laughed but Mary did not. She did almost smile though.

"You certainly didn't forget how to fight. So, have you considered when you are going to talk to the commander about your request?"

"Soon, but not yet. I want to time it just before the wizard gets here."

"You might want to do it sooner rather than later."

"Why?"

"Go talk to the scouts." Mary waved and left the room.

She couldn't tell me herself, could she? Probably still hurting from losing the unfair duel.

Alyx left the room promptly, striding down the corridor quickly. Thankfully, they hadn't given her any active duties, just the usual training. She hadn't been assigned to a squad either.

Maybe she is protecting me?

It was all odd, but Alyx didn't want to question too hard when it suited her just fine. The scout's office was at the front of the building. It had two rooms, one of which was more a reception area, and a back room. That's where all the scout reports were filed and compared. A small group pored over all the reports and tried to draw out larger trends or things of interest.

Alyx entered the reception area and nodded slightly to the staff manning the desk. The two men saluted and went back to their duties. She continued to the back room, marvelling at the rapid pace of activity.

They do never stop.

At the back of the room, she spotted Baker.

He'll be my best bet.

Alyx weaved through the many desks and scouts rushing around. Nobody paid her any attention, which was how she liked it. Baker was running his hands through his thinning hair, reading some paperwork.

"Baker, it's been a while." Alyx stopped right in front of his desk and waited. He continued reading.

"Nice to see you, Alyx. I heard all about your big return. Sweet of you to pay us a visit."

"How are things back here? Busy as usual?"

"Probably busier. Is that why you're here?"

"I can't be here just to see you?"

"You never did before, so why start now?" Baker's eyes were still on the paperwork. But Alyx could tell she had his full attention.

"Always quick off the mark, I'll give you that. Mary said that your team had something significant."

"Oh, I wouldn't say that, not yet. But it's building towards such a statement." Baker put down the papers and looked at Alyx for the first time. His blue eyes looked tired.

"Tell me a story." Alyx walked around and moved the stack of paperwork in the chair next to Baker, placing them on an empty space on his desk. She eased herself down into the chair and made herself comfortable.

"You aren't going until you get what you want, are you?"

"Of course not." Alyx smiled.

"As you wish, I needed a break anyway."

"What's the big news? In a single sentence."

"The Blight are massing," Baker whispered. He rummaged through his papers and seized a thick wad. He unfolded it, showing Alyx a map of Valrytir. There were tiny markings all over it.

"See, each mark is a sighting of Blight activity. It's never been this busy. But they're being smart too. We're not seeing huge masses of Blighters. But when you add them all up, there's a massive force building. And it's getting bigger every day." Baker leaned back, looking conspiratorial.

"They're planning something."

"I can see that. It's not unexpected, but I had hoped we had more time." Alyx could see Baker's eyes light up. He was hungry for more information.

"Sorry, I can't add anything right now. You'll find out soon enough. But I think it's time I talked to the commander. Have you briefed him on this?"

"Of course!" Baker jerked and nearly fell out of his chair. "As per usual he said to sit on it. Nothing to do until they start mobilising and we have cause to expect an attack."

"Oh, I don't expect you'll see an attack. More of a defence." Alyx smiled. She enjoyed watching Baker trying to piece things together.

"Now that's an interesting scenario. I can look again with that in mind. Reinforcement to protect some sort of goal." Baker started digging through his papers again.

"Before I go, where can I find the commander?"

"This time of day? He's taking a walk in the gardens. Best time to catch him."

"Excellent. I think I'll do just that." Alyx waved but Baker didn't notice. He was buried in paperwork once more.

I wonder if he'll turn up anything else.

Alyx's stomach started to churn. She wasn't afraid of the commander, far from it. But knowing what she had done would make it a difficult and awkward conversation. And she needed to ask him for something too. But there was no choice. She had to press on.

Willing to die by the sword, but hesitant to talk to a superior officer. Doesn't make sense.

Alyx dismissed the thought and charged through the hallways, heading towards the garden. She needed to not dwell on such thoughts and get to it. The sooner she confront the commander, the better.

There were more and more soldiers out in the gardens training. More than when she had taken advantage. It was a good sign, but surprising. Alyx stopped and looked over the scene. If she was the commander, she'd focus on the secluded patch near the back. It would be the best place for a quiet interlude before going back to the heavy burden of leadership.

As she wound her way through the gardens Alyx saw fewer and fewer soldiers and recruits until she found the garden she sought. It was leafier than she remembered, the tall trees bigger and more plants were in between. The whole area felt cooler and more at peace. She naturally slowed her pace and tried to enjoy the walk. There was no point wasting such a nice spot, and she figured that the commander would get quite annoyed if she burst in and destroyed the sense of calm.

She found him seated on a stone bench in the middle of the garden. Small hedges were to each side of him, and he leaned back, looking into the distance. He looked exactly the same as she remembered, the short-cropped grey hair and the tidy moustache. His eyes were hard, the brown irises looking like volcanic rocks. His uniform was almost the same as hers, save for a few decorative elements on his shoulder. He had pioneered this style of uniform and armour and led by example. It gave him more credibility amongst the troops.

"Commander Brady." Alyx gave him a small bow and stood ready.

"Alyx. So, the rumours are true, you have returned. And you're in uniform. This is a surprise."

"It's been a turbulent time. I hope you've been well."

"A turbulent time indeed. Yes, I've been as well as can be expected. Luckily, there's been nothing out of the ordinary to test us. Until recently."

"You mean the new massing of Blighters?"

"You heard about that? News travels far too quickly." Brady shook his head softly.

"I don't think it's travelled that far, but I do still have my contacts."

"Of course you do. I won't dredge up the past, but I just want to ask. Was it worth it?"

"Yes. But the cost may have been too high."

"I expected as much. Don't worry, I'm not as sentimental as Mary. I knew you'd leave suddenly one day, though the situation did surprise me." Brady paused for a moment, collecting his thoughts. "I could see that you wouldn't stay with us above your personal mission. Though I had hoped you would come back." Brady looked her directly in the eyes.

"Are you really back?"

"Honestly, sir, I don't know. I have a job to do, and after that..."

"Tell me about this job. Is it as extreme as your last one?"

"Possibly. I'm assisting a wizard, who will be here soon."

"For what purpose?" Brady shifted his posture, leaning forward.

"To cure the Blight." Brady let out a barking laugh.

"That's preposterous. You've been taken in on another suicide mission."

"No, it's not like that. I've seen him do it. I've seen him clear the Blight from people. He even saved me." Alyx watched Brady's reaction. He was hard to read, but she could tell he was shocked. He knew Alyx didn't lie.

"This is rather sensational news."

"It's why the Blight are massing. They know he will be coming, and they are preparing their defences. We'll need to meet them head-on, to bear the brunt of the attack so that the wizard can make it to the source of the Blight."

"Stop right there." Brady held out his hand and spoke with annoyance. "I will not commit any of my men or women on such a fool's errand. It was flights of fancy like this that created the generals of the Blight. I will not sacrifice my personnel on another disastrous venture." Brady stood abruptly.

"I know you've been through a lot, but I expected more from you."

"You'll see that I'm right. I'm only here to prepare you." Alyx met his gaze without faltering.

"Is this uniform a joke to you?"

"No, although, right now, it's a means to an end."

"So be it." Brady started to walk away but stopped before he passed her. He turned and addressed her.

"Is this because of what happened to that young man? Do you feel responsible?"

"I am responsible. But this is not because of that."

"You are on the bench. Let Mary know when you're available for active duty." Brady stiffened his back and marched off. Alyx watched him go wordlessly. Once he turned the corner, she let herself relax. She let out a deep sigh.

Still not good with people. And I didn't communicate the situation that well.

Alyx started to walk back. It wasn't the time to beat herself up. She had achieved her aim, planting the seed with the commander. He was quite astute and would start to put things together. Hopefully, when Alrion and Lara arrived he'd be more inclined to support them.

Alyx wandered back through the gardens, ignoring the soldiers training. She didn't want to spot anyone that she'd have to stop and talk to. She just wanted to walk and let her mind wander. As she reached the street, she stopped suddenly.

Who is that?

She spotted a monk walking around. He stuck out like a sore

thumb, but it seemed like he was looking for something. Unsuccessfully.

What an oddity.

Alyx dismissed the thought and kept walking. But within moments the monk ran up to her.

"Excuse me," he said.

"Yes?" Alyx said. The monk had a worldliness about him that suggested he hadn't been just confined to a temple or monastery. And he was on alert and active, like a soldier. She could feel his presence. Relaxed, but ready to pounce at a moment's notice.

"Where did you get that sword?" The monk pointed at the blade. Sheathed at her waist, the diamond on the pommel was quite prominent.

"A friend of mine let me borrow it. Why?"

"A wizard?" the monk said.

"Maybe."

"That's Alrion's sword, I was there when his father presented it to him. Is he well? Is he with you?"

"That's correct. How do you know him?"

"I'm Certan. I'm the monk that travelled with Alrion and guided him to our temple." Certan held out his hand. "And you are?"

"Alyx." She shook his hand, noting his strength. "I met Alrion after that, and we travelled together for a while. He gave me his sword for a time. I do remember him mentioning a monk, it's good to meet you."

"This is quite fortuitous. I came here to find Alrion, but I have no idea where he is. Is he here?"

"Not yet, although he's on his way. Did you arrange to meet him here?"

"No, the elders directed me here. They said he needed my help at Valrytir. I've journeyed quite a way to be here."

"Interesting. That's why I'm here as well. Do you drink? No?" Alyx was surprised by Certan's strong reaction. He shook his head and looked annoyed.

"No matter, let's go for a walk. We can share a few stories."

"Don't leave me out," a voice said from behind. Alyx whirled quickly to see who it was.

No way.

Vincent stood there on the street, smiling. He was dressed in a travelling cloak and had the companion Runesteel sword strapped on his back.

"I think we all have a lot to discuss. Alyx, I'm delighted to have you restored back to full health." Vincent winked. "And I'm glad that you two have met. It's good to have you both here." Vincent started to approach, Alyx still shocked at seeing him.

38

REFORGING THE LEGEND

"How did you get here?" Alyx said. Vincent gave her a mysterious smile.

"I should ask you the same question, I'm sure you've had quite the journey. Weren't you with Alrion? That's his sword."

"I was. Alrion gave me this temporarily to use. We were with Branthor for a time as well, as crazy as that sounds." Alyx noticed Vincent's features change, a look of concern crossing them.

"He was completely focused on destroying Rindale. He finally succeeded but at the cost of his life."

"I'm sorry to hear that. Let's go somewhere we can talk. You too, Certan." Vincent started walking away and gestured for them to follow. Alyx looked at Certan, who shrugged and started following. Vincent led them through the city into the trades district. They passed several blacksmith workshops before he stopped in front of one.

"Balzar's Blades. This place is an institution," Vincent said.

"I know this place, it's impossible to get a weapon from here." Alyx wasn't joking either. This blacksmith was for the elite of the elite.

"I go way back with the owner. Follow me." Vincent entered the shop, Alyx and Certan keeping close. The shopfront was lavishly decorated. Gleaming weaponry of all types hung on the walls. The main floor was clear save for a nicely finished wood underfoot and a counter down the end for the staff to use. Vincent waved, and they waved back. He stopped midway down the room, opening a door and ushering them through. They entered a plain room with some benches and notebooks.

"This is just a planning room, it's not being used right now. Take a seat." Vincent pointed to a bench with a few stools around it in the far corner. He waited until Alyx and Certan were seated, then he eased down into a stool.

"I have something to discuss, but first let's hear your updates. Certan?"

"Well, after you all left, I stayed to help rebuild the temple and heal those who could be saved. A surprising number recovered fully, although we lost so many."

"I'm sorry for the loss, the bravery of your order was astonishing. And I'm sorry I couldn't get there sooner."

"You did what you could. I was content with doing the hard work, trying to build myself a place there, but the elders had other ideas." Certan chuckled softly to himself, shaking his head.

"They asked you to leave?" Alyx said.

"In a fashion. They said that I had unfinished business. I was to complete the trial within the Vault of Silence then travel to Valrytir to support Alrion in completing his quest."

"Congratulations!" Vincent stood up and offered Certan his hand. They shook firmly.

"Can you fill me in?" Alyx said.

"It's a special trial designed to test a person's Will. It is the pinnacle of achievement for a monk and designates mastery over one's self and the world."

"Alrion completed the trial as well," Vincent added.

"I see. Can outsiders be admitted?" Alyx was very interested in this trial. She had heard stories of how the monks could fight, and what they could do. Things that would be incredibly useful for her to know.

"I suppose, yes, that is how I was first introduced. But you'd have to undergo the full training. I'm not sure if they accept students who don't plan to stay with the monks."

"Perhaps I'll travel after all this is done and see for myself."

"I'd be delighted to take you." Certan bowed.

"We're very lucky to have you joining us. Alrion is going to need all the help he can get," Vincent said.

"I can't agree more. The forces that the Blight are massing here in Valrytir, it's unheard of." Alyx noticed that she had Vincent's undivided attention.

"What did you say?"

"The scouts have been tracking Blight sightings. They are massing within Valrytir. They're sticking to smaller groups, but we've picked up on what they are doing. I'm not sure we've ever faced a force this big."

"Perhaps the elders had some insights," Certan mused.

"We're all here for a reason, we each have a role to play. Alrion can't face that alone." Vincent looked determined.

"The three of us are a good start. We're worth far more than our number," Certan said.

"I couldn't agree more. I think I have a way to improve our odds too." Vincent rose and took a few steps towards another door. "Come and see."

"I'm intrigued." Alyx stood and followed along, waiting for Certan to catch up. Vincent led them through to another room. It was an active workshop. At the far end of the room, blacksmiths were hammering or working metal in different stages of completion.

"I'll never get tired of that sound. It's so welcoming," Vincent said. An older man was overseeing the work, thick glasses sitting atop his grey hair. He was well-built and looked strong despite his age. He noticed their presence and approached quickly.

"Vincent! When I received your letter, I couldn't believe it. But here you are, in the flesh." The man encircled Vincent in a huge hug.

Vincent returned the gesture. They parted, and the man slapped Vincent hard on the back.

"Who do you have with you?"

"This is Certan. He's a monk from the order of a thousand eyes. He travelled all the way here from the desert." The man nodded.

"This is Alyx. She is a weapons master that made a name for herself here, before going on to taking down the Skull King single-handedly."

"Oh," the man said, his eyes alive with interest.

"This here is Balzar himself. We worked together many years ago." Vincent and Balzar exchanged a smile. Balzar started to shake his head.

"This one couldn't stay put! Just when he was starting to get good, he ran out on me!"

"Sorry, I was young and impulsive."

"Oh, you think you've changed now. Has he?" Balzar laughed.

"Not that I've seen," Alyx joked. Certan refrained from saying anything. Balzar let out a few additional peals of laughter then composed himself.

"Right, well, Vincent, I was able to satisfy your request. Come with me," Balzar started off, weaving through the various work-benches. He brought them to a heavily fortified metal door. He produced a key and unlocked it, heaving the door open. Alyx marvelled at the size of it, the door was as thick as a man. Balzar charged ahead, stopping midway through the room.

Alyx stopped dead still. Everywhere she looked hung legendary weapons. Ones she had heard about as a child, or when she was training. The Foe Lance, the Sparkling Blade, and even the Haunted Hammer.

"What is this place?"

"This is my collection of legendary weapons. A few of them I had the privilege of making myself, but the vast majority I've sourced from across the land. Vincent here asked about a particular item. I thought it was lost, but once I made enquiries it wasn't as difficult as I imagined." Balzar waited patiently and Alyx approached, curious. As she reached the table, she let out a gasp. It was a giant sword, broken into three pieces.

"This is..."

"The sword that slew the Skull King. The sword passed down by your family."

"Andrylir," Alyx said with reverence. "Why are you showing me this?"

"I asked Balzar to retrieve it for a purpose. I'm going to reforge it." Vincent looked Alyx directly in the eyes. She could see the fire and passion in his look. She felt overwhelmed.

"Is that even possible? It was enchanted."

"I won't be able to restore the power it used to have, but I don't think that it's appropriate anymore. You need a weapon you can use, correct?"

"Yes." Alyx reached out and glided her hand along one of the pieces. The feel of the metal was familiar, reassuring. It was like a part of her. She had carried it her entire life. She remembered suddenly what it had been like, and the emptiness became apparent.

"I need this," she whispered.

"You will have it, I swear."

"Is there anything I can do to help?" Certan said.

"No, not with this. I will consult with Balzar and do the work myself."

"I will then focus myself on helping Alyx with her task."

"Just let me know when you would like to start, Vincent. I'll reserve whatever equipment you require," Balzar said.

"Later today, I have something else to finish first."

"As you wish. I look forward to working with you again." Balzar smiled and directed them out of the vault. After they had all left, he locked the door once more. He was called by a member of his staff and quickly left to address the issue.

"What task is on your list?" Alyx said. She wasn't just keen for him to start, she was curious about what Vincent had planned.

"I need to get the armed forces mobilised for when Alrion arrives.

With all that talk of the Blight massing, we're going to need a few extra hands."

"I've already done that. Why do you think I'm in uniform?"

"Don't worry, I think together we can crack this. Who did you speak with?"

"Brady, commander of the special elite unit. He was quite dismissive."

"Take us there again. Please." Vincent looked determined.

"Sure." Alyx started off leading them back.

They arrived back at the building quickly. Alyx knew that Brady would no longer be wandering the gardens.

"Let's try his office, I'll show you the way." Alyx entered the building, weaving her way through the corridors.

"This is much bigger than I expected. How many are in this special elite unit?" Certan said.

"I think the name is a bit misleading. Although the soldiers here are specially trained, it's more a distinction from the main forces. There are a few thousand in total, although not all are stationed here at once."

"Still, very impressive. And this commander is the one in charge of them all? What about the main army?"

"Yes, he's the leader. The general runs the entirety of the armed forces, general and special unit, but Brady has a lot of influence. We need his support first."

"Then let's get it." Certan smiled. Alyx sighed.

I was just with him before, he won't change his mind so easily.

Before long they were outside the office. The door was closed.

"Here we are. He's probably busy, are you still keen?" Alyx said.

"Absolutely." Vincent opened the door and strode in. Brady was sitting at his oversized desk, deep in conversation with a man not in military uniform. Brady looked up, annoyance on his face and his moustache skewed on an angle. Just as he was about to speak his expression changed to complete surprise.

"Vincent?" Brady said. He rose immediately.

"It's been a long time, a lifetime. I'm surprised you still recognise me." Vincent laughed. Brady looked to his guest.

"I'm sorry, Marlin, let's finish this off tomorrow. Same time?"

"Of course." Marlin nodded to Brady, acknowledged the rest of them and quickly left the room.

How does Vincent know Brady? He never said anything about being a soldier.

"We always wondered what happened to you." Brady looked to Alyx and Certan.

"How do you know Alyx? And is that a monk?"

"We ran into Alyx at an opportune time, while surrounded by Blighters. She's been an invaluable ally on our travels. Certan, likewise, has proven himself an able fighter and reliable companion." Vincent took a seat, and Brady sat down as well. Alyx and Certan stood at the back of the room.

"I'm a family man now. Busy blacksmithing, before I made this trip. I'm helping my son out."

"I thought you were against making weapons." Brady pointed to the Runesteel blade.

"An exception had to be made. I crafted only a few for people that I trust. Alyx is currently wielding the one I made for my son, Alrion."

"Alrion, nice name. He must be grown up by now. Where is he?"

"He's on his way here, but I'm not sure when he'll arrive. I wanted to see you before then, on official business."

"Official business?" Brady looked at Vincent with suspicion. "Does your son want to be a soldier?"

"I doubt it, although he's keen on learning how to wield a sword properly. Alyx has been extremely helpful in that regard. No, I want to talk to you about your assistance in tackling the Blight." Vincent's expression lost the smile and became quite stern. Alyx watched Brady shift his focus from Vincent to her.

"Is that what this is about? Alyx has already talked to me." Brady leaned back in his chair, unimpressed.

"My son is a wizard, Brady. This is real."

"What?"

"Yes, my father was Granthion."

"Hang on, really?" Brady looked completely thrown.

"You never told him?" Alyx said incredulously.

"It's not something I advertised, I was trying to live my own life. But, as it turns out, you can't get away from your past."

"This story about the Blight is true? Your son is a wizard who can cure the Blight?"

"Yes, I've witnessed it myself. So has Alyx."

"It's true. Did you hear the reports of the Skull Queen?"

"Of course. We were preparing ourselves in case we were targeted. Some were discussing options for going after her. Suddenly though, she disappeared."

"That was me. They infected me and transformed me into that thing, as payback for what I had done."

"What? No, it can't be."

"The Skull Queen wielded a great sword. I destroyed the Skull King. It's not a coincidence. But Alrion cured me."

"It's fantastical, but it's true. Alyx has mentioned reports of the Blight massing. It's for one purpose. They know Alrion is coming and they mean to block his passage. This is our chance to end this cycle." Vincent spoke with real passion, and Alyx could see Brady starting to be swayed.

These two must have had some sort of bond back in the day.

"I trust you, Vincent, even though you abandoned us. It seems like that's a bit of a trend in this room." Brady glanced at Alyx. "But I can't promise you support without some proof. Have Alrion demonstrate his power to cure the Blight when he arrives, and I'll declare my forces and recommend that the general do the same."

"Thank you, that's all I can ask." Vincent started to rise, but Brady motioned for him to sit.

"You can't drop this on me and leave. Stay and let's catch up."

"Sure, that's only fair. I bet you have a lot of great stories to share." Vincent turned to Alyx.

"I'll come find you when it's ready. In the meantime, why don't you two go acquaint yourselves."

"Sure. Let's go, Certan." Alyx was about to say goodbye to Brady but he was fixated on Vincent already.

I can't believe that just happened.

Alyx walked out, trying to make sense of it all.

39

THE MAKING OF A WIZARD

T he boy entered the cave, the dark consuming him. He pushed forward, knowing each step intimately. Following the twisting of the path, the light behind him soon faded and he kindled his Spark, creating an orb of light and floated it ahead of him. Quietly, his steps resounded within the cave, and he observed the interesting formations on the walls.

There were multiple ridges and geometric constructions that looked unnatural. But at the same time, they didn't appear to be made by human hands or tools.

I'll have to ask him about that.

But the boy shook his head immediately. That would not do. He knew the answer he would get. None at all. He continued to progress through the cave, the depth of his exploration no longer causing concern. But deep within he could still remember the terror he had initially. There was something wrong about venturing that deep into the bowels of the earth.

In no time he had arrived. He could see his father standing and waiting. No matter what expression was on his face, the wizard always had fierce piercing eyes.

"You're late."

"Sorry." The boy knew not to use any excuses. They just made his father angrier.

"We've discussed this. Punctuality is paramount."

As is everything else.

"Have you selected a name?"

"Yes." This was actually a task he found interesting. He had pored through all the old tomes, looking at old names and the old language.

"And?"

"Aydan." He tried to say it with confidence, but it still felt strange. The wizard laughed.

"How poetic, *Lost One*. Is that how you really feel?"

"Yes. I'm kept away from everyone. I feel so alone. I don't understand." Aydan sighed.

"I've explained it to you countless times. I have powerful enemies, and they would do terrible things to you knowing you were a wizard. This is for the best, for both of us."

"Can't you just teach me to defend myself?"

"I can and will. But today I will teach you something much more important." The wizard closed his eyes. Aydan closed his eyes also, waiting. He felt something, like a prodding at him. But it wasn't a physical sensation. It was more like a magical nudge. The more the feeling continued, the more he tested it. Suddenly he understood, it felt like his Spark. But not, at the same time.

"Is that your Spark?" he said.

"Yes. Wizards can sense each other's power. Sometimes from great distances, if the wizard is particularly skilful. I was amplifying that sensation, hitting you over the head with it so you could feel it properly."

"I did. I couldn't tell it was you though. Only because we were here alone."

"That's true. But with practice, you could learn to recognise mine and distinguish it from others."

"That could be useful. For finding you."

"Yes, but that's not the purpose of what we are doing today." The wizard stepped forward.

"Today, I am going to teach you how to hide your Spark."

"Hide it?"

"Yes. You need to be completely invisible. Indistinguishable from a normal boy."

"Why is that important?"

"I cannot protect you all the time. If you are hidden in plain sight, then that is the best protection I can provide. It will deflect attention away from you. I expect great things of your potential, and if they even suspected what I think is possible..." The wizard looked away, staring out into the distance. He didn't even try to hide the concern on his face. He rarely showed it.

Maybe he's trying to worry me?

"My enemy will stop at nothing. They will never rest, never lay down their fight." The wizard stepped closer, putting a hand gingerly on his son's shoulder. Aydan almost jumped and looked up at his father.

"One day you will understand when you have a son of your own. But for now, you have to trust that I'm doing the right thing." The wizard cleared his throat and stepped away again, putting his hands behind his back.

"Now onto the lesson. I need you to focus and feel the Spark within you." He paused and watched Aydan closely.

"Good. Now, this is a visualisation exercise. It's remarkably simple, but as far as I can tell nobody else has achieved it. They never even thought it necessary. But this, this will save your life." The wizard waited until Aydan nodded then he continued.

"You need to take your Spark and wrap a metal box around it. A box so thick and heavy that the flame of your Spark doesn't even heat the box a tiny bit. A box so tight it suffocates the air from your fire. Imagine that you can touch the outside of the box and it feels completely cool." The wizard paced around the room, observing Aydan from different angles.

"More. Your Spark is a core of flame, but it is being stifled by the box. It's going back to a smouldering ember, waiting for ignition." The wizard poked Aydan in the back.

"Good. But you're trying too hard. It needs to be effortless, something you can slip on and off. You need to create a mental state of the box and, once placed, maintain it automatically."

Aydan let out a deep breath and bent over, panting.

"Was it working?" he said between breaths.

"Almost perfectly. You have a talent for this. But you need to go to the next level. You need to create a reality that supports this state. As you can see, it requires too much concentration. Do you know why?"

"Because I'm thinking about it so much?

"Yes, you're trying to actively maintain an abnormal state of being. Instead, you need to declare a new state of being and simply activate it. Do you see the difference?"

"Maybe." Aydan shifted his feet and looked at the ground. The wizard sighed and started pacing again. He stooped down and picked up a rock, striding over to Aydan. He opened the boy's hand and placed the rock onto his palm.

"Where is the rock?" the wizard said.

"It's on my hand."

"Close your eyes." The wizard watched Aydan comply. Then he added, "now, where is the rock?"

"It's still in my hand."

"How do you know?"

"Because I can feel it."

"And if I made you stand here for an hour until your arm and hand became numb. Would you still wonder where the rock was?" The wizard loomed over Aydan. He thought carefully before answering.

"No, because I had no reason to think it had moved. I could always just look if I wanted to confirm that."

"Good. Now, you know." The wizard stepped away and put his hands behind his back once again. Aydan closed his hand around the rock.

"I think I see what you're saying. I can create the change, like holding the rock then my mind will think it's still there until I change it. Or I can peek to double check."

"Close enough. That's your new instruction. You are to practice until it becomes second nature."

"For how long?" Aydan could feel his stomach starting to protest. Some of these magic lessons had gone on for entire days.

"As long as it takes. It's the best way to immerse yourself. The next time you leave this cave, I want to be confident that you'll have mastery over this. You must be invisible." The wizard locked his gaze onto Aydan's eyes, making him want to look away.

No, not this time. Aydan stared defiantly back.

"Fine, I can do this. But you need to explain why you're so paranoid. I've seen what you can do, you're a powerful wizard." The wizard stepped back and leaned against a nearby wall. The energy seemed to drain from him.

"Boy, I'm playing with things I should not be. Things that will change the world. I can't have that knowledge lost forever. I have a plan to ensure that it is not. But I also do not want to endanger you. I believe you will have a part to play in this too."

He's not concerned about me. He's more concerned about what I can do for him.

Aydan's cheeks felt hot. He flung the rock at the wizard as hard as he could. Instinctively he used force to propel the rock even faster.

"I'm not your tool." The rock stopped suddenly, inches from the wizard's face. The rock started to crumble, turning into dust. The wizard's face softened.

"Son, what I feel like I need to do is of paramount importance. And I'm hard on you, I know. But please, believe me, it is all for your own wellbeing. I could not live with you coming to harm above myself." The wizard smiled weakly, momentarily breaking up the bleak expression he always wore.

I have to trust him for now. Maybe after I master this, he will relax a bit. This can't go on forever.

Aydan returned to the lesson, stopping and starting the suppression of his Spark. He had to make the transition effortless, otherwise, he would never achieve the level of perfection his father demanded.

40

STARTLING DISCOVERY

C eles rushed down the tunnel as quickly as she could without stumbling. She kept a hand on the walls, making sure she was heading in the same direction and using it as a way to stay balanced.

Wherever this ends up, I'll be happy to be away from there.

She didn't blame the farmer, in that situation anyone would act the same. But it showed that the Blight was more advanced than anyone realised. They were proactively trying to gain the advantage and close off routes.

I hope Alrion finds a safe way in.

It made her quest for the mysterious wizard more important. If he truly was an ally, then they needed his help directly, rather than from the shadows. And if he was truly a danger, better that he be confronted and dealt with now before the end of the quest.

Alrion needs a way to do the spell safely.

Time became hard to judge as she pushed forward in the tunnel. She tried looking back once or twice but there was no sign of any pursuit and she didn't hear the tell-tale rumbling. Finally, she started to see glimmers of light in the distance.

I hope that's an exit.

Celes kept up the pace, spurred on by the possibility of escaping the tunnel. As she approached, she noticed what looked like a stone staircase leading up. She rushed ahead as fast as she could handle and surged up the stairs. As she ascended, she could see signs of a room up ahead. But she couldn't quite make out any details.

Celes reached the top of the stairs and stepped out into the room. It was all stone, with a single torch lit and hanging on the wall. There seemed to be old supplies in the room, going by the crates, sacks, and other storage she saw. There was a wooden door slightly open at one end. Celes walked towards it, carefully peeking through the door. Beyond was another room, organised like a storeroom. Or a library. There was a robed man reading a book at one end. Celes slipped through the door and assessed the situation.

This looks like a Wizard Store. Is that man a wizard? He must be.

"Hello," Celes said. The man looked up, surprise and alarm on his face. He closed the book immediately.

"Who are you? How did you get here?"

"I'm Celes. Is this a Wizard Store? In Valrytir?"

"Yes, it is. How did you get in?"

"Through an underground tunnel." Celes pointed to the back room she had entered through. The wizard looked puzzled.

"I've looked through there, it's a long tunnel with a dead end. There's no way out."

"That's good to know. But you should know that there's a way in!"

"How curious. I've never had anyone come through there. By the way, my name is Magnus, I'm the assigned wizard representative for Valrytir." Magnus bowed. "What business do you have here? Did you just stumble through? I'm quite curious what leads here."

"It's a house in Stonebridge, that used to be a wizard residence."

"Ah, yes I know the one."

"I entered the house via the Wizard Gate, and then discovered the underground tunnel. Quite fortuitously, it would seem, as the owner of the house had tried to lock me in."

"Really? For what reason?"

"Seems like he's been coerced by a representative of the Blight. He was to detain any who came through the Wizard Gate." Celes walked closer so she could converse from a more comfortable distance.

"How odd. I think I need to pay this man a visit."

"I think that's wise. But before then, perhaps you can help me."

"I will do what I can. After you describe how you used the Wizard Gate." Magnus gave her a stern look.

"Another wizard activated it for me. His name is Ashra."

"The desert wizard? He's still alive?"

"Very much so. He was quite helpful. I'm actually on the trail of a wizard."

"Go on." Magnus looked intrigued.

"He has the alias of Aydan, and the trail leads here. But it's an old one, probably twenty years old."

"You're looking for this wizard, but you're following a trail from twenty years ago?"

"Exactly. I'm trying to find out his real identity. I believe there's a clue hidden in the past." Celes looked at Magnus and gave a small shrug. He started to rub his chin, thinking.

"How odd. Well, I've been stationed here for at least twenty years. Chances are, I met him long ago. The name does not mean anything to me off the top of my head."

"Do you keep notes here in your ledger? He's appeared in other Wizard Store ledgers, so maybe there's some information here?" Celes hoped that Magnus would be helpful. This was the first time she'd encountered someone else in a Wizard Store that she didn't know.

"That's a fair request. Let me dig it out." Magnus walked into the corner and searched through a small cabinet. He withdrew a dusty book and placed it on a table for Celes to review.

She flicked through the pages, examining the contents.

"There's no entry logs?"

"No, since this store is usually occupied there was no need. There should be a notes section though."

"Let me see." Celes flipped through the book, sampling different sections to see what was there. She skipped a few that seemed to be inventories of things then discovered a note section. Not all the entries had a date, but enough did so she could figure out the chronology.

"Now we're close." Celes tapped a page dated just over twenty years ago. She started looking more carefully. It could be a mention of his name or something suspicious that would trigger her interest. And there it was.

"He was here. The wizard at the time recorded where he was staying, The Innhospitable Inn."

"That place is an institution, I can't believe it's still standing. It's near here if you'd like to investigate."

"I may as well." Celes closed the book.

"Aydan, you say? I'll keep an eye out for any references."

"Thanks, Magnus, that's a great help." Celes headed for the main door.

"Good luck," Magnus called out. Celes waved and left.

She found herself on a main street, almost knocked over by a rushing pedestrian. Looking back at the Wizard Store, it was almost invisible. The building was run-down and blended in with the scenery completely. She studied it and the surrounding buildings well just to make sure she could find it again.

Off we go.

It didn't take long to find the Inn. It was a large establishment with the named painted on the wooden exterior and had lots of people milling around outside. Celes navigated her way inside and was surprised to see it was nicely decorated. In an older style, but well-done. Tasteful furniture and clean floors. She made her way over to the bar and looked at the bartender. The woman had to be in her fifties with her long grey hair tied back and was expertly wiping down the bar and collecting empty glasses.

"Hey, love, what can I get for you?"

"A minute of your time, to indulge my curiosity." Celes smiled and watched for the bartender's reaction.

"It's fairly quiet so I'll hear you out, so long as you buy a drink after."

"Deal, I happen to be on the hunt to track down an old friend of mine. I know that he stayed here a long time ago, and I just wondered if there are any clues as to where he went next. I can't find any trace of him here."

"How long ago?"

"Twenty years or so." The bartender laughed.

"That's some hunt you're on."

"It's important, so if I can dig up anything that would be much appreciated. Do you have any records from back then?"

"Hmm." The bartender had a think. "Jones keeps ledgers of all those staying. Let me see." She started rifling through a drawer under the bar.

"No, that's too new. Nope. Oh, this is probably about right." The bartender emerged holding a rectangular leather-bound book.

"May I take a look...?"

"Christie. And yes, of course, you can. It's ancient history, knock yourself out." Christie chuckled and walked off to serve a customer.

Celes eagerly opened the ledger and flipped through. The system was quite easy to read, it was simply names and dates of check-in and dates of checkout. There seemed to be some additional markings next to some names, presumably to reference something.

This I can work with. Knowing more precise dates might help track down something more concrete elsewhere.

Celes carefully pored through the pages, starting close to where she expected an entry and working backwards. There were so many names, and she was starting to expect that there wouldn't be anything. But there it was.

Aydan! So, you did come here, and now I know when. What's this though?

Celes noticed the letter 'j' circled at the end of the entry. She looked up for Christie, waiting for the bartender to be free.

"Christie, I have a quick question before I get that drink."

"Sure. Did you find something."

"Yes, my friend definitely stayed here. What's this at the end of the entry? It's some sort of code." Celes spun the book around and pointed out the spot to Christie. She examined it for a moment.

"Well, I'll be. Lucky for you we still use that system of notes."

"What does it mean?"

"It stands for junk. It's our way of saying that the guest left stuff behind. We usually keep it for a while, in case they come back. As long as it's not decomposing or something." Celes' heart rate just about doubled. She tried to gather herself.

"Would it be silly of me to think that maybe you still have that stuff?" Christie laughed.

"You know, there's a chance if it was just shoved in a corner. There are things here that I have no idea where they came from."

"Make it two drinks and a hefty tip. If it's at all possible I have to see. This could be incredible." Celes could see Christie weighing things up.

"I am a bit curious to see if we still have that stuff. C'mon, let's be quick about it." Christie waved her over and walked to the end of the room and into a corridor. She rushed down to the last door, opening it with a key from her belt.

"This is long-term storage, I think it's mostly guest related. If we kept that box, it'll be here." Christie paused for a moment. "Good luck, I'll see you back at the bar. Please don't make a mess here, it'll just cause trouble for me."

"Absolutely, I promise it'll be like I was never here."

"Good." Christie left promptly and Celes surveyed the room.

So many boxes. Better get started.

She began by examining those closest to the door, she wanted to avoid another situation where the thing she needed was near the entry and she looked there last. After checking a few boxes, she noticed a definite trend. A lot of boxes had a big 'J' on top and tacked on somewhere else on the lid was a piece of paper with a name. Unfortunately, there were no dates. And none bore the name she needed.

I need to look for dusty boxes, probably up the back.

Celes had a good look and determined that there was a cluster of older boxes in the far-right corner. She carefully picked her way through, making sure she didn't disturb any shaky towers of boxes. It didn't take long to look over the boxes. It definitely wasn't the ones on top.

Here we go.

Celes systematically moved boxes around carefully to examine the ones on the bottom of the stacks, or near the bottom if they were particularly high. It all came down to the last box in the corner.

Please, please be this one.

"Aydan, I've got you," Celes whispered as she read the label. She set the box aside, pushing down the sudden urge to rifle through it.

The box has been here this long, I can wait a few moments before opening it. She focused on setting the room back to what it was, then carefully opened the lid. It was mostly empty. She found a few gems of different types, and some slips of paper. They looked to be receipts, but it wasn't clear what was purchased. One, however, stood out. It was a receipt from the Valrytir Restricted Library. It was confirmation of a restricted loan book titled *The History of The Blight.*

This looks interesting. If it's a restricted library, there's probably some records there too. I can feel it, this is a good lead.

Celes emptied the contents of the box into her satchel and returned to the bar.

"Hey, any luck?" Christie said.

"Yes, thank you. I couldn't believe it, but there you go. Just a few papers and some gems, but so interesting."

"Wow, that's quite lucky. Glad to be of help. What'll I get you?"

"Two shots of your best spirit, and some more information." Celes sat down at the bar. She watched Christie select a bottle and start pouring out shots.

"What else were you after?"

"The Valrytir Restricted Library. Is it nearby?"

"Oh, yes that's at the end of the main street." Christie picked up both glasses and set them down before Celes.

"Is it restricted access?" Celes retrieved some coins from her pocket, holding them in her closed hand.

"I don't believe so, just more security." Christie was eyeing off Celes's hand. Celes dipped her hand in again and grabbed a few extra coins. She pressed them into Christie's hand.

"Thanks again for your help." Celes threw the shot down, letting the burning sensation pass through her. She stood quickly.

"The other one is for you. Take care." Celes waved and walked off.

"Thanks, and good luck," Christie said. Celes quickly left the inn and started down the street.

Much more hospitable than they let on.

Celes could feel the case closing in. She was practically running down the street. It wasn't hard to find the library, it was a large stone building with an impressive dome on top. She rushed up the stairs and into the massive foyer.

The stillness of the room was a stark contrast to the hustle and bustle outside. People moved slowly and with purpose, and even the staff were quiet with whatever they were doing. Celes located a reception desk and walked over.

"Hello, I'd like your help with something."

"Good day. How can we assist you?" The librarian looked somewhat disinterested and moved her brown wavy hair off her face. Celes judged the woman was only in her early twenties.

"A friend of mine borrowed a book from here years ago. He wants to read it again, and I'd like to borrow it as well."

"What's the book?"

"The History of the Blight." Celes handed over the borrowing receipt.

"It's available. You can find it in the stacks." The librarian handed the slip back.

"Good. But, before I get it, I just need to double check. I need to make sure it's the same exact one."

"We only have one with that exact title, although there are similar books." The librarian seemed annoyed.

"If I could just look at the list of people who borrowed it, then I can make sure."

"I'm not sure I should do that."

"It's nothing, I'll just glance at the list. I'll see my friend's name and I'll be confident when I take it back that it'll be exactly the one that he wants. I'd only be looking at the names from a long time ago, nobody cares about the fact that they borrowed a book twenty years ago." Celes smiled and watched the librarian's reaction. She seemed to be coming around, despite being uncomfortable.

"You can look at the list while I'm here." The librarian turned and walked over to another section, rifling through different books. She returned within a few minutes with an old-looking book.

"This is the borrowing ledger. Let me see the slip again." The librarian checked the slip and carefully looked through the ledger.

"I've identified the appropriate entry, as expected. Take a look." The librarian spun the ledger around and guided Celes on where to look. Celes could feel her heart pounding. She read the name and suppressed a gasp. It wasn't Aydan. It was a real name.

"Thank you so much, you've been incredibly helpful. That's the exact confirmation I needed. You were so professional as well, I respect your devotion to the library."

"Why, thank you. I hope your friend enjoys the book as much as he did the last time." The librarian smiled and Celes thanked her again while she left. She made a show of walking over to where the library books were kept, but once the librarian was distracted, she left the building.

I actually did it! I've got you now.

Celes couldn't believe that she had solved it. Everything was coming together at last.

41

THE WAY TO VALRYTIR

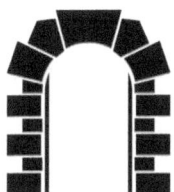

The Wizard Gate shimmered in front of them, revealing a hot dusty scene.

"Here we go." Alrion grabbed Lara's hand and stepped through the gate. The strange sensation that was starting to become familiar washed over them, light and heat and blankness.

The heat was all he expected.

"This is definitely the desert," Lara said. "I hope you have an idea of where this next gate is?"

"I do, but I also have a theory." Alrion started walking through the old temple surrounding them. It was largely destroyed, random pillars slowly eroding away, providing little to no shelter.

"What's the theory?" Lara said as they walked. Soon the temple was behind them, and a barely noticeable path stretched out ahead.

"It needs a bit more time to test. Hopefully, I'm not wrong, or this is going to be a really unpleasant journey."

"I agree with you on that point." Lara stopped and pulled out a small flask of water. She offered it to Alrion first then had a sip. They walked on without conversation, the dry heat and oppressive sun was too much. Alrion was content with just walking forward. He knew there were ways to reduce the effect of the heat, but he was happy just moving forward. Not grappling with the environment and just moving through it.

Eventually, he noticed what looked like an oasis.

"Ah-hah!" Alrion said, pointing.

"There's something familiar about that," Lara mused. As they walked closer, Alrion noticed a figure standing there.

"Ashra?" Alrion said.

"The very same. Welcome back, Alrion." Ashra smiled and waved them over.

"I knew you had to be located close to the Wizard Gate here," Alrion said.

"Lucky for you, even luckier for your mother."

"You saw her?"

"Yes, I helped her on her way. A most interesting hunt, looking for a wizard by following an old trail."

"Was she well?"

"Yes, perfectly well, although she would have struggled in the desert had I not found her. She wasn't properly equipped for it."

"Where did you take her? Another gate?"

"Of course. Come inside and we can talk more." Ashra led them into the house and down into the coolest space. He served water and Alrion drained a few cups.

"How is everything going? Are you ready to complete your quest?"

"Did she tell you Falric was alive?"

"Yes, that was a good surprise. Although I admit I half-expected something like that. It seemed odd that he fell so quickly and easily."

"I'm doing pretty well, I just need to complete my travel to Valry-tir." Alrion poured himself another cup of water.

"He's lying of course. We had to track back to the Pool of Knowledge because Alrion couldn't pull the location of the Blight from his accumulated knowledge."

"Hang on," Alrion started but Lara cut him off again.

"And when he finally found that out, he also found out that completing the spell will kill him." Lara stared at Alrion defiantly.

"Why?" he said, not even bothering to hide his annoyance.

"Ashra can help you. He's probably the wisest wizard you've met yet, and he trained you so much in the little time you were here. He's more practical than Falric."

"Practical? Because he lives in the desert?"

"Please, be still. Calm yourselves." Ashra got their attention then focused on Lara. "Thank you for being so blunt. I suspected something serious was up, and I appreciate the opportunity to discuss it." He then turned to Alrion. "You should thank her for saying what you could not. It is not a sign of weakness to ask for help."

"I'll be honest, I'm not sure what you can do to help."

"You've got it all figured out then?" Ashra smiled and gave Alrion a funny look.

"No, but I can figure it out then."

"That worked well for you before didn't it, when we duelled?" Ashra started with his gaze on Alrion, but then shifted it to Lara. She shivered noticeably.

"Lara doesn't have fond memories of that."

"Well, he did obliterate the area. Lucky you saved us."

"What's that got to do with this?"

"You weren't prepared and acted on instinct. And you lost control. Had I not intervened, it would have been tragic. Are you going to leave the fate of the world to chance?"

"No. I've come a long way. I've passed all the trials, I've cured myself and others of the Blight. And I've learned the details of the final spell and where to perform it."

"And you're confident then? No doubt whatsoever?"

"Of course not."

"Then you're not ready! Nobody is taking away from your considerable achievements. I can see the depths of your knowledge, perseverance, and willpower. But as you have no doubt noticed, having those abilities is not all that is required."

Ashra is making too much sense. In a way, it's a relief, but it doesn't make me any less annoyed. Why am I so affected by what he's saying?

"You're right, as much as it pains me to hear it. I'm not confident. I don't know how I'm going to avoid death. That doubt, you've just increased it."

"Good."

"What?" Lara said.

"He's in the right place. Mentally, and physically." Ashra gave them a mysterious smile.

"What are you planning?"

"One more lesson. Are you game?"

"Yes." Alrion nodded.

"Good. Let's go at once. Afterwards, I'll take you to the next gate." Ashra stood and immediately headed off. They followed him out of the house and back into the desert. Alrion suspected they were heading back to the same place where they had duelled before.

"Before we reach Valrytir, there's something you should know." Lara looked quite apprehensive.

"What is it?" Alrion stopped suddenly, looking at her with concern.

What has she been hiding?

"Um..." Lara stumbled over her words, "well, you're going to need military support. There's no way you'll be able to walk up to the source of the Blight without an army behind you."

"I hadn't really considered that. Can I count on them?"

"Not for sure. They're quite adept at fighting the Blight and are geared up and have the numbers to do so. But they'll be quite reluctant."

"Hmm, I suppose that's something I can think about. Do you have any special insights?" Alrion watched Lara's reaction. She still looked uncomfortable about something. And this revelation about the military didn't seem quite like it was what she meant to discuss.

"Not really. Not anymore, I've been away for a while."

"Right. Well, do let me know if you remember something." Alrion noticed Lara's face relax a bit when the conversation wound down.

I'll have to ask her about it later when I get an opportunity. Something about Valrytir is troubling her, maybe it's in her past.

Alrion hurried to catch up to Ashra. Soon enough they emerged into the arena. Despite the shifting sands, Alrion could still tell what he had done here. He felt a shiver go down his spine.

"Lara, please go wait up where you did before. You can observe and report back after the duel."

"Sure. Good luck." Lara gave Alrion a quick peck and jogged off to find safety. Alrion watched until he could see her reach the right area. Then he gave his attention back to Ashra.

"What's this going to involve?" Alrion said.

"Where's the fun in that? Just know that I'm going to test you. I want to see how far you've come." Ashra looked mischievous. Suddenly, he dropped the expression and became quite focused. Alrion started to notice darkness covering the area.

Another illusion.

Within a minute, the entire area was dark, with minimal light shining through. A swirl of dark sand surrounded Ashra. When the sand subsided, Alrion couldn't really see anything. But he did notice movement. He activated his enhanced vision, and then he could see.

Ashra wasn't there anymore. Instead, it was a dark humanoid shape. Alrion expected to see the tell-tale signs of Ashra's Spark, but it was hidden or invisible. The shape didn't look or move like a Shade, it felt like something else. Alrion prepared a fireball and shot it over. Black tendrils shot out from the shape and grabbed the fireball, squeezing it into nothing.

Now that's strange. What is he playing at?

Alrion decided to up the ante. He built up his Spark then unleashed waves of fire, followed by a seismic fissure, splitting the earth on a path to intercept. The black figure spawned more and more black tendrils. Simultaneously they swept away the fire and stopped the earth spell. Before Alrion could start another, the black shape suddenly multiplied. There were now four of them, and they all started to advance on Alrion.

He spun quickly, throwing waves of force at each one. Bit by bit he increased the Spark imbued into each one. But even these new figures had the same ability to knock away Alrion's spells. He reached for his sword and remembered he didn't have it. He had loaned it to Alyx.

I can't underestimate these.

But he already had. Something grabbed him from behind. Alrion turned his head to look back and saw one of the shapes behind him. It had grabbed him and was now spawning more tendrils to wrap around him.

There were five. *How did I get cornered so easily?*

Alrion struggled and struggled. But the hold on him became tighter and tighter. He noticed the other shapes advancing. They would be on him soon. He lashed out with waves of force, but they just cancelled out when they reached the black shapes. He forced fire into his arms, hoping to shake the figure off him. But the fire just dissipated as soon as it touched a black tendril.

Alrion started to panic. He was being smothered, and soon he would be completely enveloped. He thought about using the light bomb again but remembered how poorly he had done before, employing it in desperation. Images of Branthor using it flashed through his mind, but he didn't have the patience and presence to carefully control it, and his arms were not free to try to target it precisely.

What do I do? I can't be helpless.

The shapes were almost on him now. He saw one of them oozing a black substance.

Not again. Never again!

Alrion felt the Spark swelling in him. He was panicking. He felt the composition of the spell. It was a light bomb. He felt powerless to stop it. But he needed to. He needed to soften it somehow, to hold it in.

And then he felt his Soul Power. He knew that could help. Purely by instinct, he started to let it out, he let it infuse and mix with the Spark that was becoming a light bomb. He imagined a sphere surrounding him. It would suck all the dark shapes in like a magnet, and it would also contain the light bomb. His Soul would act as a container, keeping the force within a tight radius. He completed the visualisation and had a microsecond of peace and calm before he let it loose.

As he planned, the black shapes were drawn closer in. He was smothered completely. But it was by his choice. They were prevented from moving, and the altered light bomb exploded. Its effects were restricted to that small sphere he had set out, so the excess power and light shot up straight into the air like a beacon.

The darkness was dispelled instantly in a flash of white. Alrion looked around. The ground was cleared near him, but the rest of the arena was untouched. He saw Ashra standing off in the distance. He started approaching immediately.

"How did you find that?" Ashra said.

"Intense. How did you do that?"

"Trade secret, sorry." Ashra chuckled softly. "You really surprised me there. What's with you and light bombs?"

"I don't know. I guess deep down I know that they can wipe anything away."

"That they can." Ashra stopped in front of Alrion and put his hands on the young wizard's shoulders. He stared into Alrion's eyes. "Well now, do you feel any different?"

"Yes." Alrion searched his feelings. "I feel less burdened, a little more resilient."

"Good. You have the right instincts, but you need to be more aware, and more in control. Do you agree?"

"Yes, I know. I felt the panic there. But it was good to find a way out. That was horrible, by the way. Where did you come up with that?"

"I've listened to a few good stories in my day, thought you might appreciate it." Ashra grinned.

"You could say that." Alrion turned when he heard footsteps. It was Lara.

"I couldn't really see much, until that burst of light. Was that you, Alrion?"

"Yes. I think I passed?" He looked at Ashra. The wizard nodded.

"Good. Did it help?"

"Yes, it did. I must admit though, I didn't expect that."

"What did he do this time? Another illusion?"

"He outdid himself. Black figures with long dark tendrils advancing on me and smothering me." Alrion saw Lara recoil. "My reaction exactly."

"Ashra, you have a wicked imagination."

"Thank you for the compliment." Ashra bowed then walked past them. "We better get moving, you don't want to get stuck out here."

"Agreed." Alrion started walking, Lara by his side. Images from the recent confrontation kept bubbling up but he pushed them away. There was something terrifying about it that he didn't understand. For another time.

They found their way back onto another trail. It was slow going along the path, up and down dunes. Suddenly Ashra stopped and waited for them to catch up. Once they had, he reached down and pulled up a trapdoor.

"Wow, that's sneaky," Lara said.

"One day I'll forget how to get back here," Ashra said. He gestured at the ladder down. "After you."

Alrion climbed first, creating some orbs of light to dispel the complete darkness. They were in some sort of stone underground structure. Ashra closed the hatch and climbed down, before leading the way. They passed through nondescript passages until Ashra slowed, inspecting a wall.

"This way." He led them around a corner and there stood a Wizard Gate, glowing and at the ready.

"This is where we part ways. This gate only goes to one location. It's a small town that will get you close to Valrytir."

"Thank you." Alrion held out his hand and shook Ashra's.

"It was a pleasure. I look forward to your success."

"Thanks again," Lara said. Alrion reached out and activated the gate. It flashed and shimmered into existence, showing a dark scene beyond.

"Any last words of advice?" Alrion said.

"Say hello to your mother when you find her. Also, be careful. I suspect you'll meet that mysterious wizard that's been following you around once your quest is done." Ashra wasn't giving anything away with his expression. Before Alrion could ask a follow-up question he found himself tumbling into the gate.

Alrion found himself in darkness. Only the light of the gate was illuminating the area. Luckily, Lara was with him.

"That Ashra, can't help himself," Alrion said.

"He's just trying to help you. And look, we definitely made it here. Wherever here is." Lara started to explore, so Alrion created more orbs of light and attached them to the walls. He noticed stairs leading up to somewhere else, somewhere where there was light. As he approached the stairs, he noticed two shapes waiting up the top. They started to descend, one of them was carrying a torch.

Lara gasped before Alrion could see them. But he soon saw why. The one carrying the torch looked like an old farmer, the other was clearly a Shade. They seemed to be working together.

"Well, well, well. More through the gate," the farmer said. He licked his lips and looked nervously over at the Shade. The creature didn't notice, it was fixated on Alrion.

"I think we can work with this," Alrion said to Lara. He then turned his attention back to the farmer. "Before we start, I'd like to hear about a woman who passed through here recently." Alrion noticed the farmer's eyes widen.

Time to get to the bottom of this.

42

THE PRODIGAL DAUGHTER

Alrion emerged into the room, full of curiosity. It looked oddly familiar, the stacks of books and the small selection of equipment in the corner. Once he spotted a wizard, he knew where he was.

"This is a Wizard Store," Alrion announced. The wizard flinched, a look of annoyance passing over his features.

"Another one? Is that becoming a thoroughfare now?" the wizard grumbled.

"A woman passed through here recently?"

"Yes, are you related to her?" The wizard looked suspicious.

"It's his mother," Lara said. The wizard looked like he remembered something.

"Oh yes, she was on the trail of another wizard. She found a lead for a local inn, and I haven't seen her back."

"Glad to hear she passed through here. My name is Alrion, and you are?"

"Magnus. I'm the caretaker here and representative for Valrytir."

"Great to meet you. I may need to call on your help." Alrion gave him a small bow.

"Of course, anything for a fellow wizard." Magnus inclined his head slightly to acknowledge Alrion and went about his business.

"Let's go find this general that needs convincing." Alrion noticed Lara's features pale a little. Even though she seemed onboard with his plan, she seemed quite nervous about the whole thing. He started off towards the door, just as he was about to open it, he heard Magnus again.

"Sorry to be a bother, but what is that?" Magnus pointed to the large wooden box floating behind Alrion.

"Oh, it's just a magic trick for the general."

"High General Wynston? Commander of all the forces of Valrytir?"

"I believe that's the one." Alrion grinned.

"He's not one for magic, son. Or tricks. Or anything not rooted in reality. I don't know where you got your information." Magnus sighed.

"Don't worry, he'll love this one." Alrion smiled and opened the door. Lara left soon after, and the box floated out after them.

Alrion took a moment to revel in the scene. Valrytir was a huge city. There were clearly different districts and styles of buildings. But everywhere was busy. What drew his attention most was the large keep at the rear of the city. It gleamed white and sandy, the two types of stone used in its construction.

"I take it we head into the keep?"

"We should, but perhaps it would be wise to make one stop beforehand."

"Such as?"

"There's an elite unit of special troops in their own base within the city. Winning over their commander would help your cause."

"If you think it's worth the stop, I'll do it. But he or she would need to come along with us, I'm not wasting this on anyone less than the general."

"Fine, hopefully, we can convince him."

"Lead the way." Alrion waited for Lara to head off. He kept close but continued to marvel at the sights and keep tabs on his box. He was getting some attention for it, but clearly, the population weren't that surprised by wizards and they went back to their business.

After a brisk walk, they were in another district. It seemed more sedate and reserved than the one they had been in. A bit more polished as well. Lara confidently led him through the streets until they reached a large building. It looked almost like a school. He saw a lot of people his age going in and out in special uniforms. It reminded him of the academy.

That was a lifetime ago, and such a brief stay. Could I go back there?

Alrion's train of thought was interrupted.

"Alrion!" a voice shouted. He looked over and saw Alyx waving and running over.

"Alyx! You made it!" He couldn't believe it. Alyx was already here! And she was wearing the same uniform as those training.

"Lara, good to see you too," Alyx said.

"I see you signed up." Lara was sizing up Alyx's outfit.

"I used to be a member, it made sense given that we need their help."

"How'd you get here?" Alrion said.

"That gate went straight here. I've been trying to prepare things as well as I could." Alyx paused and lowered her voice. "Did you get what you needed?"

"Yes, I did." Alrion didn't add any extra detail and he maintained a straight face. He could see Lara giving him an odd look but ignored it.

"Has Lara filled you in on Valrytir?" Alyx said.

"Barely. But she did suggest quite rightly that we would need military assistance to approach the source of the Blight, and that the general would need some pretty strong evidence of our mission." Alrion noticed Alyx give Lara a questioning look, but it passed quickly. Alyx went on.

"As it so happens, I've started the campaign for you. Brady, the commander of the special unit, has agreed to voice his support, as long as you can demonstrate evidence of your need."

"That's amazing!" Lara said, genuine surprise on her face.

"We had a stroke of luck. Vincent and Brady know each other from a long time ago, that tipped the scales in our favour."

"My father is here? Already?"

"Yes. He's working on a special project. And Certan is here too?"

"What?" Alrion couldn't believe it. What were the odds of everyone being here?

"Your team is coming together when you need us the most. It's how it should be."

"Have you seen my mother?"

"No, can't say I have. Vincent didn't mention anything either. Is she here?"

"Yes, but maybe she hasn't been lucky enough to run into you all yet." Alrion took a deep breath. "Alright, well we can't just stand around in the street. I need to go see the general. Do you think you can get your commander to come along?"

"Absolutely, just let me get him. And I'll send a runner for Vincent as well." Alyx jogged back over to the large building.

"It's really happening." Alrion sighed. He was so relieved that his friends were there to support him. But part of him had hoped he would have more time to get things ready before he moved ahead. It looked like he wouldn't have much time at all.

The more time you wait, the more the enemy can prepare as well. Maybe this is for the best.

"Are you sure you want to do this now?" Lara said. She looked anxious again.

"I don't really see another option. How long are we going to lug this box around?" he said.

"I suppose you're right." A look of resignation passed over her face. Alyx didn't take long to return. She had Certan with her, and a man with grey hair and a moustache. Clearly the commander.

"So, you're the wizard I keep hearing about?" the commander said. He held out his hand and Alrion shook it.

"That's me. Alrion, nice to meet you."

"Brady. And likewise. I'm very curious about what you can do."

"All in good time. Let's go see the general."

"I'm sure he's keen to see what you can do as well." Brady chuckled. "I'll follow your lead," he said to Alyx. She nodded and took two steps away, before stopping and returning.

"It's time you had this back." Alyx unbuckled the Runesteel sword and handed it back to Alrion. He hesitated before accepting.

"Are you sure?"

"Yes, it has served me well, but now you need it back. Don't worry, I have other options."

"If you insist, I won't say no. I can see the value in having it back." Alrion adjusted the belt and slung it over his shoulder. Alyx started off again, leading them through the city towards the keep.

"Certan, I'm so surprised to see you here."

"It's great to see you," Lara added.

"Thank you. My heart is warmed to see you restored. I must apologise to you for not helping you more. I realise now that you needed my help more than the temple did. It's a mistake I won't repeat again."

"Don't worry, I had enough help and you had an opportunity to reclaim your life. What brought you back here?" Alrion let his attention lapse momentarily, taking in a giant gate that they were going through. They were passing through a much more fortified area of the city, the keep had to be close.

"The elders insisted. They said it was a job unfinished. I cannot return until you are successful with your quest. I'm afraid you're stuck with me." Certan smiled and Alrion returned it.

"That's a fate I can live with."

"One other thing." Certan paused and made sure he had Alrion's full attention. "I passed the Vault of Silence."

"Wow, that's amazing. We'll have to compare notes a bit later." Alrion could see Certan's eyes light up.

It's a simple thing but having someone to talk to about it will be quite novel. I wonder how much our experiences differed?

Alrion returned his attention to the environment. They were drawing near the keep now. Alrion could see the giant stone entryway. It was guarded by two very heavily armoured soldiers. One had his visor up and was conversing with people going in and out. The other just stood perfectly still, waiting for something.

"Papers," the guard said as they approached.

"We don't have papers," Alyx said. She pointed at Brady.

"Commander Brady, of the special forces unit. We need an urgent audience with the high general."

"Absolutely not," the guard said. "Only people with pre-approved business with authorised paperwork are getting in today." The guard folded his arms to reinforce what he was saying. Alrion was about to say something when Lara strode to the front. She looked the guard up and down.

"Francis, cut the act and let us in." Lara glared at him, and his face drained of blood. He looked completely white.

"Certainly, please make yourselves at home." Francis made a quick bow and walked over to the other guard, giving them plenty of space.

"What was that?" Alrion said to Lara.

"We go way back." Lara led the way, walking into the door. Alrion followed, ensuring the box stayed close.

"Uh, I'm going to have to look inside that box," Francis said. Alrion stopped and let the box rest on the ground. Lara walked up to Francis.

"Are you sure?"

"Yes." Francis licked his lips. "Sorry."

"Be my guest." Lara gave him a wicked grin, and Francis walked over to the box.

"I wouldn't open it all the way," Lara advised. Francis pried the lid open and raised it just enough to look inside. He suddenly let the lid drop closed and stepped away.

"Uh... alright. Go on." Francis spoke in a broken fashion and joined the other guard.

"You heard the man." Lara took off, and Alrion followed closely behind.

This is all very strange. The gate guard is scared of Lara? And we're meeting the general in the keep? Wouldn't it make more sense to be in a military building?

Alrion wasn't that familiar with Valrytir and pushed his concerns aside. This was a meeting they needed to get. They entered a large reception area, with a main hallway leading into another great room with big doors. A finely dressed man stood in front of the door, his dark hair slicked back. He smiled as Lara approached.

"Welcome back, milady."

"Thank you, Rogers. Kindly open the doors please," Lara said. Rogers nodded and threw open the giant doors. Alrion's mouth gaped open. It looked like a throne room. It was long and narrow, with various nobles clustered on the sides, discussing things amongst themselves. At the back of the room, an older man sat on a giant silver throne, looking bored. A couple were retreating from the throne. Rogers ran ahead.

"The Lady Lara attends with retinue," Rogers announced. There was a silence that passed through the crowd. Alrion drew close to Lara.

"What's going on?" he whispered.

"Later. Trust me." Lara strode forward with confidence. She walked halfway up the carpet leading to the throne, paused and bowed.

"I am here to present myself and my companions to his highness, Regent of Valrytir."

"No need to be so formal, my daughter." The man stood and walked slowly over to her.

Daughter! Isn't he the king? Or acting king?

Alrion was stunned. He looked at his companions. Alyx didn't seem surprised, Certan was his usual reserved self. Alrion heard footsteps behind them. He noticed his father rushing in.

"Apologies for my lateness." Vincent gave a bow at the entrance to the room then joined them. The Regent was conversing quietly with Lara.

"My daughter says that you have business here with Valrytir. As a thank you for ensuring her safe return, I will hear your business."

"Thank you, Your Highness." Alrion hoped he wasn't making a fool of himself. He had never addressed a king before.

"Please, I prefer my name, Wynston. Or if you must, use my regular title: High General."

"As you wish, High General." Alrion collected himself and started to speak again. "My name is Alrion and I'm a wizard. I've come a long way to be here, and my quest is almost at an end. Your daughter has been instrumental in helping us reach this point."

"And your quest is?"

"Cleansing the Blight." Alrion saw Wynston raise an eyebrow.

"That's quite a quest. Is it a real quest? Or a fanciful waste of time?" Wynston looked at Lara.

"It's real. Alrion can demonstrate so."

"Ha! The only way he could do that is cure the Blight in front of my eyes. Who are these other people?"

"All these people can vouch for the importance and legitimacy of this quest. This is Alyx, a formidable fighter. She is best known for destroying the Skull King." Alrion hoped that Wynston was impressed. But his face darkened considerably.

"I am quite aware of ALL her exploits. Who else?"

"This is Certan, a master monk that hails from the desert temple. And this is my father, Vincent. He is a master blacksmith, one who can work with Runesteel." That point captured Wynston's attention.

"Interesting. I'm quite familiar with Brady. Tell me, Commander, what's your link to this quest?"

"It's only very recently come to my attention, High General. Alyx brought the matter to my attention, and I knew Vincent as well, who added legitimacy to it. I was not aware your daughter was involved until just now."

"Very well." Wynston nodded and looked them all over. "What is the nature of this quest? Why have you come here?"

"My quest is to cleanse the Blight at the source. As you are likely aware, the source is not far from Valrytir." Alrion was about to continue speaking but he was cut off.

"Hearsay. I will not have you spreading such rumours!" Wynston bellowed. Alrion wanted to argue, but Lara touched his arm and shook her head. Alrion adjusted his approach.

"Nevertheless, I need to pass through to reach my destination."

"And scout reports show extremely large numbers of Blight massing just outside Valrytir," Alyx added.

"Brady?"

"That is true, High General. They avoided our detection initially because each Blight sighting is quite small, under our threshold. However, the scouts started to notice so they adapted their reporting to include all sightings. Now we're getting a real sense of the number." Brady finished speaking and waited for further questions. Wynston sighed and started to rub his chin.

"Let's assume that your quest is legitimate, and you need our assistance to reach your destination, due to the numbers of the Blight. I need something else, other than your word to commit so many lives to such an undertaking."

"Absolutely, High General. That is why I have organised a demonstration." Alrion stepped to the side and gestured for his companions to do the same. He brought the giant box into the middle of the carpet.

"Please, keep your distance." Alrion ensured everyone was a safe distance away, and he pried the lid off the box. Next, he reached into the box. There was a scream, and a dark shape climbed out. It was a Shade. Terrified screams rang through the room. The high general drew his sword instantly, as did his retinue. Alrion quickly wrapped up the Shade in waves of force, pinning it in place. The Shade was strong, but Alrion's Will was stronger. As much as it struggled, the Shade was unable to move.

"Is everyone satisfied that we have a Shade here?" Alrion looked around the room. No one said anything.

"I am satisfied. But keeping a Shade at bay, whilst impressive, is no mere demonstration, young wizard." The high general sheathed his sword and waited.

"Nor should it be. I am merely showing you that the Shade is real, but I do not wish to endanger anyone during the demonstration. Be prepared for what happens next." Alrion walked closer to the Shade. He stepped up until he was incredibly close.

"I am going to release you from your prison," Alrion said softly. The Shade shrieked again, but Alrion ignored it. He wrapped his hand in a force spell, at the same time mixing in his Soul Power. Reaching forward he placed his hand on the Shade's chest. Using his Spark as the conduit, he poured his Soul Power into the Shade. Activating his enhanced vision, Alrion took note of the key points of concentration of the Blight and took care in directing his Soul Power to wash them away. He kept Branthor's words in his mind, trying to minimise the damage to the person within.

As he worked, the room was silent, watching. Alrion wasn't sure how much of what he was doing was visible by an observer. But he was too caught up in what was happening to worry too much about that. Suddenly, he had finished the job, the last Blight retreating from the Shade. The chain reaction began.

After a quick burst of light, the Shade started to fall. Alrion adjusted his force spell to let the creature down slowly. The black exterior of the Shade started to flake away, turning to dust and disintegrating. Alrion watched the whole process with his enhanced vision on. He could see the body rebuilding, replacing what had been lost. Soon there were no more traces of the Blight. Just a man remained, his breathing shallow and weak.

"Bring a stretcher," Alrion said. The high general nodded to an aide, who rushed off. Within moments two guards returned bearing a stretcher. They set it down gently near Alrion. He thanked them and gently lifted the former Shade, using his force spells to bear the brunt of the weight. He gently lowered the man onto the stretcher.

"Lift him up and let those who need to see for themselves look." Alrion watched as the guards lifted the stretcher cautiously, trying not to look within.

The high general strode over. He stared into the stretcher, and reached in, feeling the man's hand.

"It's warm, he's alive."

"Of course. How do you think the Blight survives? It needs us."

"What of the man within?" The high general looked up at Alrion.

"That's a good question, I haven't gotten to the bottom of it. Some have had a full recovery, others I'm not so sure about. I think it depends on a lot of factors. With luck, he can lead a normal life again."

"Brady, come look." The high general stepped back and waited for the commander to view the man.

"I'm convinced, even though I can't believe it. It seems like it should be impossible." Brady looked at Alrion, an incredulous expression on his face.

"You should keep the man here, and care for him. You can review his progress, and hopefully, he can speak to you once he's recovered. There is probably a lot we can learn for the future."

"Alrion," the high general said as he crossed the last few steps between them. "You swear you can do this for the whole world?"

"I swear. It's why I need to get to the source. I can't exactly cleanse the world one person at a time."

"Of course." The high general closed his eyes, deep in thought. He stayed that way for minutes. Finally, he opened them once more.

"I've made my decision. Whatever you need, we will provide. Today is an auspicious day. It is the start of the end of the Blight." The high general held out a hand. Alrion held out his and they shook on it. The deal was done. Alrion beamed confidence. Inside, he was a wreck.

This is really happening. There's no turning back. I have to find a way to make this work. I don't want to create a world of peace that I can't also enjoy.

43

A HEAVY BURDEN

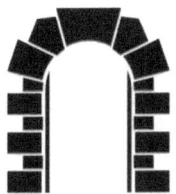

A lrion felt a hand on his shoulder and instantly awoke. It was Lara, leaning over him. She looked worried.

"Good morning. You looked restless. Did you sleep?"

"Good morning. I must have, I don't remember anything." Alrion looked around the room, remembering where he was. It was a spare apartment that his father had arranged for them. He'd arrived late at night, and it looked different in the morning sun. Alrion tried to shake off the sleepiness.

"We need to hurry. We've been summoned by the high general. There's something urgent to discuss."

"You mean your father?" Alrion glanced at Lara long enough to see her embarrassed look then sat up in the bed.

"I know, I should have told you."

"You're practically royalty, Your Highness." Alrion made a mock bow in the bed, before getting up. "Now I know why you never really talked about your family."

"It was difficult. It all happened so close together. My brother dying, the king being killed, my father being called up to the keep."

"That's why you left? All of that?" Alrion rose and started getting ready.

"Yes. It completely exacerbated my father's behaviour. He's always been so traditional, not letting me get involved like my brother. I had to read my books and do my lessons. But Leon was the son. He had the weapons training and the opportunities. And he was good, he became a squad commander in the elite unit that Brady commands. Lucky for me, he taught me quite a bit. Mostly in secret. My father didn't approve."

"You said your brother was a victim of the Blight. What happened?"

"There was a huge battle, my brother held off a whole legion of Blight, leading his men to an honourable death. Those who managed to send a message for help brought reinforcements that crushed the Blight. But they were too late to save him."

"I'm so sorry. But I'm glad that he went out doing something important." Alrion was ready, and he held the door open for Lara.

"Me too." Lara sighed, walking out the door. "Now that I'm back, I feel a bit foolish for just running away. But if I hadn't, well the world wouldn't be on the brink of being cleansed by the Blight."

"I suppose so." Alrion gave her a weak smile. They started walking towards the keep, Alrion noticed that there weren't a lot of people around.

"You're so lucky I decided to pickpocket you."

"I really am." Alrion believed it too. She had been the one constant on a journey that had surprises around every corner.

I suppose it was only natural that she had a secret too. I'll cut her a break, for now, I can see why she'd want to be clear of all this. But I don't know if I can act the same around her.

"What do you think this urgent message is?" Alrion said, changing the topic.

"Not sure. Maybe we have more information about when to make a move? I think the army will take time to mobilise."

"Time is a tricky thing. The more we prepare, the stronger the Blight gets. The more they concentrate their forces. But if we go too early, we blow the whole thing."

"Exactly. But that's what all those army men are for, they live for this."

"What do you live for?"

"I would have said liberating treasures. But now it's different." Lara gave him a mysterious smile.

"And that would be?"

"Something to be shared another time. Oh look, here we are." Lara pointed to the gates outside the keep.

"So we are." Alrion walked through, keeping an eye on the guards. They didn't make eye contact with Lara or Alrion, they just kept out of the way. It didn't take long to return to the throne room. Alrion noticed that everyone else was already there. His father looked like he hadn't slept at all.

In the middle of the room was a strange looking man. He was half height and had thick black hair. He turned to face them as Alrion arrived. The features of the man caused Alrion to gasp. The man looked like a Blighter, only with proper clothing on.

"Now I can give my message," the man rasped. He looked directly into Alrion's eyes.

"I know you are coming, Alrion. I know where you need to be. Only, I'm not going to make it easy for you. If you meet me directly, I'll face you honourably. We can settle this little disagreement like gentlemen. And it's your best chance to destroy me yourself. But if you try to sneak off, well I'll turn my army on Valrytir. We'll crush it and destroy every little piece. And we won't stop there, we'll keep on going until the whole world is under our control."

Alrion pondered the message for a moment.

"What you're saying is that I need to face you and your army now? Or you'll descend upon Valrytir and beyond?"

"Yes. No more hiding. No more tricks."

"And what if I don't agree?"

"There's this and more." The man finished speaking and his stomach started to rapidly expand.

"Everyone, get back!" Alyx shouted. The room almost cleared

instantly. Suddenly, the Blight-touched man exploded, and a toxic black gas started to billow throughout the room.

That looks bad.

Alrion activated his enhanced vision and saw what he expected. The gas was strands of the Blight, seeking to infect people. Alrion shuddered and started to deal with the situation.

First, he created waves of force to box the smoke in, moving it into a smaller area. Then he had an idea. He visualised an empty glass orb in the middle of the room. And to top it off, the orb attracted the smoke. It couldn't help but get sucked in. Once Alrion added some Spark to the mix, it started to work. The smoke swirled around like it was resisting. Then it rapidly flowed, being drawn into a single space. Once it was done, there was a dense sphere of something floating in the middle of the room.

Alrion approached it carefully. It looked the same in terms of it being tainted by the Blight. He reached out and touched it with his hand. He felt the slick, disgusting taint immediately. To start with, he created a flame and set the orb alight. Next, Alrion touched the flame with his hand and pushed Soul Power into the spell. It looked like it was working.

The flame burned with a golden colour and soon died out. There was nothing else left.

"I think that's it," Alrion said. He looked around the room. Nobody who was left had moved since the gas explosion. The high general was flanked by Magnus, both of whom had stayed but were a good distance away. Alrion's companions were all there but had retreated to positions behind him. They cautiously approached again.

"That was fantastic," Lara said.

"We knew you could handle it." Certan clapped Alrion on the shoulder as he returned. Vincent gave Alrion a satisfied nod and returned to his former position.

"That was quite dramatic. I think the creature made its point," the high general said.

"They're constantly surprising," Alrion said.

"Well, let's not beat around the bush. Either you're an amazing charlatan, or we have a big problem on our hands."

"Charlatan? How could you even think that for a minute?" Alrion was annoyed. The high general was a bit taken aback but launched into his response.

"You show up with a Shade that gets miraculously cured, now another Blight figure threatens everyone and blows up. Sounds like a good way to get us committed, and if you were an agent of the Blight it would all be easy for you to arrange. I'm just saying that this all looks rather convenient for you?"

"This isn't convenient in the slightest. And you know what? I almost understand you doubting me since I did just come out of nowhere. But your own daughter? And Alyx, a soldier that served in your own army?" Alrion watched the high general's anger bubble over.

"I'm actually being quite accommodating, really. My daughter ran off when things became too difficult, hardly a reliable person. And Alyx? She's the reason my son died. Wasted on a trifling skirmish. Again, hardly someone I want to rely on." Wynston pointed at Alyx and practically shouted the last part. Lara gasped and countered.

"What are you talking about? Are you mad?" Lara said.

"Go on, ask her." The high general was fuming. Lara looked to Alyx.

"It's true. The man I fell in love with, the one that was killed during our scouting mission. He was your brother, Leon. I thought you knew." Alyx spoke softly and looked away from Lara.

"But you said he died in a great battle? He died saving others?" Lara started approaching her father.

"I said that to protect you. But in truth, the scouting mission did save lives."

"You made me feel even more worthless than I was, by saying he died for a great cause? And then you turned around and said the exact opposite to her?" Alyx said to the high general. He didn't look concerned.

"I don't answer to you." He looked over at Lara. "Or you either." Lara shook her head muttering under her breath.

"What will it be, High General? Are we moving forward or not?" Alrion was sick of the discussion and hated how his friends were being treated.

If only we didn't need these forces. But we can't walk into that alone, it'd be suicide.

"I don't see that I have a choice. Our forces will be ready to march at first light. But you, little wizard, need to be up front and centre."

"Fine, I'll be there." Alrion left in disgust. He could hear his friends leaving too.

"You can see why I didn't want to stick around," Lara said. Alyx closed in and pulled Lara aside.

"I'm so sorry. When we spoke about my past, I spared the detail so that I would not bring up old wounds. I had no idea that you didn't know."

"I don't blame you, I blame him. It's too much to sort through right now. Let's just go ahead with what we need to do." Lara started walking again.

"Let's figure out what we are doing." Alrion led them back to his temporary quarters. They needed to be clear about what was happening.

"If you don't mind, I'll find you later? I need to finish that project." Vincent was apologetic and started walking off before they could respond.

"That's fine," Alrion said to nobody in particular. He walked the path deep in thought, not looking up. Soon enough they were in the little apartment. There wasn't even anywhere to sit, so they all stood in a circle to discuss their plans.

"Here we are, my companions. You have stood by me on this journey and saved me. None of you has any connection to me, except that you chose to help. I owe you all my life."

And I'll be paying that price most likely.

"Before we begin this final planning, I just want to thank you all. Truly. It's been a long road and I wouldn't be here without you."

Alrion smiled and received smiles and acknowledgements from them all.

"Now, on to business. Will the high general be riding with the army?" Alrion looked to Lara and Alyx.

"I expect so, but not up front. Maybe at the rear. Lara?"

"Agreed. He will be present but at the back."

"It's amusing then, that he wants me at the head." Alrion chuckled.

"To reinforce the Blight that you're there, no doubt," Alyx added.

"That's fine, it's not a danger to me. We can deal with the army, and then I can proceed to the source."

"Who should go with you?" Lara said.

"Nobody." Alrion noticed some surprised looks. "You can't help me in there, and it would be an additional complication. I shouldn't need backup, that's the benefit of taking out their forces."

"True, but shouldn't we at least guard the entrance?" Alyx said.

"That is the minimum I would do," Certan said.

"Let's assess on the day, but my preference is to have nobody there if we can help it."

I can't let them interfere. Certan and Alyx don't even know that I may die. Should I tell them?

Alrion looked at the expressions on the faces of his friends.

I shouldn't have even told Lara. I'll hold off for now and see how I feel tomorrow.

"I have preparations to make, so I'll meet you all early tomorrow morning for the ride out. I'm going to be extremely focused, so please just leave me be."

"What about offering you good luck?" Certan said.

"Maybe do it now, instead." Alrion cringed as Certan came in and gave him a big hug. But he felt reassured and was then surprised by Alyx then Lara coming in.

"You can try as you might, but I'll never leave you," Lara whispered into his ear. Alrion smiled.

"Alright, thanks, everyone. You know how to best prepare, I won't pretend to advise you on that. But, Certan, please stay behind for a moment. I have a special assignment for you."

Alyx and Lara said goodbye and left the room. Certan approached his face a mixture of curiosity and surprise.

This should work, but it's a bit of a gamble.

44

END OF THE INVESTIGATION

Celes wandered through the district, looking for Vincent. She knew he'd be working on something, which is why she had left him alone. But with her new discovery, it was time to finally look him up.

There's just too many blacksmiths and related trades around here. This could take a while.

Suddenly, she spotted him leaving a shop.

"Vincent," Celes said as she ran over. He beamed a wide smile and gave her a warm hug and kiss.

"Well, aren't you a sight! You must have had an amazing adventure."

"I sure have."

"I hope you weren't in the desert too long. That's where it sent you, right?"

"Absolutely. Lucky for me I ran into that wizard, Ashra." She watched Vincent's reaction. He smiled and nodded.

"He's a good one. Has his own ideas about how to do things, but always does the best for people."

"Best in his own opinion." Celes laughed and Vincent joined in.

"Come on, I've borrowed a small residence and I was about to eat.

You can tell me about the rest of your investigation." Vincent led her through the hustle and bustle into a side alley then into a tiny little dwelling at the end. It consisted of a bedroom, and just outside it two chairs and a table. There was some bread, cheese, and fruit laid out on the table.

"Did you prepare this?" Celes said.

"No, I've been working. Thankfully, they organised this for me." Vincent pulled out a chair for Celes and she sat down graciously. He joined her and offered her the food. She started picking at the fruit.

"That Ashra, let me tell you. He's a real trickster. He told me he knew the identity of the wizard, right before pushing me through the next Wizard Gate." Celes shook her head at the memory.

He was right to tell me that much, as infuriating as it was.

"That does not surprise me one bit. I've heard so many stories. So, another Wizard Gate. Where did that take you?"

"A basement of a house in Stonebridge." Vincent looked surprised.

"That's quite unusual but convenient."

"Yes, Ashra thought that perhaps the wizard had taken that route for speed and to keep away from established routes, not that there were any particular things to find on the way."

"It's a good theory. What sort of house holds a Wizard Gate?"

"An old wizard's home. Only there's a farmer living there now. Polite fellow, he even gave me dinner."

"Oh, that's a nice surprise." Vincent smiled.

"Oh, the surprise wasn't nice. He locked me in the basement and went to fetch some sort of Blight assistance." Vincent paused mid chewing and stared at her.

"Lucky for me, there was a secret tunnel that sealed behind me." Celes grabbed a hunk of bread and started chewing. It was surprisingly tasty. Maybe she was just hungry.

"Had I known this would happen, I would have insisted we travel together. I still would have made it here, and you would have had help."

"How were we to know? And I think in a way it was good. I had to rely on myself again. I succeeded, you know."

"Succeeded?"

"Yes, I found out the identity of the mysterious wizard."

"Really?" Vincent looked surprised, and a bit anxious.

"Yes. Lucky for me the secret tunnel linked up with the Wizard Store. By reading the log and conversing with a helpful wizard called Magnus, I was able to track the mysterious wizard to a local inn."

"That's a good lead. How'd you identify him from that?"

"It wasn't the inn itself. But the inn did have a box of his belongings. And in those belongings was…"

"A signed confession?" Vincent offered.

"No, even better. A library receipt."

"A library receipt?"

"Yes. And when I tracked that down, I found the original borrowing ledger. It turns out that book was a restricted loan."

"What was the book?"

"History of the Blight."

"Makes sense." Vincent reached for the fruit now. "How did that solve the puzzle?"

"As it turns out, our mysterious wizard signed his real name for the book." Vincent froze and stared at her.

"He signed his real name?"

"Yes. Can you believe it? I caught him with a twenty-year-old trail. Using a library receipt!" Celes was beaming. Finally, she could share her elation at the find. Vincent looked deep in thought.

"Hmm yes, he would have needed a real identity, not an alias, to borrow a restricted book. And you found the receipt in his belongings, identified by the alias." He looked up at her. "I knew you were a genius. This is phenomenal!"

"It is, isn't it."

"I knew you'd do it. Who else could return on such a long shot?" Vincent smiled at her, and she felt warm inside.

"Alrion needs to know." Celes watched Vincent's face become more serious.

"I agree. I'll tell him at the right time. Things are progressing."

"What do you mean?"

"Darvin has issued an ultimatum—Alrion must meet him face-to-face or he will bring his army to Valrytir and beyond."

"And what did Alrion decide?"

"He had no choice. The high general is mobilising the army at first light, with Alrion at the head."

"I see. We will protect him."

"I must protect him." Vincent stared at her with intensity.

"From an entire army?"

"There's always a way, you should know that. I must go with him and keep him safe. Until he sees it through. Only I can do it."

"If you insist. I can still help." Celes didn't like where this conversation seemed to be going.

"Of course you can, you can support his other companions in their fight. I'll be the one to follow him into the unknown and protect him while he performs the spell. That is the way it must be." Vincent had a sad expression.

"Well, look at us, then. Working together as a family. I never expected it." Celes smiled, hoping to break Vincent out of the mood he was in.

"You're right. It reminds me of the Blind Tiger heist."

"Yes, that was amazing."

Such a clever reference, there are so many parallels with our current situation. Only...

"Wait." Celes studied Vincent's expression. And she thought about the story he had referenced and his last few comments. "You're not coming back, are you?" Celes stared in horror and watched him nod his head.

"I don't expect to, save a miracle."

"But why! This doesn't make any sense." Celes started shaking her head subconsciously.

"I can't get into the details. And maybe I'm wrong, but I don't think so."

"There has to be another way. Surely." Celes searched Vincent's face for some sign of hope. He seemed resigned.

"Darling, what would you do to save our son? What would you give?" Vincent looked up at her.

"Anything."

"As will I." Vincent rose and fetched something from his belongings. He handed it to Celes. It was a few leather-bound books.

"I've catalogued everything I've learned in here. If I don't make it back, there will be answers within. Just promise me you won't read it yet." Vincent held her hand. She stood slowly and embraced him.

"You've been planning this for a while, haven't you?" she whispered.

"Yes. Just in case. I fear the worst."

"I refuse to say goodbye."

"What then?"

"I'll think about it. I have until morning." Celes hugged him tighter, a tear sliding down her cheek.

This can't be it. We must find a way.

45

THE MAIN ASSAULT

Alyx had a restless sleep. It was filled with images of the Skull King, and Darvin. Right at the end, to make matters worse, she experienced what she thought were memories of the brief period that she was the Skull Queen.

Alyx awoke in a sweat, her hands shaking. She steadied them and looked up. It was almost first light. She was in a single room, a luxury for a soldier. Mary had organised it, an uncharacteristically nice move. Alyx wasn't ready to bunk with other soldiers yet.

She quickly dressed and left the room, not fussed about eating. There would be snacks later if she wanted. To her surprise, there was a well-dressed messenger waiting outside her room. Upon seeing her he became quite animated.

"Good morning, Lady Alyx. I have been dispatched to bring you immediately to Master Balzar." The messenger gave her a deep bow and waited for her response.

"Sure, lead the way." Alyx started walking and had to increase her pace to keep up with the messenger. He wasn't joking around.

This must have something to do with the sword. At least, I hope it does. There's no more time.

Alyx had become accustomed to having Alrion's Runesteel sword, and her lack of a weapon right now felt wrong. She was still incredibly deadly without it, but it was still something to be fixed.

The messenger led her expertly through the city, taking some side roads and shortcuts she didn't know about. Before long they had reached Balzar's workshop. As before, she was led into the back area and down to the large vault. Balzar was standing outside, arms crossed. He beamed her a smile as soon as he saw her.

"This is an auspicious day. Welcome again, to my humble store." Balzar bowed.

This is hardly humble, but I'll let him have his pomp and ceremony.

"Thank you for the invitation and being ready so early in the morning. I need to be out as soon as possible."

"Of course, we've all heard. Lucky for you, Vincent worked some magic." Balzar paused, "figuratively speaking of course. But you'd be forgiven for thinking otherwise." Balzar opened the massive door and eased it open. He disappeared inside, and Alyx followed him in. She found him standing next to a table. He was sporting a huge grin and Alyx could see why. She ran over to the table.

"Andrylir," Alyx whispered under her breath. The sword was gleaming and looked strong. She ran her fingers along the blade feeling it. There were no hints of the previous fragments, it was completely restored.

"Go on, pick it up," Balzar urged. Alyx carefully reached for the sword, remembering its weight. She used two hands, lifting it carefully. She almost dropped it and looked at Balzar sharply.

"Don't look at me, it's all Vincent's work." Balzar held his hands up. "I couldn't believe it either."

"How could it be lighter? It doesn't make any sense?"

"Vincent did say something to me about the blade. He said it won't be the same as it once was but, in some way, he's made it better. Something about Soul Power?" Balzar looked confused.

"I know what he means. I wonder..." Alyx looked around the vault.

"Woah there, I know that look. If you're after something to try it on, I'll set you up outside, not in here." Balzar looked concerned, his eyes tracked hers almost manically.

"Don't worry, I was just seeing what else was here of comparable strength. A more mundane test is fine." Alyx let Balzar lead her out and excuse himself. Within a minute, he had two assistants hauling in a large piece of stone.

"Not sure what we're doing with this. Feel free to test your blade." Balzar's apprentices looked shocked at the suggestion, but they stayed and stared at Alyx.

This is a risk, knowing that I could damage the blade. But I need to know how strong it is, and how sharp.

Alyx hefted the sword and swung diagonally at the stone. It was almost effortless. The sword passed through the stone like it was water, and she felt something as it passed through. A warmth came through the blade.

"Excellent!" Balzar was clapping enthusiastically. His apprentices just stared with their mouths open. Balzar rushed over and inspected the stone.

"Incredibly clean cut, look at this, boys." He called them over and they ran their hands over the stone.

"Do you have something I can use to strap this?" Alyx said.

"Certainly. I had a colleague whip something up. It's not flashy, but it'll work well." Balzar disappeared again and returned with a leather strap system. He helped Alyx put it on, then she was able to almost clip the sword in. After a few more adjustments she could relatively easily remove the sword and return it.

"This works. I cannot thank you enough for what you have done."

"I was merely the facilitator. Give Vincent your thanks, and mine, when you see him."

"I will." Alyx finished her goodbyes and rushed out of the workshop. She needed to get to the rendezvous point before Alrion left with the main force.

Alyx found Lara at the city gates. Just beyond, the forces were massing.

"Am I too late?" Alyx said.

"No, we're just about to move." Lara was peering into the distance.

"Where are the others?"

"Alrion is out there already, I can see him mounted. Certan, I'm not sure. Maybe his special assignment is taking longer. I haven't seen Vincent either."

"Vincent had a special assignment also," Celes said, approaching them both.

"Celes!" Lara ran over and hugged her. Celes smiled.

"You're looking well. You too, Alyx."

"Thank you." Alyx bowed.

"And I can see you're equipped well. At least my husband hasn't been slacking off." Alyx drew Andrylir and let Lara and Celes examine it.

"This sure beats my Runesteel dagger." Lara looked impressed.

"Phenomenal work, I'll have to compliment Vincent." Celes looked out into the distance. "I think they're starting to head out?"

"You're right. Why don't we get started then?" Lara looked at them each in turn. Alyx and Celes both nodded.

"We should push through to catch up to Alrion." Alyx didn't wait for agreement, she started moving out. She could sense the others just behind her. Alyx could recognise the different sections of the army. Even though they were on the move, it was relatively easy to slip between them with their smaller group focused on moving faster. Within half an hour they had reached the front. Alrion was riding out front alone, on a horse. However, he still stayed relatively close to the main force.

I wonder what he's thinking? He looks like he's deep in thought. Almost meditating.

That made sense, he needed to prepare himself for the coming conflict. Although something looked different. Alyx couldn't quite pick it. Until suddenly she realised.

"He doesn't have his Runesteel sword."

"Oh, you're right. That's odd, isn't it?" Lara said. She paused for a moment before continuing. "I didn't see it back at the apartment."

"Do you think he left it somewhere else on purpose?" Celes said.

"Perhaps. Maybe Certan is taking it somewhere for him?"

"It's not cause for concern, his power greatly outweighs what he can do with the sword." Alyx didn't want to upset the others, she was just surprised. He had seemed genuinely relieved to have the sword back, despite freely giving it to her.

After a short while, Alrion stopped completely still. He didn't say anything, just remained on the horse. Alyx could see why.

The Blight forces were visible now. They had massed into a seething horde that stretched as far as the eye could see.

"The Blight are here. They weren't messing around, I did not expect them to march this far," Alyx said.

"Just as well we mobilised quickly. As much as the city is designed to withstand a siege, it would be devastating to the population."

"I'm no soldier, but do you think we can handle such a large number?" Celes looked at them both.

"Normally, I would say no, but we have Alrion up front. He can decimate their forces before we even engage." Lara turned to Alyx. "Do you agree?"

"Yes, that's an accurate assessment." Alyx was about to speak more when she saw movement from the Blight. There was something rippling through them. Suddenly Darvin burst from the front lines, storming forward. He stopped when he was near Alrion.

"Thank you for heeding my call," Darvin shouted, addressing the army at large. He focused his attention on Alrion. Lara started creeping forward, and Alyx and Celes joined her.

"It's time we put aside this misunderstanding and allow each other to peacefully coexist," Darvin said. Alyx looked to Lara.

"What's he on about?"

"I'm not sure."

"I've encountered him before. He's not one for peace, but he is one for manipulation. Don't trust a word he says." Celes shook her head, glaring at the Blight General.

"No response, young wizard? Nothing to say for yourself?" Darvin started approaching. He drew his sword and shield.

"Perhaps I should beat it out of you?" Darvin laughed and started running forward. Alrion skilfully leapt off the horse, holding his footing. He stepped forward, his eyes focused on Darvin. The Blight General leaned in with a giant swing. Instead of fighting back, Alrion merely stepped to the side. Darvin continued by slamming his shield at Alrion. The young wizard held out a palm and blocked the strike. A ripple seemed to roll through Alrion.

"That's odd, I didn't realise he could enhance his body like that," Alyx said.

"I haven't seen that either. I know he can enhance himself with the Soul Power, but he's never really demonstrated it." Lara looked concerned. Celes crept further, looking like she had noticed something.

"I need a closer look," she said, creeping forward again. Darvin attacked, again and again, Alrion just dodged and blocked where required. The movements were simple but skilful and completely efficient.

I've never seen him move so well.

"We have a problem. I'm sure of it now." Celes turned back and looked at Lara and Alyx.

"What's wrong?"

"I don't think that's the real Darvin. Vincent cracked his shield when they fought. Now there's no sign of it."

"Couldn't he have just fixed it?"

"A shield like that? I don't think you can. Vincent did something strange to it, drawing on his Soul Power." Celes looked like she was thinking it through. "I bet it's not him and that's a lookalike shield. If I'm right, Alyx should slice right through it."

"I'm up for that. For some reason, Alrion isn't fighting back either." Alyx strode forward, preparing to draw her blade. Again,

Darvin was pressing the attack, and again Alrion was dodging around. He didn't make a single offensive move.

"Time for me to show you how it's done." Alyx drew her sword and launched into a wide arcing strike. Alrion retreated, and Darvin threw up his shield. Just as Celes had predicted Alyx sliced through without issue.

It felt even less resistance than the stone. This is not the same.

"You're not Darvin, are you?" Alyx said. Darvin laughed.

"Of course I'm Darvin, my dear. I remember all about you. It's just, well how do I put this, I'm not the original." Darvin threw her a cackling laugh and retreated into the mass of Blight.

"Good work, Alyx," Celes said as she approached. She was about to speak again when Alrion dropped to his knees. He was in intense concentration.

"Let it go, Certan." Alyx watched as Alrion's features flickered and disappeared. Certan was there, kneeling before them.

"What?" Celes said. Lara too looked shocked. Certan rose, taking a deep breath.

"I apologise for the subterfuge, it was at Alrion's request. He did not expect Darvin to fight fair, so he thought he shouldn't either. I guess he was right."

"If Darvin isn't here, then he must be waiting for Alrion. With his entire strength and who knows what else." Lara looked panicked. Alyx felt the feeling too. It was a dread realisation in the pit of her stomach.

Alrion is alone behind enemy lines, and the enemy commander is likely preparing an ambush.

"He needs backup, but we're in even more trouble here now that we don't have him to help thin them out." Alyx was in two minds about where to go. But Lara had no such hesitation.

"I'm not a front-line fighter, please do your best here." Lara dashed away at speed, threading her way through friendly forces. Alyx looked to the enemy.

I can do a lot of good here, but I feel like Alrion needs me.

Just as she felt herself leaning towards joining Lara, she saw a shape emerging from the crowd.

It can't be.

The creature was wearing exactly the same twisted grin. It was like no time had passed at all.

"The Skull King is mine," Alyx said as she began to advance.

46

A FALSE BATTLE

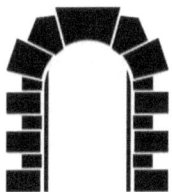

A lrion stumbled through the undergrowth, not seeing one of the tree roots. It was so hard concentrating on his spell, and he was so tired. All night he had worked with Certan to perfect the illusion spell in a way that Certan could maintain it. Now he was keeping himself invisible and masking as much noise as possible.

But he was weary. The effort was taking its toll, slowly but surely.

Maybe I'm far enough away from the armies to relax a bit.

Alrion leaned against a tree trunk, taking a moment to catch his breath. He decided to push on a little further. He could rest soon once he saw the cave. Once he entered, that would be it.

I hope the plan worked. If Darvin thinks I took the bait, I might be able to get in and finish the spell before he can intervene. If I'm incredibly lucky.

It was a lot to ask for, but it was worth a shot. He almost tripped again and swore.

Time to let the invisibility go. It's not worth it anymore.

Alrion let the spell go, feeling a huge weight lifting from his shoulders. There were a few ways to create and maintain an invisibility spell. He had chosen one with a strong Will component. He didn't want to burn too much of his Spark too soon.

Noises of the conflict reached him from afar, but he tried not to think too much about it. That battle was important, but not what he had come here for. His battle would be entirely different. Alrion saw a clearing ahead and charged towards it. Maybe he was closer than he realised.

The cave looked exactly as he expected. A rather ordinary looking entrance flanked by rough rocks. The grass didn't grow on it, the ground above was dry and lifeless, and the rest of the stone was free from any greenery. But there was a feature he had not anticipated. Darvin was standing in front of the entrance.

"Come out, Alrion, no need to be shy." Darvin grinned and beckoned into the distance. Alrion stepped out of the trees into the clearing.

"This is a surprise and not a welcome one." Alrion looked Darvin in the eyes.

"I would say almost the same thing. All reports were that you were heading up the attack force. But you see, I wasn't worried about that. I wanted to make sure if you made your way here, we could have a little conversation. And here we are." Darvin stepped a few paces closer then stopped.

"I have other business to attend to. What do you want?" Alrion made himself sound wearied and disinterested, which was quite easy to draw upon. He was weary of games, and Darvin no doubt had another.

"Your business is my business if you don't mind. You know, my orders are to let you through. Collectively, we think that you'll help us, not hinder us. But I'm not so trusting. There's no way I'm letting you in there until you become infected." Darvin drew his sword and shield and took up a ready stance.

"I see. In this situation, it's not in my interests to kill you when I can save you. But I'll do whatever I need to in order to get inside and fulfil my quest. It's best you step aside now. Wait it out, and you'll be free from these burdens in no time."

"That's a matter of perspective. In my eyes, the burdens will be brought by you!" Darvin took another step forward.

"It's a fight then?" Alrion drew his Runesteel sword. He glanced at the diamond and it was shining brightly.

Maybe I can wear him down without using too much Spark. I don't want to be in a position where I can't perform the spell.

Alrion started a standard form, warming himself up. Darvin seemed to know it well, he moved at the same pace and anticipated each strike, blocking or parrying with ease. Alrion did notice that Darvin's shield seemed especially strong. He expected his Runesteel to do more to it than it did. If Darvin wasn't so able with the sword, Alrion would have believed that Darvin just relied on the shield.

After a few exchanges, Alrion realised that Darvin was just too good. Even as Alrion got faster and more involved, Darvin just upped the tempo and was always one step ahead.

I'm not a sword fighter, how can I beat him this way? I can't ignore my talents.

Alrion dismissed the option of using his Soul Power. He needed to conserve it as much as possible. There was no knowing how much he would need to perform the spell. That left his Spark. He was a wizard, after all, he'd have to win this fight like one.

Alrion stepped back and sheathed his sword.

"Giving up already? We've barely started!"

"I know where this is going. At my best, I couldn't really trouble you with the sword, not for more than an instant."

"Very wise, you have good instincts." Darvin sized Alrion up. "What are you going to do now?"

"This." Alrion focused his Spark into a quick release fireball that hurtled towards Darvin. He held up his shield and the spell fizzled into nothing. Darvin laughed.

"Did your encounter with the Skull Queen teach you nothing? You thought you could just waltz in here and blow me away?" Darvin's laughter turned into cackling. Alrion was furious.

He's getting under your skin. Just think carefully.

Alrion could see that the direct spell was dispelled by the shield. He did remember that the Skull Queen had done something similar with that sword she had wielded.

Direct attacks won't work. But other things will. And my Will should still be effective.

Before Alrion could plan another attack, Darvin was on the move. He launched into a flurry of strikes, weaving his shield into the attack pattern. Alrion used his Runesteel sword to block and parry, but he was losing ground quickly. And the exertion on his already tired body was worrying. He stumbled back, and Darvin used that as inspiration for another string of attacks.

Alrion acted on instinct. He raised a chunk of earth, upsetting Darvin's footing and using the distraction to roll away. He drew in deep breaths, taking the time to recover.

"So now you're thinking like a wizard. About time." Darvin grinned.

Is he enjoying this? Probably. He's been consistent in that. Taunting and such the whole way through. Maybe I can unsettle him, maybe that will turn the tide.

Alrion had a few glimmers of a plan, but it hadn't quite formed. In the meantime, he had to keep Darvin busy.

"I can't target you with my spells, but I can have some fun myself." Alrion sent multiple waves of rippling earth at Darvin, all from different directions. The Blight General stepped aside, dodging some and using his shield to deflect the rest. He looked inconvenienced, but not concerned about the attack.

At least his shield didn't completely negate the attacks. I can work with this.

Unfortunately, Alrion couldn't use the approach he had done with the Skull Queen. He had no backup and he needed to conserve his Soul Power. But there had to be a way he could wear down Darvin using his magic.

Before Darvin could start up a new attack, Alrion was already preparing his next. He lifted chunks of stone out of the ground and hurled them at Darvin.

"You'll have to do better than that." Darvin sneered at Alrion then spun around, slicing two of the large stones and battering another away with his shield. Alrion wasn't using too much Spark, but it was adding up and he wasn't really damaging Darvin at all.

I need something better. Can I use my Will to influence the environment more?

Alrion had an idea, but it was going to be hard to do. He took in a deep breath and steeled himself. He started building up his spark and preparing a visualisation. Darvin started approaching.

"Why are we fighting like this, Alrion. Surely you know what you're up against." Darvin kept approaching, his shield and sword in a relaxed position by his sides. "Why are you so insistent on completing this quest? The Blight can be a tool for your use. Join us and influence us from within. Together we can make the world a better place."

"No. I've already had a taste of that, and it sickens me." Alrion kept his concentration. Darvin came closer still. Time was running out. Alrion reached down and slapped the ground with his hand. It wasn't necessarily required, but it was an easy focal point for him. At that moment, he enacted a change in the area's gravity. Darvin started to stoop slightly and moved a lot slower. He started to raise his arms. Outside the area of influence, Alrion was building stone spears from the ground. More and more and more. Soon he had ten, twenty, fifty spears. Each honed to a razor point.

Consider this my thanks and acknowledgement of you, Branthor. Alrion lifted them all into the air, all aimed directly at Darvin. The Blight General was still lifting his shield and sword to protect himself. Alrion sent his stone spikes in, and at the last moment changed the space around him. Suddenly, everything moved incredibly quickly. It didn't last long, but it was enough to have an enormous impact.

Almost instantaneously the array of spikes appeared next to Darvin, on a collision course. There was no way he could block or strike them all. But then he did something unexpected. He tapped his shield and it expanded its size. Much faster than Alrion could track. And as the spikes impacted, Alrion heard a giant clang sound, like an ominous bell.

Once the dust settled, Alrion saw that Darvin was not there. Instead, his shield was spread out like a small dome.

"Are you under that?" Alrion said, incredulously.

"Of course. Did you think I would let you hit me with all that?" Darvin's voice echoed from within the shield dome, sounding harsher and more unusual than ever before. Alrion looked around, seeing the broken bits of stone spikes all over the ground.

"I'll break through eventually; your shield isn't perfect. Look, it even has a crack in it." Alrion noticed the crack and his hope increased. But the more he looked at it, the stranger it appeared. It had to be older than just now, and it didn't look like his stone spears had done the damage. It was too clean.

"Yes, but not by your hand. I can last long enough to bring more pain to you, mark my words."

"Fine, I'll just walk by you." Alrion stopped walking but he heard Darvin's laughter and stopped.

"Be my guest. When you least expect it, I'll be there, interrupting your plans and forcing you to our side." Darvin kept laughing.

I didn't expect this. He obviously did. He had this stalemate as a fall-back.

"This is what you get for sneaking off without me," a voice said from behind. Alrion whirled around. It was Lara. She did not look impressed.

It's good to see her.

"Impeccable timing. I have a cowardly Blight General to deal with." Alrion pointed at the shield.

"I know, I've been watching this fight. You had us fooled for a while, I didn't expect that. Nice trick with Certan." Lara glared at him, but he could see some small amount of surprise and respect in there.

"It was necessary. Unfortunately, Darvin had plans too."

"He sure did. Certan was fighting another Darvin before I headed over."

"Another one?" Alrion glanced back at the shield. Nothing had changed.

"Yes, it didn't elaborate. But we figured out it was not the original."

Lara walked past Alrion and pointed at the crack in the shield. "And I know how that shield was damaged."

"How?"

"Your father used some sort of strike that used Soul Power. Have a think about it." Lara looked at Alrion then at his sword. Then she pointed at the crack. He nodded.

She's not speaking additional detail out loud.

"That's all well and good, but I can't waste Soul Power on this. I don't know how I could break that shield." Alrion said the words for Darvin's benefit, but quietly drew his sword.

If my father could enhance his blade with Soul Power, I can too. He tried pushing some through his hand into the blade. It felt strange, but it began to work.

"I can likely only create the opening, you need to complete the job," Alrion whispered to Lara. She nodded.

"Maybe you have some sort of potion that will damage the shield?" Alrion said to Lara. She winked at him and started rummaging through her things, retrieving her Runesteel dagger and holding it ready.

"Oh, perhaps. Let me look." Alrion smiled back at her and focused on his sword. He could spare a bit of Soul Power, enough to work on that crack that was already there.

"Take your time, I don't think he can actually bring any help here." Alrion advanced slowly, nodding at Lara. She followed too. He hoped that their conversation would distract Darvin, or at least invite him to focus on communicating with others. Once they were close, Alrion made himself stable.

Here goes.

Alrion focused the Soul Power in his blade towards the tip, and it seemed to collect more there. Next, he leaned back and thrust forward as hard as possible. The Runesteel impacted with the shield with a great crash but didn't bounce off. It found space within the crack and started to press further. Lara stood at the ready. As the shield started to give way, it started transforming.

Oh no, he's changing his stance. I'll probably miss completely.

Darvin rose as his shield reverted to its normal size. The transformation threw Alrion's strike off, and he lost his balance. Darvin started cackling. He dropped his sword and withdrew a black dagger with a thick inky substance dripping off the blade. As he prepared to attack Alrion, he suddenly dropped to his knees.

Lara stepped back, admiring her handiwork. She had circled around Darvin and thrust the Runesteel dagger into the creature's heart, from behind.

"This cannot be," Darvin muttered, before falling face down into the ground. He started transforming once again, a black dust flaking into the air. His body was returning to what it once was, before the Blight.

"I'm sorry that I couldn't save you," Alrion said.

47

A LONELY PATH

L ara drew Alrion aside, and they walked away from both the cave entrance and Darvin's body. She sat him down on some rocks in a nearby glade. They hadn't spoken at all since the fight.

"What were you thinking? You could have died back there!" Lara shouted at him, pounding his chest with her fists. Alrion let her.

"I'm sorry, it's my journey to take. Nobody else can do this for me."

"What was your plan? I saw what he did to your spells. He wasn't afraid of you at all. What would you have done if I hadn't shown up?"

"If I couldn't wear him down enough? I'd try to cure him."

"Wouldn't that weaken you for a long time?"

"Yes. But it would have worked if I needed it." Alrion looked away. He couldn't argue with her, she was right. But there was another reason he had snuck away. A more painful one.

"I'm just glad I found you in time."

"Have you used what I gave you?"

"Not yet." Lara retrieved the two small glass vials. They almost looked empty. Alrion activated his Soul Power and saw the power within them.

"Still looks good. That will help you in a pinch."

"I'm going with you." Lara gestured back towards the cave.

"You can't. Nobody can."

"I think you just proved that you can't be left alone." Lara looked annoyed. But she stopped glaring at him and looked worried instead. "There's too much at risk. Can't you trust me?"

"Of course, I trust you. I don't trust myself." Alrion looked past her, towards the cave.

"What do you mean?" Lara sat closer, holding his hand in hers. He didn't look at her, not yet.

"I need to be alone in there. If I have you with me, maybe they can use that against me."

"That's not a good enough reason, it's worth the risk." Lara reached over and turned his head, so he was looking at her.

She's right. She must suspect something else is wrong.

"Fair enough. Let me put it this way." Alrion sighed and collected his thoughts. "If I must sacrifice myself for this, I need to be at peace with that. And having you there will make it much harder to do. I'll probably cling to my life and make a bad choice. I need to keep my focus and do what is required." He let himself look into her eyes. She had tears in there.

"The world is not your responsibility. There's always another way." He could see the sadness behind her eyes, he knew the extent of what the Blight had meant for her and her family. It was not easy for her to say those words.

"I don't want to die. I don't want to be sacrificed for everyone else. But if that makes all this go away, I'll do it. You said there was another of Darvin, the Blight will keep reinventing itself until it wins. I have to stop it here." Alrion felt his resolve harden a bit more.

Maybe I'll get taken by this process, but it would protect Lara and everyone else. That's worth it, isn't it?

He saw Lara wiping away her tears. He gave her a hug and felt her warmth seeping into him. He put everything aside for a minute and basked in it. Alrion then pulled away, standing up.

"I need to keep going. I'm sorry."

"What if I..." Lara said, but Alrion raised a hand.

"You can't enter the cave, that's final. But you can help everyone else. Isn't that worth doing? We don't know how my actions here will affect the battle being fought elsewhere." Alrion saw Lara thinking it over. She looked like she was coming around.

"I don't like this, but I can see you won't be swayed. I'll search the area out here for more forces or traps, then I'll rejoin the others." Lara gave him a weak smile. Alrion walked in close and leaned in. He kissed her deeply and gave her a hug. She held him tightly for a long time. Eventually, she pulled away.

"You better come back, or I'll be forced to find a way to drag you into the light. And you won't enjoy that!"

"Doesn't sound like it." Alrion forced a chuckle. They started walking back to the glade where they had fought Darvin. His body had completely returned to a human one. Alrion forced himself to look for a moment.

"Good luck," Lara said. Alrion reached into his pocket and retrieved a small bag. He threw it to her.

"What's this?"

"It's the ring you stole from me."

"Why are you giving it back?" Lara had a confused look.

"You can hold it for me."

"I will. Although, it's not as fun if you just give it to me."

"Sorry about that. Thank you." Alrion turned and started walking to the cave entrance. He turned back just before he reached it, and saw that Lara was still standing there, waiting. He gave her a short wave then entered the darkness.

The cave was pitch-black. Alrion created an orb of light and had it hover just above him. Now that he could see better, the cave was completely featureless. It was just dark and boring. He walked on, listening for any signs of life. Nothing was there, save for the echoes of his footsteps. As he walked, he felt like he was going down. But the cave seemed to be getting lighter. Soon he started to see rays of light, then areas of the cave bathed in natural light. He pushed forward, curious.

Alrion emerged into an impossible space. It felt like he was outdoors. Lush trees and shrubs grew thickly around the path, and he could see glimpses of blue sky through the tree coverage.

Where am I?

This was not what he had expected. He was supposed to be heading to the source of the Blight. Darkness and decay are what he expected.

Did I go to the wrong place?

Alrion looked behind him. The cave tunnel he had travelled down was still there. It didn't look like a trick.

Time to march forward, see where I end up.

Alrion slowly progressed through the dense forest. It was eerily quiet. After a time, he picked why it seemed so odd. There were no signs of life. No animals at all. And there wasn't any wind either. Everything seemed so static.

Maybe there's a reason this is here.

Alrion could see something up ahead. It looked like a big rock formation. He made his way over, carefully. The light and life, as still as it was, felt refreshing. He soon found himself before a large lake. The water was light blue, and it almost glowed. Alrion knelt and ran his hand through the water. It tingled.

Is that Soul Power?

Alrion activated his enhanced vision and looked at the lake. It was definitely infused with Soul Power. He cupped his hands and tried drinking some. It was refreshing and energising.

This doesn't make any sense. But I may as well use it.

Alrion took a moment to drink and rest. But he didn't completely relax. There was still something strange about this environment. And he couldn't waste too much time. He stood and looked for a way around the lake. There didn't seem to be one.

Let's just try.

He started to wade through, instantly sinking down to his waist. It was slow going, but he managed to progress. Step by step he progressed through the lake. He didn't trust himself swimming and pressed forward. Slowly but surely, he made his way across. He expected it to get dark, but the light and environment remained unchanged.

As he reached the other shore, he noticed a small opening in the rock formation. It was another tunnel. Alrion climbed out of the water and used a bit of his Spark to dry his clothes.

Now, let's see where this goes.

Alrion started off, creating another orb of light to see. He noticed a change instantly. There was a strange architecture in this new tunnel or cave structure. It looked like there were places where it was narrow and other places where it expanded. There was almost an odd geometry in the walls. Regular shapes such as rectangles and squares were formed out of the rock.

It doesn't make sense.

Alrion pressed on. One section was pitch-black, another bathed in light. He lost track of where he was, and where he was going. Onward and onward he walked, no signs of any other life.

Then he saw it. It began with an uneasy sensation running down his spine. Something he felt before he noticed it. He almost didn't see it. But in the distance, in a darker section, he saw something that was blacker than black. A mass of living shadow.

"The source," Alrion whispered. Even from this distance, he recognised it from his dreams. His destination was so close. He steeled himself and took a step towards his destiny.

48

DARKNESS IN NUMBERS

Certan watched the Skull King emerge from the opposing army. He turned and witnessed Alyx's reaction. It looked like a mix of fear and rage. She was trembling.

"I don't want you to interfere." Alyx was fixated on the Skull King. She started to advance.

"As you wish. Is it another copy?"

"It has to be, but I don't care." Alyx kept advancing. The Skull King was laughing, an evil sound that made Certan's skin crawl.

If Alyx has bested this creature before, she should do so again. I doubt it is as strong as before. But she will need backup.

Certan noticed that a retinue of creatures followed the Skull King out. Not only that, but the Blight forces were losing their tight formations. At any moment, they could break out into open warfare.

"I don't like this. Chaos is about to be unleashed."

"I suggest you do what you do best," Celes said, joining him. She had a dagger in one hand and a vial of orange liquid in the other.

"I will." Certan removed a vial of his own. It looked empty, but he knew it wasn't. It was a gift from Alrion. Certan opened the vial and poured it over his hand. He felt the Soul Power wash over him like a warm glow, and it enveloped his hand, using that as a way into his body. He let the sensation settle and prepared his approach.

Certan counted two Shades and a Shade Wizard supporting the Skull King. Alyx would struggle with that combination. But he could do something about it.

"Try not to engage too soon, save your firepower for when they break loose." Certan saw Celes's acknowledgement and he instantly ran off to assist Alyx.

The Weapon Master had drawn her sword and began a duel with the Skull King. However, the creatures following the Skull King around had started flanking, looking for an opportunity to interfere.

"Not on my watch, foul creatures!" Certan shouted. They looked over at him, surprised. Certan composed himself for a moment, winding himself up. Then he shot out at surprising speed.

This power works fantastically.

Certan practically appeared in front of the Shade. He used a single punch to breach the creature's heart and watched it drop instantly, a shocked expression on its face. The other Shade began to fight back but Certan swept its leg out with his, causing it to stumble. Using that moment of weakness, he performed the same attack, killing it instantly.

The Shade Wizard was not to be caught the same way. It started throwing fireballs at Certan at close range. He rolled away, using his speed to create some distance between them. Wizard fire was hard to judge, and it could burn him quite badly if he miscalculated or the Shade Wizard was more powerful than expected.

The Skull King looked over, distracted by Certan's attack. Alyx used the moment to gain an advantage, forcing the Skull King back and getting a strike on the creature's arm. It howled with pain and rage then regrouped, attacking Alyx with twice the ferocity.

She can handle this. I need to shut down the Shade Wizard quickly.

Certan wheeled around, looking to close the distance quickly. The Shade Wizard was throwing fireballs, and waves of force. Certan saw the attacks coming and shifted his heading and stance to avoid them with minimal loss of momentum. The Shade Wizard started to panic and created a wall of fire.

Be faster.

Certan focused himself even further and pushed through the fire. He felt a searing pain for an instant but passed through. The Shade Wizard was stunned and struggled to throw more spells. But Certan was close enough. He knocked the Shade Wizard down with an open palm then broke its neck. With utmost precision, he destroyed its heart before it could recover.

Looking up, Certan could see that while he was fighting, the main Blight force had entered the fray. The battle lines were now muddled, with Valrytir soldiers and Blight fighting everywhere he could look. The Blight had overwhelming numbers. He heard an explosion over his shoulder and saw Celes throwing some of her vials. Clumps of Blighters were knocked away or retreated while on fire.

It's not enough. We need to create an advantage.

Certan considered joining Alyx's fight, as she would add considerable might to the general fight. But he decided not to, it wasn't arranged and could put her in danger if he upset the balance. Certan scanned the crowd and noticed something unusual in the distance.

"Celes, what's that?" Certan pointed.

"That's another Blight General I'd say. My guess would be Rindale?"

"Rindale. The architect of their creatures?"

"Yes, the very same."

"He might be behind these copies of the generals."

"Very astute." Celes threw a flurry of daggers over Certan's shoulder. Two Blighters dropped to the ground.

"Let's change the course of this fight." Certan didn't wait for Celes to reply. He launched himself into the Blight lines. He could feel the Soul Power draining, but he continued to use it. He focused his body completely, wasting no motion at all. He glided forward, each movement advancing him and becoming an attack. He stepped forward and kicked a Blighter over, tripping another. He elbowed another, slamming it into two more and used the collapsing heap as a springboard to launch himself into another cluster of Blighters. He landed on one and quickly rose into a spinning kick that cleared the area and killed some Blighters instantly. Others backed away immediately. Certan heard a blood-curdling cry and looked back anxiously.

Alyx was throwing herself at the Skull King, her blade gliding through the air as though it were a leaf. He was managing to block the strikes, but he was being pushed back. Any Blighters that were close were just cut down in the process. Certan thought he saw something golden on the blade, but an instant later it was gone.

"Eyes on the prize, monk." Celes pointed to Rindale. He was trying to sneak away. Certan took in a deep breath and composed himself once more.

It's too inefficient fighting the whole army. I need to be smarter.

The master monk planned his course, prepared his muscles and steeled his will. Then he launched himself into the air. He cleared a group of Blighters and landed on another. He picked up a nearby Blighter and charged forward, using the Blighter as a shield to bludgeon away anything in his path. As fast as Rindale retreated, he was held up by the sheer number of bodies surrounding him. Before long Certan had caught up. He threw the Blighter he was holding, clipping Rindale's leg just enough to make him stumble.

"I'm not so weak, monk." Rindale stood quickly and readied himself. Certan walked up slowly, not trying to attack. Rindale watched him suspiciously. Once Certan was right in front of Rindale, he held out his hand.

"What is this?"

"There is no honour in this chase, this fight. I will spare you if you come back with me."

"Come back where?"

"Back to beyond the intense fighting. I believe you have valuable information." Certan watched Rindale's reaction. The creature was intrigued. He flicked his eyes left and right, clearly evaluating his chances of getting away.

"I'm not so easy to kill, just so you know."

"I know." Certan left his hand outstretched. Rindale reached for it. As his hand closed around Certan's, the monk noticed a strange black nail. He felt it soon after.

"Ha! You're mine now." Rindale cackled. Certan was not impressed. He grabbed Rindale by the wrists and hauled him away. No matter how Rindale struggled, Certan's grip did not waver. He methodically strode back through the battlefield. The Blighters all stayed out of his way, terrified. Once they had reached a safer spot, Certan put Rindale down on the ground.

"You haven't won, you're infected."

"Am I?" Certan showed Rindale his hand. There was no wound.

"Impossible! I injected you with the Blight."

"Try again." Certan left his hand out. Rindale snatched at it and tried again. But his nail could not pierce Certan's skin. The black liquid oozed away with no effect.

"This cannot be."

"Perhaps the original Rindale could have done the job, but you're not him. What are you?"

"A shadow of my former greatness, I'm afraid," Rindale muttered.

"How did you do it?"

"You wouldn't understand." Rindale shook his head.

"I'm sure you can explain in a way we'll understand," Celes said. She approached, twirling one of her daggers.

"It was a contingency plan to keep control of the Blight. I managed to preserve the look, personality, and power of each of us. But none of the host bodies could manifest them with the right strength. We're all weaker. Lesser." Rindale shook his head.

"How many are there?"

"Just one of each. It takes time." Rindale looked around. He pointed at the Skull King. "He was a great success."

"How so?" Certan asked for curiosity's sake, but he could see what Rindale meant. Even though Alyx was fighting the creature furiously and with incredible speed and accuracy, the Skull King was not letting up or tiring.

"Darvin pushed me to find a way. The Skull King was the first of us to fall, he was missed the most. After much experimentation, I managed to succeed. Great power, at great cost."

"What was the cost?" Celes said.

"Many lives. And his personality. It's a mere shadow of him. Fine for this, but not what any of us wanted." Rindale sounded disappointed, and perhaps even sad.

"Keep questioning him. I need to stop this." Certan walked off, towards Alyx. He dispatched any lone Blighters in his path, his attention fixated on the fight. The more Alyx pushed, the further they went into enemy territory.

She will tire and be overwhelmed eventually. She needs to cool her head.

Certan jogged over and drew in close.

"Alyx, this creature is not him. It's just a monster with his appearance and attributes."

"No, this grin. It haunted me for years!" She increased her intensity again. There were nicks and breaks on the Skull King's blade, but he seemed to be fine.

"Rindale himself admitted that it's just a shadow, but an incredibly strong one. You need to fight smarter." Certan shadowed her movements, trying to figure out how to get through to her. But he could see it now. She was in a blind rage. The Skull King's reappearance had tapped into something else. He knew what he had to do.

Certan watched carefully, then he made his move. Alyx had a fantastic opening and she lurched forward with a massive overhead strike. Certan dashed in, one hand catching her blade, and another stopping the Skull King's. He could feel both weapons surging ahead, trying to eat through his hands. But he steeled his will and held firm.

"Alyx, listen to me." Certan could see her blindly pushing on. "Alyx, you can't defeat him like this." Alyx barely noticed him. She just pushed harder with her sword.

Nothing else to do then.

Certan let go of each sword but guided their path as soon as they jumped free. Both swords were thrust into the ground. Certan shoved them even further, to ensure they were hard to dislodge. As Alyx struggled to free her sword, Certan tapped into the minimal Soul Power left in his body. It felt so close to his own life force. He mixed the two and prepared a special technique. He turned and faced the giant tower of evil, the Skull King. It wasn't even trying to reach its sword, it was reaching towards Certan. He ducked under its hands and moved in close. He placed both palms on the creature's chest and let loose a blast of pure energy. He stumbled back with the effort, but the Skull King fared much worse.

A large hole was created in the creature's chest, and it toppled to the ground. Instantly, the body started to flake away. Certan turned and regarded Alyx. The rage seemed to have subsided. She tugged at her sword and managed to free it. She looked up at Certan.

"I owe you my life. I'm sorry, I lost myself."

"We all have, at one time or another. There's no time for that now, let's turn the tide of this fight." Certan pointed to a large cluster of Blighters heading towards where he had left Celes and Rindale. Alyx nodded and they jogged along, carving a path through the mass of Blighters. Certan looked back to gauge the rest of the battle's progress. It was hard to see, but he thought it was evenly matched.

Hopefully, we can change the momentum now.

"They're after Rindale, there's no time!" Celes shouted. Certan launched into a sprint. He noticed Alyx by his side.

"Follow my lead." Certan didn't even bother to look at Alyx's response. He knew she would follow. Certan aimed at the middle of the pack. He wasn't focused on killing them, he was more focused on knocking them down and keeping them occupied. After he had their attention, they changed their focus to try to swarm him. But then Alyx swooped in.

With large arcing slices she decimated them with ease. With their attention divided, they had no way of avoiding her blade. Any that tried to run, found Certan knocking them back into the path of Alyx's blade. Within minutes, the group had been dispatched.

Certan drew in more deep breaths. His stamina was running out. He looked over and saw Celes questioning Rindale. She looked concerned. He rushed over as fast as he could.

"You look concerned. What happened?"

"That push happened because Rindale started to spill. I hope Lara found Alrion."

"Why, what is it?"

"Not only did the real Darvin go to intercept him, but there's another surprise lying in wait. Something dark and horrible." Celes didn't bother hiding the dismay on her face. Certan understood the feeling completely. He looked up at the battlefield.

"We need to trust in their strength, there's too much to be done here." Certan stood and started his return to the fighting.

Be safe, Alrion, and may wisdom guide your path.

49

STRUGGLE

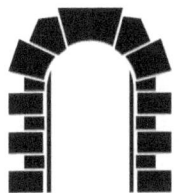

Alrion moved forward, one step at a time. He didn't want to make a wrong move. There was something incredibly unsettling about the darkness beyond. He couldn't make out any details, perhaps that is what made it worse.

Definitely in the right place.

He couldn't see anything past the mass of black. It seemed like it sucked the light out of anywhere nearby, it was that dark. Quiet too. Completely silent, save for his footsteps. They echoed around on the rocky floor. He decided to create an orb of light and send it over to get a better look at what he was heading towards.

The orb floated over towards the darkness. The closer it moved, it seemed as though something was pulling the light from it. Alrion waited and watched. Soon enough the orb was dimmer.

That's strange. I better investigate.

Alrion's mind started imagining some crazy scenarios and dreamed up some ridiculous monsters. But he pushed that aside.

I've seen this before, it's just a wall or gateway or something like that. I don't need to build it up more than it needs.

As he approached, he cast another orb of light and floated it over near the first. The extra light helped a little, although it began to fare the same as the other one. But he did catch sight of something.

There was movement. That shouldn't be happening. He took a few more cautious steps. He sensed movement again and turned sharply. Nothing was happening, but he knew there was something.

"Show yourself," Alrion said, his voice stronger than expected. He didn't hear any response or notice any motion. He stepped forward again. Suddenly there was movement. From multiple directions. Alrion sent out a wave of fire and watched it alight several things at once. But he couldn't get a sense of what they were. He activated his Soul vision and gasped.

They were black sinewy tendrils of darkness, full of the Blight. They looked as though they were somehow made from the Blight itself. They snaked through the air, shrugging off the flames which soon died out.

I can't believe it. This is what Ashra sent at me!

Alrion was stunned. His body went numb.

Don't freeze up! Fight them!

He channelled his Spark into another fire attack. He knew it wouldn't do much, but he needed to keep moving. The tendrils were accelerating now, and he couldn't count how many there were.

Did I fight them the right way last time? Isn't that a waste of Soul Power?

Alrion tried waves of force, trying to batter them around so they tangled one another. It did work a little, but the tendrils seemed to coordinate perfectly, never quite coming into contact with each other. He pulled at a rock jutting out of the wall, and wrenched it free with a force spell, throwing it towards the biggest mass of tendrils. One was knocked about a little, but the rest expertly dodged away.

They started to converge now and sped towards him in a tight clump.

Maybe I can get them with a more intense heat.

Alrion gathered his Spark and created a beam of condensed flame. It shot out at incredible speed and blazed across the space. The collection of tendrils fanned out, then came at him from different angles. Alrion knelt and worked the earth beneath him. It formed a protective barrier that they all smashed against. But they were strong, and the barrier wouldn't hold for that long.

Maybe there's no choice?

Alrion took a moment to compose himself. It was difficult with the vast number of creatures banging against his defensive wall. But he knew that he had a few moments.

Think through the spell and try it.

Even though he had succeeded in Ashra's trial, it wasn't a very targeted spell. It had been a lot safer to use, but he hadn't exactly wielded it with precision. This situation, however, required more finesse. He didn't want to bring the whole place down on him. Alrion started to gather his Spark and create the basis of a light bomb. But as before, he fed in Soul Power. This seemed to somehow contain the energy a little. The two powers were in equilibrium in a glowing sphere. He pushed it out against his wall. The sphere passed through the wall, burning it away like it wasn't there. It must have hit one of the tendrils because he heard a sizzling and wailing sound.

At least it works. Alrion sensed that the bomb was still intact, so he sent a pulse of Spark into it. This upset the balance and the light bomb exploded. After a flash of white Alrion opened his eyes. His defensive barrier was gone, and there was a small piece of floor removed. There seemed to be fewer tendrils than before, but still a lot. And they were completely spread out now.

Well, that worked. A little too well. Even that small size and the Soul Power didn't make it that safe. Maybe I can use it as a tool, rather than an explosion.

The spell had taken out one of them by merely making contact. Alrion created another and dubbed it a Soul Bomb. It floated in the air before him. It shone so brightly, he could barely look at it. The tendrils of black seemed to avoid it as well. Just as he started to feel like he had a handle on the situation, he felt something wrapping around his right leg. He looked down and saw a tendril had snuck up on him. As he turned, it wrapped around tighter, causing him to drop to his knees. Alrion used a wave of force to tug at the Soul Bomb, bringing it around to his leg. With a quick adjustment of its trajectory, it burned through the black tendril, turning it to ash.

That's better.

Only Alrion saw that his leg was quite damaged by the attack. It was quite weak and he almost stumbled when getting up.

They're not trying to infect me, they're trying to weaken me. And it's apparently quite easy to do.

Alrion directed some Soul Power to the injured leg and lamented yet another drain on it. He didn't have an unlimited amount. More tendrils had circled around and were going for his legs. Alrion drew his sword and took a swipe. They expertly dodged and came in close. Alrion pulled his Soul Bomb closer and managed to clip one before the other flew away.

I wonder if this would work.

Alrion used his hand to channel Soul Power into his sword again. This time he found a way to manipulate it so there was a bigger area of coverage. It extended beyond the blade's edge. When the next three tendrils attacked, Alrion carefully aimed his sword to look like he was just missing. The tendrils did not dodge but were knocked down by the Soul Power attached to his blade. While they were incapacitated, he swung his Soul Bomb down, burning them away.

That was more effective.

Alrion took a few steps back, surveying the scene. There were still more enemies, but they were more cautious now that he had defeated quite a few. But it was taking a toll on him. He decided to end it quickly. He sheathed his sword and let the Soul Bomb dissipate. He closed his eyes and waited.

He could hear them howl as they flew in. They seemed to delight at the opportunity. He wanted to run, to defiantly fight back. But it would be too draining. This would be better. He drew all his Soul Power into a small spot, condensing it. He was thinking about the barrier that his grandmother had done. Only, he wasn't going to overcharge it. This would be something else.

He felt them attacking now. First his legs, then his arms. Then his torso, and even his head. They had completely wrapped around him. A wave of panic ran through him. He was being smothered.

Control the situation.

Alrion pushed his Soul Power out as a barrier, just far enough to encompass all the tendrils of black attached to him. They shrieked in agony as it passed over them. But it did nothing more. However, he then used his Spark to build a light bomb. He mixed in a tiny bit of Soul Power, then triggered an explosion. A flash of white, a bang, then nothing.

Alrion pulled himself up off the ground. There was a ringing in his ears and he could barely see. His eyes had to readjust to the darkness. It took a long time. Or there was more darkness, which was just as likely. He couldn't see or sense any more of those things. His body was battered and sore. He had some Spark left, and some Soul Power, but nowhere near as much as he would have liked.

Nothing ever works out as you'd like.

Alrion found his sword and sheathed it. The darkness beyond was still there, only it didn't seem quite so dark.

Maybe those creatures had made it appear darker. He took a deep breath and pushed on. He created a tiny orb of light to help, but it did little to penetrate the darkness. Tentatively he kept walking. The geometry on the walls was here too, and there were some wild shapes that seemed impossible. But they weren't why he was here. Soon enough he saw what he expected.

A wall of darkness, in slow but constant motion. At the same time, it looked like it was oozing yet also a void of nothing. He saw in his mind the image of his grandfather touching it. He could understand why. It defied logic. There was an irresistible urge to just take it in your hand and see if you could make sense of it. Alrion forced his hands to stay in his pockets. He didn't want to be too rash.

Some of the elements of the spell came to the front of his mind. He would need to interact directly with the wall to enable the spell to work. As he considered the best way to do that, he noticed something odd. The wall itself was changing. Forming something. A head. No, more than that. An entire body stepped out of the wall, made of the same substance and connected to the wall by millions of tiny strands.

"Welcome, Alrion, we've been waiting for you." The creature of black spoke to him.

"What are you?"

"I'm the Blight. The manifestation of consciousness behind all those connected to me. We have much in common."

"I very much doubt that." Alrion didn't know what to think. He hadn't expected this. Nothing mentioned this.

"We are both born of Granthion." The thing smiled and Alrion shuddered.

"I don't understand."

"The great wizard Granthion caused all this, as you know. Our sentience is thanks to him. His power awakened the ability in us to act. And so we have. Developing our own people, our own ways. Strengthening our bond. And yet, here you are. Trying to take that all away from us."

"You have no right to those gifts when you only have them by destroying human lives."

"Destroying? No, we enhance them. Do you not believe that?"

"Of course not. I've experienced the terror myself."

"You were just afraid and rejected the bond. In time, you would accept and find joy from it. Ours is just a different way." The creature held out a hand. Alrion stepped back.

"What are you doing?"

"It doesn't matter what you want to do, you need to interact with us anyway. Hold my hand, so that we may understand each other better." The creature held out its hand. Alrion looked at it warily.

This doesn't feel right. What do I do?

Alrion stepped back again and channelled his Soul Power into his hand as a precaution. The creature of the Blight did not move, perhaps it was restrained to the source. He debated in his mind on how to move forward. He doubted he could even interact with the source without touching the creature. Just as Alrion reached a decision he heard footsteps. He turned to see who was approaching.

50

THE MISSING PIECE

A lrion saw a figure in the distance, approaching. It looked
like a man in a hood. A wizard.

It's him!

Alrion turned completely and ignored the creature of the Blight.
He started walking away. The wizard kept approaching.

"Announce yourself. Who are you?" Alrion said.

"You know me as Aydan. We've been conversing for a while now."
The wizard kept approaching at a steady rate. His voice sounded
strange, like it had been altered.

"So, you're the one that's been following me around everywhere.
And sending me messages in that book. Finally, you show yourself."
Alrion was annoyed.

*Now this wizard shows up, at the critical time. A time when I can't use
help from anyone else. A time when this wizard would just be a hindrance.*

"I came at the appropriate time. I apologise for all the subterfuge,
I needed to keep my identity secret."

"I could have used your help before. Now, it's pointless. Even five
minutes ago would have been helpful. What comes next is just for
me, as you should know."

"I am sorry, I was supposed to be here. I thought you had

returned to the battle, but I made a mistake. That delayed me getting here." The wizard had approached Alrion and was standing right before him. His face was still hidden by his hood.

"Now you're here, you could at least show me who you are."

"Yes, you should know." The wizard spoke without the voice masking. Alrion gasped.

"No, it can't be. That's impossible."

"It's not impossible. You and everyone else just accepted a false truth." Alrion stepped forward and thrust back the hood. He was staring into his father's eyes.

"I still don't believe it. Prove it."

"As you wish. We are safe for a time." Vincent held out his hand and a small flame appeared above it. Alrion shook his head, not impressed. The flame grew larger then morphed into three different-sized flame spheres, all rotating at different speeds.

"Must I go on?" Vincent said. He let the flames dissipate.

"I don't understand. Why do all this? You've spent your entire life lying to me, lying to everyone." Alrion's voice sank. This was not the revelation he expected, or even wanted.

"It was my father's idea. At first, he was scared of me being targeted by the Blight. And then he wanted me kept secret to keep his progress on a cure secret."

"What do you mean cure? You?"

"You know I can use Soul Power. My father knew that too. He intended on us curing the Blight together, as father and son."

"But he died saving you?"

"Yes, because I left him alone. Then I was captured by Rindale and infected. My father knew he would lose his chance at saving the world from the Blight, but he could save me instead. That was his gift to the world." Vincent wore a sad smile. Alrion thought about it, he let the thought sink in.

I know what it's like to have that weight on your shoulders. Has he carried it all this time?

Alrion stepped back.

"I can't believe you lied to me again. Is there anything else you haven't told me?"

"No, nothing important. I left some papers with your mother, that will explain more than we can discuss here."

"Does she know? Weren't the two of you investigating the mysterious wizard?"

"We were. We parted ways so that your mother could continue the investigation. She found me out, as I had hoped."

"But why not just tell her?"

"It is easier to come to the understanding yourself, rather than being told." Vincent paused, thinking before he continued. "Also, there is a great danger in this information becoming widely known. I was genuinely interested to see if there was any evidence that she could find to tie me to that identity."

"And was there?"

"Yes. But now it is safe with us." Vincent looked past Alrion, to the darkness beyond. "You've seen it?"

"By it, do you mean the wall or the human-like figure?"

"The human one. Whatever you do, don't hold its hand." Alrion looked over at the creature, and back at his father.

"What do you mean?"

"It's the wrong connection to make. You'll be compromised too quickly, and unable to complete the spell."

"What do you suggest I do instead?"

"Something else. Together with me. As my father intended." Vincent smiled again, this time it was warm.

"Together? You keep saying that. There was no mention of two wizards in what I read."

"The information from the Pool of Knowledge is quite selective. As you know, it tells you what you need to know, not what you want to know. It's like a wizard in that respect." Vincent chuckled. "It was always designed for two. One as a conduit for the Light, one as a conduit for the Darkness. Guess which one dies."

"Knowing as much as you do, having lived this for your whole life. Are you willing to just resign to that fate? Why must death be a part of this spell?" Alrion challenged his father, daring him to keep up that line of thinking. Vincent looked thoughtful.

"Well, my son, I suppose we should keep an open mind. When my father designed this, he was imagining one wizard with Soul Power, not two. Perhaps there is a way." Vincent gave Alrion a slight shrug.

"I'll take that, it's something I can work with. I've done enough impossible things already, that this can just be another one."

"Very well, I won't argue the point. You've certainly grown into a resourceful man and a wonderful wizard. As I always knew you could be."

"Yet you kept trying to get me to be a blacksmith?"

"It's a good life, you should try it. And remember, there's a lot of overlap between what I taught you like the keys to blacksmithing and being a wizard." Vincent looked distracted.

"Is something wrong?" Alrion looked around himself, trying to see what was happening.

"We can't delay any longer. We need to do what we came to do." Vincent held out a hand to gesture Alrion forward, and they walked side by side towards the darkness. The creature tilted its head, regarding them.

"Two wizards from Granthion, how odd. I did not expect this."

"It's not going to go down as you expect." Alrion clenched his right fist then relaxed it.

"Whatever you think you are planning, you cannot avoid the inevitable. Your family's history of sacrifice will be continued." The creature spoke solemnly, but its eyes seemed to tell a different story. They appeared to be mirthful, almost laughing. Alrion stepped forward, but Vincent held him back.

"Don't take the bait. The Blight is masterful at manipulation. We can engage on our own terms. Observe." Vincent stepped forward and the Blight creature extended its hand again. Vincent stepped around it, and the creature couldn't follow. Before Alrion could say anything, Vincent had thrust his hand into the darkness beyond.

51

SOUL OF LIGHT

Vincent felt himself immersed in the other world, that of the Blight. It was overwhelming. But he didn't let himself be taken in completely.

"Alrion, quickly now. Follow my lead and hold my hand." Vincent couldn't see clearly back into the space he had been, but he sensed the movement. A shining light weaved around the space then grasped Vincent's hand. He instantly recognised his son.

"Well done, let's navigate this together." Vincent pulled Alrion with him, and the two were thrust into a dark void. After a few moments of disorientation, Vincent found himself in a different space altogether. Alrion thankfully was by his side. As they surveyed the strange stark horizon, they noticed a pool of darker substance to one end.

"Did you read about this?" Alrion said. He looked out in wonder over the strange place they were in. Vincent shook his head.

"No, I think this is new territory. Nobody has been here before. Let's investigate the black mass over there." Vincent led the way, his son staying close.

We can do this. Maybe he's right about finding a better way.

As they neared the black mass, Vincent had a good idea of what it was. He stopped before and turned to Alrion.

"I think this is quite clear."

"Yes. That's the essence of the Blight. It's that substance they use to turn people really quickly." Alrion looked disgusted. Vincent looked out over the expanse. He couldn't see where it ended.

"There's nothing else here."

"Not quite," a voice said behind them. Vincent whirled around quickly. A black figure was standing there, watching them. It had to be the same one that had confronted them outside.

"It was clever of you to infiltrate our space. But you still won't succeed." The figure moved in a bit closer.

"We may need to take our chances." Vincent looked at Alrion. He was staring intently at something in the distance.

"Agreed." Alrion dove into the blackness, surprising Vincent. He didn't hesitate and joined his son. They were engulfed in the thick black liquid, which was like tar. It was very hard to move through and seemed to pulse with a regular beat of energy. It felt alive. Vincent wanted to say something, but he couldn't. He dragged Alrion back up to the surface and they managed to get their heads above the inky substance.

"This is not good. But I see an opportunity further ahead." Alrion didn't wait for confirmation, he surged forward.

He's got good instincts. Let's see where this takes us.

Vincent followed along, turning occasionally to see if the figure was following them. It was. Soon enough though, Vincent saw what Alrion was hinting at. There was a platform in the middle of the Blight. It was simple stone and had a tiny altar upon it, also made of stone. Atop the altar sat a strange orb.

"That's the ticket." Alrion powered ahead and reached the platform first. He bent over the orb but didn't do anything. Vincent sped up and reached the platform as well. The black figure was still advancing, hovering over the black substance.

"Look in here. What do you see?" Alrion said, peering within.

Vincent looked and gasped. It looked like people. Images of faces flashed by fast.

"This must be the link to all those who are infected. What do you think?"

"This is it, this is how we can help them all."

"I doubt you have enough Soul Power for all that. You're going to need help." Vincent looked around. He knew there had to be something else. There was a tugging on his mind, reminding him of an extra element that they would need. He walked around the platform staring out, then he saw it. A glimmer of white amongst the sea of black. He instantly knew what it was.

"Alrion, I know what we must do. Look out there and tell me what you see." Vincent directed Alrion's gaze. After a few moments, he almost jumped.

"There's something down there. Soul Power?"

"Precisely. It's all coming together now. You need to reach it and drag it back here. We can use that to cure all those people."

"It's pretty deep, I'll be drowned in that stuff. Unless." Alrion concentrated and focused on the deep sea of Blight. Vincent watched with curiosity. Nothing was happening.

"This isn't right. Try using your Spark on the Blight there." Alrion kept staring at the spot he had been focused on. Vincent gathered his Spark and tried using a wave of force to part the Blight, making a path. The flows were absorbed by the black mass. He tried again and looked closer. It was more like the Blight was drawing in the spell. Vincent tried flames, and it was the same result.

"Still trying those old tricks?" The figure of Blight was close now, but it didn't move onto the platform.

"We get it, old spells don't work in your place." Alrion didn't bother turning to look at the creature. It burst into horrific laughter. The sound was like loud gongs being banged right near their ears.

"You don't get it at all. Why do you think we made Shade Wizards, but not Shade Mystics?" The figure regarded them with curiosity. Alrion looked thoughtful.

"It was easier for you, no Soul Power."

"Close, but you're so far away from the truth. Why do you think your first experience of your Spark was triggered by feelings of frustration and anger?" Alrion turned and looked at the creature, shocked. Vincent was starting to put it together.

"We don't just target wizards for no good reason. Your grandfather wasn't involved for no good reason. Everything needs an equal and opposite force. Soul Power fuels the Myotics, the Blight Source powers your Spark." The figure leaned its head back and cackled, delighting in the revelation.

"That's why our spells are ineffective. That's why I needed to use Spark as a method for transmitting Soul Power." Alrion was nodding along.

"Don't be fooled by this creature. It speaks the truth, but it omits what it wants. There is a greater truth here." Vincent approached Alrion and put his hand on his son's shoulder.

"The source and origin of your gift do not reflect on you, nor what you can do with it. Take away the utility of that knowledge. Your Spark cannot be a weapon against them here, at the source. We must use the other tools that we have." Vincent gave Alrion a reassuring smile. He nodded one more time.

"Soul Power it is. Let's go get some more." Alrion concentrated for a moment, and Vincent did the same. Soul Power, when channelled correctly, should keep the Blight at bay, for a time. Alrion climbed down, the Blight parting just enough to avoid touching him. Vincent followed then grabbed his son's hand.

"Let's be quick about it. Support each other and we can make the trip."

"We just need to make it there, no need to conserve for the way back." Alrion set off, slowly drifting through the space. The Blight parted for Alrion's path and stayed back. Vincent tried reducing the amount of Soul Power he was emitting, and it worked.

Good, we may need some extra down the road.

It was slow going, and hard to gain glimpses of where they were headed. But they kept going and reoriented themselves when required. Finally, they reached something.

Before them was a stone circle, floating amidst all the Blight. It was glowing with Soul Power.

"Doesn't look like much, does it?" Alrion examined it. Vincent could see the Blight starting to encroach. He forced some Soul Power into Alrion, causing the Blight to shrink back. Alrion touched the circle.

"There's Soul Power in here, but I don't know how to open it." Alrion felt all over the circle, looking for something. Vincent could see the Blight massing behind them. It was in motion, trying to find an opening.

"Try using Soul Power to open it." Vincent turned back to watch the Blight. It seemed to be forming into a denser material.

It's trying to compensate for our barrier and will likely overwhelm us soon.

Vincent looked over at Alrion. He seemed to be making progress.

"It's working, but it's taking a lot of Soul Power. I think it's a kind of lock."

"Keep going, I'll pass you as much as you need." Vincent found it easier now, to flood Alrion with the Soul Power.

"Almost there." Alrion was completely focused on the Soul Power. He didn't notice the danger looming around them. The Blight started its move. Part of Vincent's barrier failed. He could feel it beginning to wrap around his leg.

"Alrion, we're almost out of time." Vincent pushed out the last of his Soul Power then drew more from his life force. A dangerous, and potentially deadly move.

I just need to hold out a minute longer.

He could feel the strain on his body, on his life. He would burn out soon. Suddenly, a flash of light emanated from Alrion.

"I did it. This is incredible, Dad. It's the source of the Soul Power. They're connected!"

"Draw it out, we're out of time." Vincent felt the Blight consuming more and more of him. He turned to look at his son. Alrion was glowing brighter. The Blight was shrinking back. Alrion turned and looked at Vincent, noticing for the first time what was happening.

"Not on my watch." Alrion held out a hand and blasted all the Blight from the area. He then placed his hand on his father's back, returning Soul Power. Vincent could feel his body recovering from the Blight. But he still felt weak from burning his own life force.

"It's my turn to protect you," Alrion said. Glowing like a being of light, with an incredible aura, Alrion led the way. As he progressed, the Blight shrank away. Vincent looked behind them. There was a thick visible cord of Soul Power linking Alrion back to the source. The other source.

Vincent looked upon his son in awe.

He's come into his own. To have that much Soul Power flowing through him requires tremendous strength of Will and control, it's incredible.

The return trip to the stone platform was faster. Vincent didn't even feel the passage of time. It was like a strange dream experience. Alrion reached the platform first and pulled Vincent up onto it. The figure of Blight looked upon them in horror.

"What have you done?"

"I've brought light to the darkness." Alrion disregarded the creature after he spoke. But it continued.

"How dare you? This is my domain. I built this. You have no right to come in here and do this!" The Blight creature was furious. It looked like it was trying to bully Alrion into doing something. But he ignored it.

"So be it. You've underestimated the Blight once again." The Blight figure closed its eyes and concentrated. Vincent sensed movement and looked over at where they had come from. The gigantic black mass of Blight sludge was on the move. But it wasn't targeting them.

The avatar of the Blight was absorbing it all. It looked to be growing darker and stronger. As it strengthened it became less and less affected by the light that Alrion was producing. Finally, it let out a satisfied sigh.

"Your power is not stronger than mine. You have the entirety of your source at your disposal. As do I." The figure finally stepped onto the platform. It was oozing the black sludge, and its eyes were like black pits of eternity.

"I'm not afraid of you. But you're afraid of me." Alrion stared at the creature defiantly.

"You're not strong enough to hurt me."

"Maybe not. But together we're strong enough to do this." Alrion held out his hand and Vincent grabbed it. Together they put their hands on the strange orb on the pedestal. Vincent could feel all the Souls of those who were trapped by the Blight.

"Now!" Alrion started drawing the Soul Power through the source and funnelling it into the orb. Vincent could feel the torrent, it was frightening how fast and powerful it was. He couldn't match it, but he could help. He reached out with his Soul Power and touched Alrion's chest. Their Souls bonded, and their collective glow more than doubled.

"This is as it should be." Alrion smiled.

"Yes, my son." Vincent smiled back. As the orb was overflowing with Soul Power, they could start to sense the effect it was having on people. They had used the Blight's system of control and connection against it, hijacking the link and using it to cure people.

The Blight avatar wailed and shrieked. It seemed to lessen in darkness, strength, and stature.

"You feed off them, don't you? How much of this is borrowed power?" Alrion said, surprise on his face.

"A mere drop in the ocean." The creature sneered at Alrion and tried to press forward. Vincent stepped in front of the orb.

"Don't even think about it." Vincent watched the creature pause, and he held his ground. Between staring off with the creature of Blight and being a party to the Soul Power curing, Vincent had no sense of how long everything was taking. But after a time, Alrion sighed and looked at him.

"Dad, there's only one soul left." Alrion looked to the avatar of the Blight.

"That thing? It has a Soul?"

"Of course I do. I'm more like you than you realise."

"I think it has a fragment of Granthion's soul. And built upon that."

"Really?" Vincent walked back to the orb and placed his hand on it. He could sense the last soul, and what Alrion had said.

It's true. Unbelievable.

"You've stopped because you can't do this through the orb, can you?" Vincent looked at his son. Alrion nodded. He pointed behind them.

"See?" Vincent turned to look at what Alrion had been pointing out. It was a similar stone circle, but it was filled with endless darkness.

"You've sealed the Blight from all those people back into the source?"

"Yes. But that thing can't go back for some reason." Alrion pointed at the creature.

"I understand now. It's why my father wanted to be a part of this." Vincent walked forward to the Blight avatar. It was giving him a curious look.

"In the name of my father, I return you to where you belong." Vincent reached out and grabbed the Blight Avatar. It laughed and readily accepted his touch, leaking a black substance into him. Vincent held strong though and kept pulling at the avatar. It started to lose its form, and as it melted it was sucked into Vincent

"No! What are you doing?"

"I'm incorporating it into my Soul. It's the only way I can destroy it, from within me."

"But what will it do to you?" Alrion looked distraught.

"I can't say for sure. My Soul will survive, but my body might not handle this concentration of Blight." Vincent stepped into the avatar's body and sped up the process. He could feel the creature rebelling within him. But at the same time, he could sense the part of his father that had created it.

I hope you'll forgive me.

52

THE BREAKING OF A WIZARD

Aydan stepped into the forest. He had never been here before, and it was a break from routine. Something must have changed,

Father has been so occupied lately. Maybe he's had a breakthrough.

It had been long enough. Aydan was a boy no longer. Yet he still suffered the same restrictions. The same need for complete secrecy. He walked amongst his father and the other wizards, and none of them had a clue. He had perfected the skill of hiding in plain sight, but it was eating him away inside.

Maybe we're at a turning point. Maybe I can finally emerge from the shadows.

Aydan continued through the forest, moving towards the meeting point. Once he arrived there was no doubt. There was a small glade that was a lot more open, but it was still masked well with tree cover.

At least it's not a cave.

Within moments he heard footsteps behind him.

"Punctuality is a virtue. Glad to see you've finally embraced it."

"Nice to see you too."

"I'll overlook that comment, today is an auspicious day. Today, we kick off a new endeavour." Father looked excited and energised. That was a good sign. He led Aydan to the middle of the glade, then removed a lantern.

"I've made a bit of a breakthrough, and I need you to verify it for me."

"What's that? It looks like an ordinary lantern."

"I can assure you it is not." The wizard turned the lantern around then handed it to Aydan.

"What's it for?"

"It's particularly sensitive to a wizard's Spark. Try it." The wizard gestured to Aydan. He looked the lantern over, wondering how it worked. He started gathering his Spark and nothing happened. He looked over at the wizard.

"Not that sensitive. Just apply a little." Aydan nodded and applied the tiniest amount of Spark to the lantern. It roared to life, a medium-sized flame dancing within it. Aydan stared at the flame.

"That's quite sophisticated. What's it for?"

"I'm thinking of using it as a test for new wizards. What do you think?"

"It should work, it's quite sensitive. If a wizard can't light it, they may not fare well with training." Aydan thought the conclusion was quite obvious.

"Exactly my thinking." The wizard held out his hand and Aydan returned the lantern.

Why has he got me testing such obvious things?

"That was just the warmup. I've got something much more interesting next." The wizard reached into his robe and removed a white stone. Aydan received the stone, turning it over in his hand. It didn't take long to see the black streak through it.

"I haven't seen anything like this before."

"Take a close look, tell me what you think." The wizard studied him, waiting.

So, it's another test. Let's see.

Aydan peered into the black substance. It didn't look natural, but it also didn't look painted on or separate to the stone. It was somehow part of the whole piece. The more he stared, the more he started to get entranced by the blackness. He imagined it pulsating and beating like it had a heartbeat. He started to become terrified by it and started to reach for his Spark.

What is happening to me?

He felt an uncomfortably warm feeling inside, and a rush of heat. And then, out of nowhere, a gigantic white flame spewed from the stone, rushing into the air and lighting some of the tree cover. The wizard quickly doused the flames. Aydan was in shock.

What just happened?

"Fantastic!" The wizard was looking up at the area that the flames had burned, then turned his attention to Aydan. "Better than I expected."

"That was a bit surprising." Aydan wanted to say frightening, but he didn't want to admit that.

"The reaction was a little stronger than I expected but good. This we can work with."

"What does that mean?"

"It means you can cure the Blight. Well, in theory. More testing is required. But no matter how I approach it, I can't do what you can do."

"Cure the Blight? That's not possible." Aydan stared in disbelief.

"It shouldn't be, at least the way that I'm thinking, but somehow it is." The wizard started pacing, talking to himself.

"This is what you've been working on all these years? Some trippy test for a fairy tale?" Aydan was just getting started. He'd lived a double life from childhood, suppressing who he was, all for this?

"This is no fairy tale. I've done many successful experiments, small scale mind you, using the stored Soul Power I have available. The results are consistent. Applying enough Soul Power to a person infected by the Blight should cure them."

"What is this Soul Power? I'm a wizard, I have Spark."

"Oh, but you have both. Soul Power is a gift from your mother. Perhaps it's time to make a trip to see her." The wizard resumed his pacing.

"I thought you lost contact with her, and it was all too difficult to talk about."

"It is difficult to talk about. And she lives at the end of the world, she may as well be lost." The wizard spoke carefully. Aydan could not believe what he was hearing.

"Let me get this straight. You know exactly where my mother is and haven't bothered to contact her. Only now, when it's convenient for you, you're thinking of going to see her?'

"Don't be silly. Where do you think I received the orbs charged with Soul Power? We've been corresponding for some time. It's slow and strictly business, but she knows and supports what I'm doing, even though we have our differences."

"This just gets better and better." Aydan threw his hands up in frustration. "You've kept me in the dark about everything. I'm not a child anymore."

"Easy, son, I was just protecting you. There are burdens you don't need to bear."

"I feel like I've been bearing them anyway. Why have you spent both our lives on this fool's errand?" Aydan glared at his father defiantly.

"It's better you don't know. Let's just leave it at that."

"I refuse to do any more until I know the truth. Either include me or admit that you're just using me as a tool, and I'll be gone for good." Aydan's heart was racing. He wasn't sure where this had sprung up from, and it surprised even him. But he meant it." The wizard sighed and walked in closer.

"Son, this is not an easy thing to discuss. But you deserve to hear it. Many years ago, on my travels, I was researching the power of Spark, and looking for sources of it. I must admit I was jealous of the Mystics, they were able to build around a source of great power, and I had visions for what wizards could do with that same sort of organisation. My research brought me to something strange." The wizard had a faraway look in his eyes, then he continued.

"Something didn't feel right, but I couldn't put my finger on it. So, I investigated. And I found myself standing before it. The source of the Blight. There was no question." The wizard started to shake his head. "My curiosity drove me forward. Why had my search brought me there?" The wizard looked pained.

"What did you do?" Aydan almost whispered.

"All I did was touch the wall with my hand. But my contact changed it, irreversibly. In that instant, the fate of the world was altered."

"What happened?"

"My touch created a being of intellect. I saw it form before my very eyes. And it spoke. It spoke of the wonder of creation, of the opportunities that now awaited it. But the creature was very new, very immature. I knew it would take time to grow, take time to realise its own aspirations. But it was the beginning of everything."

"Everything? Like what?"

"The Blight was a force of nature. Unpleasant, but random and contained. But I gave it the means to act independently. It started to organise, it created enough trouble that Valrytir sent the four generals. They were turned to the Blight's cause and have started to wreak true havoc. Who knows what will happen if we let this continue!" The wizard looked weary. Truly, the burden was weighing him down. And he didn't look eased by sharing it with Aydan.

"You really are responsible for all this. All the terror, and the Blight activity." Aydan was amazed. It hadn't seemed possible, but now. Now he knew. He understood.

"Yes. I cannot allow my legacy to be one of darkness. I must right my wrong. Together, we must solve this." The wizard held out his hand. Aydan shied away.

"This is too much. I've gone from being hidden and ignored, to being required for your redemption. I can see your pain, your sense of responsibility. But I'm not the answer. I've lived enough of my life under your thumb, trying to compensate for your mistake."

"Don't you dare walk away from me. I've given you everything. You will save our family and save the world."

"In secret still? I thought it could be different. But I see now nothing will change. True, I know the reasons why. But you'll still keep me hidden away. I'll still have to pretend to everyone that I'm not what I truly am. All to protect you and your plans. I've had enough." Aydan turned to walk away.

"Andar. Stop. Please. Let's talk about this." Granthion grabbed his hand and stopped him from going. Andar turned and shook off his father's hand.

"Calling me by my true name won't make a difference. You took everything from me. I have no relationship with my mother, I cannot be my true self with anyone. I can't do it anymore. I need to start living for myself." Andar walked away, forcing his legs to move before he lost the willpower to follow through.

I can't keep going like this. I need to try living for myself. He will find a way to do what he must, he always does.

Andar kept walking through the forest, trying not to think about what had just happened.

53

LEGACY

Alrion opened his eyes and peered into the gloom. It looked like they were back in the cave. He found his Spark and manage to create a weak orb of light and attach it to the wall. The effort almost made him pass out.

Why am I so exhausted?

The memories of what happened flooded back. Particularly the torrent of Soul Power that had flowed through him. That probably did something.

Father!

Alrion looked around for his father. He almost missed him. Vincent was lying on the ground, and his skin was incredibly pale. Alrion ignored his pain and rushed over, gently lifting his father up into a sitting position against the nearest wall. Alrion collapsed next to his father, the effort sapping the last of his strength.

"Dad, you're still with us."

"For now. I fear the worst." Vincent weakly pointed at his leg. Alrion could see a glimpse of his father's foot, and the skin was pure black.

"You can fight this. We won." Alrion frantically searched his body for any semblance of power or magic. He found nothing.

"I don't think we can, not now. But you're right, we did win. That creature is gone. Look at the wall." Vincent leaned back and closed his eyes. Alrion looked over at the dark wall of Blight. It seemed almost inert now, it didn't have the same vitality and motion that it did before. And there certainly wasn't a figure in black addressing them.

"We did it, I can't believe it." But Alrion couldn't revel in the moment. He could see that his father was dying.

"Alrion, what will be, will be. We must accept our fate."

"Surely there's something I can do."

"Yes, there is." Vincent paused, a pained look on his face. "Listen closely." Vincent drew in a few sharp breaths. Alrion held his father's hand.

"Son, now's the time to discuss what happens next. My body is failing, I will be gone soon. But not lost. I will live on in you, and your mother. Your memories, and the feat we achieved here today, that will give me eternal life."

"But you won't be here."

"Not in the same way, but just trust me. Also, I need you to promise me something."

"Yes, what is it?" Alrion leaned in closer.

"Don't tell anyone about me being a wizard. This is your quest and your achievement."

"Your story deserves to be told!"

"No, it does not. I can be the supportive blacksmith that followed his son to the end of the world. That's good enough for me. There's no need to confuse things now." Vincent coughed, a ragged sound that pained Alrion just to hear it. After a few moments, he settled down.

"Now, I left your mother with some writing that explains a lot. Some you will already know. But it may help fill in the blanks and understand me better. I'm sorry for hiding so much from you. In that way, I was too much like my father."

"Dad, it's alright. I know you were trying to do the best for everyone." Vincent shook his head.

"No, I was a coward. And angry. And I ran away from my responsibility. And yes, my father was not an easy man to work with, but he was brilliant, and he gave me impeccable training. And I still couldn't step up. So, I lived a whole new life. I changed my name and pretended my old life didn't exist. But you can't just close the door on your past, as we have discovered." Vincent opened his eyes and stared directly at Alrion.

"But you, my son, you achieved all this with minimal training and minimal information. You used your instincts, you took chances, and you trusted people. You succeeded where I could not. I am so proud of you, and I know your grandfather is as well. You are the true hero, and it was my pleasure to be here to witness you." Vincent cried, the tear turning black as it ran down his face.

"Dad, I had the best preparation. You taught me everything I needed and gave me the desire to be better. You're my hero." Alrion could feel his father's life slipping away. His pulse was weak and fleeting.

"What do I do now? I need your advice." Alrion wanted to ask his father so much, but there was no time.

"Alrion, I can't possibly tell you that. But I can get you started." Vincent closed his eyes. "Go back to our home and investigate my workshop. I've left something there for you. It will show you the way." Vincent's face tensed. He gripped Alrion's hand hard.

"Dad?"

"Goodbye Alrion. Be free and find your own path." Vincent sighed and relaxed. His body started to disintegrate and turn into a fine black dust which floated away. And within a few mere moments, there was nothing left of him. Alrion couldn't hold the tears back, and he lost track of time. Until everything became black.

54

AFTERMATH

Alrion felt an overwhelming warmth. He opened his eyes and saw a figure standing over him.

"Dad, you came back?" As his vision improved, he saw the dark shape next to him was someone else.

"It's me, Lara. Are you alright?" Lara sounded incredibly worried.

Maybe I'm in worse shape than I realise.

"Mostly. Don't touch the black stuff."

"I figured that. Can you stand?" Lara bent down and put her arm around him. With her help, he managed to get himself to a standing position, albeit hunched and leaning on her.

"I lost my dad." Alrion sobbed into her shoulder. He couldn't help it, he didn't even intend to say that.

"I'm sorry, Alrion. Let's get you out of here, then we can figure this all out." Together they took a step forward. It wasn't as hard as Alrion thought it would be. His body felt numb and worn out. But at least it was moving. They struggled wordlessly through the cave, Alrion not knowing what to say, or having the energy to mutter any words. After an age, they came to the strange lake, the one infused with Soul Power.

"Stop." Alrion eased himself down near the water's edge. He

leaned in and cupped water in his hands, drinking it carefully. The hydration was nice, but the Soul Power burned as it flowed through his body.

"This water has Soul Power in it."

"I thought there was something odd about it."

"I'm all burnt out, so let's try to keep this quick." Alrion knew he wasn't fully explaining what had happened, but he couldn't say any more. He was just too tired. Lara seemed to understand though.

"We'll be quick through the water, don't worry." Lara took the lead, letting Alrion travel in her wake. The lake did seem to have a restorative effect, even though his body couldn't handle the Soul Power. The burning feeling came and went, and when they emerged at the other end Alrion dropped to the ground and lay on his back.

"I feel like I've just run for a week straight." He tried to slow his breathing, bit by bit. His body was not really paying attention. It was doing whatever it wanted.

"I'm not going to pester you with questions, but... did it work?"

"Yes," Alrion rasped. Lara nodded and didn't ask any follow-up questions. Alrion closed his eyes and rested a little. After a few moments Lara woke him, and they were off again.

Once they finally reached the exit, Alrion stumbled. His body wouldn't go any further.

"Don't worry, I've got a horse." Lara smiled.

"Have you got rope? I doubt I can hold on."

"Usually do. We'll organise something." Lara busied herself then helped Alrion up into the saddle. He swayed immediately, but she seemed ready for it and, before he knew it, he was tied to something.

"Rest if you can, it's a bit of a ride." Lara nudged the horse off and Alrion closed his eyes immediately, losing track of anything else.

Alrion awoke with a start and sat up immediately. He was in a clean bed, in a room he didn't recognise. Lara looked up sleepily.

"You're awake!" She smiled and rose from the chair she was

slumped in and walked over. She peered into his eyes and examined his face.

"You look better. More alive. How do you feel?"

"Like everything in me has been squeezed out and nothing is left."

"We'll have to do something about that." Lara looked out at the door, deep in thought. She looked back to Alrion. "Can you handle a few guests?"

"Sure." Alrion wasn't sure, but he couldn't say no. He was pretty sure his mum was waiting outside. Lara walked over to the door and opened it, saying something to someone.

True to form, Celes entered the room first. Certan and Alyx were close behind.

"My son, I'm so relieved you're alright. Celes rushed to his side and almost crushed him in a hug. Her eyes were full of tears.

"I'm sorry but..."

"I know, there's no need to go into it now."

"Alright." Alrion had a panicked thought and looked over at the group. "It worked, didn't it?" They all nodded. Certan stepped forward.

"It was a sight to see, Alrion. I'm not sure if you caught sight of the Blight army, but it was huge. Despite intense fighting and having some successes, they were still ridiculously strong. I didn't think we could turn the tide. But when it started happening, wow. It was incredible!"

"What did it look like?"

"It looked like rays of golden light raining from the heavens. One for each creature. They were enveloped in the light and fell to the ground. The darkness was driven from them and dispersed into nothing." Alyx spoke with such wonder like she still couldn't believe it.

"It's true, Alrion. It's a day that nobody will ever forget." Celes gave his hand a squeeze and she stepped back to join the others.

"I'm glad. Please, can I have some water? Then I will tell you the tale of what I encountered." Alrion was eager to tell the tale, and to be free of telling it.

Alrion spoke at length of his experience but took care to leave out any parts that referenced his father. Only at the end did he mention how Vincent had shielded him from the Blight while he completed the spell, and how that had enabled him to be successful. He noticed many sad looks at that part, and he exchanged a knowing glance with his mother.

She will need more details when we can talk privately.

"What of that mysterious wizard? Was he a problem?" Lara said. Alrion sighed. He had forgotten about that thread, especially since both he and his mother knew the truth of that.

"He did make an appearance and was helpful. I can't say more about it right now."

"I see. It's not a problem anymore?"

"No." Lara looked relieved, and the others seemed content with that. Once Alrion had finished the tale, the rest of the talk came quickly.

"I'm so sorry I left you there. Even though you asked me to. Only when I reached the others did I realise that Darvin had left other horrors for you to encounter. I should have been there." Lara looked pained. Alrion held his hand out and enclosed hers.

"It was as it should have been. You already helped me immensely with Darvin."

"He was a tricky one, that's for sure."

"I have a question for you all: what became of those who were cured? Are they lost?" Alrion was a little apprehensive at what the answer might be. He knew there was a chance they had all died, and all he had done was reduce their suffering.

"Many seem to have survived. The copied Blight Generals, however, were a different story." Lara looked to the others. Alrion spotted many awkward expressions.

"I don't know much about that."

"I know the most, I questioned the other Rindale," Celes explained. "He was unable to replicate the Blight transformation in a simple way, so those copies were made using multiple people. I'm afraid they had no chance to return, and there's also no chance for the original person to return from that creation."

"I see." Alrion thought over what his mother had just said. "What you're saying is that any generals of the Blight that died are gone forever."

"That's right. It's a small price to pay, isn't it?"

"On the scale of what we did, yes." Alrion resumed his thinking. He almost forgot they were all there.

"You're all probably wondering what's next?" Alrion looked and saw nods from his friends. "I have an idea, I just want to fully form it first. Could you all return tomorrow?"

"That's fine," Celes said, speaking for the rest. They took this as a cue to leave, but Alrion held on to Lara.

"Can you stay for a moment?"

"Of course." She waved to the rest then pulled up a chair next to Alrion.

"What did you want to talk about?"

"I'm going to ask everyone tomorrow, but I need to know now about you. What are you going to do now? You're home at last." Alrion watched Lara's face and saw a pained expression on it.

"My father is going to try to keep me here. Something about lineage." Lara shook her head.

"Is that what you want?"

"No. You've seen what he's like? They can find someone else. I'm sure there are other members of the royal family that can be substituted."

"As long as you're sure. I'd like you to come with me."

"Where to?" Lara looked extremely curious. He had her full attention.

"I'm not quite sure yet. Wherever the wind blows us?"

"Sounds good to me. I've travelled the world by myself, without a purpose. There's a reason I latched on to you and your quest." Lara laughed. "But now I'm not sure what to do next. I'd like to find out, with you." Lara suddenly reached into her pocket and pulled out a soft pouch. "This seems like a good time to return your ring." She handed it to Alrion. He opened the pouch and took out the ring, examining it. He chuckled to himself.

"My father said this would keep me safe. I know why, now." Alrion noticed Lara's face go pale.

"What is it?" he said nervously.

"There's something I never told you. About that mysterious wizard?"

"I'm listening."

"He met me several times. In fact, he was the one that suggested that I stick with you, and work with you directly." Lara looked down. Alrion was shocked. He didn't expect it. But the more he thought about it, the more it made sense.

"Well, that's a surprise, but it's all coming together now. A wizard with the appropriate knowledge can track that ring." Alrion was amused at Lara's surprise. "Now I understand why the mysterious wizard was delayed reaching me. He was tracking the ring, and you."

"Oh, really. Was that a problem?"

"No, not at all." Alrion handed the ring back. "Will you take the ring? I can promise that it will keep you safe." He smiled.

"Not that you'll get a chance to use it, I'm not going to leave your side ever again." Lara winked at him. Alrion let out a small chuckle.

"And don't worry about working with that mysterious wizard. There's something you'll need to know if we're going everywhere together." Alrion leaned in and whispered into Lara's ear. Her eyes widened, and she gasped.

"No way! I can't believe it!"

"It's true. I find it hard to say out loud, but yes it was my father. But he asked for secrecy. That is not the legacy he wishes to leave. Can I trust you on that?"

"Absolutely, I'm a vault. You didn't even need to ask."

"I know, I just wanted to be clear, for his sake." Alrion sank back into the bed.

"I think I'm going to drift off again. Let's talk a bit later."

"I look forward to it." Lara gave him a quick kiss and left the room, closing the door behind her. Alrion drifted off into a dreamless sleep.

The next morning his companions were all gathered once more. Alrion was better recovered, fully dressed and sitting on his bed. He awkwardly stood when they were all gathered, to address them properly.

"First, I need to thank you all again. We really did achieve the impossible, and we've set the world on the right course." Alrion smiled and took in all the smiles in the room. "I know you all have plans, I just have one more request for you all." Alrion paused before continuing. "I want you all to accompany me to the Wizard Academy. There's a special announcement I'd like you all to be part of."

"It would be an honour," Certan said.

"For me as well," Alyx added.

"I already told you I'm following you to the ends of the world." Lara winked at him.

"I never saw the place before, I would enjoy the opportunity to come," Celes said.

"Great, I'm glad that it's settled. I'll see if there are any ways to speed up our journey." Alrion thought about consulting Magnus for more details concerning local Wizard Gates.

This feels right. I'm excited at what might happen next.

55

A NEW ERA

Lara was excited by the Wizard Academy. She had seen it from a distance but hadn't dared sneak in when she was following Alrion. The main building looked like a miniature castle, with an impressive tower rising behind it. A small welcoming party waited out the front. She recognised Falric. He waved them over.

"Great to see you all. Congratulations." Falric embraced Alrion and wept tears of joy. Lara couldn't help smiling.

"I'm just glad we could lure you back here, even if only for a limited time." Alrion stepped back and gave Falric a broad smile.

"I owe you this much. And I must admit I'm intrigued by what you are planning."

"You'll find out the same time as everyone else. I'm assuming since you stepped down, I can do what I want."

"Well, you are Granthion's heir, you've earned your place. The wizards are all assembled."

"Let's not keep them waiting then." Alrion and Falric took off. Lara sped up to stay close. The trip here had been an interesting one. Fast, yet slow at the same time. Travel between places was very fast, as Alrion extensively used Wizard Gates. Yet he often stopped at odd places and talked to different people. It was all very secretive, he didn't involve them in any of it. Whenever Lara probed too much, he told her 'don't ruin my surprise'. Lara had even compared notes with the others, and nobody had much to add. Not even Celes.

But it was good to be here, and once Lara walked out into the courtyard the sight took her breath away. The outside of the court-yard was lined with wizards in white robes. The tower stood tall behind. Alrion walked out with confidence. Lara slowed and stopped, wondering what her part in all this was. Alrion seemed to notice the slackened pace of his companions, as he stopped and looked back.

"Come on you lot, you can't hide in the back." Alrion grinned and started off again. Lara exchanged glances with Celes and shrugged.

I suppose we just follow along.

Once they reached the centre of the courtyard, Alrion stopped. He pointed to a spot nearby.

"Please stand there, if you don't mind." He watched them all take their position, then he conferred quietly with Falric.

"It is time," Falric announced. He used his normal voice but must have enhanced it with magic. It reverberated around the space effort-lessly. The wizards quietened down, and soon silence reigned over the Wizard Academy.

"We come together today at the request of Alrion. As you should remember, we recently welcomed Alrion into our number. He was charged with a special task, one that seemed incomprehensible. The quest to cleanse the Blight." Falric paused and let that last sentence sit upon the audience.

"Against all odds, he succeeded. His only request was a special audience with you all, and to play his part in the future of the Acad-emy. Please all give Alrion a hero's welcome." Falric started clapping and the wizards joined in. Most of them were restrained, but a few were quite enthusiastic. Once the clapping died down, Alrion stepped forward.

"Thank you, Falric. The last time we were all here, Falric stepped down as your leader. He adopted a new role, to guide me through the trials and my own training on this incredible journey. Falric's task then took on a new dimension, assisting with research into the Pool of Knowledge, so that we could most effectively glean its secrets and apply its knowledge to the problem of the Blight." Alrion looked out at the wizards, watching their reaction. After a few moments, he started again.

"Falric's reign quite rightly came to an end, as he was ready to move on to his next challenges. His successor, Branthor, was also a pivotal part of my quest. Unfortunately, he was lost to us, losing his life in trade for that of the General of the Blight, Rindale." Alrion paused and let the commotion swell up then die down again. He started pacing around the area.

"This leaves us with a void of leadership. I have learned an incredible amount in a short time and have much to share with you all. But I'm not the right person to lead the Academy. But I did find the right person." Alrion held out a hand like he was presenting someone. But there was nobody there. Suddenly there was a bang, and the silhouette of a man appeared out of nowhere, obscured by smoke. Slowly the smoke cleared. Lara stared, her heart thumping faster and faster.

Who is it? It's Ashra!

A strange silence settled over the crowd. Alrion walked over and embraced Ashra, ending with a handshake. He stepped back and addressed the crowd again.

"Many of you won't recognise this wizard, but you have all heard of him. Your new leader is none other than the legendary desert wizard, Ashra." As Alrion finished his proclamation, a series of fireworks exploded in the sky above. Ashra bowed with a flourish. He cleared his throat and offered a few words.

"Meeting and helping Alrion on his quest activated a part of me that I thought was lost. I had been a hermit for so long, an outcast of my own doing. I didn't think that I'd miss the world of men, or the simple act of sharing another's hopes and dreams. But I was wrong. It is with great pride and honour that I take up this post. I vow to personally help each and every one of you take the steps you need to become wizards of great strength and character." Ashra turned to Falric. "Thank you for this opportunity, I will do my best to continue your legacy." Ashra then bowed. Falric returned the bow.

"Now I believe Alrion has an announcement." Falric stepped back and beckoned Alrion to step forward. He did a little nervously. But then something changed, he adjusted his posture and projected confidence.

That's the way. Whatever this is, just own it.

"To say I've just been on an incredible journey, would be an understatement. And by myself, I would have failed. Several times over. But I had this group of people to help." Alrion used his arm in a sweeping gesture to represent his group of companions.

"You've already met Falric and Ashra. They were my mentors and guides in my development as a wizard." Alrion acknowledged them both then turned back to face his companions.

"Before I address my companions, I must speak of one that cannot be here." Alrion took a deep breath.

Be strong. You can do this.

"I speak of course about my father, Vincent. He was a master blacksmith and a former soldier. He supported me every step of my quest, created legendary weapons to support myself and my companions, and followed me into the abyss itself. He sacrificed himself so that I may live, and for that, he has my eternal thanks." Alrion kept his eyes closed and looked deep in thought. He slowly opened them and looked over at his companions again.

"First, I must speak of Lara. Treasure Hunter, Scout, and an expert climber." Alrion looked at her and chuckled. Lara blushed as she remembered her exploits climbing over that gigantic wall.

"Lara was the first companion to join my quest, and the most important. She came at a time when I needed help the most and was there through every major trial. She was the person I didn't know I needed." Alrion gave her a smile and she flashed him one back.

"Next, we encountered Certan, the monk. He was facing demons of his own devising, which is why we were fortunate enough to find him. But Certan proved himself to be a loyal and key member of our team. He led us to the sacred temple in the middle of the desert and helped fight off hordes of Blight forces. He mastered himself, bested the Vault of Silence, and became a master monk in his own right. And he still came to my aid." Alrion bowed to Certan. "You taught me a lot about Will and mindset, lessons I will never forget." Alrion turned next to Alyx.

"Alyx is likely the best fighter in the whole world. Not only is she a weapon master, but she single-handedly took down the Skull King. Alyx intervened when we were going to be overrun by a massive Blight attack and risked herself for no good reason. She suffered dearly for her assistance to us but rose above it and continued to help us when good sense would have been to run away. Thank you for showing me how to fight and being a rock-solid ally when we needed you the most." Alrion bowed to Alyx. Finally, he turned to Celes.

"Last, but not least, we have Celes. She happens to be my mother, but her contribution was much more than that. In another life, Celes was a master thief and treasure hunter in her own right, and she not only tracked us all down and helped expose Blight conspiracies, but she also revived a twenty-year-old trail to unmask the Hidden Wizard." Alrion paused and watched the crowd. Confused murmurs ran through the group. Lara was alarmed.

What's he doing? Surely, he's not going to reveal anything?

"The last companion that you don't see here is known as the Hidden Wizard. He helped us from the shadows, fighting battles we weren't aware of, and ensuring that we as a group could continue to advance in our quest. He asked for nothing, save that his identity is kept secret. To thank him, I have a special announcement." Alrion closed his eyes and concentrated. Suddenly a pillar of light appeared in front of him and shot up into the sky, exploding into a shower of golden sparks that dissipated above the crowd.

"Today, I am announcing the formation of a new organisation. I am calling it the Order of the Hidden Wizard. As a tribute to that wizard's mission, this organisation is dedicated to watching and preventing the spread of the Blight. The world has been cleansed, but without a watchful eye, it could easily slip again." Discussion started immediately, the square filling with the sounds of multiple conversations. Lara looked at Alrion, confused.

"Is that it?" she said. Alrion smiled at her.

"No, there's more." Alrion held up his hand and the commotion slowly died down.

"That's not all. There's little point creating an organisation, but not empowering it. So, I am therefore opening all the Wizard Stores to members of the Order of the Hidden Wizard. For the first time, we will openly share our secrets and resources. And, once I figure out a way, I'm also going to open access to Wizard Gates." The commotion was a lot louder now.

"You've certainly got this lot talking," Lara said. Alrion laughed.

"I think it's what my grandfather would have wanted. Open cooperation against the Blight, preventing another disaster. It's the only way to protect the world." Alrion looked over to Falric, and the master wizard smiled and nodded. Ashra, too, seemed to agree. Alrion walked over to his companions.

"I hope you are all fine with this?"

"Of course we are." Alyx spoke up but looked at the others and nobody raised a complaint.

"Good. I'll work with Falric and Ashra to figure out how to provide you with the entry tokens you need for Wizard Stores, and the locations of each. But for now, where will you go?" Alrion looked to Certan first.

"No surprises here, I will return to the temple. My service is promised there. But I will take a meandering path. I wish to see for myself the fruits of our labours. I want to see the new world we have created together." Certan stepped forward and offered Alrion his hand. They shook and Certan stepped back.

"I'm going to visit my hometown. It's been a long time. After that, who knows. I think I'll spend some time in Valrytir. I owe them that much. If I run out on them again..." Alyx smiled sheepishly. Alrion walked over and gave her a big hug.

"I'm sorry again for everything we put you through."

"Don't apologise, I was party to it all. I made all my choices, and I stand by them."

"I was going to go home. It's been a long trip, and I don't know what I'll do next. At the least, I'll spend some time with what Vincent left me." Celes sighed. Lara could see the tears welling up, but they were being held back.

"Do you mind if we join you? I'd like to go visit as well. And maybe I can look through the papers too."

"Of course, I would be delighted." Celes looked at Lara then back at Alrion. "And you're bringing a girl home? I'm not sure if I approve." Celes winked and laughed.

"You better win her over," Alrion whispered to Lara loud enough for everyone to hear. They all laughed. Falric and Ashra walked over to join them.

"Enjoy a break. You've done enough for a lifetime. When you're ready for something else, we can work out all these things you promised." Falric slapped Ashra on the shoulder. "Or should I say, Ashra will work them all out. I have urgent business to attend to." Falric waved goodbye and wandered off.

"I've never seen anyone run so fast to paperwork," Lara said.

"Exactly. I fear I have maybe committed to too much." Ashra grinned. He wished them well, and the companions all walked to the main gate together.

"You know where to find me." Certan waved.

"Me too. Don't be a stranger." Alyx waved as well. With that, the two rode off on horses supplied by the Academy. Alrion and Celes wanted to walk.

I don't think they're in a rush to get home. Especially with him gone.

56

THE RETURN

They made the wise decision of borrowing horses at Carford. As much as Alrion had enjoyed the walk and the change of pace, he was now eager to get home. It felt like an age since he had ridden out with his father and Falric.

One of them I thought had died, the other one now has.

"This is new territory for me, I never travelled this far," Lara said.

"I felt the same way, long ago. I'm not quite sure why Vincent insisted on us living here. It was quite an adjustment, coming from the big cities. But we built a nice life here. It was a different pace, and a different focus." Celes looked around as she spoke. Alrion recognised the terrain quite well. They would be back in Hamley soon.

"Is that it?" Lara said, pointing. Alrion peered into the distance.

"That's it. That's where I lived my entire life until recently." Alrion realised just how small the town was. It looked like nothing from a distance, and as they approached, he realised that unlike other places, it didn't really expand into something else. What you saw at long range, was it.

"Cute sign," Lara commented as they rode by. They were entering the town proper now.

It's like I never left.

The usual hustle and bustle of the small town continued. Men and women travelled from place to place, visiting artisans and buying or delivering goods. The familiar smells of the carpenter and leather-worker wafted over before he spotted the buildings. The noise and smells from the blacksmith were noticeably absent. He couldn't remember a time when the shop hadn't been open.

He noticed a few townsfolk regard them, but nobody said anything.

"Why aren't they greeting us?" Alrion said to his mother.

"You and your father left in a hurry, and then I left. There's been no word, and we're returning without him. They don't know what to think, let alone say. Don't worry, that'll change. They just need a few days to get used to having us around again."

"I suppose that's fine." Alrion turned to Lara, "It's not much, but this is home."

"I have a good feeling about it. Don't worry about a few people you haven't seen in a while." Lara gave him a reassuring smile.

I wasn't sure what she would think, but I'm glad she's giving it a shot. Even if we don't stay a while, this will always be home.

Soon Alrion pulled up before his home. It looked exactly the same. The white paint was a little more faded, as was the red door. But it was minimal. They dismounted and tied up their horses, and Celes approached the door, unlocking it.

"We're home," she announced as she walked through the front door. Alrion noticed a musty smell from the house being closed, but otherwise, it was unchanged.

"Don't worry, I wasn't sure when I was returning so I prepared the house appropriately. The only downside is that there's no food." Celes disappeared into the rear of the house, and Alrion sat on the couch, inviting Lara to sit with him.

"It was here that Falric announced I was a wizard. A lifetime ago."

"Your father was quite surprised. Although now I'm not sure what to believe." Celes started to keep talking, but she abruptly stopped.

"Don't worry, I told Lara. She needed to know."

"Well, yes that's fine." Celes gathered her thoughts and began to talk again. "He must have known you were a wizard, perhaps he was surprised at Falric appearing to take you away."

"I think so. Have you had a chance to read through much of what he gave you?"

"Not really. I've been waiting. Now that we're home, it makes more sense." Celes started to cry and turned away. Alrion was about to rise to comfort her when she quickly turned around, hiding it. Celes sat on the nearest chair.

"You discovered it was him, didn't you? In your investigation?" Lara said.

"Oh yes, it was quite a shock. I suspect he intended it that way."

"He did tell me that it was the best way to make you believe it. And, he wanted to find if there was any evidence tying him to that persona." Alrion watched his mother. She shook her head and chuckled.

"I suspect he didn't know how to tell me. It's quite a secret to keep all those years." Celes looked far away, lost in some sort of memory. She abruptly addressed them again.

"When I confronted him with the information, he didn't even formally acknowledge it. Even though we both knew. It was like he didn't want to say it out loud. But he did reference a story about the Blind Tiger heist. That said a lot."

"I'm not familiar with that story," Lara said.

"It's an interesting one. Well, perhaps it's worth sharing." Celes eased back into the chair and made herself comfortable. "It all started with a thief, who was part of a larger group. His name was Michael. He was tasked with stealing a pristine jewel, known as the Coded Citrine."

"I've heard of that!" Lara said, excited.

"What is it?" Alrion asked.

"It's an orange gem inscribed with tiny characters. We're not quite sure what it's for, but it looks incredible. Anyway, it was held in a special vault, and only one man knew the precise method to open the vault. And he never did it in the presence of anyone else. This group had investigated every angle, and they had no way of breaking it out."

"How did Michael play into it?" Lara said.

"Well, he proposed a plan whereas he was introduced to them as a blind man. But a specialist servant, one who could assist with tasks in a way that was capable, but also discreet. The thieves weren't convinced by the feasibility of the plan, but they let him try it. Michael found a way into their service. He was an advisor as well as an organiser. They tested his blindness in every way they could conceive, and he passed."

"Wow, so he found a way to convince them he was blind, even though he could see."

"Precisely. Although in many respects, he needed to almost be blind, to continue his cover. As he gained their trust, he became enamoured with the family's niece, who had come to stay at the estate. Over time, they developed a relationship and married. And had a daughter."

"Over what period? What happened to the thieves?"

"Years. The thieves were split apart by a rather terrible heist gone wrong, and Michael believed that he could just abandon his mission and live out the new life he had made for himself." Celes paused and shifted in her seat. Alrion was about to ask another question but she continued.

"You're probably wondering what went wrong? Well, one day he was confronted by two men. The leader of the thief group, and the man who had assigned the task to Michael. They had remembered about him and had come to collect what they were owed. When Michael refused to help them, they took his daughter hostage."

"What happened?" Alrion asked.

"He was forced to help them. He had seen the way to open the vault and helped them get the jewel. But he confronted them both and died in the process."

"But what of his daughter? And the jewel?" Lara said.

"The head thief fell in the tussle, but the other man got away with the jewel. The daughter, thankfully, was left in the middle of nowhere by the gang and found her way home. She was fine but traumatised by the whole ordeal. The family, however, did not discover Michael's treachery. They assumed that he had been coerced by the thieves and died honourably."

"How did you get involved?" Lara said.

"I overheard the thief that got away bragging at an inn. His name was Morgan, by the way. It didn't take much to convince Vincent to help me. I can see now that he obviously identified with Michael."

"What did you do?" Alrion said.

"It wasn't hard to liberate the jewel. We just followed Morgan home. Vincent kept watch while I located and stole the gem. Morgan was so out of it we had no trouble."

"And the gem? What of it?"

"Vincent wanted to return it to the original family, but we didn't get around to it right away. It was some distance to travel. Over time, we just ended up keeping it. I think it's stowed away here somewhere." Celes finished the story, and the energy seemed to leak out of her. She slumped back in the chair.

"So that's how I figured out that he wasn't coming back. And he was right. Of course, he was right."

"I thought we had a chance to do it, and both survive. But I think deep down he knew what would be required. Maybe that's why he couldn't work up to it until Falric involved me."

"Maybe that's true." Celes stood up and walked into another room.

"Are you alright?" Lara said. She looked really concerned.

"I'm alright, it's just weird being here. I keep expecting him to walk in the door, returning from the workshop." Alrion paused, remembering something. "If you don't mind giving me a moment, there's something I need to do." Alrion stood abruptly.

"Of course, I'll be here." Lara gave his hand a squeeze and let it go.

"Thanks." Alrion strode over to the door and left immediately.

He left something for me at the workshop. I need to see what it is. It must be important if he didn't include it with what he left for Mum.

Alrion saw people he recognised in his peripheral vision. He ignored them and kept walking. Strangely, though, they didn't pay him any attention either.

Maybe they don't recognise me?

For now, it was one less distraction. Alrion stopped before the workshop and fished around for the key. He found it and unlocked the door. He slowly swung it open, surveying the shop.

It looked exactly as they had left it.

Dad knew we wouldn't be coming back. That's why he was so adamant about finishing everything.

Alrion walked through the workshop, running his hand over some of the counters. Everything was packed away, nothing was left out.

He left something for me. Where would it be?

Alrion stopped and looked over the room. Perhaps he had left something, but it had always been there. If that was the case, it had to be in a safe location.

Where was he always working?

Alrion walked over to the bench that his father always worked at. Without fail. In fact, he always ensured Alrion used another bench.

It must be here.

Alrion slowly pushed the workbench away, sliding it into an open space nearby. There was a rough, threadbare mat underneath it.

That's curious, why put a mat under a workbench?

Alrion pulled the mat aside and noticed a trapdoor. He gingerly pried the top off, sliding the cover off. There was a ladder leading into a dark area.

Now, this is promising.

Alrion stood and walked to the front door, locking it from the inside. He couldn't afford to be interrupted. Returning to the open trapdoor, Alrion peered inside. He could see a ladder leading down. He created an orb of light and sent it down before starting to climb.

This is oddly reminiscent of that place in Stonebridge.

He climbed down carefully and took stock of where he was. It was a tiny stone cellar. Completely empty save for one thing.

There's a Wizard Gate under the workshop!

Alrion couldn't believe it. All this time he had lived and worked here, never knowing that a portal to another place was just sitting here. He rushed over, curious to see it. The gate looked like any other. He impatiently examined the pillars and saw only one symbol. He activated it, curious to see where it went. The gate roared to life, the blinding flash subsiding quickly. Alrion could see what looked like a room, but there wasn't a lot of other details he could glean from it.

Is it wise to take this? I have no idea where it goes, or how I could get back.

Alrion paused before the open gate. He thought carefully. If this was a place his father used, it had to have a return function. Because his father never went on strange unexplained trips. He was always around.

He asked me to find something here, I must try.

Alrion stepped through the gate, unsure of where he would end up.

~

Alrion stepped into a study. It was made from stone, the walls filled with shelves and books. A single window lit the room. But what caught Alrion's attention was the desk in the middle. He recognised that desk.

It's Granthion's desk. From the dreams.

Alrion rushed over, spotting something on the desk. He touched it reverently.

"Granthion's spellbook," he whispered. His father had had access to this the whole time. Alrion stepped back, curious about where he was. He walked through the room, seeing no entrances or exits. Just the Wizard Gate, and the window. He wandered over to the window, peering out. It looked like Avaria. There was a rather large hill that dominated the view.

You don't suppose.

Alrion let the thought mull over. Was that hill the place his grand-father had cast the spell over Avaria? He walked back to the desk, looking at the spellbook.

I have so many questions now. I wish I could talk to someone about it.

But Granthion and his father were gone. Alrion started leafing through the spellbook. He could read all the words. Mostly they were mundane spells, but he had a realisation.

Now I can find more spells that I need and consciously learn them. This will be amazing!

He set the book down and turned to leave. As exciting as it was, he needed to go back and make sure everything was fine at home. He would have plenty of time to come back and forth, as his father had.

57

DREAMING

Alrion was dreaming. The realisation was sudden, but also confusing. He was in the same room that he had discovered that day. His grandfather's desk prominently sitting in the middle.

Is the Pool of Knowledge trying to tell me something else?

Alrion saw a wizard looking out the window. He started to approach, and the wizard turned to face him.

"Dad?" Alrion said, not sure if he believed it.

"Hello, Alrion. How are you doing?" Vincent smiled. Alrion had to suppress the urge to run up and hug his father.

"Oh, I get it. You're not really there, you are a manifestation of my mind trying to help me realise some crucial knowledge from the Pool." Alrion sighed.

"I take offence to that, I made considerable effort to get here." Vincent shook his head and chuckled.

"What do you mean? You died. Unless..."

"No, I'm pretty sure I really died. But I did arrange to have a conversation with you, so I'm glad we are here talking."

"That doesn't seem possible. Say something that nobody else would know?"

"Let's see here. Your mother knows I'm the mysterious wizard that's been following you around all this time. Does that work?" Vincent smiled. Alrion felt himself grinning. He couldn't help it.

"So, it is you!" Alrion ran over and hugged his father. It did feel like him too. The pain at losing him suddenly arced up and Alrion had to fight back tears.

"I'm so sorry, Alrion, to be so secretive and then disappear from your life. It all worked out, didn't it?"

"Yes, we did it. The Blight is back to what it was, and the world is cured. Many people have awoken, although there are also many who didn't survive the transition back." Alrion tried not to think about those.

"Good, good. I'm glad it wasn't in vain. Who is running the academy now?"

"Ashra. Falric came back to help initiate him but won't stay long."

"Hah!" Vincent laughed. "I suggested to Ashra that he should do that. Glad to hear he's there."

"I suggested it too, I guess great minds do think alike."

"I think we just don't want to be responsible for a group of wizards." Vincent grinned.

"I think you're right." Alrion sighed. "How does this work? How long are you here?"

"I'm not entirely sure. I think it's a one-off short-term type arrangement. To be honest, it was very much luck on my side. I wasn't sure it was going to work."

"What did you do?"

"Remember when we were in the thick of it? Saving the world? Well, I grafted a piece of my soul onto you while we were linked. And here we are." Vincent shrugged.

"You didn't know what would happen?"

"Not at all, but I had suspicions. It was all a bit desperate really, but it worked. So I'll claim it. Anyway, I want to hear what you're doing now. Did you follow my instructions?"

"Yes, I found this place." Alrion gestured at the room they were standing in. "And I found Granthion's spellbook."

"Amazing! Hopefully, you'll get more out of it than I did."

"What do you mean?"

"Well, since I never advanced my study of Soul Power, a lot of it was unavailable to me until recently. And I didn't exactly have time to sit down with it. But you do."

"Yes, I have nothing but time at the moment."

"It's good, enjoy it for the rest of us." Vincent paused, then his eyes brightened. "You know, Alrion, this is the part where I'm supposed to wish you a long and prosperous life and tell you to follow your heart and discover your true path." Vincent watched Alrion, gauging his reaction.

"That would be a nice thing to say. But instead?"

"Instead, I'm going to ask a tiny favour." Vincent walked over to the desk and opened up Granthion's spellbook. "It's not even a favour, it's just a recommendation. When you do have time to look at the spellbook, I suggest this one. It looks quite interesting." Vincent tapped the page and stood back. Alrion walked over and carefully leant over, looking at the page.

Resurrection Spell

"You know, I think I could find time to look at something like that." Alrion looked up, but his father was gone. Nowhere to be seen.

"You have impeccable timing." Alrion laughed to himself. But his father was right. The spell did look quite interesting. And he needed a new challenge. As the dream started to fade, Alrion smiled and started planning his next move.

WANT MORE FROM THE HIDDEN WIZARD?

While this story is complete, I am working on other stories in the world of **The Hidden Wizard**. If you are interested in reading more please check out the below page on my website:

http://vaughanwsmith.com/finished-the-hidden-wizard/

ABOUT THE AUTHOR

Vaughan W. Smith is a fiction writer from Sydney, Australia, who explores big life questions through story. His favourite genres are Fantasy, Mystery, Science Fiction and Thrillers.

www.vaughanwsmith.com

www.ingramcontent.com/pod-product-compliance
Lightning Source LLC
Chambersburg PA
CBHW030327120726
47901CB00007B/1709